Chronicles of the Human Sphere:

By Fire and Sword

T0277041

By Mark Barber

ZMOK
BOOKS

Chronicles of the Human Sphere: By Fire and Sword
By Mark Barber
Cover by Bagus Hutomo
Black & White drawing by Tommaso Dall' Osto
Zmok Books is an imprint of
Winged Hussar Publishing, LLC, 1525 Hulse Road, Unit 1, Point Pleasant, NJ 08742

This edition was published in 2024 Copyright ©Winged Hussar Publishing, LLC

PB ISBN 978-1-958872-54-3
EB ISBN 978-1-958872-64-2

Library of Congress No. 2024946706
Bibliographical references and index
1. Science Fiction 2. Space Opera 3. Action & Adventure

Infinity and *Chronicles of the Human Sphere* are the properties of Corvis Belli
This book is published under license
Winged Hussar Publishing, LLC All rights reserved

For more information on Winged Hussar Publishing, LLC, visit us at:
https://www.WHPSupplyroom.com
Twitter: WingHusPubLLC
Facebook: Winged Hussar Publishing LLC

Chronicles of the Human Sphere: By Fire and Sword

Chronicles of the Human Sphere & Infinity Timeline:

N1

N2
Campaign Paradiso

N3
Uprising
        -*Outrage*
Third Offensive
        - *Downfall*
        - *Team Zed*
        - *By Fire and Sword*
Daedalus' Fall
        -*Defiance*

N4
        - *Basilisk*
Raveneye
        -*Aftermath*
        - *Airaghardt*
Endsong

"Thanks to everybody who helped and supported me over these last two novels; I hope I've given an already popular figure just a little more backstory and character for the MO fans."

Prologue

One Mile East of Mauritius
Earth
0100 local time

The conflicting growls of the powerful engines meshed poorly, giving an almost doppler-like effect. Even that noise created by the powerboats seemed to clash in competition as they hurtled across the water. Both vessels were crammed with oversized power plants, flickering blue flames from lines of exhausts illuminating the boats' sides as they carved across the calm, black water of the Indian Ocean. The smaller of the two speeding vessels - a wedge shaped powerboat painted in vivid shades of electric blue - was perhaps two lengths ahead as the sleek racers rapidly approached the next corner in the course. Behind, larger and looming over the blue boat like an angry predator, was a boxier, flame orange craft that rapidly closed on its opponent, demonstrating its superiority in both speed and acceleration on the long straight of the course.

Rapidly buttoning up his expensive, Merovingian silk shirt, Robin Gillan rushed out onto the upper deck of his sleek, black super yacht. His bare feet slapped on the oak planks of the near priceless vessel's waist as he hurried to where the small crowd of spectators had gathered at the open fo'c'sle area. His eyes only slowly adjusted from the bright lights of his extravagant cabin within the yacht's superstructure to the half-moon lit night of the Mauritian coast, despite the aid of his ocular implants. He recognized his laser blue powerboat expertly handle the corner of racetrack on the water, the waypoints highlighted on his contact lens. The aggressively cut, orange powerboat behind narrowly missed ramming the back of the smaller boat at the next corner - despite the driver's clear intentions - and then wallowed behind as it drifted wide in the wake of its agile, expertly driven blue adversary.

Gillan swore to himself as he reached the crowd packed at the front of his yacht - perhaps twenty intoxicated men and women shouting and cheering gleefully at the impromptu, high-speed spectacle playing out before them. His guests: ten potential investors he was keen to impress, and a host of stunningly beautiful young men and women he had hired to make sure they were entertained in every way. Gillan's eyes fell on the tall, muscular form of Trevithick, his head of security.

"Hey! Hey!" Gillan shouted above the excited din as he planted a hand on the shoulder of the taller, older man. "What the hell is this?"

"Boat race," the black-mustached ex-soldier smirked. "Mister Eckhart was explaining to your guests that he has only ever been beaten by professional drivers."

"I can see it's a race!" Gillan snarled. Eckhart's notorious, orange powerboat struggled to regain the racing line and accelerated in an aggressive pursuit of the smaller boat gliding smoothly into the next straight of the course. "Who the hell is racing him?"

"Gabby," Trevithick replied evenly.

Gillan's eyes widened in shock.

"Gabby?!" he exclaimed. "Less than an hour ago he was high as a fucking kite on Old Steely, downing an entire bottle of gin! Why the hell did you let him get behind the wheel of a fucking powerboat?!"

The aging ex-soldier's dark eyes narrowed just a little, and the sparkle faded away from the grim smile beneath the thick mustache.

"You pay me to keep you safe, Rob," Trevithick grunted, "there isn't enough money in the Human Sphere to pay me to keep all of your stupid friends and associates safe as well. Besides, Gabby knew what he was doing. He did that thing he always does. Plays the part of the stuttering computer nerd to draw his prey in. He's a shark, you know that."

"Fucking hell!" Gillan snapped, leaning forward to plant both hands on the gleaming, chrome rail running around the upper deck of his yacht.

A collective gasp washed over the small crowd as the angular, orange powerboat pulled ahead of its smaller opponent along the penultimate straight, leading into a tight hairpin bend digitally laid out on the lens of drivers and spectators alike across the moonlit water. Gillan's jaw ached as he clamped his teeth together, his hands tightly gripping the rail. Eckhart's orange boat extended its lead. On the one hand, keeping Eckhart in a good mood was beneficial to him; hell, it was the whole point in this social gathering - to keep his investors happy and coming back for more business. On the other hand, the blue boat was his, and watching it come in second over the line was a personal failing. Then there was the man at the wheel. Gillan's head of IT was nearly as gifted behind the helm of a powerboat as he was at protecting the company from hackers working for rivals - but not when half of his brain was being blitzed by Class A narcotics.

"Come on, Gabby!" Gillan exhaled.

Eckhart flung his speeding boat into a tight turn on the final bend. Gillan allowed himself a smirk. He was no racer, but even he could tell that Eckhart had entered the bend too fast and outside the racing line. The orange boat listed violently to starboard, skidding out of the turn as the thunderous engines roared in protest at their mis-handling. It was an easy overtake. The assembled crowd shouted and roared as the small, blue boat slipped easily inside its flailing adversary on the bend before smoothly accelerating out of the turn and along the final straight. Eckhart's recovery was good - possibly even masterful - and the hulking orange powerboat might even have stood a chance of a comeback if there was another lap to play with. But without that chance, Eckhart could only stand up in the cockpit of his boat and slam his fist against the windscreen as the blue powerboat streaked across the finishing line only meters from the crowd on Gillan's yacht.

Despite the obvious financial penalisation that would inevitably come from Eckhart's anger at losing, Gillan found himself laughing in relief. He stood up on the rail of his yacht, waving his arms over his head at his friend as the victorious blue boat sped past. He saw the familiar figure of De Fersen at the wheel, his tasteless floral shirt open to expose his lean, bony figure. The young computer prodigy whipped the powerboat around in a tight turn; foam blasted up from the vessel's stern as it was expertly skidded into a flamboyant circle of spray only yards from the packed deck of the yacht.

The crowd cheered and waved as De Fersen stood up in the cockpit, one hand on the wheel while the other raised a clenched fist above his head. Gillan laughed again. He could practically hear the victorious howls of glee from the ostentatious computer programmer. His smile faded. He could also practically see the effects of the drugs and alcohol in his friend's eyes even from this distance.

"Gabby…"

Inside the cockpit of the blue powerboat, the lean man slipped and fell from his seat. His hand still clutching at the controls of the boat, he dragged the wheel across to full lock. The boat jolted to one side, smashing into its own wake. Gillan felt a sickening fist clutch his gut as the boat was flung up into the air. He saw De Fersen tossed out of the cockpit like a rag doll, an arc of crimson fountaining up into the night sky as his head connected with the rim of the windscreen. De Fersen's lifeless body twirled off to one side and slipped beneath the waves as the boat flipped over and rolled across the disturbed seas, showering the entire area with debris. Before Gillan could even think how to react, Trevithick dove into the water and began swimming rapidly toward the spot where De Fersen's body had disappeared.

***

"How is he?"

The short doctor looked up at Gillan from her tablet as he approached the hospital room doorway. Strands of gray running through the woman's thick, black hair gave her an almost regal hint of authority that somehow calmed Gillan. Far better this woman than some wet-be-hind-the-ears junior doctor. The stern-looking physician glanced down both ends of the private hospital's second floor corridor. One side of the corridor consisted solely of tall windows, offering an unobstructed view of the curved, white buildings of Port Louis at night; to the north, the tall billboards and flickering neon blues and greens signposted the city center, where wealthy tourists would still be enjoying the final few moments of the city's nightlife scene before closing time. The other side of the corridor was made up of a row of closed doors leading to private rooms. Aside from Gillan, Trevithick, and the doctor, the corridor was empty.

"You two are his...?"

"Friends," Gillan replied, "we're Gabriele's friends."

The short woman's eyes narrowed.

"Friends. You were with him tonight?"

"Yes, that's right. We drove him here after he hit his head."

The doctor folded her arms.

"The head wound is superficial," she said, her chin jutting out. "What I'm more interested to know is how he ended up in the water, unconscious, with enough Old Steely, alcohol, and amphetamines in his system to kill a horse. Some friends you two are, letting him get in that state."

Gillan took a step forward, his face twisted in anger. Trevithick had dove into the water to save De Fersen; Gillan had driven them to the hospital at breakneck speed to ensure he received the best medical care money could buy. Gillan was paying this woman's wage, and he was not doing it to be lectured like a child.

Trevithick slammed a hand firmly on Gillan's shoulder.

"Rob," the big man warned sternly.

Gillan stopped. He took a breath. Throwing money at a problem he caused did not make him a saint. He needed to accept some responsibility for what had happened.

"You can go in and see him," the doctor said. "He's up now."

Gillan watched the short woman head off toward the next room before turning to look up at his head of security.

"You wait here," he nodded to Trevithick before turning to enter De Fersen's room.

The plush, private room was perhaps the same size as a four-pa-tient ward room in Port Louis's general hospital. De Fersen sat upright on a broad bed, a line connecting his bandaged arm to a sleek, glossy white palbot stood next to his bed. The medical robot slowly pumped clear fluids into its patient, a series of numbers that were meaningless to Gillan were displayed on a black screen on the bot's head and repeated holographically above it. The walls of the room were colored in a calming, tropical turquoise that gently pulsed and waved as if reflecting sunshine off of calm waters. An entertainment suite lay dormant opposite the bed.

De Fersen looked across at Gillan as he paced slowly over. Only twenty years old, he looked a decade older thanks to his heavily receding hairline and gaunt features. Gillan's IT security man forced a smile as he sat further upright atop his clean, white sheets.

"Hello, Rob!" he croaked wearily. "I appear to have made a bit of a tit of myself again!"

Gillan's face cracked into a smile.

"Don't worry about that." He smiled. "I'm just... well... I'm just glad you're okay."

"Yeah. Okay. Nearly not, though. I'm sorry about your boat."

Gillan sat down on one of the three plush, beige armchairs in the corner of the room. He winced as he looked across at the younger man.

"Precisely," he agreed, "nearly not okay. Come on, Gabby. What were you doing? That race was only going to end one way."

The young programmer's pale features hardened a little for a second, and Gillan braced himself for one of his friend's rare, but volatile outbursts. Then the frown faded away again.

"I know." De Fersen nodded wearily. "I know. It has to stop. All of it."

Gillan placed the fingertips of both hands together and rested his elbows on his knees as he leaned forward.

"I wouldn't go as far as to say 'all of it'," he countered. "You don't need to become a bloody monk! I just think you should... I think it was a fucking stupid idea to race a powerboat at night on drugs. There. I've said it. Powerboat racing - fine. Steely and amphetamines - yeah, in moderation. But the two shouldn't mix."

The room fell silent. De Fersen spent several moments staring at the foot of his bed until his sunken eyes turned to face Gillan.

"No," he said, his tone almost apologetic. "No. It's not enough. It all has to stop. Robin, I need to go. I need to do something different with my life. Something better. I need to change."

Gillan shot to his feet and took a pace forward.

"Gabby! Come on! You've just had a serious knock to the head! Now is not the time to be making huge decisions and changes in your life! You need to rest."

De Fersen's head turned again. He looked back at the end of his bed and took in two long, deep breaths. The silence of the room was broken only by a faint ticking from the palbot and the fans of the room's environmental control system. De Fersen's thin lips opened and he muttered words that Gillan could only just make out.

"And immediately something like scales fell from his eyes..."

Gillan's face twisted in confusion.

"What?"

De Fersen looked up again.

"It's from the Bible. The Acts of the Apostles, I think. It means that one really bad night can force you to change your life for the better."

"Oh, come on!" Gillan scoffed. "That's your dad talking! When the hell did you suddenly flock to the NeoVatican's banner?"

"About an hour ago," De Fersen answered calmly, "when I smashed my head open on that boat and realized how much of a prick I've been for the last two years."

Gillan sank back down to his chair again, the faux leather creaking beneath him. He folded his arms across his lap and leaned forward, staring down at his ludicrously overpriced, designer boat shoes.

"You haven't wasted the last two years," he said slowly, deliberately. "You've spent the last two years working for me. I pay you a fantastic rate because you are the best at what you do. I pay you fairly. I treat you with respect. I give you time off whenever you want it. I give you benefits beyond what anybody else would. I take you to different worlds to see places you'd never see without me. And on top of all of that, I'm your friend. I'm not just a good boss. I'm a good *friend.*"

De Fersen looked across at Gillan, his cool eyes fixed uneasily on his. For the two years he had known him, De Fersen had always come across as a boisterous, confident man. But rarely a confrontational one. Yet, at that moment, as the gaunt computer programmer nodded slowly, eyes unflinching, Gillan saw a look he had not seen before. Woven amidst his assertive countenance was a clear hint of anxiety.

"Yeah. Yeah. You are a good boss. And a good friend. But I know what you are, Rob. I know what you do. There was no way I could protect your assets forever without one day finding out what was going on behind the curtains."

Gillan froze in place. His eyes narrowed. De Fersen continued to meet his gaze fearlessly. Gillan slowly, calmly, pulled his cuffs out from beneath his jacket and drew in a breath.

"You've always known what I am, Gabby. It's impossible to get this far in this industry without getting one's hands a little dirty."

"What you do is illegal," De Fersen declared coolly.

"The narcotics you took tonight that nearly killed you are illegal, Gabriele. You have no moral pedestal from which to lecture me."

"But I'm doing that to myself!" De Fersen spat suddenly. "I've never hurt anybody else! Never! What you do destroys other people!"

Gillan shot to his feet for a second time.

"Enough! Enough of this! Fucking hell! You're throwing accusations around as if I'm a drug dealer or an arms smuggler or some bastard like that! I twist my financial figures, Gabby, nothing more! I know the business, I know what I have to declare and what I can hide behind smoke and mirrors! I keep money for my company that the government says they should have. They're none the wiser and nobody gets hurt. The PanOceanian government loses a few million that would be spent on guns, bombs, and TAGs for their bloated military-industrial complex! I can look myself in the mirror, knowing I've illegally kept some money back from the PMC's war juggernaut!"

"That's how you justify it?!" De Fersen croaked. "You tell yourself that you're a Robin Hood recreation? Keeping the money away from the corruption of the PanOceanian government and its war machine? Come on, Rob! You are committing fraud on a huge scale, and as a result, you are crushing small businesses underfoot as you expand, putting countless honest people out of work! You are wrecking their lives and those of their families! And I don't want to be a part of this anymore!"

Gillan turned away. He looked out of the private hospital room window, across the brightly lit night skyline. He saw a billboard for private medical care and a green light on his wrist-mounted comlog signaling that his cutting edge geist had blocked a pop-up advert from forcing itself onto his contact lens. Below the billboard, an ambulance threaded its way skillfully through the automated vehicles controlled by ALEPH's traffic system. The world of Earth continued to play out, minute-by-minute via the people of Mauritius, just as life did across the stars on the handful of other planets inhabited by humanity. Countless people continuing their existence; 99.9% of them less wealthy but more honest than Gillan. He turned back to face the younger man.

"Gabby, you've bumped your head. You shouldn't be rushing into any rash decisions. You need me and I need you. This works. Don't do anything stupid."

Gritting his teeth, De Fersen carefully edged over to the end of his bed and sat up straight, breathing heavily from the exertion.

"This isn't a whim. This isn't an ill thought out, rash decision. Rob, I'm done. I need to do something different with my life. Something good. Something worthwhile to help people instead of leeching off them. I could have died tonight, and for some reason, I've got another chance. I need to do something good before it's too late."

"Too late for what?" Gillan exclaimed.

De Fersen winced, let out a despairing breath, and looked down at the floor beneath his bare feet.

"Too late for my soul."

"That's your dad…"

"No, it isn't. It's me. It's me talking. I've got to move on."

Gillan nodded slowly. It was not the words. It was the focussed, bitter determination in his friend's eyes that convinced him. He did at least respect that. After another long pause, he stepped across and offered his hand to De Fersen.

"Best of luck with whatever you decide to do, Gabby. If you change your mind, you know where I am. I'm always your friend."

De Fersen looked at that hand, then up into Gillan's eyes.

"Tell me you'll at least think about what you're doing. Promise me you'll at least consider the impact of what your actions have on others."

Gillan shrugged and nodded slowly.

"I'll think it over," he said, not even sure if he was lying to himself.

Seemingly content, De Fersen accepted his hand and shook it firmly.

"What's your plan?" Gillan asked quietly. "What are you going to do?"

De Fersen looked out of the window and across the sprawling, neon city stretched out on the dark canvas below him.

"I don't know," he murmured quietly to himself, "I really don't know yet. Something... something where good people benefit... and evil bastards get hurt."

Chapter One

Thirty-five years later
Vedi
Septentria Continent
Paradiso
2137 Local Time

The wailing of sirens was audible even over the howling wind, announcing the road convoy long before the flashing blue lights appeared over the horizon. Vehicles on the tall, long bridge spanning across the River Odme peeled off to the left and right; the majority - those fully automated and controlled by synched micro-AI Logic Programming and Artificial Intelligence devised by ALEPH - parted neatly and efficiently to form a clear path for the rapidly approaching emergency vehicles. The small number of cars driven manually by people were slower to react, their drivers almost robotically following the example set by the dozens of LAI controlled road vehicles.

The six lanes running across the bridge were washed in flickering blue lights as the first vehicles appeared; two sleek, curved police patrol cars in blue and silver, followed by a taller, bulkier ambulance, its angular frame painted in high visibility yellow and green. A third patrol car brought up the rear of the rapidly moving convoy, but another vehicle sped almost awkwardly along ahead of it and just behind the ambulance. A tall, long, boxy vehicle that sat somewhere between a van and a heavy goods truck, its slab sides colored black and devoid of any markings. The five vehicles hurtled across the apex of the bridge, down the other side, and then turned sharply off the freeway and onto a minor road. That road in turn curved away from the brightly lit main route from the sprawling, coastal city of Vedi and toward the notorious jungles of Septentria Continent, Paradiso.

The flashing lights of the patrol cars and the ambulance flickered against the walls of vegetation to either side of the narrow track, the pale blue bouncing off the dull browns and vivid greens of tall palms, crawling vines, and dense bushes sprouting up out of the sandy earth beneath. The road snaked on, up a shallow hill and toward a plateaued peak less than a mile ahead, where a luxury hotel complex was visible even from this distance. The lights all but disappeared beneath the arching canopy of green, reduced to a mere pulsing of azure tracking purposefully through the darkness.

A trio of police officers stepped out to meet the vehicles at the hotel complex's main entrance, pushing back the handful of correspondents who had managed to arrive at the scene with almost suspicious rapidity. A young police officer held up one hand to the drizzle-soaked journalists, gesturing for them to stay back while beckoning with her other hand to invite the vehicle convoy through. The first two patrol cars, their sirens now silenced and their lights dimmed, headed up the gravel drive toward the hotel's main entrance. The black van peeled away to the right and, its lights extinguished, continued alone around the back of the complex and into an underground parking area beneath the hotel's health spas. The vehicle came to a halt.

From the cab's passenger seat, Father-Officer Gabriele De Fersen looked across at the driver. Mother-Officer Britt Heijboer, De Fersen's executive officer, glanced back across at him from behind the steering wheel of the van. In her early thirties, her sharp, stern facial features were accentuated by swept back, red hair that was cut short at the nape of the neck. Like De Fersen, Heijboer wore black combat fatigues, partially covered by a civilian jacket - in her case, a stylish three quarter length coat of shiny, faux red-brown leather.

"Get operations set up as a priority," De Fersen ordered his second-in-command, "then get the kit sorted, and then domestics. I'll be in touch as soon as I've got anything."

"Do you want them booted and spurred?" Heijboer queried, nodding her head toward the soldiers secreted in the back of the van.

"No, not yet," the veteran knight replied, opening the door to the van's cab. "I think we might be here for a while. A good few days, in fact. And there's a fair chance we won't even be activated."

De Fersen stepped down from the cab, the humid, dense night air of Paradiso immediately enveloping him. Drizzle pattered audibly off his jacket as he fastened it up while a powerful gust of wind rustled the soaked trees to his left, providing some mild respite from the hot, night air. De Fersen walked briskly toward the main hotel building, thrusting his hands into the pockets of his bulky, red civilian jacket. He sneered to himself as he remembered some of the lighthearted abuse he had received from a pair of the younger knights for still wearing whatever brand the jacket was; apparently 'Pearl' was the designer brand of choice these days for covert military operatives conforming in their self-perceived non-conformity.

De Fersen tapped at the comlog on his wrist, ensuring that his IFF was set up to register on both military and law enforcement networks. Unarmed and unarmored, even the light handguns carried by police would be enough to ruin his day if some trigger happy cop saw him wandering alone through a hotel complex with a reported terrorist seizure, and jumped to the wrong conclusion. Within an instant of activating the Friend or Foe Identifier, the law enforcement network transmitted the positions of every police officer within the complex to his comlog; in turn, this data was uploaded to his tactical contact lens. Through the drizzle, foliage, and brick walls of the hotel complex alike, every police officer now showed up as a vivid blue outline. The path from the parking area wound up through a gap in the trees, heading uphill toward the brightly lit main complex; a smooth, oval building of cream-white with brightly lit balconies and impressive water features flanking the main promenade leading up to a grand entrance. At the foot of the steps were four police cars and a collection of pistol armed officers. Having identified his presence to the officers from his comlog, he saw one jogging over to him as a line of text scrolled across the top of his lens.

- *Broadsword Zero Identified. Silver Zero requesting communication link.*

Tapping his comlog to accept the request, De Fersen paced out to meet the approaching officer. A young man, barely out of his teens, with a pock-marked face partially hidden behind a thin, ill-advised attempt at facial hair came to a stop before him, the drizzle soaking his dark blue uniform into near black. The short police officer narrowed his eyes in suspicion as he took in De Fersen. No doubt the rookie had been dispatched to meet the 'SF guy,' and was therefore expecting a hulking mountain of muscle encased in camouflage, with a cliched scraggy beard, baseball cap with PanO flag, tactical body armor, and a Combi Rifle dripping with expensive tactical rail attachments. Instead, he was presented with a lean, bald, middle-aged man in a hill-walking jacket who looked as though he was lost and had wandered accidentally into a counter-terrorism operation.

"Are you... are you...?"

"Re-entry Team Leader," the hospitaller nodded curtly. "Silver HQ up here? Better take me to your boss."

The shorter man led De Fersen away, staying well clear of the main building and the surrounding ring of pistol-armed police officers. An alert appeared on De Fersen's lens, informing him of incoming files from Silver HQ. He accepted them and immediately set about reading through the headline details of each file as he walked.

The information of the hotel building was identical to that which had been provided to De Fersen on the drive across: three floors, the lower consisting mainly of a sprawling reception area with a small number of staff and storage rooms, while the upper floors were made up of luxury accommodation suites. So far seven terrorists had been picked out by the hotel's own security system before it was shut down, as well as surveillance drones which continued to drift noiselessly in the night sky overhead. The terrorists were armed with pistols and a handful of submachine guns; some wore light body armor. De Fersen scoffed at the thought - their weapons would struggle to penetrate the armor of his soldiers, while their own armor did not stand a chance against the hospitallers' weaponry. Clearly their plan hinged on a resolution before an assault.

But that was not De Fersen's problem. Dead hostages were his problem.

The incident HQ was set up in the reception of the health spa building, only a couple of minutes walk from the main hotel. The plush but spartan room was decorated with a liberal smattering of framed, calming photographs of hammocks on sandy beaches and mountain-top sunsets - De Fersen suppressed a gruff laugh as the irony of the current scenario was not wasted on him. The three-dimensional, holographic schematic of the hotel building was projected in the center of the room, the walls and floors shimmering in a pale blue while the last known position of each terrorist was marked in bold red. The holographic display also showed perhaps a dozen figures crammed together into a large suite on the middle floor, surrounded by three of the red terrorist images. The seated figures were highlighted in green - the hostages.

Six uniformed police officers surrounded the flickering image in the center of the pale, marble walled reception area. One of them, a tall woman of perhaps forty years of age with smooth features and a mop of unruly, black hair tied back in an attempt to tame it, looked up at De Fersen and then walked across to meet him.

"Broadsword team leader?" she greeted, offering a hand. "I'm Superintendent Perez. I have tactical control here."

"Gabe," the tall soldier nodded, shaking her hand firmly, "my team is setting up and prepping kit. What have you got for me to brief them?"

"Broadsword is a Hospitaller callsign, isn't it?" the veteran police officer asked warily. "I was expecting PMC SpecOps for a counter terrorism op, not soldiers from the NeoVatican's Military Orders."

"The Military Orders are fully integrated into the PanOceanian Military Complex," De Fersen replied coolly, fighting to keep the annoyance from his tone. "The Order of the Hospital happens to have a main base of operations here in Vedi, so it made sense for us to respond as we'd be the quickest on scene. What have you got for me to brief my team?"

Given how rare it was for the police to work hand-in-hand with the military, De Fersen could forgive Perez for her ignorance. It was common enough even within PanOceania's armed forces for the typical misunderstandings of the Military Orders to present themselves, as De Fersen had encountered countless times over the past decades:

"So, you guys are warrior monks?"

"No. Even in Earth's medieval era when the Orders were established, it would be a gross oversimplification to term knights of the Orders as warrior monks. We're soldiers for the Church. We swear holy vows, but we are not ordained. We serve God and God's people, but we are not clergy."

"But… you just fight for things that the Christian NeoVatican is involved in?"

"No. The NeoVatican is fully aligned to the PanOceanian government and no other faction within the Human Sphere. That agreement is mutually beneficial. Where the PanOceanian armed forces go, the NeoVatican's Military Orders go."

"The terrorist cell consists of at least seven people," Perez began, turning to face the shimmering holographic display in the middle of the room and tapping on her wrist-mounted comlog to bring up security footage from earlier in the day. "They entered the building at sixteen thirty-seven this afternoon from two vehicles; one disguised as a safety inspection team while the other posed as a maintenance team. After revealing their intentions and drawing weapons, they locked down the main building and began a controlled release of most of their hostages."

De Fersen nodded slowly as he watched the footage of a brown van reverse up to the hotel's rear entrance before disgorging a trio of men in trade overalls, accompanied by an array of convincing looking maintenance and cleaning bots and drones. All of which were large enough to conceal small arms.

"The terrorists have taken George Hayes - a prominent Member of Parliament - and his campaign team," the police superintendent continued, "they arrived in the hotel yesterday as part of the election campaign. Details of his team should be in the briefing pack, along with facial recognition data for your weapon safety systems. There are twelve hostages in total. The terrorist team have identified themselves as a cell from Equinox. They have already released a list of demands, and seem to have targeted Hayes specifically due to his progressive politics. They've asked for…"

De Fersen held up one hand.

"I'll stop you there. Just to save some time. The briefing pack I read through on the drive over included details of the two security guards killed by these fuckers. Whatever their cause is, whatever their demands are, save all of that for your negotiator. If my team gets the green light to go in, be under no illusion that their 'causes' and 'demands' won't matter anymore."

The room fell silent for a moment. De Fersen was more than familiar with Equinox. A sprawling, well organized techno-terrorist group committed to bringing down the perceived 'evils' of ALEPH; the sole legitimate Artificial Intelligence network that was as close to sentience as De Fersen would ever like or admit, which carefully controlled and directed a significant fraction of all affairs of the Human Sphere, irrespective of faction.

The assembled police officers looked up at De Fersen.

"I suppose forgiveness and mercy look good on your Order's billboards, but it's a little harder in practice. Perhaps." Perez smiled without humor.

Despite being mentally armed with a plethora of instant responses to the tired, cliched attacks on the aggressiveness of the Hospitallers, De Fersen did not bother to answer. He could snap back with some snippy comment about forgiveness being reserved for those who asked for it, or mercy only for those who deserved it. The truth was that he did not care for any validation from Perez or any of her subordinates.

"What live intel have you got from inside the building?" De Fersen demanded.

Perez looked across at a young, dark-haired man sat at a terminal at the edge of the shimmering, holographic depiction of the hotel's main building.

"We've got satellite and drone imagery giving us live feed updates of every side of the building," the police officer replied, "as well as human surveillance on all doors and windows. The locations of the hostages and terrorists were last updated just over an hour ago using cameras we managed to push up into the environmental control ducts, but those ducts have since been covered up, and we now have no live intel inside the building."

De Fersen folded his lean arms and glowered down at the young police officer.

"The terrorists covered up the air ducts an hour ago, so you all just gave up on live intelligence from inside the building?" he grimaced.

The police officer looked up at Perez. The superintendent planted her fists on her hips.

"We have intelligence specialists en route as we speak," Perez declared defensively, "so the very fact that my first response team have provided us with this level of intelligence in the first place is..."

"Your intelligence specialists still aren't here, several hours after a major terrorist incident," De Fersen cut in, "and what's stopping you from using the building's own power bar grid to emit a low energy pulse within each room to identify any obstacle that isn't identified on the security and emergency floor plans? As a rule of thumb, a big group of people are hostages. One or two on their own, wandering around freely, they're the terrorists."

Perez looked back at the officer by the terminal. The officer looked down at the controls on his desk.

"There is no power bar, sir," he replied. "Cutting the power was the first thing the terrorists did once they sealed the building. We've seen them with flashlights, most likely infra-red, meaning they're using IR lens..."

"Then hack it," De Fersen grunted.

The dark-haired police officer looked awkwardly up at De Fersen again.

"That would fall within the remit and skillset of our intelligence specialists, sir," the young officer said quietly. "They'll be here in..."

De Fersen tapped a finger on his comlog and brought up the shimmering, pale-blue holographic control wheel of his hacking device's programs in the space above his wrist.

"Leave this to me."

***

Sergeant Anja Nilsson glanced around the subterranean carpark that could well act as her home for the next few days. A squat, square space constructed of drab, gray concrete and given just a hint of life via its neon blue strip lighting, the park housed the hotel's pool of vehicles that were left behind from before the evacuation. A motley collection of rugged, adventurous four-by-four trucks and more luxurious, glossy black sedans for ferrying wealthy clients to and from meetings were neatly parked in rows beneath the low ceiling. Two curved vehicle access ramps led up to the world above. In and around these, the small group of Hospitaller Knights and sergeants set about their business; establishing areas for communications, planning, prayers, and sleeping. Nilsson herself was responsible for the armory - as a soldier with just under two years of experience, she had recently qualified as an armorer and was now capable of maintaining a unit's weapons and equipment.

Nilsson, like her seven comrades, wore plain black combat fatigues decorated only with the white cross of her order. As with her fellow three sergeants, she wore the three chevrons of her rank on her thin epaulets. That in itself was something of a concession; over a thousand years ago, the division between knight and sergeant in the Order of the Hospital was based on social standing; non-nobles would join the Order as sergeants and were a lower rank, both in terms of the military hierarchy and the weapons and equipment they were provided with. The use of the word 'sergeant' as a senior NCO rank came centuries later, yet in the modern day Order, sergeants wore the same badge of rank as their regular PanOceanian military counterparts, to avoid the abject confusion injected into the PanOceanian Military Complex by the elite, NeoVatican fighting orders.

Exhaling slowly, her pale arms folded across her narrow torso, Nilsson looked down at the collection of weapons and armor lined up before her, ready for maintenance and adjustment. Combi Rifles, MULTI Rifles, pistols, a Boarding Shotgun, a Spitfire... all hurriedly loaded into the van when an emergency unit of knights and sergeants was hastily activated and assembled in response to the terrorist threat in the hotel. In peacetime, duty teams of soldiers and carefully prepared and maintained pools of weapons would be at the ready for a counter-terrorism activation, but on a planet where the already warring factions of the Human Sphere were threatened by the external force of an alien invasion, one hotel full of terrorists fell a long way down the priority order, no matter how important the politician they held hostage was.

Leaning over the fold-out desk that served as her armorer's bench, Nilsson picked up the first weapon. A CineticS Radjun MULTI Rifle, 4.5mm, capable of firing APlus, ultrashock, and double action ammunition. Just as the assault rifle was the next step in weaponry evolution from the semi-automatic rifle, and in turn the Combi Rifle was a technological leap again, the MULTI Rifle was the pinnacle of general use, anti-personnel firepower for the modern soldier. Ammunition was standardized at 4.5mm caseless, but these compact, high-velocity rounds could be interchanged either from multiple magazines or from separate compartments within the same magazine, all at the flip of the thumb at the top of the weapon's pistol grip.

Other innovations included a smart squeeze-breech system that instantly and automatically configured to any manufacturing defects or variations in ammunition to ensure that every last iota of propellent was exploited in firing every round. Whereas the Radjun's predecessor, the Koryos, managed a respectable average of one chamber stoppage for every thousand rounds fired, the Radjun's squeeze-breech improved this to an unprecedented one stoppage in five thousand average, leaving other similar rifles practically half a generation behind.

Nilsson's job with each of the rifles was twofold - first off, to remove the standard barrel and replace it with a shortened, carbine barrel designed for close quarter battle. Moving rapidly in the close confines of the hotel - should they be given the green light to proceed - could result in the longer, standard barrel of the Radjun becoming a mobility hindrance, and the increased power and accuracy it afforded would be completely wasted at such short ranges. That task was quick and easy enough.

The second job was to adjust the iron sights on each weapon to match the individual requirements of the firer. While the weapon system's battle sight - mated in combat with the firer's contact lens and helmet visor - provided reflex, zoom, IR, night vision, and a host of other options, the battle sight could be hacked or simply fail, and the backup system was nothing more complex than a notch-and-post adjustable sight, similar to that fitted to rifles in the great wars of Earth's twentieth century. However, whereas soldiers would need to test and adjust their sights to align them to that exact rifle, more modern rifles could at least be set up correctly based on standardized metrics taken on firing ranges during basic training.

Nilsson took the first MULTI Rifle - a weapon assigned to Brother-Sub Officer Luca Romano, a knight she had only met in the drive across to the hotel - and released the magnetic locks on the weapon housing. This allowed her access to the main release clips, which in turn enabled her to detach the bulky housing from the weapon. Now with access to the working parts, she set about inspecting the trigger mechanism, main magazine housing, rotary upper magazine housing, breech, gas-parts, and safeties. Then it was simply a case of unclipping and detaching the barrel before sliding in and securing the shorter, carbine barrel. This could all easily be carried out by any knight, but with Nilsson's additional qualification as an armorer, she could also incorporate extra inspection measures and sign the weapon off on its six-month safety assurance check.

"Hello, Anja."

Nilsson looked up from her task and saw Mother-Officer Heijboer walking across from the bank of portable computer terminals that had been set up to form the unit's operations hub. Before their hurried reunion only three hours before, Nilsson had not seen Heijboer since her basic training where the intimidating woman had been one of her weapons and tactics instructors.

"Hello, ma'am," Nilsson smiled with a respectful nod of the head, "I'm just working through the Radjuns now. I'm giving them all their six-monthlies while I'm at it, it's only a few extra minutes work. I'll get straight onto the other weapons after that, and then the armor."

"No problem," Heijboer folded her arms, "but get them sorted quickly. I know it's fifty-fifty at best whether we'll be activated, but if we are, then we need to be ready in all respects at a moment's notice. Those weapons are all already in date for their six-month checks, so don't waste your time if you don't need to."

"Got it, ma'am." Nilsson nodded.

Heijboer grabbed her own weapon - the sole CineticS Preman Boarding Shotgun that had been brought with the team - and set about dismantling it herself to swap the long barrel for a shorter variant.

"I've read over your file. Seems you've been kept busy since graduating. Counter insurgency in Varuna, ops against the Yujingyu in Svalarheima, even a couple of months on Dawn... You've seen a fair bit."

Nilsson finished her adjustments on the iron sights for Romano's MULTI Rifle, digitally signed its safety inspection, and then grabbed another weapon to repeat the process.

"It's certainly been a busy couple of years, ma'am," she shrugged, "but I've never had any involvement in counter terrorism, so I'm not going into this one with any complacency."

"I've no doubt. While this team has been put together very quickly, we still had a good number of soldiers at the ready. Father-Officer De Fersen hand picked you, just as he did everybody else here."

Nilsson tapped her wrist-mounted comlog to bring up the firer's biometrics, noted his sight settings, and quickly adjusted the weapon on the bench in front of her to meet those requirements. Heijboer's words were complimentary, certainly, but it did not pay to be proud. It was not the Hospitaller way. One reflected on failure or substandard performance and tried to do better; success, on the other hand, did not need fixing so therefore did not require any thought. Nilsson, who in her childhood and adolescence had always prided herself on her optimism and high spirits, found this disposition somewhat grim and miserable, but she had fought hard to become a Hospitaller Sergeant and was more than willing to adjust her temperament to suit the Order.

"Yes, ma'am." She nodded simply as she finished adjusting the sights and set about changing the barrel. "I suppose that is one of many advantages of our Order. I have only worked with Sergeant Kilpatrick before. Aside from yourself, ma'am, everybody else here is a stranger. But as brothers and sisters of the Order, I at least know I can trust them with this op. Just as they can trust me."

"It's not our lives I'm worried about, Sergeant," Heijboer said, handing over her shotgun for Nilsson to carry out her safety checks on, "it's the hostages. If we go in, we'll go in with superior arms, armor, training, and experience. Those Equinox terrorists don't stand a chance. But if any of them want to prove a point before they die for their cause, it'll be easy enough to put a bullet in a hostage. And I'd imagine only the MP himself will be able to afford resurrection, even if he is eligible."

Nilsson nodded silently. She half agreed, she supposed. It was very easy for an Order Knight to feel safe in their state of the art, fully enclosed ORC combat armor, providing the user with enhanced speed, strength, and superlative protection from modern battlefield weapons. But for the second rate sergeants of the Order, their light armor provided only a fighting chance at best of surviving a gunshot. And just as the Order's seemingly limitless finances suddenly met a backstop when it came to armor for its sergeants, so too was that the case with firepower, as sergeants were armed with effective but mundane Combi Rifles rather than the versatile, harder hitting MULTI Rifles and Boarding Shotguns often employed by the Order knights. The knights only took Combi Rifles into battle when stores of the cripplingly expensive MULTI Rifles were low. So, easy for a knight not to worry about being killed in a counter-terrorism operation. Not so easy for a sergeant to place the same faith in their arms and armor.

"Have you thought of reapplying for a position as a knight?" Heijboer asked suddenly, as if somehow reading Nilsson's inner turmoil and doubts.

Nilsson finished signing off the MULTI Rifle in front of her and then grabbed the half-finished weapon left by Heijboer. Of course she had thought about it. When she left school at the age of eighteen, she applied to become a knight. She took the same selection exams as any other aspiring Order soldier. She passed the written tests to become a knight. She passed the interviews. She passed the stringent medical examinations. Then she failed the physical tests by the smallest of margins. It was so close that she was granted the exceptional courtesy of a re-test. Having mentally piled so much pressure on herself, with just one barrier between her and her goal of becoming a knight, her re-test was an abhorrent disaster with an even lower grade than her first test.

She was lucky that the Order of the Hospital counted that first, narrow failure on the physical tests and she was offered a place to train as an Order Sergeant. Twelve months of training instead of the four years demanded of knights. She gratefully took the offer and passed the training. Two years of combat experience later, and the gifted few men and women who took the tests alongside her and managed to pass were still a full year from graduating as knights.

"I consider myself blessed to have any place in the Order, ma'am." Nilsson smiled. "*In all thy ways acknowledge him, and he shall direct thy paths.* God has put me where I am supposed to be."

That seemed a far better answer than the truth - although she did believe wholeheartedly that God had placed her there for a reason. The truth was that she was terrified of facing those trials and tests again.

Before Heijboer could answer, her eyes flickered to one side, and she raised one hand to her ear. Nilsson watched as Heijboer turned away and muttered a few words in reply to whoever was calling her on her comlog. After a few moments, the older woman turned back to Nilsson.

"That was Father-Officer De Fersen. We're on. We've just been given the green light."

***

The same holographic image that De Fersen had seen in the police incident HQ at the health spa was now projected in front of him, across his own team's briefing area in the car park. The image, perhaps two meters cubed, hovered at waist height and showed the detail of the ground floor, the first and second floors above, and the basement area below. De Fersen stood with Heijboer on one side of the image while his six other soldiers assembled opposite them. He cast his eyes across the hastily assembled team. Any man or woman capable enough to pass the selection process to become an Order knight or sergeant, let alone the brutal, relentless training that followed, could already be relied upon for this task. But the two knights and four sergeants who had been assigned to De Fersen and Heijboer were all known quantities - mostly with years of combat experience, although in one case only a few weeks - and to De Fersen, they stood out even within an already elite group.

"Listen in," Heijboer began, "the parliament green-lit our operation seven minutes ago. We brief now, prep for entry, with E-Hour planned for 2300 local time. You've all confirmed to me that you have read and understood the intelligence briefing provided by the Black Friars, so I'll go straight into the operation brief."

De Fersen folded his arms and looked across at the holographic projection of the hotel building. Thanks to his hacking skills, they now at least had a live feed on movement within the building.

"We've been blessed with a relatively simple scenario," Heijboer continued. "You've all read the operation order and the detailed plan, so this briefing is merely to confirm the overview. Twelve hostages are being held in one room on the first floor. After the latest hack of the building's interior, we now know we are facing nine terrorists, not the seven we were first briefed on. The hotel is a roughly rectangular building of three floors, one basement below them, and one main entrance on the ground floor with two smaller entrances. There are numerous balconies on the first and second floors, highlighted in yellow, here. Our operation will consist of four simultaneous entries - two on the ground floor, one on the first floor, and one on the second floor. Four teams, each consisting of one knight and one sergeant."

Heijboer clicked a button on her comlog, and the four pairs of soldiers appeared in green on the three dimensional projection of the plan.

"Alpha Team will take the main entrance, that will be the Boss and Sergeant Kilpatrick. You'll be entering at the main entrance on the ground floor, here at the central point on the eastern wall. Bravo Team - that's Brother-Sub Officer Romano and Sergeant Aubert - will be entering at the service entrance on the south wall. The last entrance on the ground floor, here on the north wall, will be covered by a police unit."

De Fersen scratched his jaw. Kilpatrick was an experienced, dependable soldier and one of the Order's most senior sergeants. As for Bravo Team, Romano had a decade of experience and was already under consideration for promotion to Father-Officer - he was the right man for the job. Aubert was an unknown to De Fersen but came highly recommended by Heijboer. Superintendent Perez had informed De Fersen that a police special weapons unit was already on the way to the hotel. They could cover a single entrance and ensure nobody hostile came out of it. He hoped.

"Charlie Team," Heijboer continued, "will be me, with Sergeant Nilsson. We'll ascend into position from the ground floor to enter the hotel at this first story balcony. Finally, Delta Team - Brother-Sub Officer Hawkins and Sergeant Alvarez - you'll enter directly above, on the corresponding second story balcony."

Charlie Team would be straight into action on the critical floor housing the hostages, but Heijboer was one of the best soldiers De Fersen had worked alongside. If anybody could secure that floor, ready for the final assault on the hostage holding area, she could. Nilsson had a lot less time under fire, but she had earned a solid reputation with a good breadth of operational experience.

Delta Team's job was more simple. The top floor housed at least two lookouts at all times. Security sensors and cameras were easy enough to hack - the Equinox terrorists knew that much - and so relying on the human eyeball was in this case a safer bet. The rudimentary sensor sweep De Fersen had conducted on the building placed two terrorists on lookout on the top floor, with not a hostage in sight. For not the first time that evening, De Fersen found himself clenching his jaw in frustration at his team's lack of sniper support. None could be made available in time. None...

De Fersen switched his concentration back to the holographic map and briefing, and the details of his fourth team. Of the two soldiers in Delta Team, Alvarez was a fantastic soldier - five years' front line experience resulting in a performance that had marked her out from her peers for selection for knight training. Hawkins was a different matter entirely. His experience could nearly be counted on one hand - in weeks, rather than years - but his involvement in a high profile border conflict with the Yujingyu had proved that he was more capable than he looked.

"Simultaneous entry into all four points." Heijboer clicked on her comlog to begin the holographic animation of the plan. "Alpha Team will enter through the main hallway and proceed immediately up the main staircase. Charlie Team will by this point have entered through the first story balcony and eliminated resistance along the first floor corridor. Alpha and Charlie Teams will then proceed to the last suite here, where the twelve hostages are being held. Meanwhile, Bravo Team will eliminate all resistance on the ground floor before securing the main entrance as a hostage extraction point. Delta Team will take all hostiles on the second floor and hold position at the main stairwell, ready to provide assistance to any other team as required. Alpha and Charlie Teams are then to enter the hostage holding area and eliminate any final resistance. Hostages are then extricated via Bravo Team at the ground floor main entrance."

The six soldiers stood opposite the holographic mission projection stared through the flickering, three-dimensional image at their two leaders. The animation projected in the center of the subterranean car park showed the simplified, almost childlike representations of the eight Hospitallers move into the building and engage the red projections of the terrorists. De Fersen suppressed a grimace. If only it were that simple. He looked up at his waiting soldiers.

"The plan is simple enough," he began, "you know the score. The plan has to be simple because we have to be flexible. There's nine terrorists who, in an ideal world, we would watch and draw up patterns of life to anticipate when to strike. It's not an ideal world, so we're going in within the hour with what little intelligence we have. For those of you who haven't faced Equinox before, don't underestimate them. They'll only be lightly armed and armored compared to us, but remember why they are here. They are fully committed to their cause. They are willing to die for it, and they are willing to kill civilians without flinching."

De Fersen paused for a moment. He considered bringing up the two dead security guards, but he knew all of his soldiers would have read about that in their intelligence briefs.

"Priorities from Command are clear. First - hostage casualties are unacceptable. None. Second - all terrorists are to be eliminated. Facial recognition profiles have already been uploaded to your weapons for those terrorists that are identified - by all means feel free to read up on these people as individuals, but you'll quickly find that they're all complete bastards. And none of you will need a history lesson on what happened in Madrid in eighty-six, so remember: these bastards have had plenty of time to plant explosives in the building, and they have the motivation to fire them off. Leave it to God to show them mercy. That's not our job. Our job is to protect innocent lives. Any one of them could have a remote detonator, so every one of them must be killed without hesitation. Understood?"

Various affirmations were nodded or uttered quietly by the assembled Hospitallers. De Fersen understood their collective apprehension. No mercy was not a message that rested easily on the shoulders of some of the younger soldiers of the NeoVatican.

"Five minutes for individual prayer. Then get booted and spurred."

***

Twenty three minutes to go until entry. The hastily improvised base of operations within the car park was silent, save for the knights and sergeants finishing their prayers and making their way over to their equipment. Brother-Sub Officer Kyle Hawkins made the sign of the cross with his right hand before standing and walking over to where his weapons and armor lay by his bunk. Three hours. That was how long he had been back from leave before he was activated for this task. Three hours. He had not even finished unpacking his clothes.

Hawkins looked down at where his ORC heavy armor lay ready at his feet. The hiss of escaping air sounded from his left as Mother-Officer Heijboer set about preparing her black combat fatigues for suiting up. To his right, Sergeant Kilpatrick fitted his breastplate over the top of his combat jacket, tightening the buckles beneath each arm. Another hiss of expelled air sounded as De Fersen tightened his own fatigues. Hawkins glanced across at the exit to the car park and the pathway leading to the hotel. Nine terrorists. He had only ever faced legitimate combatants from another faction of the Human Sphere. Never terrorists. Never men and women willing to kill helpless, unarmed civilians for their misguided politics.

Hawkins reached down to the small, thumbnail-sized valve on the belt of his combat trousers. He twisted it a quarter turn and immediately felt his clothes tighten to his skin as the air within them was expelled. The weave of his combat trousers and hip-length jacket contracted, forming a water tight body glove that was close enough to the skin to now allow the fitting of ORC armor above. He reached down and lifted up his breastplate, clipping it in place around his muscular torso. He then took the left arm of his armored battle suit and slid his hand down into the alloy tubing, feeling the lines of artificial muscle contract tightly around him. He reached up and slid the power connection guide out of its flush housing and clicked it into place above his collar bone. A red light illuminated silently at his elbow to signify a successful connection. He repeated the process for his right arm before then fitting his pauldrons and gauntlets. Exercising the joints, he found the full and smooth freedom of movement a knight should expect from fully functioning armor. No resistance, no noise - certainly not the ugly, mechanical whirring of joints that was featured in those awful but enjoyable Father-Inquisitor Mendoza Maya-movies. If ORC armor was really that noisy, the team would not stand a chance of sneaking through the night to position themselves for their explosive entry into the hotel.

On the other side of the car park, Aubert and Alvarez exchanged a few words as they completed fitting their armor. Hawkins took off his combat boots and then fitted his greaves and armored boots to his legs. He connected and tested them, rewarded with red lights at the joints to demonstrate to the wearer that full power and functionality had been successfully achieved, backed up by a green light on the built-in test function on the indicator unit on his belt.

The BIT's successful diagnostics report was repeated, with more detail, on a scrolling diagnostics list on his contact lens, confirming the full functionality of every subsystem - power, back-up busbar, twenty channels of communication, personal navigation, injury detection, Chemical-Biological-Radiological-Nanotechnological Shield, targeting detection, automated medical serum dispenser... every feature that a suit of modern armor needed, with monthly software updates from Omnia Research & Creation Corporation keeping every subsystem at the peak of technological development for the modern battlefield. A recent software update had drastically reduced the time it took for a knight to suit up and be fully prepared for battle.

Hawkins looked down at the surcoat on his bunk. A simple, sleeveless garment of red smart-fabric, adorned with a white cross. Save the modern technology of the smart-fabric, it was in essence identical to the surcoats worn by his spiritual warrior-forefathers on Earth a thousand years ago. Hawkins pulled the surcoat over his armor and wrapped a similarly archaic looking brown leather belt around his waist.

Four weapons and a helmet remained on his bunk. Hawkins picked up the smallest of these - a TauruSW Ferro 8.5mm pistol. If the Order of the Hospital had economized anywhere, it was perhaps with this simple weapon - a conventional, automatic handgun carrying a single magazine of twenty caseless, rectangular rounds in its bulky pistol grip. Hawkins slotted the Ferro into the holster on his right hip, together with a spare magazine. The second pistol was more of an oddity. A Huntley Mk.VIII MULTI Pistol, over fourty years old in its design, its bulky ammunition cylinder making it resemble a heavy revolver of earth's twentieth century world wars. The weapon was not issue and therefore not permitted by regulations to be carried, but the memories that came with it were worthy of the inevitable reprimands. Hawkins broke open the frame at the hinge just forward of the cylinder and loaded six heavy DA rounds before snapping the weapon shut and magnetically attaching the heavy handgun to his belt, behind his holster.

If the Huntley MULTI Pistol did not appear anachronistic enough, the Hospitaller Knight's sword Hawkins slid into the sheath at his side certainly would. To the casual observer, the sword looked almost identical to the heavy longswords carried by Military Order knights of the crusading era of Earth's medieval period. The modern knight's Switech sword, however, had its lethal blade augmented by an almost microscopically fine laser edge, capable of cutting through any personal armor. The technology was old, but with each generation, the power source and the lethality found new heights.

Content he was ready in all respects, Hawkins dropped to one knee to quickly whisper a Hail Mary before grabbing his short-barrelled MULTI Rifle and helmet. The other seven soldiers were waiting at the car park exit. De Fersen stood with Alpha and Bravo Teams, ready to move to their positions by the ground floor entrances. Hawkins jogged over to where Heijboer waited with Sergeants Nilsson and Alvarez. Alvarez nodded a curt greeting to Hawkins as he approached before pulling her helmet on over her shaved head. Nilsson flashed a warm smile, her plaited blonde pigtails giving her the look of an ancient, Viking shield-maiden.

"You all ready?" Heijboer asked.

"Yes, ma'am." Hawkins nodded respectfully.

Heijboer looked down at Hawkins's waist.

"Is that your grandfather's handgun?" Heijboer's brow furrowed. "You're not content with the weaponry issued to you by the Order, Sub Officer?"

"Perfectly content, ma'am," Hawkins replied uneasily, "just an extra weapon if needed."

"It's non-regulation, sir," Nilsson said quietly. "I can't requisition parts or ammunition for that weapon, let alone sign it off on a safety check."

"Minds on the job!" De Fersen called across from his group. "Let him have his six-shooter, Britt. Besides, some of us do well using weapons we've acquired on our travels."

De Fersen patted the bulky, CineticS Bagyo Spitfire slung over his shoulder to emphasize the point. Heijboer shrugged in acquiescence.

"Alright." She looked across at her three soldiers. "Subdue your colors and follow me."

Hawkins tapped his comlog and brought up the color wheels on his lens for the surcoat's smart-fabric. He selected night subdue and, like his comrades, the vivid red of his surcoat faded to black, the white cross of his faith similarly fading to a barely perceptible gray. The eight Hospitallers walked silently up the ramp toward the hotel building.

Chapter Two

Romano and Aubert broke away and disappeared into the wet foliage to track around the hotel ground's perimeter. De Fersen saw them on his lens, highlighted in blue, as they stealthily picked their way through the carefully maintained, neat line of trees toward their entry point. He checked his comlog - five minutes to E-hour. Up ahead, four police cars formed a barrier across the broad, gravel driveway in front of the hotel's main entrance. Just as they had been briefed, six police officers remained by the vehicles - some of them engaged in conversation to give the appearance of complacency, of letting guards down. Anything to stop suspicion rising.

De Fersen looked up at the hotel. His sensor hack was still providing the vital information the team needed - all hostages clumped together in one room on the first floor. Two terrorists guarding them. Two on the ground floor, two on the first floor corridor outside the holding room, and now three lookouts on the second floor. De Fersen swore under his breath. Having locations of the enemy was a good start, but it was nothing more than the absolute basics for a counter-terrorism operation involving hostages. If they had time to establish proper intelligence, his lens would also be highlighting the real time fields of view of each terrorist based on the position of their heads. But that was beyond what he had been able to provide with a few brief minutes of hacking in the incident room HQ from long range, and without the benefit of an information repeater.

"Broadsword Zero, this is Silver Zero," De Fersen heard Perez's voice in his helmet earphones, "my team is in position and has the north entrance covered."

De Fersen saw four bright blue figures on his lens to his right as Heijboer led Charlie and Delta teams across to position for climbing up the south wall to the balcony entrance points. He tapped his comlog to reply to Perez on the police secure emergency channel.

"Broadsword Zero, copied."

Two alloy rope lines shot up on the far side of the building, one securing to a first floor balcony rail and the other to the second floor. He changed his active communication channel back to his team's tactical frequency.

"Zero, four minutes," he warned.

Looking over his shoulder, he nodded to Sergeant Kilpatrick to follow him. Crouching low, both Hospitallers dashed around the northern edge of the gravel driveway, just inside the line of decorative trees flanking the open area. De Fersen reached a corner in the meticulously manicured, vivid green foliage and dropped to one knee again, now only a few meters away from the hotel's main entrance. He looked up at the building. The three lookouts remained in place at their posts on the second floor. One of them, given a decent multispectral visor, would possibly be able to see him now. De Fersen uttered a brief prayer and hoped these bastards had not managed to acquire military-grade hardware.

"Zero, three minutes," he called as Kilpatrick dropped down by his side.

On the far side of the building, he saw Hawkins dashing up the alloy rope toward the second floor, quickly outpacing the other three Hospitallers. He nimbly rolled over the balcony rail and took position by entry point Delta. Heijboer stopped dead in place on the next line. De Fersen looked across, his interest piqued. But, not time for full anxiety just yet. On the balcony above, the red outline of an Equinox terrorist moved along the corridor toward entry point Charlie.

"Charlie Team, hold position," Heijboer whispered across the tactical channel.

Alvarez continued on up the second alloy rope line and took position on the balcony next to Hawkins.

"Delta team, in position," Hawkins reported.

"Bravo team, in position," Romano called in from the east wall of the hotel.

De Fersen watched silently as Heijboer and Nilsson hung motionlessly on their line on the south wall.

"Two minutes," he warned.

"We're all in position!" Nilsson whispered. "Why don't we just go in now?"

"Charlie Two, hold position!" Heijboer said sternly. "Give it a minute."

De Fersen looked across to the main entrance. He now had ninety seconds to sprint the distance, allow Kilpatrick to set the explosive charge, and then enter the building. They only needed ten seconds for that. The other option was to just hold and delay as long as was required, until that damn terrorist lookout moved to a new position. But that could take hours. Or, worse still, more lookouts could move and their position could become even more tenuous. No. They were going in at E-hour. Their orders were to enter at 2300 local time, specifically. And there was, no doubt, a very good reason that time had been selected.

"Charlie Team, moving," Heijboer reported.

De Fersen watched as Heijboer and Nilsson continued to climb up the line, content now that the terrorist above them had walked back along the corridor to exchange words with a comrade. The two Hospitallers crossed the balcony and took position by the double doors leading into the adjacent suite.

"Charlie Team, in position," Heijboer said.

"One minute," De Fersen whispered.

He waited in the tall bushes for another thirty seconds and then sprinted forward across the edge of the driveway to the northwest corner of the building before carefully following the wall around to the main entrance. He paused at the foot of the grand marble steps leading up to the tall, elaborately carved double doors.

"Alpha Team, in position."

De Fersen looked over his shoulder. Kilpatrick waited patiently behind him. De Fersen gave him a thumbs up. The Order sergeant quickly and quietly made his way up the stairs and grabbed his explosive charge from the pouch on his belt. De Fersen crept behind him, his Spitfire tucked in at the hip, and dropped to one knee to one side of the doors, clear of the explosive's path. Kilpatrick set the charge.

"Five seconds," De Fersen issued his final warning.

***

With the small charge set securely against the locked balcony doors, Nilsson quickly tapped in a timer. The whole thing seemed overkill, given that one sturdy kick would probably open the thin, white doors. She thumbed the activation circuit into life and stood to one side, her back against the wall and her Combi Rifle held up and ready.

"Five seconds," she heard De Fersen's voice on the tactical net.

Heijboer waited on the other side of the door, her shotgun held against her chest. Nilsson took in a breath. Despite two years of experience, she still found her heart thumping as adrenaline coursed through her body. Somehow, the timer still had three seconds to go. The world had seemingly paused. She willed it to move on.

Four explosions simultaneously detonated across the hotel. The balcony shook as the night was lit up with a small, brief whoosh of yellow flame, blasting back out from the entrance. Heijboer and Nilsson both turned and rushed through the shattered doors, their weapons held up to their shoulders. The suite inside was enveloped in darkness; the fuzzy outline of Nilsson's view sharpened into focus as her helmet's visor adjusted from the cultural lighting outside the building to the absence of lighting within. She heard screaming from somewhere to her left. Gunfire erupted from the floor below.

"Tango down," De Fersen reported over the communications network as Heijboer and Nilsson fanned out and quickly crossed the room. Through the wall, Nilsson could see a figure outlined in red sprinting toward the suite door from the far end of the corridor.

"Set charge!" Heijboer ordered, pointing at the locked door ahead.

Nilsson ran forward and planted another explosive charge on the door before dashing to one side and remotely detonating it. The door burst open with another brief blast; Heijboer hurtled through the smoking debris, dropped to one knee, and fired two booming shots from her Boarding Shotgun into the terrorist sprinting toward them along the corridor. The tall man's arms were flung out to either side as the first shotgun shell stopped him dead in his tracks; the second flung him back a pace as blood erupted from the impact points. The terrorist had only just fallen to the floor when Nilsson saw a second figure highlighted in red dash across the far end of the corridor. She fired a burst from her rifle, knocking two holes in the pristine, white plastered walls before a third round caught the man and span him around. He disappeared from view around the corner of the corridor. A moment later, the red silhouettes of all enemy positions disappeared from view.

"I just winged him!" Nilsson reported, sprinting forward.

"Watch your flanks!" Heijboer warned, rushing forward to catch up with Nilsson.

Nilsson rounded the corner and looked down to see her prey. A pale-faced, terrified man in his mid-twenties, dressed in brown overalls and with one hand pressed against a bloody wound in his chest. The dying man raised a shaky hand in an attempt to aim his pistol at his killer. Nilsson fired a long burst into him.

***

De Fersen barged through the main entrance, his Spitfire raised to his shoulder. His helmet visor instantly adjusted light levels to the near blackness of the hotel's lobby, illuminated only by the infra-red flashlights carried by the two submachine-gun-armed terrorists in the room. One stood startled at the foot of the grand, main staircase leading up to the first floor; the second man was at the right hand side of the room, already bringing his weapon up toward the two intruders.

Pivoting in place, De Fersen aimed his own weapon at the more apparent threat - the brown overalled, rotund man swinging his submachine gun up toward them - and centered his sights on the terrorist's center of mass. The Spitfire erupted in De Fersen's armored grasp, spewing out a torrent of rounds into his target. The terrorist span around in the hail of fire, his own submachine gun blasting haphazardly into the ceiling in his death throes.

"Tango down," De Fersen reported, turning in place to line up a shot on the second adversary.

Kilpatrick was already in position, firing a three round burst into the second terrorist's gut, and then a second burst of two rounds into the lean man's head as he crumpled down at the foot of the stairwell.

"Clear," Kilpatrick called dispassionately.

Out of the corner of his eye, De Fersen noticed a black, fist-sized object not unlike a peeled open, metallic sphere affixed to the wall by the main door. A repeater. The terrorists had a hacker. The sound of running footsteps echoed above along the first floor corridor, quickly followed by two blasts of a shotgun and a falling body. A moment later, a Combi Rifle chattered.

***

"Five seconds," De Fersen's voice came through Hawkins's earphones as clearly as if they were stood next to each other.

Hawkins and Sergeant Alvarez stood on the second floor balcony, their backs to the hotel wall to either side of the double doors leading inside as the last few seconds ticked away on the explosive charges. The whole world was silent. Hawkins stared out toward the horizon, concentrating on keeping his breathing slow and measured. He saw the distant lights of Vedi, a neon jungle encroaching on the edge of nature's grasp of Paradiso. The elegant sweep of the coastline meandered past the endless sea of trees to embrace the city limits where Vedi grew from its low suburbs up to the peak of its brightly lit skyscrapers in the center. For a moment, a silent moment, Hawkins contemplated what his normal, everyday counterparts would be doing only a few miles away. In the city, twenty-two year old men would be heading out to nightclubs, watching movies or playing games with loved ones, willing their babies to sleep... and here he was, a killer encased in metal, rifle held across his chest, seconds away from taking yet more lives...

The charges detonated. The balcony doors blew inward. Hawkins and Alvarez moved inside the adjoining suite, their rifles raised as they advanced rapidly past the room's plush furniture. The thumping of gunfire from somewhere below them began before they had even reached the doors to the main corridor outside. Up ahead, projected onto his visor from the intelligence feed from De Fersen's hack, Hawkins saw three red figures on their floor - all of them in separate suites. All three moved toward the central corridor.

"Two seconds!" Alvarez warned, attaching another charge to the locked door ahead of them.

Hawkins backed against the wall to one side. The charge detonated, blowing the door open in a shower of wooden splinters. Alvarez rushed forward ahead of Hawkins and into the corridor. Hawkins was only a pace behind her, his MULTI Rifle raised, when he saw a red silhouetted figure dart out into the corridor ahead, carrying a flashlight and a pistol. Alvarez fired a short burst from her Combi Rifle, catching the terrorist in the chest and throat. The man was dead before he hit the floor.

Both soldiers advanced quickly and cautiously through the corridor, Alvarez stopping momentarily to check a locked door to her right.

The next door led to another suite with a red silhouetted figure. The last figure, too, had elected to remain in their room. The dull sounds of gunfire thumped away from the two floors below as Hawkins pressed his back to the side of the next doorway, his rifle held against his chest and ready. The red silhouette remained stationary in the center of the next room. Hawkins glanced across at Alvarez and nodded. She acknowledged and raised her rifle.

Hawkins darted in through the door, his rifle tucked into his shoulder. He stopped dead. A short woman, barely out of her teens, stood in the center of the room. The woman threw her pistol to one side and raised her hands high above her head, staring up at him through tear-streamed, green eyes.

"Please!" the woman begged.

In the briefest fraction of a moment, Hawkins remembered just one thing that was hammered home in training and reinforced in his weeks of fighting against the Yujingyu. Act. Do not freeze. Act.

"Down on the ground!" Hawkins yelled, rushing forward to jam the muzzle of his rifle into the young woman's chin while he grabbed her comlog wrist with his other hand.

The crying woman shakily lowered herself to her knees.

"Please!" she repeated. "Please don't kill me!"

"Face down!" Hawkins forced her to a prone position, wrenching her comlog off her wrist before reaching up to yank her earpiece from one ear and throw it aside.

Behind him, Alvarez let out a guttural grunt of frustration.

"Charlie Team from Delta Two!" she called across the tactical net. "We've got one Tango down and one restrained on the second floor - last Tango is at the stairs and heading down to you!"

Hawkins looked up and saw the red silhouette of the third terrorist dash across the corridor outside to the top of the stairwell. A moment later, all red indications of enemy positions faded from view on his visor.

***

"Zero, Bravo One," Romano's voice cut through the tactical net, "ground floor is secure. Moving to main entrance."

De Fersen checked the ammunition counter read out on his lens. Still plenty. Tapping his wrist-mounted comlog, he brought up a three-dimensional schematic of the building in the top corner of his view to check on the progress made by his teams. Ground floor secured by Alpha and Bravo Teams; first floor, two terrorists eliminated by Charlie Team; two further terrorists were still in the hostage holding room. Top floor - one terrorist killed, a second terrorist captured, a third on the move. De Fersen's eyes widened. A terrorist captured. He let out a groan.

"Fucking hell, Kyle!" he spat.

"Charlie Team from Delta Two!" Alvarez called. "We've got one Tango down and one restrained on the second floor - last Tango is at the stairs and heading down to you!"

"Charlie One, copied," Heijboer replied calmly.

Already at the foot of the stairwell, De Fersen took several paces quickly up to the landing halfway to the first floor. Looking up, he briefly saw the red silhouetted figure projected onto his visor as the highlighted terrorist bounded toward the top of the stairwell from the second floor. Then the red silhouette faded to nothing.

"Bastard," De Fersen breathed.

That was their hacker. His simple surveillance measure had been discovered. De Fersen brought up his comlog and rapidly opened his holographic control wheel. As if on queue, his hacking device sent an alert message to his lens.

"Charlie One!" De Fersen warned. "Britt! You're being hit with a carbonite program!"

"Got it," Heijboer replied, "attempting to reset."

Swearing again, De Fersen looked up toward the top of the stairwell. If he just had a weapon with more punch than his Spitfire, he might be able to shoot straight through the marble stairs and gun the bastard down. No, he would have to use another skillset to stop the enemy hacker from shutting down Heijboer's suit in place. De Fersen pressed a finger against the holographic wheel projected above his wrist and activated his hacking device's Hacker-Killer software package. Rapidly navigating through menus, he quickly selected a Trinity counter-hack program and directed it toward the terrorist hacker who stood two floors directly above him. His device easily located the terrorist's own comlog program and initiated a hostile connection. In immediate response, a line of defense coding scrolled across De Fersen's lens.

"No you don't," De Fersen whispered, "you'll have to do better than that."

Quickly picking holes in the logic operated by the enemy hacker, and dragging a series of nodes in place to plan another quantronic attack, De Fersen re-routed his hostile program into the power supply of the terrorist's comlog. De Fersen saw another change in defense code input, but it was too little too late. The aging knight issued a dark smile, amused at the irony of the religious connotations behind the word 'trinity' as he used the program to overload his adversary's comlog power supply. De Fersen was instantly rewarded with a high-pitched scream from his target above as he directed the entire source of his target's comlog power in one, concentrated burst into the wearer's body.

A moment later, a lithe body toppled over the banister of the stairs and plummeted down to land with a bloody thump next to the terrorist Kilpatrick had gunned down only seconds before.

"Tango down," De Fersen muttered with a dark grin.

He paused to reassess their situation. All looked good so far - the ground floor was confirmed as secure; save any rogue enemies who had evaded detection, the second floor was also clear. Eight Hospitallers were still in the fight, no injuries, with only two terrorists remaining. But they were locked in the room with the hostages. And it was all about the hostages.

"All teams, from Zero," De Fersen called. "Two Tangoes remaining in the holding area. Bravo One, move to the foot of the stairs and be prepared to handle hostages for extraction. Bravo Two, secure the entrance to the basement. Delta One, sweep and clear the Second Floor. Delta Two, secure the prisoner. Alpha and Charlie Teams: move to the first floor holding area."

Kilpatrick made his way quickly over to rejoin De Fersen as Romano appeared through a doorway on the east wall of the main lobby. De Fersen activated the emergency channel to Silver HQ.

"Silver Zero, this is Broadsword Zero," De Fersen began. "Ground floor is secure. We're moving to the hostage holding area. Move a police team to the main entrance and be prepared to handle hostages during extraction."

"Broadsword, copied," Perez replied, "I have a team moving to the main entrance now."

Content that the operation was proceeding as planned, De Fersen made his way quickly up the stairs to the first floor.

***

Muffled, angry shouts emanated from the far side of the locked door, only just loud enough to punch through the seemingly ceaseless screaming. Nilsson followed Heijboer across to the door where De Fersen and Kilpatrick waited, her armored feet padding against the thick, plush red carpet. She glanced up a floor and saw Hawkins standing guard above, while Romano waited at the foot of the stairs below next to two crumpled bodies. Blood seeped out from the corpses in an expanding circle of rusty red into the white carpet below them. De Fersen looked across at Heijboer and Nilsson as they arrived, his piercing stare practically boring through the red visor of his helmet.

"Set Combi Rifles to low velocity," he commanded. "Britt, we'll take the lead with pistols."

"Already done, sir," Nilsson replied.

For the majority of scenarios, full power was desirable for a firearm; for moving into an enclosed space with more friendlies than hostiles, the risk of a penetrating shot going through the intended target to then hit a friendly was unacceptable. The Combi Rifle had the capacity to tap off a greater proportion of the propellent gasses to reduce the force of the round; this same capability was not available on Spitfires or the CineticS Preman Boarding Shotgun.

Heijboer slung her Boarding Shotgun to her side and unholstered her pistol. Nilsson watched as De Fersen tapped his comlog to bring up his shimmering blue control radial menu.

"Their hacker shut down my surveillance program before I got him," the knight said gruffly. "There's two of those bastards left in there. Give me a moment, now that I'm close enough, I can spotlight them."

Nilsson checked anxiously over both shoulders as De Fersen hurriedly programmed in his hack. Seconds passed by as the screams and threatening shouts continued from the far side of the door.

"Gabe!" Heijboer whispered. "We need to go in!"

De Fersen silently continued his work, his fingers dancing nimbly across the blue holographic display projected above his comlog. One of the terrorists on the far side of the door appeared in red on Nilsson's screen. Whereas the last target highlight was merely a location, this hack now provided clear data - an outline of the opponent with perfect clarity, including details of the weapon held. Most importantly, the spotlight hack provided the Hospitallers with aiming data - a red line projected on Nilsson's lens connected the muzzle of her Combi Rifle to the target's center of mass, including a virtual assist giving simple advice on her lens to tell her how far to alter her aim. A moment later, the same details appeared on the second terrorist. Both terrorists were holding hostages in front of them in preparation for the Hospitaller assault, pistols held against the heads of their screaming victims.

"Alpha Team left, Charlie Team right," De Fersen commanded, unholstering his Ferro pistol. "Charlie Two, set charge."

Nilsson grabbed another small charge from her utility pouch, pressed it against the door, and set the timer.

"Three seconds!" she warned.

Both teams stood aside. Fighting again to control her breathing, Nilsson's fingers closed tightly around her rifle. Two more terrorists to go. Eight of them. Just two more...

The charge detonated. Somehow the screaming grew louder. Nilsson followed Heijboer in, her Combi Rifle raised. Ten terrified men and women were bundled against the north wall of a room cleared of all furniture, its windows boarded up. Two young women in expensive but disheveled suits stood screaming by the east wall, each involuntarily shielding a terrorist with their bodies. Both terrorists flashed red on Nilsson's lens, the extra targeting data connecting her rifle's line of fire to them now flashing as obstructed. A warning scrolled across her lens.

- *78% chance of friendly fire! 78% chance of...*

De Fersen fired a single shot from his pistol. The terrorist on the left braced up as his head was flung back, a bloody hole appearing in the middle of his forehead. The final terrorist, a thin woman with red hair, screamed in panic and dropped to her knees. She pathetically dragged her hostage down in a futile attempt to hide beneath the yelling, struggling body of the politician's assistant. Heijboer rushed forward, grabbed the hostage by her arm, and roughly flung her clear. The veteran Mother-Officer then brought her pistol down in a two-handed combat grip and shot the final terrorist repetitively in the body and head. The screaming continued as shot after shot was fired in quick succession. Nilsson's eyes widened as she lowered her rifle. She stopped counting how many times Heijboer fired her pistol after ten rapidly delivered rounds.

"Get them out!" De Fersen yelled. "Alpha Team! Charlie Team! Get the hostages clear of the building!"

Galvanized into action again, Nilsson stepped forward and grabbed the first hostage by the back of the neck; a heavy set man with graying temples and blood dripping from his nose.

"Out," Nilsson yelled, "get out and down the stairs! Move! Move!"

The terrified, battered, and bruised procession of hostages were slowly herded out of the room and across to the stairwell, where Romano continued the yelling until the line met the police team at the main entrance.

"Zero to all teams," De Fersen called, "hostages clear of the building. Extricate via the main entrance."

It was only once Nilsson was out of the building, past the line of police cars, and back out of sight in the subterranean car park when she allowed herself to remove her helmet, take in a deep breath of fresh air, and run her fingers through her sweat-soaked hair.

***

The driveway in front of the hotel was lit up with strobing lights of blue. The number of police cars had doubled and were now joined by an armada of ambulances. The recently freed hostages had been moved to the police incident HQ in the spa building; some received medical treatment while others were carefully and tentatively questioned by Perez and her team. It was into the early hours of the morning now, and as De Fersen wandered alone around the edge of the driveway, he found himself thanking God that the police perimeter had been robust enough to prevent even a single journalist from sneaking anywhere near the hotel.

De Fersen had already received his orders to return to the Hospitaller base of operations at Vedi. No less than Eloïse Gerard, the recently promoted Grand Master of the Order of the Hospital herself, was currently flying in to discuss the operation face-to-face. De Fersen thrust his hands back into the pockets of his coat, his image now reverted from

God's armor-clad, vengeful angel of death to an aging bald man in a walking jacket. A passing police officer eyed him fearfully; she had, no doubt, seen the effects of De Fersen's work inside the hotel with her own eyes.

"Father-Officer?"

De Fersen turned around. He was confronted by a stocky, middle-aged man with dark skin, a neat mustache, and a disheveled pinstriped gray suit.

"Mister Hayes, sir," De Fersen took his hands back out of his pockets and folded his arms. "Superintendent Perez informed me that you wished to talk to me before my team departed."

"Yes," the politician smiled uneasily, "yes, that's right. I... well, the whole night is understandably a bit of a blur. I... we were in the dark for the whole thing, they took our lenses."

De Fersen silently watched the politician, waiting to see where the line of dialogue was heading.

"...I just remember hearing the explosions, and then the gunfire. We couldn't see anything when your team came in through the door. I just heard gunshots and screaming."

"Probably best none of you saw much, sir," De Fersen said curtly.

"Yes," Hayes said again. "Yes... I... I wanted to thank you personally for everything you did here. My campaign manager, Judy... she said one of them was using her as a human shield when you all came in. She said one of your soldiers fired over her shoulder to shoot her captor in the head. She's understandably shaken, but she's also terrifically pleased that your soldier didn't miss!"

De Fersen suppressed a grin. He had made that shot. As soon as they moved into the hostage holding area, the clock was against them. They needed to move quickly and ruthlessly, capitalizing on the surprise and terror they caused in entry. No time to give the terrorists the capacity to come to their senses. No time to fuck around. That was why he made the shot as soon as he was confident he had it.

"I'll pass that on to the man who saved your campaign manager." De Fersen shrugged. "Anything else before we leave?"

The battered politician looked down at the ground and took in a breath before continuing, the flashing blue lights of the stationary emergency vehicles illuminating his grimy skin and clothing.

"Some of my people would like to thank your team. Personally, when it is appropriate. I'll be in touch with your chain of command to see if we could perhaps visit..."

"It doesn't work like that," De Fersen interrupted. "The Military Orders are not interested in PR opportunities with political..."

"I didn't mean like that," Hayes cut in. "No PR. Just a chance, when people have calmed down and recovered, to say a sincere thank you."

De Fersen tapped the fingers of one hand against his bicep thoughtfully. Over by the spa building, another freed hostage was carefully escorted toward an ambulance by a paramedic. The wind had eased off and the weather had returned to one of Paradiso's notoriously humid nights. He looked back at Hayes and carefully considered his next words. De Fersen's demeanor - all very careful and deliberate - so far had, he hoped, communicated to the Member of Parliament that he was not an admirer of politicians. Particularly those who were occasionally outspoken against traditional values. Values such as Christianity.

"Regardless," De Fersen said, "the Military Orders are somewhat secretive. We have to be, for our own security. From a professional point of view, all I can say is that you would need to feed in a request via the correct channels. It's above my pay grade, but my gut feeling would be that a request for a dozen civilians to visit an active Military Order unit recently engaged in counter-terrorism operations will most likely be rejected."

"Right," Hayes's shoulders slumped, "right. Well, I'll put in the request anyway. And personally?"

De Fersen's eyes narrowed.

"Sorry?"

"Personally?" the bruised MP repeated. "You said that those views were issued from a professional point of view. What would you want to say to me personally? Between you and I?"

De Fersen slowly unfolded his arms and brought them around to clamp his hands at the small of his back. It had been a long night, to put it mildly. And he still had the debrief with Grand Master Gerard to face. If Hayes was looking for a sycophantic young soldier to praise his work in government, he had picked the wrong man. De Fersen pulled his handgun out of his pocket, thumbed the magazine release and slid the magazine out of the pistol grip. He then removed a round and held it up in front of the MP. A boxy, rectangular prism of caseless propellant leading to a snub-nosed, solid alloy bullet.

"Personally," De Fersen began, looking past the round he held up between them and down into the shorter man's eyes. "Personally, I think you and your team can take a lot away from this. I know about your personal politics. But if you and your people can't muster the faith to go to church and pray to God, what you can do is put your hands in your fucking pockets and put something in your church's donation box. God's work is bloody sometimes. You've just seen that for yourself."

De Fersen saw Hayes visibly deflate in front of him as he continued to deliver his personal opinion, as requested.

"And while I don't believe the devil is red, with horns and a trident, I do believe we're here to stop the devil's work. Evil, if you want. And to stop evil, my people and I need bullets. And bullets aren't free. So if you want to take anything away from your experience, stop criticizing the NeoVatican and start throwing more money at it so we can carry on doing our job."

"Father-Officer." Hayes smiled. "You make it sound so simple. It's not as easy as that. Believe me! If I could, I would..."

"Good night, sir," De Fersen said, thumbing the round back into the top of the magazine before replacing it into his pistol and walking back toward the car park.

Muttering obscenities to himself, De Fersen walked away from the hive of activity at the driveway and down the ramp leading to the car-park. He found his seven soldiers busying themselves with loading the van again; Kilpatrick and Hawkins handling crated suits of ORC armor and weapons up to Alvarez and Romano and into the back of the vehicle while Nilsson stock checked every item. Heijboer walked across to meet him as he reached the bottom of the ramp.

"You talk to him?"

"Yeah." De Fersen shrugged.

"Anything interesting?"

"No."

"Were you a dick to him?"

De Fersen hesitated to consider his answer.

"Yeah."

"Oh. Right."

"How are they all?" De Fersen asked as he walked briskly toward the van. "The whole thing was pretty successful, so I'm guessing there's nobody to worry about."

"No, all good," Heijboer replied. "Romano and Aubert are a bit pissed off that they didn't even fire a shot. Opportunities to be a part of an operation like this don't come around very often."

"Yeah, I get that," De Fersen grunted as he reached the van.

"Look," Heijboer said, her tone suddenly a little more severe, "about being a dick to an MP. Gabe, you can't keep..."

De Fersen cut his comrade off by whistling loudly to attract the attention of everybody in the car park. His soldiers stopped loading the crates and turned to regard him silently. De Fersen pointed a finger in accusation at Hawkins.

"You. Come with me."

Heijboer sighed as Hawkins jumped down from the back of the van, straightened his black, hip-length battledress jacket, and walked across to meet them.

"Gabe," Heijboer said quietly, "I've already spoken to him about..."

De Fersen turned to look down at Heijboer.

"Thanks, Britt. Now *I'm* going to talk to God's special fucking idiot about it."

Heijboer let out an exasperated sigh and threw her arms out to either side before walking away. De Fersen paced angrily away from the van, hoping Hawkins would at least pick up on the non-verbal cue to follow him. De Fersen waited until they had walked far away enough from the van to be out of earshot, and then turned to face the young knight.

Hawkins was, on the surface, the very poster boy of what a modern Knight Hospitaller should be. Deeply religious, top of his school in every sporting event he tried his hand at, youth martial arts champion at a planetary level in multiple fighting styles, academic grades good enough that he could have attended a reasonable university, and a package all wrapped up aesthetically with a clean-cut, youthful handsomeness that literally turned heads wherever he went. De Fersen gritted his teeth in frustration. If only the idiot's performance equaled his potential.

"Which part of our orders didn't you understand tonight?" he growled.

Hawkins looked across, his dark eyes as vapid as ever beneath his long, dark fringe.

"Sir," he began slowly, "I'm sorry that my actions have caused complications tonight. But I am not sorry I did not fire my weapon at a helpless woman. I'm not sorry for taking her prisoner."

De Fersen turned half away and let out a cry of frustration.

"You just don't fucking get it, do you?" he roared. "You genuinely think you did something morally upstanding and altruistic? Our orders were to eliminate all opposition immediately! You gave that woman a chance to detonate a bomb!"

"The police bomb disposal team have already swept the building, sir. There was no bomb."

"You didn't know that at the time!" De Fersen shoved a finger of accusation at the younger man. "We have SOPs for a reason! We learn from past mistakes! We always, *always* assume that the place is rigged to explode! That's why as soon as we had eliminated every threat we were aware of, we still evacuated the entire building as quickly as we possibly could, rather than shoulder our weapons and start high-fiving each other!"

Hawkins exhaled slowly, his eyes sinking to look down at the broken cement of the floor.

"Kyle, do you think that nine fucking idiots with pistols and a couple of submachine guns were expecting to repel a full counter-terrorism assault spearheaded by elite, heavy infantry?"

"No, sir."

"Exactly! Something else was going on here! They were not equipped to deal with us, not even close! Their plan did not involve a shoot out! And I'm pretty sure that's why we were moved here in such a rush, so secretively, and given the green light so quickly! Pistols were never the threat here, something else we don't know about was! *That* was why our orders were to go in quickly and eliminate all opposition without hesitation!"

Hawkins looked up again, his features suddenly hardening into a mask of resolve.

"No."

"No? What do you mean, no?"

"No. I entered a room. I saw an enemy. That enemy threw away her weapon and pleaded for her life. At that moment, I could have pulled the trigger, or spent one extra second - *one second* - grabbing her wrist and pulling off her comlog. One second to make the difference between ensuring that terrorist had no way of..."

"One second of risk!" De Fersen snapped. "One extra second to give a terrorist the option to detonate a basement full of explosives to kill you, me, the entire team and twelve innocent hostages! But that's okay, we could have explained that to their spouses, children, parents! Sorry your mother is dead, but there's a silver lining! Kyle Hawkins, with all of his six fucking weeks of combat experience, can now look himself in the mirror and know he gave some murdering bitch of a terrorist a chance at redemption, and now he has the moral high ground!"

De Fersen stared at the younger soldier, his eyes narrowed and jaw clenched. Silence ensued for several seconds.

"Just... get in the damn van. We're leaving."

His face a mixture of sadness, resentment, and anger, Hawkins turned and walked back to the van. De Fersen looked up to see the rest of the team continuing to load the crates, doing a poor job of pretending they were not trying to overhear the conversation. Given De Fersen's volume, they would not have to have tried particularly hard to do so. Swearing to himself again, he walked toward the front of the van.

Chapter Three

The corridor leading up to the office was an odd concoction of hyper modern attempting to blend with heritage. A sonic wave swept smoothly across the gleaming, smooth white floor to push any traces of dust and grime into the cleaning vents at the base of the polished, white stone of the walls. Paintings, the most recent of them at least a century old, hung from the pristine walls. Each painting was accompanied by a wall terminal that allowed a double tap connection to transmit a recorded history of the events depicted to a viewer's geist. A smattering of original artifacts were carefully displayed on plinths at irregular intervals along the corridor.

De Fersen looked up at the same painting that captured his imagination every time he found himself in this corridor; the original *The Martyrs' Refusal* by Archer, painted in 2067. It depicted events immediately following the disastrous Battle of Hattin in 1187 - one of the major contributing events leading to the Third Crusade - where the Christian forces under the command of Guy of Lusignan were defeated by the Muslim forces of Saladin. The painting showed a line of captured Knights Hospitaller, battered, bloodied, and exhausted in their mail armor and black surcoats, being dragged before an executioner and given the chance to renounce their faith and convert to Islam, or face execution. Not one of the knights turned their back on Christianity.

His hands clamped at the small of his back, De Fersen leaned in to inspect the brush strokes of the painting, the light artistically shining from a gap in the clouds above to illuminate the indignant faces of the captured Military Order knights. Historians still debated over whether there was actually an opportunity presented to the Holy Order knights to convert; certainly, with the exception of the Grand Master of the Knights Templar, all of the Military Order knights were beheaded on Saladin's orders. While some other Christian prisoners were spared, it was said that Saladin feared the ferocity and fanaticism of the Military Order knights to such an extent that mercy was never an option.

De Fersen glanced across to the pitted, battered thirteenth century great helm on its shelf next to the painting. The painting only showed Hospitallers queuing bravely to die. Of the two hundred Military

Order knights executed that day, a significant number were Templars. De Fersen took in a long breath. In 1307, King Philip IV of France ordered the arrest of dozens of Templar knights on false, trumped up charges of blasphemy and heresy. It led to the violent dissolution of the entire Order. Yet, lightning was not supposed to strike twice. De Fersen recalled his own bitterness when, only four years after his fateful power boat crash, as a young warrior of God, he was forced to hand across his Templar surcoat when the Order was dissolved for a second time.

At least the Hospitallers showed him more mercy than the French court showed to his predecessors in the fourteenth century. At least Saladin executed Christian knights in the belief that it was in the defense of his faith and principles; Philip IV did it for nothing more than greed. Yet, the one time De Fersen had met ALEPH's modern Recreation of Saladin - now a naval liaison officer with O-12 - the painting by Archer was all he could think of. It seemed odd to hold the actions of a man who died over a thousand years ago against his modern Recreation; yet, De Fersen was fairly certain that the baseless accusations against the Templars influenced the thoughts of some in the judgment against the modern Order. History had a certain way of repeating itself - it might not always echo directly, but it did perhaps rhyme.

"Gabriele," a familiar voice in De Fersen's earpiece dragged him back to the present, "come in."

De Fersen straightened his black uniform jacket and walked to the end of the corridor, past the paintings of the Battle of Arsuf and the Siege of Acre, to open the door to the Grand Master's office. The office itself was relatively spartan, with a grand desk flanked with a cabinet on one side and a suit of ceremonial - some would say ostentatious - armor on the other. The newly elected Grand Master of the Order of the Hospital, Eloïse Gerard, stood up from her chair behind the desk. In her mid-forties and with a crown of dark red hair framing a wide, pale face, Gerard wore the same plain black uniform as De Fersen, adorned only with her badges of rank on the epaulets and a Hospitaller shield on one sleeve.

"Sorry for keeping you," Gerard began. "I know it's late and you've had quite a night. Take a seat."

De Fersen sat down in the simple, black armchair opposite from Gerard. The short woman walked over to the cabinet and produced a plain, wooden box from a shelf. She opened it on her desk and took out a pair of matching, bulky goblets of polished gold.

"I know you're not much of a drinker these days," she continued, "but one glass of wine won't kill you. My husband bought these bloody awful goblets for me to celebrate my promotion. I can't stand the things, but out of respect to him, I'll try to make some use of them."

Gerard drained a crystal decanter of red wine into the two goblets and passed one over to De Fersen.

"Thank you, ma'am," he said formally, accepting the gaudy receptacle.

"Oh, don't stand on rank when it's just the two of us," Gerard said from where she stood at the edge of her desk, eyeing her own goblet with obvious disapproval. "We've known each other too long for the formalities. You can switch the rank back on when we're in the presence of our juniors."

De Fersen took a sip of the wine, uncomfortable with both drinking alcohol and remaining seated while his Order's Grand Master - a woman he had once commanded in battle - stood over him. He placed his heavy, archaic goblet back on the desk and looked up at the younger woman.

"I've got a couple of things to talk to you about," the Grand Master said, taking a seat opposite him again, "both of them important. We'll come on to this evening's op at the hotel, but more pressing is what I'm sending you off to do next."

This evening. Things had been so hectic that bursting through the hotel's main entrance, Spitfire blazing, already seemed like it had happened a week ago. De Fersen checked his lens's chronometer. It was only just past three am. Only a handful of hours, on Paradiso's twenty-eight hour day, since the assault.

"Where are we off to?" De Fersen asked.

Gerard tapped her comlog, and a map of the planet was projected above her desk, between them. The map was centered over the middle of the Barrier Sea; the vast expanse of water that sat between Paradiso's two main continents of Norstralia and Septentria. The territories of the planet were divided between the three most powerful factions of the Human Sphere - PanOceania, Yu Jing, and the Haqqislamite.

However, an area spreading out from the Barrier Sea onto the coasts of both major continents - an area known as the NiemadsZone - had been home to a shock alien invasion that, via three successive and brutal offensives, had extended out to take territories from all three human factions. The alien Combined Army consisted of a number of allied species, their only commonalities being their merciless brutality in waging war. Yet, even with the arrival of an alien military in the midst of the Human Sphere, the conflict between the rival factions of humanity sporadically continued.

De Fersen regarded the holographic map with grim interest. In over three decades of fighting, he had gone to war with every flag on that map outside of PanOceania. In answer to his earlier question, Gerard tapped her comlog again.

"I'm sending you there, to Hill One-Five-Two," she replied as a marker appeared on the map, "or more specifically, to work from a forward operating base set up by the Black Friars in the southern Moravia suburbs."

A small, yellow cross appeared in Eastern Norstralia, in an area of jungle in between the city of Moravia and the base at Taarsa-6, both of which were now abandoned after the advances made by the Combined Army during the Second Offensive. De Fersen nodded slowly. The dense jungles that enveloped most of Paradiso made it impossible for either side to wage a conventional war. The Combined Army foothold on Paradiso was indeed firm, and all of their offensives had met with success, but the naval blockade in space above the planet prevented any significant reinforcements from reaching the alien invaders. The war currently hung very much in the balance. Asymmetric warfare, bordering on guerilla campaigns in the jungle, was how each side traded blows. But this? Yes, the front lines of fighting were vaguely defined and easy to cross at the best of times, but Gerard's yellow cross on the map was way, way behind those lines. That area of Nostralia was not contested. It very clearly belonged to the Combined Army.

"Orders from the secretary of defense himself," Gerard added. "Approved by the prime minister, sent to me via the Pope. And now I'm choosing you to carry them out."

De Fersen leaned forward, planting his elbows on the desk and resting one clenched fist inside the other open hand.

"What's the job?"

The corners of Gerard's thin lips tugged up slightly.

"Make a statement. The prime minister is concerned that Pan-Oceania is seen as being constantly on the defensive. We're losing territory to the Combined Army, and any victories reported in the media are nothing more than heroic defenses or line holding actions. We need to be seen to be on the offensive."

De Fersen leaned back again and smiled grimly.

"So we need to be seen to get behind enemy lines and blow some shit up?"

"Bit of a crass way of putting it, Gabriele, but in essence, that's exactly what I'm sending you out to do."

"Any target in particular?" De Fersen asked.

Gerard tapped her comlog again, and the holographic map zoomed in before expanding out and twisting to present a three-dimensional look at a fifty cubed mile area, complete with terrain contours.

"This is your target. It's a munitions depot, a major one. With the naval blockade above, the flow of supplies to Combined Army forces on Paradiso is being strangled so every strike we make on their supply chain will be felt. I appreciate that the Combined Army takes great pride in their ability to live off the land and fight without a rigid logistical chain, but even they have their limits. You'll be one of a series of coordinated attacks, all part of Operation Aphek. But, in the interests of honesty and transparency, be under no illusions: this is not just about causing a major logistical disruption to front line enemy units. This is about showing the Human Sphere that PanO are still *the* Human Sphere's hyperpower. This needs to be… loud."

De Fersen leaned in and regarded the map. The depot sat in an industrial site on the outer suburbs of Moravia. Getting across the area did, at least, appear simple enough. The city was held by the Combined Army, but there was a good enough route to it - a valley amidst dry, rocky terrain, providing some respite from the dense, aggressive vegetation that sprawled across most of the planet. That dry ground would at least be far easier to traverse on foot, although counter-surveillance assistance would be required to keep his team out of view from the enemy's network of drones. Getting into the area… that would prove trickier. Their best bet was most likely to be airlifted to a forward operating base near Damburg, and then to look for a covert, low level air insertion from there.

"And there's more suboptimal news," Gerard tilted her head with an element of awkwardness. "This is part of a larger, combined operation. There's a lot of concurrent activity. Long story short, I can't spare a demolitions expert for you. We've weighed up the priorities for our assets, and I've employed them elsewhere. It's a building full of bombs. I'm sure you can blow it up without a dedicated specialist."

"Alright," De Fersen nodded, "I'll get together with Britt and we'll come up with a plan. When do we leave?"

The Grand Master's eyes narrowed.

"Mother-Officer Heijboer won't be joining you. I've already chosen your team."

De Fersen leaned forward across the desk, his eyes fixed on Gerard's.

"What do you mean you've chosen my team, Eloïse? This is a tactical mission! I wouldn't expect this level of long-screw driving micromanagement from an operational commander, let alone a strategic one! And what's wrong with Britt?"

Gerard met De Fersen's aggressive stare without flinching.

"I told you that I had two things to discuss with you. This is one. Your assault on the hotel is the other. I have some issues with the latter."

De Fersen threw his arms to either side.

"Issues? What issues? We went in to rescue hostages. We recovered every hostage without an injury, let alone a fatality! That sounds pretty successful to me! Aside from one idiot taking a prisoner, we also made sure every last one of those bastards was dead! What issues, Eloïse?"

The Grand Master gritted her teeth, her plain face twisted in anger.

"I'll tell you what damn issues!" she spat. "Do you know how many times Britt Heijboer shot a combat ineffective target in front of those hostages? Fourteen, Gabriele! Fourteen fucking shots at point blank range! I'm pretty sure that less than half of that would have made sure the target was neutralized!"

"She's aggressive," De Fersen shrugged, "nothing wrong with that."

"Aggressive?! Don't patronize me! I'm a front line soldier, too! But I'm not done there! Let's look through a few choice lines recorded by your soldiers in the post operation interviews! Brother-Sub Officer Romano commented, *'the op went according to plan, but I was disappointed that I didn't even fire my weapon'*! Gabriele, who the hell thinks like that? And this, from Sergeant Aubert! *'The ground floor was secured efficiently in accordance with the plan, but unfortunately I didn't get to kill any of the fuckers myself'*."

De Fersen folded his arms across his chest.

"Eloïse, I think you've spent too long away from the front line..."

"That's bullshit, Gabriele!" Gerard slammed an open palm on the desk between them. "We're supposed to be God's warriors! A force for good! Protectors of the helpless! Not a gung-ho bunch of fucking psychopaths that empty nearly a full pistol magazine into a prone target, or go on record as lamenting their woes over the lack of opportunity to take a human life!"

De Fersen leaned back in his chair, shaking his head slowly. He ran through a dozen responses, but faced with the angry, immoveable lack of reason or pragmatism displayed by his superior, he was left in a stunned silence. Gerard took in a deep breath and exhaled slowly before standing up and pacing across to idly inspect the gaudy, ceremonial suit of armor hanging opposite her desk.

"This is my Order now," she said quietly, "and I'll run it the way I see fit. Things have gotten out of hand. We've lost our way. We are God's warriors, and the thing which is supposed to separate us from every other soldier in the Human Sphere is our Christian virtue. Our mercy. Our humility. Only one of your soldiers demonstrated that this evening; your pretty boy protege. Gabriele, the reputation of the Military Orders is in the crosshairs of the Pope. The rumors have reached the NeoVatican. The bullshit stories about Military Order soldiers literally hammering crucifixes into the hearts of our enemies."

De Fersen slowly raised himself to his feet and took a pace across to stand next to his commander.

"Everybody there must know that's bullshit," De Fersen began. "I mean, the morality aside of disrespecting Christ by using a cross for such a thing... there's the sheer practicalities. When we go to war, we go in dripping with modern, state of the art weaponry. Why would we bother using crosses when we have guns and blades? You can't believe these stories. Neither can they. As far as I'm aware, this all stemmed from a PR story about ten years ago when a knight referred to his sword as his cross, and later in the interview he mentioned using it to stab at the hearts of the Church's enemies. That's all that is."

Gerard turned and looked up at the taller knight, the anger from a few moments ago now dissipated.

"I know, I know. I don't believe any of that. But that's what our citizens think of us, and that's what they see us as. So when Britt Heijboer empties fourteen rounds into a surrendered foe, I worry. When Francois Aubert says he's disappointed he didn't kill anybody, I worry. Gabriele, I need to turn this Order around, and I need your help to do it. I need you on my side."

De Fersen leaned back to sit on the edge of Gerard's desk, folding his arms again. While he certainly saw her point, he did not agree with it. But phrasing that would be the difficult part.

"Eloïse, look... what we do, it's... We're in dark times. We can't be virtuous, shining knights of justice. That's the stuff of those ridiculous Maya-movies with that prick Mendoza. The reality of war is that we face the most dangerous foe that humanity has ever encountered in the Combined Army. There is no room for mercy. If we hesitate, we lose."

De Fersen paused, his expression neutral, waiting for another aggressive response. None came.

"So, if you want my opinion as one of your most experienced soldiers, well, my opinion is that coming in and implementing major changes in your first month in post would be ill-advised. We don't need to ease off the aggression. We need to foster it and encourage it. My 'pretty boy protege,' as you described him, he fucked up tonight by taking that prisoner and not firing his weapon. He needs to be more like Britt and Francois, not the other way around."

Gerard's eyes closed for several long seconds. She clasped her hands together and muttered something under her breath. Then, finally, she looked up again at De Fersen.

"Gabriele, you are part of the problem. For Heaven's sake, you lectured a Member of Parliament a few hours ago. An MP! In this Order, you are a legend. Your opinion holds far, far too much sway. I need you on my side, and right now, you are not. You've told me for years that you're stuck at the rank of Father-Officer because of your past with the Templars. That's just not true. Anybody who judged you back in the day is long gone. The reason you are stuck at your rank is because you rant and rave at prominent politicians, and you defend gung-ho killers who have truly, truly lost their way."

Clenching one fist in frustration, De Fersen recalled Hayes' words; *'Personally... between you and I.'*

"I didn't speak to him in a professional context."

"Then there are two clear lessons here," Gerard interrupted, "both of which shouldn't come as a shock to you. First off, don't trust politicians. Second off, don't shout at them. I fully understand that we work for the Church and not for the government, but this should still be common sense to a man of your age and experience."

De Fersen felt an ache in the sides of his face as his jaw clenched. He found himself standing up straighter, towering over the shorter woman. He remembered her as a freshly qualified Sister-Sub Officer; ambitious, serious-minded, but just as naively altruistic. He remembered dragging her, bleeding and dying, from a Nomad ambush. He remembered hurtling across a decimated starport, Ariadnan bullets kicking at his heels, to rescue her when her fireteam was cut off and surrounded. She owed him more respect than this.

"Eloïse," he exhaled, "you need to..."

"I'm not discussing this with you," Gerard said sternly. "I'm giving you orders. Go and get some sleep. Be here at ten hundred and we'll go into more detail on your next task. As I said, I have chosen your team. I understand your frustration at my involvement in the finer details of your job, but I wasn't elected to lead this Order through incompetence. I know my job and, more importantly, I know my people. That's all for now. Go and get some sleep."

Failing to hide his bitter resentment and disappointment, De Fersen silently made his way out of the Grand Master's office.

***

Sitting on a damp, wooden crate in front of the green aircraft hangar, Darius Stanescu flicked a finger across the holographic display above his comlog, cycling through various potential playlists as he patiently waited for an update on his flight. On the civilian side of the aerospace port, another airliner noisily clawed its way up into the sky and lazily turned away from the runway, momentarily disappearing inside a thin layer of cloud as it headed north and away from Valkenswijk.

On the other side of the gray, perimeter fence in front of him, a mother walked along the road with two small children. The older child, a boy of perhaps eight years of age, stared through the fence curiously at the lone figure in the dark hood, sat in front of the closed hangar in the restricted military area.

Stanescu flashed the boy a friendly smile and a wave. The boy waved back excitedly. The boy's mother grabbed him firmly by the arm and quickened their pace. Stanescu watched them go. As a boy, he too would have looked with curious envy into the secretive areas he was not allowed into. Now he looked back out, envying the simplicity of a normal life.

Stanescu's attention was diverted back to his lens as a message scrolled across to alert him of an incoming call. He tapped his comlog and the familiar image of a short, gray-haired woman in her eighties appeared in a communications box in the corner of his lens.

Stanescu smiled.

"Hello, Grandma!"

"Darius! You look tired! Always so tired! Are you not getting any breaks?"

Stanescu saw his own image in the opposite corner of his lens. His thin face and prominent cheek bones were just visible beneath his dark hood, his olive skin complimented with a neat, goatee beard. He smiled at his grandmother.

"I get a little bit of…"

"They work you too hard!" the old woman continued, her face a picture of concern. "It was just the same when I was your age, working in the hospitals! And it's always the junior staff! Never the managers! Never the consultants! Are you still on track for your exams? You've been qualified for three years now! Surely you should be a registrar, they must see that, they…"

Stanescu held up his hands in an attempt to placate the agitated woman. Yes, he had technically been qualified as a doctor for three years now. But no, he would not be a registrar. The truth, carefully hidden from his grandmother, was that he had never worked a single day in a hospital.

"Grandma, it's okay!" he said softly. "There is nothing you need to worry about! Work is going just fine, I…"

Another alert flashed up on his lens. His flight was landing in five minutes.

"Grandma, I have to go," he winced, "I've got to get back to work. I'll be in touch as soon as I can, okay? I promise."

His grandmother's face fell in disappointment. Stanescu felt a tightening in his throat. It was not technically lying - he was always careful to ensure that hiding the truth from the woman he owed everything to was not a direct lie - but even the equivocation left him feeling hollow.

"Just take care, Darius. I worry. I made a promise to your father."

"And you are keeping it." Stanescu forced a smile. "I'm sure dad would agree. I'll talk to you soon. All my love."

A tightness gripping the center of his chest, Stanescu terminated the call and stood up, slinging his long, heavy kitbag over one shoulder. He checked the flight details and saw that his aircraft would be taxiing into the far side of the military quadrant of Valkenswijk aerospace port. Tapping his comlog, he selected a playlist of piano based rock and roll that reminded him of his father and began the long walk around the hangars.

***

Her eyes staring numbly out of the car window, Marianna Cortez watched in disinterest as the streets of Valkenswijk crawled slowly by. The early afternoon sun reflected from the curved, white buildings leading to the city center; tall, graceful office buildings and plush accommodation blocks led to a more grim, angular industrial site housing a succession of grimy warehouses. All were described in brief detail with lines of text flashing across her lens, advertising services, buy-to-let housing options or storage 'solutions' - all things that were useless to her.

"Do you know how long you'll be away for this time?" Owen asked from where his tall frame was crammed into the driver's seat.

"No."

Cortez looked ahead and saw the long lines of traffic converge onto the freeway ahead, the automated vehicles almost polite in their gentle movement into the three lanes on each side of the central divide. Advertisements flashed on billboards above the freeway; optimistic reminders to buy tickets for the resurrection lottery; prices for viewing rights to next week's Aristeia! season finale depicted with the heroic figures of Maximus, Gata, and 8-Ball; the annoyingly angelic, pious face of Joan of Arc plastered on advertisements for health insurance with the Order of the Hospital. Only a mile ahead, Cortez saw the freeway exit for the aerospace port.

"This is really how you want to leave things?" Owen looked across from behind the automated wheel of the white sedan. The steering wheel turned gently to follow the road, the accelerator pedal easing off as the LAI controlled vehicle obediently followed its pre-planned route. Cortez found herself resenting Owen even more, somehow, for offering to drive her to the aerospace port and then not even bothering to manually drive the car.

"It's not how I've chosen to leave things," she replied bitterly, "it's how things are."

The tick-tock tone of the indicator annoyingly sounded as the car peeled out of the flow of traffic and down the freeway exit ramp toward the aerospace port. More adverts flashed across Cortez's lens:

*- Frequent flier? Sign up to Nortra-line's Gold Plan! Enjoy exec-
utive lounges, reduced price on cabin upgrades…*
*- We all have relationship problems. Sign up to a counselor who
cares…*
- Holiday insurance need not be a pain in the…

The car pulled up into an unloading bay by the aerospace port's
first civilian terminal. Cortez wordlessly opened the door and stepped
out into the afternoon sun. The pavement was still wet from the morning's downpour, but only a few wispy clouds now remained in the purple-blue sky above. Cortez opened the back door of the car and took
her heavy bag out to sling over her shoulder. A small bus ground to a
halt behind her vehicle, its interior filled with excited looking children
who queued impatiently to wait for the doors to open. Cortez looked up
at the line of children in silence.

"Let me help you with that."

She felt Owen's hand on her shoulder. She recoiled quickly.

"I can carry my own bag."

The tall, red-haired man looked down at her.

"Marianna, we can talk about this when…"

"Don't bother," she cut in, taking a step back and up the curb
behind her. "Just… don't bother."

"So this is really how you're ending this?" Owen threw his arms
out in exasperation to either side.

"No. It's how you're ending this."

Cortez turned her back and made her way into the busy passenger terminal. And with that, a two-year relationship and engagement ended. Her first relationship since her divorce. Cortez entered the
cavernous, brightly lit terminal building and stepped onto the travelator
by the main entrance, placing her bag down by her feet as the moving
walkway ushered her and a line of a hundred brightly clothed tourists
toward the central terminal. She tapped her comlog, bringing up her
personal geist's radial menus and selecting her work profile to identify
herself as military, initiating the security check process. Her lens highlighted a travelator exit up ahead in red. Animated pictures on the walls
around her showed sunlit beaches with gentle waves and palm trees,
complete with smiling, jumping dolphins; brightly colored powerboats;
and dramatic kite-surfers. The irony of the images, considering her location, added to the sickening feeling already left by her confrontation
with her now ex-fiance.

Stepping onto the red-highlighted travelator, Cortez let out a
sigh of relief as the platform led her through an automated security
station and into the military terminal. The walls were now devoid of the

sickeningly optimistic animations. The low ceiling did a far better job of keeping the atmosphere cool and bearable; the long tunnel leading to the central hub was nearly empty, with only one other small group of passengers.

The tunnel opened out into another tall, brightly lit room with one entire wall made up of tall windows, allowing the day's sunlight to pour in unobstructed. Robust, utilitarian chairs lined the walls, bolted to the gray floor. Cortez was willing to bet that the chairs in the civilian terminal were twice as comfortable looking. The trio of passengers walked away to the far corner of the room, their footsteps echoing across the near empty space as a huge, six-engined airliner taxied slowly past the windows. Two familiar figures walked out to meet Cortez from a pile of bags dumped by the unappealing chairs on the far side of the room.

"Sergeant," Corporal Lois greeted, a typically uncomfortable smile on the thick lips hidden beneath his dark beard.

"S'arnt," Crosier May nodded, her long, blonde hair tied back in a pony tail but styled with an almost pompadour bulge atop her head which left Cortez wanting to cringe. She looked around the terminal.

"Where's Kalal?" Cortez asked.

Lois exchanged a brief glance with May.

"He's not coming, Sergeant. His father died this morning. Lieutenant Moreno has been trying to contact you."

Cortez saw another individual step off the travelator and into the tall room; a gaunt-faced man in his late twenties, his features obscured behind a dark hood and an intense stare accompanying his goatee beard. She watched him walk over to a line of chairs and sit alone.

"I've had my comms switched off," she replied to Lois, careful to keep the anger out of her tone. "I've had other things on this morning. Who's replacing Kalal?"

"Well... nobody. There hasn't been time to get a replacement. It's just the three of us."

Cortez swore under her breath. Her eyes drifted back to the man in the dark hood.

"Then we'll go with what we've got," she muttered. "What was Kalal responsible for? Armor, wasn't it? Is that all sorted?"

"Yes, S'arnt," May nodded, "it's all here and checked, with the weapons. The aircraft landed a few minutes ago and is just taxiing across. But it'll be another hour before we leave."

Cortez's eyes widened.

"An hour?! Why?"

"Something to do with air traffic slots and availability." Lois shrugged. "We've got to wait our turn in the queue to leave here."

"Wait our turn?" Cortez snapped. "We're a military unit deploying on a deliberate op! And we need to wait by the vending machine and watch Maya-series so kids can go on vacation without delays? That's seriously where we're fucking at?"

"I guess the travel companies are paying more than the air force," Lois offered quietly.

Cortez swore again, walking over to the dumped pile of bags. Through the window she saw a small van drive up to the terminal, its passenger compartment filled with half a dozen men and women in the black uniforms of Hospitaller soldiers.

***

The blast of cool air from the terminal building provided a welcome respite from the afternoon heat. The Paradiso air was close and sticky, the moisture content driven uncomfortably high after a downpour from the heavens during the flight from Vedi to Valkenswijk. Hawkins looked back over his shoulder as he held the door open for Sister-Sub Officer Sonia Tocci - De Fersen's new second-in-command - and watched as a fuel bowser trundled a lackadaisical path over to the black, bulbous POC-9 Rhincodon heavy transport aircraft. It seemed a waste of resources to move a mere ten soldiers, two dronbots, and their equipment across Paradiso. Their next stop would be Damburg, then into smaller aircraft for a tactical insertion behind the front lines. Hawkins looked across at a line of tourists boarding a civilian liner on the far side of the dispersal area. In a few hours, they would all be on vacation. In a few hours, Hawkins would possibly be in a firefight for his life.

"Kyle?"

A familiar voice from behind Hawkins brought his attention back inside the terminal building. Hawkins's eyes widened in surprise as he recognized the hawkish features of Darius Stanescu. The lithe doctor leapt forward with an outstretched hand, his thin features lit up with a friendly grin. Hawkins shook his hand warmly.

"Darius! I was not expecting you to be joining us! How've you been? Where've you been? How… it's great to see you!"

The older man removed his hood to reveal his cropped short hair. His dark eyes lit up with excitement.

"I haven't really been anywhere!" he explained. "I've been at Skovorodino all this time. I only graduated last week."

Hawkins quickly suppressed a sympathetic smile that he feared would seem patronizing. Having been friends with Stanescu for the doctor's two years of training at the fortress-monastery, Hawkins knew that he had struggled in several areas. A late graduation could only have come about from the requirement for remedial training to meet the final standard. But Stanescu had made it; he had graduated after all of the challenges he faced. Now he was Brother Surgeon-Sub Officer Stanescu.

"It's good to have you here!" Hawkins said genuinely as the two made their way over to one of the lines of spartan, white grill metal chairs bolted to the ground. "How is your grandmother?"

"Oh, fine," Stanescu replied as he sat down, "she was worrying about you when all of the fighting at Glottenburg was all over the news. You'll have to tell me how it all went."

Hawkins felt color warmly rise to his face at the mention of the fighting at the Alpha Four-Four research facility, followed by the familiar, gnawing guilt at the thought of those who did not survive. That guilt was immediately replaced with exhilaration as a communication alert appeared on his lens, followed by directions to the terminal building's closest call room. He glanced quickly around and saw De Fersen talking to the trio of plain-clothed Coadjutor Crosiers who were joining their force. He had time.

"Darius, I've got a call coming. I'll explain everything later but I've got to take it. I'll just be in the call room round the corner, okay? Shan't be long."

Hawkins sprinted away from the waiting area and to a door leading to a bank of private communications rooms. He could take the call on his lens, but the opportunity to see her virtually in three dimensions, he could not miss that. Hawkins bounded into the first of the rooms - a simple cube, perhaps three or four meters long - and shut the door behind him. He sat down and accepted the call.

"Hi!"

"Hey!" a voice chimed into his ears. "I got through to you! I was worried your stop off wouldn't be long enough."

Hawkins smiled. The feminine, heavily accented voice of his fiancee pushed away the fear of the unknown ahead and the weight of uncertainty of De Fersen's erratically unpredictable approval.

"I've got a little time. I still can't see you, the image hasn't come through."

"Ja, same here," Beckmann replied. "How are you coping? Has everything died down since the hotel?"

"Yes... officially, at least. There's no action being taken against me, anyway. I think Gabriele is still disappointed in me. I... The picture still hasn't come through. Are you getting a good reception at your end?"

There was a pause; an uncomfortable pause, before a reply came through.

"I told you you'd be fine. Kyle, I'm going to turn the visuals on now, and I want you to stay calm, okay?"

Hawkins leaned forward in the comm room seat, his eyes narrowed suspiciously.

"Yes, certainly. I'll stay calm. Erm... what's happened?"

The visuals flickered as a signal worked through to the room from the far side of the planet. Hawkins recognized the tall, slim figure of his fiancee sat opposite him as the pixels gained resolution and clarity. He saw the electric guitars hung on the wall behind her, as if he was in her music room with her at her home. She wore faux leather jeans and a shredded t-shirt with the logo of one of the many vintage heavy metal bands she was trying to encourage him to follow. Then her face materialized. Her flawless face had its beautiful perfection marred by a huge swelling over one reddened, heavily bruised eye. Hawkins leapt to his feet.

"What the hell happened to you?!"

Beckmann smiled.

"You should see what I did to them."

"Lisette, this isn't funny! Who did this! Who hurt you?"

"Look, just calm down, I...."

"Calm down?! Don't tell me you walked into a wall! I recognize an injury from a fight when I see one! Who the hell did this?! I'll..."

"Kyle! Calm... down."

Dejected, Hawkins sank back into the cubicle's plush chair. He knew she was no stranger to injuries, but the primitive, protective part of him raged at the thought of somebody hitting her. Beckmann's features softened from the stern admonishment to one of concern.

"Don't worry," she repeated, "I'm fine. The doctor gave me some injections. This'll all be back to normal in a couple of days."

"What happened?"

Beckmann folded her arms and let out a sigh.

"I... it's a long story. I was driving back from a therapy session. There was a car ahead of me, stopped at the lights. There were four drunk girls inside. Kids, really, about your age."

Hawkins clenched his jaw. The four year age gap between them was often nothing, but sometimes may as well have been a lifetime.

"They had the windows down," Beckmann continued, "it was evening. There were families around. Parents with young children. These four arseholes were swearing, shouting, abusing people passing by, upsetting kids... listening to shit rap. One of them threw an empty can at a bin and missed. So... I got out of my car and threw the can back on her lap and walked away. She... threw the can into the back of my head and called me a name."

"Right," Hawkins said wearily, "what happened then?"

"Well... I split her face open on the steering wheel, so they all got out and jumped me. One of them got lucky with a bottle and hit me in the face. But, as I said, I'm okay. Just a couple of injections and a few days to heal."

Hawkins swallowed. He leaned forward and found himself having to pluck up the courage to ask the next question.

"And them? What about those four girls?"

Beckmann reached into her pocket and produced a crumpled pack of cigarettes, and then a chrome-plated, vintage Zippo lighter. She lit a cigarette and inhaled before answering, her face cool and callous.

"They'll live."

Hawkins shook his head slowly.

"Lisette, you can't keep doing this! You were literally on your way back from seeing your therapist! Does she know about this? That on the way back from a therapy session, you beat four young women nearly to death in broad daylight, in front of a bunch of families with children?"

Beckmann's blue eyes narrowed.

"Fuck, Kyle, when you phrase it like that, you make *me* sound like the bad guy." She flashed a mischievous smirk.

Hawkins knew, even at the most superficial level, that he was wrong for falling for that infectious smile. He also knew exactly who and what she was when, only a week ago, he had dropped to one knee on that church tower rooftop and asked her to marry him.

"Look," he continued, "just... keep your guard higher next time, okay?"

Beckmann burst into laughter. A few seconds passed in a lighter mood, the tension seemingly broken, before Beckmann replied.

"*Ja*, okay! Got it. Look... how long have you got until your flight leaves?"

Hawkins checked his lens chronometer and keyed his comlog for an updated boarding time.

"Oh, a fair while yet."

Beckmann's eyes narrowed mischievously for a second time. She leaned closer and propped her folded arms up on her lap.

"Well... that's good," she purred, "because I've got an idea of how to productively spend the next half hour or so. You see, I've got this program ready..."

Hawkins sat bolt upright in surprise.

"What?" he exclaimed. "Here? Now? Lisette, I don't think we should be..."

"Kyle," Beckmann warned, "if you don't practice, you'll never get good at it."

Hawkins looked around at the cramped cubicle, visualizing how they could possibly enact her plan virtually with so little to work with.

"I mean, we can try? It might..."

Mark Barber

"Good!" Beckmann beamed, pressing her comlog. "Accept the program."

An invitation flashed across Hawkins's lens. He reached hesitantly across and keyed to accept. The room around him faded. The temperature plummeted. Hawkins looked up and saw snow as far as the eye could see beneath a crystal clear sky. White frosted pine trees covered a meandering, gently sloped countryside. Hawkins shivered and looked down. He wore a white winter smock and carried an ancient, wooden rifle with a telescopic sight.

"It's December 1939," Beckmann said as she appeared next to him, similarly dressed in archaic winter combat clothing. "We're just south of Petsamo, northern Finland. The armies of the Soviet Union invaded less than a week ago."

The ground shook as an explosion thudded into the hillside not far from them, showering the area in clumps of earth and snow. Hawkins stared at the smoking hole.

"That's Soviet artillery fire," Beckmann said, dropping to one knee in the snow, "and you've got a company of enemy infantry advancing through the forest to the east. It's just you and that Sako M28/30 bolt action rifle. 7.62mm, five round magazine, effective past eight hundred meters with that scope."

A second shell exploded in the trees, far closer this time. Hawkins instinctively flung himself down to the ground.

"That artillery fire is not effective yet," Beckmann continued, undeterred, "but you can't stay here. Your task is to halt the enemy advance by eliminating key members of the company's chain of command. Come on, Kyle. What's your plan?"

Chapter Four

His steady hand expanded to comical proportions when viewed through the magnifying glass, Gabriele smiled as he slid the final wire into its connection port. Directing the fiddly, miniature screwdriver into the archaic, plastic block, he tightened the connection until the screw bit down on the copper wire. He allowed himself a chuckle of victory as he pushed the magnifying glass away and stared down at his master-piece. A perfect, working replica of a GlowTech AB15X; a first genera-tion comlog, nearly a century old in design. And built using old tools and an ancient magnifying glass.

Gabriele took the ugly, angular device off his desk and wrapped it around his forearm. It was time to find out if the perfect replica did actually work. His heart thumping in his chest, he pressed down on the clunky on/off button. Nothing happened. His smile faded away. His thumping heart slowed. Then, like a ray of sunshine peering over the horizon of the darkest night, a thin white line appeared on the black screen. Gabriele's smile slowly grew again. Lines of code scrolled rapidly across the ancient, AFED screen. It was booting up. It actually worked. No holographic projection, no modern technology automatical-ly mating to the chip implanted in his arm; just a tenuous connection via a biotechnological relay of his own design. The home menu screen appeared in all of its cyan glory. Gabriele pumped a clenched fist in the air and cheered.

"I'm guessing that isn't your homework."

The victory celebrations instantly faded away. Gabriele swiv-eled around on his chair to face the door to his bedroom. The tall, thin figure of his father stood in the doorframe, his arms folded. The mid-dle-aged pastor's face was twisted in a frown of disappointment.

"I'm sorry, Gabriele, perhaps I didn't make myself clear enough. Would you like me to rephrase my previous statement into a question?"

Gabriele blinked in frustration, tearing his first generation, home-built comlog from his arm.

"No. This isn't homework. This is… history."

The room fell silent. Gabriele attempted to meet his father's stony stare and very quickly failed.

"This… this is an AB15X," Gabriele continued desperately. "I've managed to construct an exact replica! This is history! I've construct-ed a copy of something really significant, and I've done it without any

help!"

His father shook his head.

"So it's not enough that you haven't bothered going to church for five Sundays in a row; you're now not bothering with your homework and are instead wasting your time with… whatever this is supposed to be. Fourteen years old and you've got it all figured out, haven't you?"

Gabriele sighed and looked up into the far corner of his bedroom. That was phrased as a question, but it did not deserve a mature answer. His eyes fell on the old family photograph on his windowsill. He remembered those golden days when his father was a loud, vibrant, gregarious lawyer. When his mother was alive. The aging preacher his father had morphed into now muttered in despair under his breath and gently closed the door on his son.

Gabriele stared at the closed door in silence for several long minutes. Yes, he had not been to his father's church for over a month now. He was still looking for a way to tell him that he did not believe in God anymore.

The lead Tubarão flared over the landing site, its engine nacelles swinging forward to alter the vector of the thrust from forward flight to a low hover. Dust kicked out and away from the underside of the aircraft in great billows as the sleek, black aircraft sank down until its landing gear connected with the uneven surface of the cracked, crumbling road. De Fersen was the first out the cabin door, his Spitfire tucked into his hip as he sprinted clear of the landing site and dropped to one knee to take up a precautionary firing position. Four other soldiers quickly filed out after De Fersen, along with a surprisingly fast and nimble, arachnid-like dronbot, as a second Tubarão descended down to land on next to the first.

In seconds, both aircraft had disgorged their passengers and dronbot cargo. The Tubarãos then lifted back up into a brief hover before transitioning away, departing rapidly at low level over the darkened jungle canopy. His force spread out in a defensive circle on the weed-infested road, De Fersen watched as the two aircraft disappeared behind a ridgeline beneath the moonlit sky, the roaring of their engines gradually fading away. He quickly checked that his team's IFF signals were serviceable and that their location tied in with the position reported on his lens's map by the network of invisible navbots hovering in the upper reaches of the atmosphere. Ahead of them, the fractured roadway led off toward the city of Moravia; a city De Fersen remembered from before the invasion as having lit up the horizon from over a dozen miles away. Now, it was a collection of blackened, deserted skyscrapers reaching up into the darkness like black claws.

"Bravo One, on point," De Fersen ordered, "let's get going."

As ordered, Sergeant Kormea took position at the head of the column of soldiers, the rest of the team slotting into their pre-briefed positions as they quickly made their way northeast toward their lay-up position. The base of operations set up for them at map marker Mike Three-Five was just over six miles away; they would be in position well before dawn. Kormea, supported by the Sierra dronbot, led the column along the road. Even after witnessing firsthand the sheer destructive capability of the natural forces of Paradiso for several decades, De Fersen still found himself amazed by the thick, tree-trunk sized green weeds that had forced their way up through the old road like zombie arms through a graveyard ground in some terrible, old horror movie. To either side of the road was dense jungle, the darkness populated by both animals and vegetation that was dangerous even to an armored knight. As much as they risked detection by moving along the road, it was the lesser of two evils when compared to the Karava vine-traps, bloodbriars, and a thousand other dangerous examples of vegetation that lay ahead.

The line of soldiers and their two armed drones moved quickly north, crossing beneath what was left of a toppled road bridge near an abandoned industrial estate at a fork in the River Allom; a powerful sight that triggered De Fersen's memory, recollecting that this was the site of a major battle in the Second Offensive.

"Eternal rest, give unto them, O Lord," De Fersen mouthed silently as they moved quickly past the destroyed bridge, *"and let the perpetual light shine upon them. May they rest in peace. Amen."*

On the other side of the bridge, the road dipped down into a shallow valley with steep contours, running north to south. His visor set to filter out any lifeforms less than a meter in size, De Fersen saw a collection of red shapes to his right near the treeline, each nearly the size of a crouching humanoid. The live intelligence feed provided by the surveillance bots in low orbit above his team automatically confirmed that the life signs were purely biological, with no unnatural materials marking them out as possessing arms or armor. Nevertheless, De Fersen watched the trees warily in case of any ill thought out attack by aggressive animals or, worse but extremely unlikely, the group was something Shasvastii in origin. Up ahead, Tocci and Stanescu were already pointing their MULTI Rifles at the trees as they passed. The quartet of shapes bolted and darted away, their movements so fluid and fast that they could only have been jungle animals.

De Fersen's attention was dragged back to his lens as a line of text scrolled across his field of view.

- *Enemy force detected northwest of your position, one kilometer, closing. Analyzing for further details.*

De Fersen swore. He checked his map and saw the enemy force highlighted in red, not far ahead on the road. The autofeed of information from the invisible surveillance bot above provided further information as its sensors zoomed in on the opposing force. Strength seven. Infantry. Most likely a standard Combined Army patrol.

"Alpha Zero, you copying this?" Sister-Sub Officer Tocci asked.

"Yes," De Fersen replied, "and given their own surveillance network is in place alongside ours, I'd guarantee they're having a similar conversation about us."

"Are we losing them in the jungle?" Tocci asked.

"No," De Fersen replied immediately, "we're closing with them and we're killing them."

De Fersen grumbled a curse to himself. Only a mile from the landing site and they had been detected already. Given the pace of action on the Paradiso fronts, it was inevitable to a certain extent, but he was not going to slow his operation down with a dangerous traipse through the jungle. They had been ordered to make some noise. This was a decent start. He checked his map for a good position to set up fields of fire between his current location and the advancing enemy. He highlighted it on his map, only two hundred meters ahead.

"Alpha Team," he called his three fellow knights, "Core Fireteam, I have lead. Bravo Team, take the Clipper and set up in cover at my Marker Delta. Charlie Team, with the Sierra, set up at Marker Echo."

Tocci, Hawkins, and Stanescu closed up on De Fersen's position. Kormea led the three Order Sergeants and the missile launcher-armed Clipper Dronbot off toward the cover provided by the tall, thick lip of weeds at Marker Delta. Cortez led the trio of Crosiers and the Sierra Dronbot to the piles of crumbled concrete at Marker Echo, on the other side of the road. De Fersen checked his intelligence feed again; the enemy force, now identified as Morat Vanguard Infantry, were moving rapidly along the road to engage. De Fersen clenched his jaw. Morats were bastards to knock down - definitely not a powerful enough force to defeat his own soldiers, but even their basic, light infantry posed enough of a threat to thin his numbers for the task ahead. De Fersen plotted another marker for his Fireteam of knights and quickened his pace to a sprint.

**

Her lightly armored feet pounding on the cracked concrete, Nilsson sprinted after Kormea toward their designated marker - a position marked on her lens as a blue, glowing cylinder reaching up from the ground. Kormea reached the cover of the thick, twisted jungle roots first, leaning against the natural barricade of pale green that had torn up through the human-made intrusion. Poddar arrived a second later, dropping to one knee and unclipping his Heavy Rocket Launcher from his back. That explosive level of firepower was backed up by the Clipper Dronbot as the squat, spider-like automaton scuttled into cover next to them, its missile launcher appendage at the ready.

Nilsson checked her tactical map - the Morats were closing fast along the road ahead. She raised her right hand to her forehead, then to her heart and her shoulders to cross herself, thinking of the fight that was moments away. She had faced Morats before. It took a truly unique level of dark maliciousness for a foe to deliberately aim at a human's implanted Cube, going to great pains to destroy any chance of resurrection. Nilsson found herself working hard to keep hatred at bay over the thought.

"Charlie Team, in position," Nilsson heard Cortez report.

She glanced across to her right and saw the three Crosiers lying prone in the scant cover provided by the rubbled remains of a broken section of road, two Combi Rifles and a Spitfire pointing down the open pathway that snaked in between the tall, looming trees. In between the two trios, the quartet of knights shot forward across the open ground, silent and hunkered low in the darkness. Nilsson changed range scales on the tactical map projected in the upper right corner of her lens; the seven Morat Vanguard infantrymen were rushing forward in two pairs and a team of three, rapidly covering ground and crossing obstacles in their path. Nilsson felt fear rising within her at the speed of their advance - the Morats knew what they faced; a superior force in terms of both numbers and ability. Yet, without even a thought for their own safety, they rushed headlong into a face-to-face firefight. Such was their way. Fearless, ruthless to the last.

"Bravo Team, Charlie Team," De Fersen called over the tactical net, "cover north with dronbots and heavy weapons. Keep one shooter covering south in case we're being flanked."

"Charlie One, copied," Cortez replied calmly.

Nilsson peered over the cover of the thick roots. Off in the darkness, her helmet's visor automatically compensating for the low light levels, she saw a pair of the tall, hulking figures of the Morats bounding forward down the road.

"Bravo One," Kormea said from next to her, "we've got..."

Her squad leader's final sentence was cut off as a burst of gunfire echoed from the darkness of the jungle to their left, and a torrent of blood erupted out of the back of Kormea's neck.

***

The jungle erupted into a cacophony of gunfire and explosions. The Sierra dronbot pivoted in place and began spraying the trees to the right with long bursts of automatic fire from its heavy machine gun. Bullets tore into cover around Cortez and her Crosiers. A red targeting reticle appeared in the jungle to the east, projected onto her lens where the network of surveillance bots high above detected incoming fire. Cortez huddled herself further into cover and looked over the top of the piles of rubble, but she saw nothing other than a blurred, indistinct shape perhaps ten meters back from the treeline - clearly the source of incoming fire but nothing she could make out clearly. She tapped on her comlog to designate the target for her team.

"Charlie Team! My Marker Foxtrot! Open fire!"

Cortez raised her Combi Rifle to her shoulder and shot off a quick burst of return fire, her rounds joining the shots from Lois's Spitfire and May's rifle in blasting apart the trees around the hazy target.

- *Sergeant Panikos Kormea, dead. Gunshot wound, neck.*

"All positions, Bravo Two!" Cortez heard Nilsson calling from the left flank. "Bravo One is down and we're taking fire from the trees! Can't make out what it is!"

"Charlie One," Cortez called calmly, "we've got a firer on the right flank. Light automatic, possibly a marksman. We're holding position and returning fire."

Explosions sounded from the left flank as missiles and rockets blasted into the ground amidst the dense trees. Flocks of birds flung themselves up into the night sky, squawking in terror. The still, humid air stank of burnt propellant. Through her lens, Cortez could still only make out a distorted, hulking form taking cover behind a thick, felled tree, the muzzle flash of an automatic weapon spitting out short, sharp, and disciplined bursts. Through the smoke and the twirling clumps of vegetation, she made out a second enemy shooter in the darkness. A round thudded into the piles of broken road in front of May. The young Crosier recklessly ignored the threat and fired off a return burst as long streams of automatic fire from Lois's Spitfire and the dronbot's HMG carved up the jungle.

***

The pair of Morats rushed rapidly along the edge of the road, hunkered down low as their advance was covered by short, accurate bursts of fire from the cover behind them. From his position in partial cover behind a vine-covered, bent lamppost, De Fersen fired a long burst from his Spitfire, catching one of the advancing alien soldiers across the gut. The huge, brown-red-skinned soldier seemed momentarily to somehow shrug off a full burst of fire to the abdomen, taking another two paces before crumpling down to the ground. Accurate return fire slammed into the vegetation around De knightFersen, causing him to flinch instinctively, but nothing more. He quickly checked his tactical map as the lone Morat ahead diverted his path to take cover in the jungle to the side of the road.

The Fireteam of four knights was front and center, crouched behind the cover of a huge, dark green vine that had burst through the center of the ruined roadway. Behind them and to the left, the Order Sergeants were exchanging fire with a pair of enemy troopers hidden in the jungle, whose opening shots had managed to fell both Kormea and Poddar. Similarly, to the right, Cortez's Crosiers exchanged fire with a pair of hidden enemies - their ability to blend into the jungle marking them out as something more highly trained than the Vanguard Infantry who advanced toward the knights. De Fersen quickly plotted another series of markers on his force's shared tactical map as Tocci, Hawkins, and Stanescu fired at the trio of Morat Vanguard Infantry directly ahead of them.

"Bravo Team, hold position," De Fersen commanded, "help's on the way. Charlie Team, flank enemy position via Marker Golf."

"Charlie One, copied," Cortez replied.

De Fersen quickly considered sending Stanescu back to see what the doctor could do to help his two felled sergeants, but right now he needed a killer to secure that flank. He turned to Hawkins, switching to his Fireteam's communication channel.

"Kyle, get back to Marker Hotel. There's two Morats at that position with reactive camouflage, possibly Zerat Special Forces. Report in when they're down."

"Sir."

The young knight nodded, checking quickly behind him before breaking away from the Fireteam and sprinting low off to the cover of the jungle to the west. De Fersen looked around to assess his own situation. The Vanguard infantry advance was based around a central trio, with two pairs rushing the flanks. The central trio were dug into cover ahead, with the pair on his left reduced to one soldier pinned in cover. De Fersen looked to his right and saw the second pair still advancing to a better firing position. Morats were big and aggressive - ferocious combatants - but also professional and intelligent. They were far too disciplined to rush Military Order knights in close combat. No, they were just moving to negate De Fersen's team's cover.

"Alpha Team, advance to Marker India!" De Fersen shouted, jumping up to his feet and running off toward the dense, deadly jungle to the east, Tocci and Stanescu close behind.

***

Her teeth gritted as her Combi Rifle thumped away against her shoulder, Nilsson fired another long burst at the closer of the two Morats hidden in the jungle. Both enemy troopers were highlighted with red brackets on her lens, but neither showed up as anything other than a blurred, almost pixelated shape that seemingly washed across her field of vision, disrupting her attempts to aim. Both Kormea and Poddar lay motionless at her feet, smoking holes in their armor. To her right, the hunched Clipper Dronbot scuttled around the edge of cover and fired off a salvo of missiles, brief plumes of flame erupting from the back of its weapon mount before the projectiles hurtled away into the jungle. The night was lit up with yellow spheres of flame, the shockwave from the explosions giving Nilsson a gentle push in the chest even from this range. Snapped tree trunks, branches, and leaves twirled up in every direction.

Almost instantly, a burst of fire replied from the jungle, kicking shards of pale green root up only inches from Nilsson's face and sweeping across to thump into the thin, alloy carapace of the Clipper Dronbot. Nilsson ducked back down into cover and pulled the empty, curved magazine out of her Combi Rifle and grabbed a replacement from her belt before feeding it in ahead of her weapon's pistol grip. She checked her tactical map. Behind her, the Crosiers were locked in a firefight with two hidden enemies in the jungle. Ahead, De Fersen was closing the gap with the advancing Morat Vanguard Infantry. A sole knight, bracketed in blue on both her tactical map and her lens, was moving quickly back along the western flank toward the two Morats that had gunned down her comrades.

"Alpha Two, from Bravo Two!" she called. "Two targets at my marker! They've both got reactive camouflage systems and automatic weapons! I'll keep them busy if you can get in behind them!"

"Bravo Two, that's alright," Hawkins replied. "I... I can see them now, I think. You stay in cover and out of their line of fire. I've got them now."

***

"Steph, take Target Alpha!" Cortez shouted. "Johnny, take Bravo! Keep those bastards in place!"

Lois's Spitfire let out another long burst, sending streams of fire into the treeline ahead. It was joined a moment later by the deeper bark of the Sierra Dronbot's HMG, the two lines of rounds criss-crossing through the branches and leaves in the direction of the two hidden

Morat soldiers. Cortez planted a hand on the piled rubble in front of her and vaulted up and over, sprinting forward toward the treeline as she heard May's Combi Rifle join the symphony of gunfire behind her. The automatic rifle fire ahead ceased before the storm of bullets, but to the right of the first shooter, Cortez heard the telltale, deep blast of a Boarding Shotgun from the trees and felt a shot whizz past her head. She reached the treeline and flung herself down into cover as the exchange of fire continued all around her.

"S'arnt!" May shouted over the communications net. "Target Alpha is moving toward you!"

"Keep shooting the fucker!" Cortez yelled, hurling herself back to her feet and plunging into the dark jungle.

Ducking beneath a low hanging tree branch, aware of something dog-sized slithering in the darkness to her right, Cortez moved rapidly through the small spaces between the ominous trees and vines. She let out a stifled cry of pain when she felt a series of stings ripple up her left arm as thorns dug between the plates of her light armor and punctured her combat fatigues. Ignoring the pain, tensing up again as heavy machine gun fire cut up the jungle around her, she looked up and saw the combined fire of Lois's Spitfire and the Dronbot's machine gun rip through one of the Morats.

A shotgun blast echoed through the darkness, and Cortez felt a punch in the hip, half spinning her around. She dropped to one knee in cover behind the closest tree, ignoring the warning line of text that scrolled across her lens to tell her that she was bleeding from a gunshot wound to the pelvis. Her armor had taken the brunt of it. She had had much worse. The red bracketed Morat up ahead moved again, following a shallow valley in the jungle, its path either one of retreat or to take up a better firing position on the Crosiers still on the broken road. Sucking in a lungful of air and ignoring the pain in her arm and hip, Cortez rushed after her target.

The distance closed. The red bracket stopped dead in her lens. The gunfire behind her was more distant now, just the booming of MULTI Rifles from Alpha Team somewhere far ahead. The Morat turned around and rushed toward her, close enough for Cortez to make out her adversary's feminine form and distinctive armor. Zerat Special Forces. Cortez knew their tactics well enough to know that the only way was to fight fire with fire and be quicker on the trigger. Without hesitation, Cortez flung herself forward again and down into the valley. At the same moment, the Morat appeared ahead, its hazy outline shifting as the reactive camouflage of her armor jumbled its way across her lens.

The Zerat trooper raised her weapon. Cortez was faster. Her first burst blasted through the space that the Morat should have been in but succeeded only in tearing into a tree trunk to one side. The second shot winged the enemy soldier, stopping her dead. The third blasted neatly into the center of mass, punching straight through her chest. The muscular alien soldier span in place and fell to the dry earth, face down. Cortez knew the Morats well enough. There was no giving up, no surrender, nothing but a last opportunity to inflict death on their enemies. She rushed forward, unsheathing her sword, and plunged the blade straight through the alien warrior's back before twisting it, wrenching it clear and then hacking down into the felled warrior's thick neck for good measure.

***

A thorned vine swung out and wrapped itself around Hawkins's forearm as he advanced on the enemy position. Effortlessly, and thankful that the vine was not something more dangerous, he grabbed a fistful of the trailing plant and tore it free before dashing silently forward again, his rifle raised and ready. Twenty meters ahead, the two red bracketed figures shifted and jumped across his visor. He was around the side of them now; a decent enough firing position. But just adding one more rifle to the firefight was not why he had been sent back.

Another long burst of fire cut across from Nilsson's position to the left, immediately answered by a heavier rifle and the rattle of a submachine gun. Ducking beneath a low, thick branch and vaulting nimbly over a second, Hawkins slung his MULTI rifle onto his back and unsheathed his sword.

"My grace is sufficient for you," he whispered to himself, *"for my power is made perfect in weakness."*

Behind him, the fast whine of a Spitfire cut through the night, accompanied by the snaps of Combi Rifles and the dull thuds of MULTI Rifles. Ten meters. He could see them both now - tall, hulking muscular forms encased in armored plates and angular helmets. From his intelligence briefs, he recognized them as Kyosots.

"For Christ's sake, I delight in weaknesses… in hardships… for when I am weak, then I am strong…"

The closer of the two Morats turned to face Hawkins as he darted out of the undergrowth, vainly attempting to bring his submachine gun around to bear. Leading with a fluid, high attack, Hawkins swung the blade down in both hands. With an audible whoosh, the heavy sword cut through the dense air to cleave the weapon in two before ripping through the Kyosot's armor and cutting open his chest. A horrific wound torn from shoulder to midriff, the bleeding Morat collapsed heavily down to his knees. Hawkins followed up smoothly with a second strike, neatly decapitating the alien soldier before rushing forward again.

With a guttural yell, the second Morat soldier leapt out to face Hawkins, a long, curved dagger held high. Hawkins moved directly into the attack, glad to get as close as possible to his target. He planted one open palm against the attacking Morat's upper arm to push the attack aside before driving his sword straight through the soldier's abdomen, plunging bloodily out of his back. With a cry of anger that was audible and clear even through the Kyosot's fully-enclosed helmet, the alien warrior grabbed Hawkins by the neck and squeezed hard while the dagger swung down at his back.

Momentarily surprised by the sheer power of the choke rather than the move itself, Hawkins released his grip on the sword embedded in his adversary's gut. Free to move, he swept up his right hand to again block the attack from the dagger, and then reached over the choke attack to grab the Morat's wrist and hold it firmly in place. With the choking arm held fast, Hawkins slammed his free palm up into the underside of the Morat's limb, breaking the bones of the forearm.

With one broken arm and a sword protruding through his torso, somehow the Kyosot warrior leapt in clumsily for another attack. His adversary weakened, dying, Hawkins could see now that this was merely a formality, a need to go down fighting. He obliged by grabbing the back of the Morat's head and dragging the flailing warrior down to meet his armored knee as it swung up, smashing into the soldier's faceplate with a loud clang. The Morat staggered back from the force of the blow. Hawkins whipped his MULTI Pistol up from his waist and shot the staggering soldier three times in the chest. The Morat was flung back bloodily, collapsing down into the dry earth. Hawkins paced across, shot the fallen warrior in the back of the head, and then recovered his sword.

"Bravo Two," Hawkins reported, breaking open his pistol and thumbing four fresh rounds into the cylinder, "Marker Hotel is clear."

Hawkins checked his tactical map to see where the closest enemy troops now were, a feeling of unease suddenly flaring up at the back of his mind.

***

His Spitfire tucked in at the hip, De Fersen charged forward from the cover of the trees and back onto the road. His first burst of fire blasted into the closest of the three Morat Vanguards, catching the big soldier in the chest and killing him instantly. The second Morat returned fire, a burst from his Combi Rifle clanging against De Fersen's heavy ORC armor. Tocci and Stanescu, close at De Fersen's heels, fired in response as they rushed past, their MULTI Rifles gunning down the alien trooper as lines of text scrolled across De Fersen's lens, warning him of superficial damage to his armor.

Ignoring the warnings and the bruising in his chest from the impact, De Fersen let out a grunt and resumed his charge, dropping his Spitfire and unsheathing his sword as he closed the gap with the final Morat. The huge, white-haired alien roared and rushed out to meet the Father-Officer head on, swinging his Combi Rifle like a club. De Fersen twisted in place to duck beneath the strike, planting his armored shoulder into his opponent and driving the Morat back. The bulky alien planted a clenched fist into De Fersen's gut; De Fersen swept up an elbow into the Morat's face, breaking his nose in an arc of blood and jolting his head back. Given a brief opening and enough room to maneuver, De Fersen swung his sword around in a horizontal strike, slashing open the soldier's belly. The knight continued into a smooth, follow up second strike that hacked down into the Morat's shoulder, taking off the muscular, red arm.

To the alien's credit, he tried one final lunge forward to attack, a huge fist swinging at De Fersen. The knight batted it aside with his blade, allowed the momentum of the attack to carry the Morat past him, and then hacked a great wound open across his back. The Vanguard trooper fell down at his feet, dead.

Save a final, sporadic exchange of Combi Rifle fire on the right flank of the attack, the roadway fell silent.

"Alpha Zero, Charlie One," Cortez called, "final pair of enemy soldiers are retreating to the north. Shall we pursue?"

De Fersen sheathed his sword and looked down at the dead soldiers littering the broken road.

"Negative," he replied, "regroup and report in casualties."

"Alpha Zero from Bravo Two," Nilsson responded immediately, "I've got two casualties at my position, request medical assistance."

"Charlie One, I've taken a hit," Cortez added, "nothing serious, I'll take my turn after Bravo Team."

De Fersen checked his tactical map. Just the two red dots retreating rapidly away to the north. But they would no doubt be returning. Morats did not just... run away.

"Alpha One, Alpha Two, set up at Marker Juliet and watch for enemy forces coming back our way," De Fersen commanded. "Alpha Three, attend to the wounded."

Immediately, De Fersen saw Tocci pace forward to take position at his marker, while Hawkins's blue dot on the tactical display likewise moved rapidly in response to his command. Stanescu remained rigidly in place. De Fersen looked across at the knight doctor. Stanescu was staring down at a heavily wounded Morat at his feet, the alien soldier's torn chest slowly rising and falling as his milky, unfocused eyes stared up at the starry sky above.

***

His hands still clutching his MULTI Rifle, his feet rooted motionlessly to the spot, Stanescu stared down at the dying Morat. The Vanguard had caught a burst of fire across the gut - from De Fersen's Spitfire, when Stanescu replayed the events of the past few minutes in his mind's eye - and now lay on his back in a still expanding pool of dark blood. Stanescu was familiar with what a Morat looked like; with what one of these creatures was. With what they were capable of. Since the pretentiously self-titled Evolved Intelligence had decided to subsume every race in the galaxy into its plan to achieve transcendence, its Combined Army was no stranger to hostility. Humanity was merely the latest of these unwilling partners, and the warlike Morats were but one of several races that the Human Sphere faced in the Combined Army's assault on its schismatic people.

Stanescu took in a deep breath and let it out slowly, his fingers tightening around the handguard of his rifle. He stared down at the dying alien soldier. Standing taller than a human, perhaps averaging two meters in height, the average Morat was also more heavily muscled - particularly in the upper body. The ruddy, brown-red-skinned alien's head, being the same size as a human, appeared smaller in comparison. The face was a harsh, intimidating assembly of rough skin; a small, almost piggish nose; and a broad, fanged mouth that ran almost from pointed ear to pointed ear. A shock of long, white hair stood out in stark contrast to the red skin.

"Stanescu!"

The doctor jumped at the snapped mention of his name. He turned to face the speaker and saw De Fersen towering over him, only a few paces away. The harsh intonation of the Father-Officer's voice indicated that this was not the first time he had attempted to force a reaction from him.

"We've got wounded. Get to it. *Quickly.*"

Attaching his rifle to his back, Stanescu turned and jogged back down the road toward where he last saw the Order Sergeants of Bravo Team setting up behind the cover of the thick vines. As he ran, he brought up biometric status updates on all soldiers in the unit.

- *Sergeant Panikos Kormea, dead. Gunshot wound, neck.*
- *Sergeant Anil Poddar, unconscious. Gunshot wound, chest. Life threatening.*
- *Sergeant Marianna Cortez, superficial injuries. Gunshot wound, hip. Lacerations with poisoning, upper arm.*

Triaging his casualties was instant and effortless - Stanescu found himself in the bizarre position of finding comfort in the familiar surroundings of dealing with the pressure of life and death. Yes, he only had one year's experience as a doctor, but compared to his peers from medical school, that year as a Christian missionary volunteer dealing with the fallout of the Combined Army's invasion was worth a decade as a general practitioner when it came to battlefield trauma management. He paired his comlog to Poddar's and checked the wounded soldier's airway and breathing. Clear upper airway - breathing severely impaired by a punctured lung. Casualty unconscious due to a combination of hypoxia, hypovolemia, and pain.

Stanescu reached his casualty and dropped to one knee. Poddar lay sprawled on his back, a pair of blackened, smoking holes in the armor over his chest. Stanescu pressed the symbols projected holographically over his comlog and overlaid a primary survey on his lens. It showed an internal view of a minor blockage. After ascertaining that oxygen levels were acceptable, he grabbed his medikit to address the bleeding.

"Okay, Anil, I'm going to get you all sorted."

Reconfiguring his visor to zoom in on the injury and highlight his patient's veins and arteries, Stanescu took a serum syringe from his medikit and rapidly set about sealing the wound.

***

The unseen eyes of surveillance drones high above updated the tactical picture on Hawkins's map as he stared out to the north. The survivors of their earlier encounter were long gone, disappearing into the mass of biological signals that made up the jungle vegetation and the animals that swarmed within it. Hawkins's previous experience in the Glottenburg region of the Norstralia continent - thousands of miles off to the west - had been in an area of jungle considerably less dense and less frequently populated with dangers. He wondered briefly if the Combined Army had chosen such a difficult part of Paradiso for their assault just to prove to the Human Sphere how willing they were to face any dangers.

"You alright?"

Hawkins looked across to the second knight keeping watch to the north. Sister-Sub Officer Sonia Tocci was crouched behind a fallen tree only a few meters away, her rifle tucked into one shoulder.

"Yes. Fine... why?"

"Because even under all of that armor, I can see you shrugging and shaking your head as if you're debating something with yourself."

Hawkins glanced across. The more experienced knight continued to stare out motionlessly to the north. Yes, she was entirely correct.
As soon as the gunfire had stopped, the most stupid of all thoughts
forced its way into his head; and no matter how hard he tried, it was not
shifting.

*Whoever sheds human blood, by humans shall their blood be
shed; for in the image of God has God made mankind.*

It was the opening statement in one of many lectures on morals and ethics at the fortress-monastery of Skovorodino. That particular lecture had been about waging war against the alien races of the
Combined Army. A dozen lectures and their associated dissertations
had already been completed regarding waging war on other humans
- Just War theory, when it was acceptable to take another life - but the
likes of Morats and Shasvastii? The moral lessons were clear. There
was nothing to debate. They were not God's creatures. There was no
hesitation, no mercy. They were evil, as close as one could find to the
creations of the Devil himself in this modern, scientific age.

Yet now, with two Morats torn apart by his own blade only minutes before, Hawkins found himself questioning even that. Yes, the
Bible made it clear that humans were created in God's image. But the
Bible, even with divine guidance, was written by mere men. Fallible
people. People in an era when aliens were not even a concept, let
alone a reality. Could any of them really claim with any authority that
these were not also God's creatures? Was there a better way?

"Hawkins! Concentrate!" Tocci snapped.

"I'm on it!" Hawkins growled. "If they come back, we'll drop them
all over again!"

Tocci stared across.

"You really think it's that easy? You think that because we took
three casualties while killing eight of their number, this was a walkover?"

Hawkins shook his head and looked away again.

"This wasn't a walkover," Tocci continued, "they took heavy casualties because they were willing to die without flinching, not because
that fight was one-sided. Any Human Sphere opponent would have
retreated with half the casualties! But that's not their way! They push
on, even if it means death, if there is any chance of achieving even the
most minor of objectives! Do you understand?"

"Is there a problem here?"

Hawkins looked over his shoulder and saw De Fersen strid-
ing toward the two of them. The tall, veteran knight's piercing gaze
seemed to practically punch through the visor of his helmet as he ap-

proached. The Father-Officer stopped by his two subordinates and folded his arms.

"No problem, sir," Hawkins replied.

Of course there was no problem. How could he tell the legendary Gabriele De Fersen, of all people, that he was in mental anguish over cutting down two Morats? That he was facing the same internal struggle that he had after his first combat, when he had hacked down a Yujingyu warrior in the opening round of what became one of the most crucial border disputes between PanOceania and Yu Jing in recent years? So many Fusiliers had died in the weeks that followed. Yet, Hawkins found himself so wrapped up in his guilt over taking lives that it was not until days after he left the combat area that he paused to truly reflect on the people he knew who had died around him.

"You overthinking things again?" De Fersen grunted. "Don't. Keep your mind on the job."

"Yes, sir."

All three knights looked across as Stanescu made his way across from the south. Hawkins watched his old friend with admiration, wishing that he had composed himself as professionally in the moments after his first ever firefight. Then again, to an extent, it was not the doctor's first firefight. At least, it was not Stanescu's first time being shot at by Morats.

"I've done all I can, sir," Stanescu reported to De Fersen. "Sergeant Cortez is fine. Sergeant Poddar is conscious and walking. He can fire a weapon, if necessary, but he needs rest. I'd recommend getting him to a proper medical facility as soon as possible. Sergeant... Panikos Kormea was dead when I got to him. Nothing I could do."

De Fersen issued one, brief nod.

"I know. Have you recovered his Cube?"

Stanescu gently patted a pouch on his utility belt.

"Yes, sir."

Hawkins bowed his head respectfully. That Cube was now all that was left of Panikos Kormea, a man he had met only two days before and barely spoken to. The Cube - a device that was implanted into the base of the skull - was constantly updating, storing every aspect of a human's personality, memories, ambitions... everything that made them unique. The Cube could then be used to transplant the personality of a dead human into a new, synthetic body for another chance at life. That was, assuming, the person had both a resurrection license and the means to address the cripplingly expensive bill that came with the procedure. For Panikos Kormea, like the vast majority of the Human Sphere, death meant being transferred to a Cube, and that Cube in turn being placed into long term storage in the hope that the advances of technology would one day make resurrection an af-

By Fire and Sword

fordable reality for all.

"Can Poddar keep up?" De Fersen asked. "We've still some way to go."

Stanescu paused briefly.

"He can keep up, sir."

"Good. Let's go."

Hawkins found himself almost involuntarily taking a step forward. De Fersen looked down. Again, even through the visor, Hawkins felt the older knight's disapproval before he even spoke.

"Sergeant Kormea, sir."

"Yes, Kyle. He's dead. Surgeon-Sub Officer Stanescu made that quite clear."

"Can we at least bury him, sir?"

De Fersen planted his clenched fists on his hips.

"Hawkins, we are miles behind EI lines. We've got an important job to do that is time critical. The enemy now knows we are here. They are assembling another attack literally as I am speaking to you. And you want to stay here to try to dig a hole in the most inhospitable jungle in the Human Sphere and conduct a burial service? Fucking hell, Kyle, think!"

Hawkins looked down and to one side, taking a moment to control his rising anger. Of course he had bloody well thought of that! In the four years Hawkins had been acquainted with De Fersen, he had snapped and lost his temper at the older knight six times. Twice he had gotten away with it.

"Two minutes, sir," Hawkins looked up again, "two minutes. The amount of rockets and missiles that went off on the west side of the road, I guarantee there's already a hole six feet deep. Panikos Kormea has given us everything he had. He has laid down his life. Let me lower our brother into a shell hole, cover him with earth, and say a prayer. Two minutes."

De Fersen glowered down at the younger knight in silence for a brief moment. His shoulders sank a little, and then he nodded.

"Alright, Kyle, go on."

De Fersen turned to the other two knights.

"Get moving; scout ahead. Stay off the road. Call in anything you see. We'll be right behind you."

Chapter Five

"Despite the challenges we face, it is our future. Despite the wars that ravage humanity, it is our future. Despite the bleakness that eats away at the edges of our optimism, it is our future. And it remains a bright one. A hopeful one. With this graduation celebration we share, the worlds of the Human Sphere are our oyster. Our chance to make a difference. Our chance to do real good. It is our future."

The cavernous hall erupted in applause as the hundred students stood as one. Even a few cheers echoed from the back of the hall, echoing across the old walls and highly polished wooden floors that had been Nilsson's home for the past seven years. From her position behind the podium on the stage in front of them, she could not help but smile. Even the smattering of old rivals who had attempted to beat her grades and her accolades joined in the applause. Head Girl, Debating Captain, Cross Country Running Captain, Inter-Human Sphere Relations Captain... Nilsson had left them all behind. And in her opinion, she had done so with dignity and decorum.

Ms. Pedersen, the school head teacher, exchanged a smile with Nilsson and politely gestured for her to leave the stage. Nilsson took one last, long look at the hall and the faces of the boys and girls - now men and women - she had spent nearly half of her life with. Memories of school trips to the far reaches of Neoterra, of victory and defeat in sports, of excellence in academia, of drunken hilarity in parties... all of it had come to pass. Her throat felt tight as she forced a last smile and walked from the stage.

"Thank you, Anja!" Pedersen beamed as she took her place at the podium to address her graduating students.

Nilsson walked down to the alcoves flanking the hall. She saw the pictures of graduating classes running along the walls, spanning back over the decades to a time when face-to-face schooling was still the norm and not merely the province of the wealthy elite. Now, the great masses of children across the Human Sphere were schooled virtually from home, at their own pace and in the comfort of their own safe spaces, only meeting their classmates in virtual recreation areas across the Mayasphere. Nilsson remembered those days fondly, before the age of eleven when she was whisked off to St. Hallvard's Academy of Social Science. The same school her father graduated from as Head Boy.

"Good speech," Nilsson's mother whispered with a grin as she stepped down from the stage, "a little on the nose with the worlds as your oyster, perhaps. But you get that from your father."

A few of the other parents lining the hall alcoves shot admonishing looks across at Nilsson's mother for talking during the head teacher's speech, but the lithe woman showed no signs of caring for their opinions. She was head of the Board of Governors and one of the chief sources of income for the academy, so she could do whatever she wanted.

"Come on!" Her mother flashed a smile. "Let's get a drink!"

Nilsson followed her mother quietly out of the hall, linking arms with the shorter woman as the droning of the speech receded into indecipherable murmurs behind her. They walked along the corridor leading to the music department, past the large bay windows looking over the school playing fields.

"When you say a drink," Nilsson ventured, "do you mean a drink, drink?"

"Ha! Plenty of time for that later at the party! I'm sure something soft will do for now! Your father will be home from work in a couple of hours. He's got something special for you, you know."

Nilsson knew. She had accidentally overheard them talking the night before. Her father had arranged for a part-time apprenticeship at his company while Nilsson undertook her degree in Business Studies. Her smile faded from her lips.

"About that…"

Her mother stopped. The blonde woman stepped across to look up at her daughter.

"I recognize that tone. What is it? What's wrong?"

Echoes of another wave of applause drifted across from the hall behind them. Out of the window, Nilsson saw eight horses wheel around each other as fifth year students skillfully maneuvered them across the Polo field. A proper, traditional sport. None of this newfangled REM Racing nonsense. She sucked in a lungful of air. It was now or never.

"Mother. I'm so grateful for everything you and father have done for me. So very grateful. But I… but I…"

"But?"

"But… I don't want to go to university. I don't want to go into commerce. I want to join the Order of Saint John and become a knight."

Nilsson's mother's face lit up with a mirthful smile. It lasted for only a few seconds until the reality of the situation sunk in, and she evidently realized that her daughter was serious.

"I've already taken some of the examinations," Nilsson continued, "I'm sorry I hid that from you, but I needed to know. I've passed all of the written tests and the medical. I only have the physical exams left to go."

Her mother took a step forward, one eye half closed in confusion.

"You… want to be a soldier? For the NeoVatican?"

"Yes. More than anything."

Nilsson braced herself for the inevitable anger and disappointment. It never came. Her mother clasped her hands on Nilsson's shoulders as the mirthful smile returned.

"Then a knight of the Order of Saint John you will be! Your father and I will do anything we can to support you."

The outskirts of Moravia swept up the miles of gentle slopes to the dark, gray skyscrapers jutting across the green skyline. Angular buildings reached up to the dark blue heavens as if pointing in warning at the stars, and the incoming terror that might spell the doom of all human life on Paradiso. The suburbs of the Moravia eased off toward the ubiquitous jungle, cascading down in size from the gargantuan city center. The modern, abandoned metropolis gave way to smaller houses, areas of commerce, parks, and meeting venues. All lay just as cold, gray, and lifeless as the center of Moravia.

Light rain fell down from the night sky, drumming against the huge leaves of the jungle's edge. Nilsson crouched low in the cover of the foliage, her Combi Rifle tucked into her shoulder. Even from this distance, she could already see a handful of Combined Army surveillance drones hovering over the city outskirts, mindlessly following their predetermined courses as their scanners swept the empty streets for signs of life.

Nilsson glanced over her shoulder. Behind her, the knights, sergeants, Crosiers, and dronbots of her unit waited in the drenched jungle. She saw De Fersen activate a hacking menu on his comlog and then dial in a succession of inputs on the holographic wheel projected above his forearm. Seconds later, her tactical map was updated with the positions of three Morat patrols roving the empty streets within a mile radius and the scan tracks of the Combined Army drones' surveillance devices. Nilsson smirked at the live information transmitted across from the enemy drones. Perhaps the Hospitallers would be better placed for making more use of hackers after all.

A marker illuminated on Nilsson's visor, some two hundred meters ahead, quickly followed by a series of waypoints that planned out a pathway to it. She checked her map for an updated position on enemy units, glanced to both sides for a visual check in case of any undetected enemy units, and then sprinted out of the jungle and across the nearest road. She reached cover by the corner of an abandoned house and dropped to one knee, raising her rifle to cover the street as Hawkins and May ran to catch her up.

Quickly, quietly, wordlessly, the Hospitaller unit advanced from street to street until they were within a stone throw of their target building. Nilsson stopped at a small crossroad, taking cover behind an abandoned silver sedan, left in place for so long that small roots had punched up through the road and punctured its tires. The marker on her visor highlighted a long building set up on the other side of a narrow, steep valley with a stream. A quaint, wooden bridge led across to the white building; a rectangular construct punctuated with triangular beams painted black, imitating the architectural style of a public house from renaissance-era western Europe on Earth. The archaic looking building stood out in stark contrast to the smooth, sleek lines of the white houses spanning either side of the road.

Nilsson waited until the second trio of soldiers caught up to her position and then led Hawkins and May across to the wooden bridge. She winced as her armored feet thumped along the damp planks. Nilsson reached the other side and stopped by the building entrance as Hawkins took position by the door. She held up a hand to halt the knight in place before she quickly tapped her comlog to set up an entry pattern. Both other soldiers tapped to acknowledge her plan.

Hawkins edged forward, slinging his MULTI Rifle away and drawing his pistol to free up one hand for the door handle. Rain pattering off her helmet and rifle, Nilsson raised her weapon to her shoulder again as May checked behind the trio. Hawkins gently pulled down on the imitation vintage brass handle and pushed the door open. Nilsson darted inside, dropping to one knee as her visor automatically adjusted to compensate for the lower light levels. Hawkins moved in after her, his heavy MULTI pistol held in both hands and pointing over her shoulder down the entrance corridor.

"Bravo One, sitrep," De Fersen demanded.

"Zero from Bravo One, entrance corridor is clear. Moving in to clear the ground floor."

***

De Fersen placed his Spitfire and helmet down on the dust-covered table in front of him. The public house basement was more expansive than it appeared from outside, with the white-brick walled room extending into an L-shape below the main building. Just as promised, De Fersen and his soldiers found provisions, ammunition, spare parts, and bedding left behind by the Black Friar team that had set the forward operating base up. Content that they were safely out of harm's way for the foreseeable future, De Fersen took a small bottle of water from its pouch on his utility belt and glanced around at the rest of his team.

The two dronbots had been left upstairs, on the ground floor. Stanescu was helping the wounded Poddar over to a roll mat in the far corner of the room, while Tocci removed her helmet, folded her arms, and looked across at De Fersen expectantly. Hawkins propped himself up against a wall, pensively looking down at a set of rosary beads in one armored hand. Nilsson fastidiously checked her rifle. Lois and May waited silently behind their stone-faced leader, Cortez. De Fersen turned to look across at the veteran Crosier NCO.

"Sergeant, take your team back to the first floor and set up sentry positions. Double check those dronbots and make sure they are definitely powered down. I don't want that Sierra leaping into a Total Reaction program and gunning down any Morat patrol that is wandering past the building. Keep things quiet. Keep things out of sight."

"Understood, Sir," Cortez said before leading her two Crosiers back up the stairs.

"Sergeant Nilsson, check everybody's gear. Use those spares to service damaged armor as best you can."

"Sir!" Nilsson responded with an optimistic smile before turning to walk across to the supply crates at the northern end of the room.

Left with just his knights, De Fersen turned to Tocci and Hawkins. Tocci met his stare, her dark eyes and slicked back, black hair contrasting sharply with her pale skin. Hawkins remained slouched back against the wall, his focus still on his rosary beads.

"You two, get some sleep," De Fersen ordered.

"Sir?" Tocci's eyes narrowed.

"Sleep. I need you rested. I need to plan our recce of the target site. In the meantime, we need to start striking out at local patrols. That's where you two will be coming in. Go and rest up."

Tocci took a step forward.

"Sir, I don't need any sleep. I'd be more use to you with planning."

De Fersen repressed an irritated sigh.

"Sister-Sub Officer, I've extended you the respect of telling you how I intend to utilize you. See if you can't reciprocate that courtesy and trust me to lead my own team."

Tocci winced uncomfortably, nodded her head, and walked off toward one of the bedrolls against the southern wall. Hawkins wordlessly headed off to the bedding on the opposite corner. Stanescu paced across from where he had left Poddar resting.

"How is he?" De Fersen asked as the doctor approached.

"Well enough," Stanescu replied, "his armor took a bit out of the impact. But he needs rest. If Morats were suddenly to barge in here, he'd be well enough to fight. But he won't recover any time soon if you put him back in the firing line."

"Then keep him resting. We'll make do without him for now."

Stanescu nodded and turned to head back to his patient.

"Wait a minute."

The thin, olive-skinned man stopped and turned back to face De Fersen. The older knight checked that the others were out of earshot. Tocci had already discarded her armor and lay on her bunk, eyes closed. Nilsson was busily removing the outer shell of Poddar's breastplate to set about some simple field repairs. Hawkins sat on his own bedroll, still in armor, reading a small, crumpled piece of paper.

"What about you?" De Fersen asked quietly. "Are you alright?"

"I didn't take a hit, sir."

"That's not what I meant. I meant that this was your first time under fire."

The gaunt-faced man narrowed his dark eyes.

"It's my first time in combat, armed and armored. But not my first time under fire. Not even my first time under fire by Morats on this planet."

De Fersen paused. He vaguely remembered Stanescu from the fortress-monastery on Skovorodino; a quiet student who only participated in classroom exercises under duress, but always produced the goods in assessments. Academically, at least. When it came to combat - both ranged and melee - Stanescu had encountered some real problems. But, given that he was twenty-seven years old and a qualified doctor, it made sense that he had a life before the Order.

"Refugee aid?" De Fersen ventured.

"Yes, sir."

De Fersen paused before asking the next question.

"D'you see what these bastards are capable of?"

"It's why I joined the Order, sir. Healing the sick and wounded wasn't enough. Sometimes fire needs to be met with fire."

De Fersen looked down at the shorter man. His intense eyes focused on the other side of the room, or rather through it and at a point somewhere off in infinity. De Fersen clasped his hands behind his back and subtly brought Stanescu's personnel file up on his lens.

"Your father is Nøkken?" De Fersen said, "I've worked with his unit several times before. Fantastic soldiers."

"He was Nøkken, sir," Stanescu replied, a faint, fond smile tugging at his lips. "And yes. Fantastic soldiers. He was a fantastic father. He was killed fighting about two years ago."

De Fersen felt his jaw clench. He nodded and cleared his throat. Stanescu blinked and looked up, his attention now seemingly focused once more. It was several moments until De Fersen thought of something to say.

"Keep monitoring Sergeant Poddar. That's your priority. As soon as we're putting rounds down range again, I'll need you back in the firing line."

"Yes, sir," Stanescu replied evenly before walking back to his patient.

***

There were about four seconds between each of the drips. From where he sat on his bedroll, Hawkins tapped his comlog to activate the noise cancellation of his earpieces, wondering briefly how humankind ever fell asleep before the invention of such simple devices. The silence of the outskirts of Moravia was, to Hawkins, just as eerie as the sights. Just as there were no people, traffic, or cultural lighting, so too was noticeable the complete absence of advertisements forcing their way onto his lens; the constant and not always welcome intrusion of Maya and its tight grip on all aspects of the Human Sphere's society.

Hawkins glanced across at where Sergeant Poddar slept, while Stanescu quickly checked over his patient with a small scanner from his medikit. Hawkins had sat next to Poddar on the flight across to Norstralia. He was a couple of years older than Hawkins and from a large family; a quiet, seemingly thoughtful man whose evidently fierce intellect was all the more impressive given the humble background he hinted at. Hawkins closed his eyes and whispered a prayer for Poddar's recovery.

When he opened his eyes a minute later, Stanescu had moved across to talk to De Fersen. Hawkins looked across at Poddar again. The images of burying Sergeant Kormea's body by the side of the road earlier in the night jumped to the forefront of his mind. With them came the sudden and unwelcome memories of scores of Fusiliers who had died around him during the Glottenburg incursion. Priya Shankar, Jon Lanne, Aida Castillo, Stefan Mann... the guilt instantly rose up within him like bile as he recalled how much time he had spent ruminating over the lives he had taken, and how little time lamenting the comrades who died around him. The train of guilt continued when the thought of the Yujingyu lives he took at Alpha Four-Four led on in turn to the Morats he had killed only hours before. Did they, too, have families? Were their souls worthy of prayer? Hawkins reached to his side and popped open one of the brown, leather pouches on his utility belt to recover his rosary beads for the second time since they had arrived at the FOB.

His eyes fell on a small package of white paper at the bottom of his pouch, held together with a black, elasticated hair band. He pulled the soft, feather-light package from his pouch and slid off the band. A small teddy bear, half the size of the palm of his hand popped out. Hawkins emitted a chuckle as he picked the bear up, the packaging now open on his lap and revealed to be a letter.

'*Mein Liebe,*

I'm writing this as you are in the next room, getting ready to go away. I found this little guy for you, I hope he makes you smile when you find him. I don't know whether that will be on some training exercise or whether it will be for real. I don't know what you are going back to. I do know that you are tough, tougher than you think, when it comes to the fighting. It's what is inside that worries me, it's how you will cope with what you see and do, afterward when you have time to think about it all. Just remember that you are doing the right thing, and every difficult act you are forced to carry out is protecting people who deserve to be protected. You are doing the right thing. You always have since the second

I met you.

Ich liebe dich,
L'

Hawkins read the letter again, carefully hiding the tiny bear in the palm of his hand in case any of the other soldiers saw the childlike act of love in the gift. He smiled fondly as his mind swam away from the pain and guilt of both Alpha Four-Four and the fighting earlier that evening, across to happier times.

The small brass section of the band kicked in with a soft, gentle melody that accompanied the gentle brushing of the drums and the thump of the bass. The slow, melancholy song echoed across the church hall, perfectly capturing the spirit of the showers of red poppies decorating the walls, and the thought-provoking, beautifully sculpted statue of two soldiers reaching across to shake hands over a football; one wearing the uniform and peaked cap of a British soldier of the First World War, the other depicted as his German adversary. A singer - the mother of a boy Hawkins went to school with - joined in with the song as the six couples danced on the wooden floorboards of the old church hall, watched with varying levels of interest by the hundred or so dinner dance guests still sat at their tables around the central dance floor.

"I'm sorry!" Beckmann whispered. "I... learning to dance was never really on my 'to do' list. I'm so sorry about this."

"You're doing a better job of it than I am!" Hawkins flashed what he hoped was an encouraging smile.

One hand at the small of her back, the other holding her hand, Hawkins did what he thought was a basic approximation of leading a dance partner, based solely on what he saw others around him doing and what he had seen on Maya. The shirt collar and tie of his uniform itched. His black uniform was punctuated only by the simple white cross of his Order at the top of the sleeve, and the badges of rank on his epaulets. Beckmann's blue-gray dress uniform was adorned with the showier, more ostentatious badges of her higher rank, along with a row of medals for bravery and the PanOceanian Vir Chakra worn around her high collar.

Hawkins glanced at the statue by the entrance again, wondering what his English forefathers would have made of him dancing with a German soldier at a Remembrance Day charity ball, raising money for military charities and remembering the fallen of those terrible wars on Earth. He hoped and prayed that the souls of the fallen would look down favorably, realizing that they died so that nations would one day come together again and move on from the past in peace. Certainly, the smiles of friends and family of Hawkins's church community seemed genuine in their support and affection for him and the girl he had brought home from the war.

"I'm sorry about this morning, too," Beckmann whispered, looking down as her face fell. "I… I didn't mean to put pressure on you. I shouldn't have said what I said. It wasn't fair."

Hawkins tensed up at the mention of the incident, immediately hoping that she would not misconstrue his reaction. Waking up that morning to find Beckmann wide awake already, staring at him, was something he had become accustomed to. But not what she then said.

"What would you say if I asked you to marry me?"

Hawkins forced himself to relax again, feeling the small box with the engagement ring in his pocket pressing against his chest. That morning, when he had stopped to think on why he avoided answering the question, his initial thought was that after only knowing her for a few weeks, it was ludicrous to even entertain marriage. But the more he thought about it, the more it made sense. The more sure he became. He had not avoided the question because he did not want to marry; he avoided it because he refused to go through life by her side, knowing that she asked him instead of the other way around. It was he who needed to reach up and ask for acceptance from her.

"Don't worry about it," Hawkins forced a smile as they tentatively navigated their way around the other dancing couples. "I… I hadn't really…"

"But I've scared you off," Beckmann cut in, her voice panicked. "I've rushed everything and now you're going to end this. Aren't you?"

As if on cue, Father Farrah - the parish priest - appeared at the door of the church hall. The old man looked across at Hawkins and gave a conspiratory thumbs up. Hawkins nodded in acknowledgment. Everything was ready. Just across the road outside was the church where Hawkins was baptized and took the sacraments of First Communion, Confession, and Confirmation. And at the top of the tower of the church, the priest had lit the candles by all of the flowers Hawkins had laid down earlier that day, just after he bought the engagement ring. He looked across at Beckmann, the nerves of what he was about to ask now hammering his heart.

"Would you like to go for a walk?" He smiled uneasily.

"Hawkins!"

Hawkins's eyes shot open. He instinctively grabbed the letter and the small bear and hid them in his hand. He looked up to see Tocci staring down at him with angered eyes. He tapped his comlog to command his geist to switch off the active noise reduction.

"Come on, get up!" the more senior knight scowled. "The boss wants to talk to us."

***

By Fire and Sword

Huradak Krakto Zevult folded his broad, red-skinned arms across his muscular, barrel-like chest. The holographic map of the enemy area, designated 'City-B-Six', shimmered atop the table in front of him. The sweeping, curved roads, the carpet of low, twin-story buildings with their elegant architecture, the overwhelming proportion of facilities dedicated to artistic pursuits and socializing... The amount of time and resources actually wasted on inefficiencies in human settlements was utterly bewildering. Zevult grunted out a short bark of a laugh. Even the electric blue paint on the walls in the building that now served as his battalion's command center was ridiculous; reminiscent of a long-gone era in Morat society.

Zevult drew in a slow breath and refocused. He raised one hand to his jaw, tapping a finger against the neatly shaved partition at his chin that sat between the long, white strands of hair flanking his broad face. 'Sideburns,' the humans called that styling of facial hair, something that marked out a soldier in Morat society just as it had done for humans in centuries past. Zevult shook his head. From what the intelligence cell had informed his officers about what they were facing, they were in some ways fortunate not to be facing those human soldiers from centuries past, back when humans knew how to prioritize.

That intelligence briefing had driven down into the real specifics of the fighting forces of the Human Sphere. Soldiers who joined the military sometimes for as short a time period as possible, as 'something to do' while they mentally groped their way through early adulthood in a confused, entitled trance, wondering how best to make more money and increase their levels of comfort. The notion was disgusting. No thought of contribution to society, not even a moment spent contemplating how dedication to the military craft both bettered the individual and the collective. No, just a brief dalliance with uniforms and weaponry so that after a couple of years, social standing was slightly elevated in a vocational interview for some easy, overpaid job in industry. Zevult grunted again at the thought.

"Absolutely fucking disgusting," he grumbled.

Now, if the forces of the Combined Army had made footfall on Paradiso to find the technology and flexibility of the modern Human Sphere combined with the fortitude and fighting spirit of the ancient human warriors of Earth... well, they would be struggling to maintain the dying momentum of their advance even more so.

Zevult's attention was diverted away from his ill-disciplined musings - a momentary failing, but one he felt angered at, nonetheless - by a chiming at the door.

"Enter."

The door to the command room slid open to admit Ze Hamak Gehter Ryyak, one of Zevult's most senior and experienced company commanders. The tall Morat walked past the two aides working by the entrance and into the command room, his eyes half-closed, the braids of his long, white hair uneven and unkempt, his armor pitted and grubby. The soldier's disheveled appearance was not surprising; the 3rd Company had only just been rotated out of the bitter fighting on the southern front where they had kept the pressure on the enemy line for weeks longer than expected.

Rotating them to guard duty at City-B-Six was not anything as crass or pathetic as a 'reward' or a sympathy; it was a basic efficiency to return them to full fighting strength. Yet, on their very first night of garrison duty, they had sustained casualties from two separate attacks by what could only be human Special Forces units inserted behind their lines. The exhausted, depleted Morats had sustained worse casualties than they should have.

The company commander stopped a few paces from the scarred huradak, stood up smartly, and saluted.

"Sir, I..."

"Ze Hamak," Zevult interrupted, using the battle language of Kyvalad, its complexity known only to Morat officers, "basic standards of military dress and bearing are not constrained to our line soldiers. They are even more important in our leadership. Yet you, as a ze hamak, present yourself to your huradak in this state. It's not shitty ceremony. It's the basic standards that form our foundation."

"We need to discuss our response to the attacks, sir," Ryyak answered without hesitating. "Taking a few minutes to polish my armor and neaten up my fucking hair is a few minutes wasted. And we don't have minutes to waste. Sir."

The battalion commander paused.

"That's fair. Proceed."

Ryyak folded his thick, crimson arms. A truly towering soldier, even by Morat standards, Ryyak was - like Zevult - a veteran of the almost humorously entitled Rasyat Diplomatic Division. That brought with it a practically peerless level of hand-to-hand combat training on top of the natural killer instinct required to pass selection for the division. And that was by Morat standards; not the far lesser soldiers of other races of the Combined Army - let alone their inferior human adversaries. Still, it appeared sometimes - often now, in fact - that the aggressive, violent company commander had forgotten that Zevult, too, shared that same previous experience.

"We've had a patrol fail to report in," Ryyak grunted.

"Yes. I know." Zevult turned back to the flickering holographic display, gesturing at the two markers on the outskirts of the suburbs. "We're no longer looking at an isolated mission. Something bigger is going on."

Ryyak's jaw set into an uneven grimace, his dark eyes narrowing.

"I wouldn't jump straight to that conclusion, sir," he countered, "that could be the same force splitting up to cover more ground. They could…"

"Measure the distance, Ze Hamak!" Zevult snapped. "How fast do you think these bastards can move?! We have surveillance footage of the enemy contingent that forced its way through our line along Route-B-54. We can narrow down the timing and location of our missing patrol to this marker. Unless humans have worked out how to fucking teleport themselves, I think we can assure ourselves that we are dealing with two separate forces."

Ryyak leaned in aggressively.

"No."

"No?"

"No, sir. A single force could have been airlifted in below our surveillance coverage and split into two before this first engagement. I find it highly unlikely that two separate forces with two separate objectives would attack us in two locations so close. It would be more efficient to give the tasks to a single unit."

Zevult turned around and leaned against the desk supporting the map display, his fists pressed down against its smooth surface. His two aides, not holding a high enough rank to understand the conversation in the officer's language of Kyvalad, could still no doubt pick up on the tone and body language. They were not idiots. But unwise enough to fail to hide their interest. Zevult would deal with that later.

Yes, he had to admit that Ryyak's hypothesis was certainly a possibility. But it was more prudent to prepare for the worst case eventuality. That his area of operations had been selected for a series of coordinated strikes by the enemy. Zevult stared intently at the holographic map again, as if somehow a period of undisturbed, laser-focus would reveal his enemy's plans.

"How many patrols do you have in your sector, on foot, at any one time?"

"Eight, sir."

"Make it twelve."

The tall ze hamak failed to suppress a snort.

"On our current rotation of patrolling, guard duties, and rest, that's demanding more than simply another four patrols!"

Zevult slammed a fist into the desk surface, the impact echoing around the room and forcing his two aides to turn away quickly. Zevult shot up to his full height, still half a head less than Ryyak, and glowered up at the younger soldier.

"Give your bone idle bastards less rest, then!" he yelled. "Your soldiers can rest on a one in four rotation instead of a one in three! Fucking hell, Ryyak! Do you honestly think I've forgotten how to run a company?"

Ryyak met his commander's glare for a brief moment, then stiffened to stand to attention, staring straight ahead. Formally, and respectfully..

"My company has been in this location for a single day. One, sir. We were moved here because we have taken the brunt of the fighting on the southern front. Every one of my soldiers has exceeded what can reasonably be expected of them. I don't say this out of a misguided sense of care for them or expect reward. I say it as a simple matter of efficiency. They are fatigued. They need to be rested if they are to fight and kill more effectively."

Zevult paused. He could appreciate the need to keep his soldiers at peak fitness to fight more effectively. He also found himself more amenable to his subordinate's suggestion now that the younger officer had discarded that simmering veneer of petulant aggression and had replaced it with the conduct that the Morat Aggression Force demanded from its soldiers.

"Increase the number of patrols your soldiers are conducting, Ze Hamak. Return to your post."

Ryyak brought his hand up in a smart salute and departed, leaving Zevult with his map. He turned back to review his understanding of the areas of attack. After a moment, he raised his wrist-mounted golgrapt and brought up the surveillance footage of the first attack on Route-B-54. A still image he had previously zoomed in on was at the top of the list of digital files. Human heavy infantry, their hyper modern battle armor adorned with ancient surcoats, complete with the cross iconography of their deluded, ancient faith. PanOceanian Military Orders. In many ways not dissimilar to the honor-obsessed warriors of the Morats' old times. And while clearly as flawed in their outlook on conflict, also no less dangerous. This could be a problem.

Chapter Six

"Sergeant Cortez!"

Cortez snapped to attention at the call and bellowed out her response.

"Sir!"

Turning on the heels of her tan combat boots, Cortez marched smartly along the thin corridor and turned to enter the office. She stopped abruptly in front of the long desk, bringing one knee up to waist height before smashing her foot down to stand to attention, then bringing her right arm crisply up into a rigid salute. Staring straight ahead, above the heads of the seated interview panel, she brought her arm down to her side and clenched her fist.

"Sergeant Cortez, Number Two Battalion, 5th Fusiliers, sir!" she announced forcefully.

The interview room fell silent. With her dark eyes locked ahead, there was only so much of her surroundings she could see at the periphery of her vision; the two simple, wooden tables pushed together to form one long barrier between her and her assessors. The four seated figures on the other side of that barrier, dressed in the simple, black uniforms of the Order of the Hospital. The crucifix on the wall behind them. The cracks in the plaster of the wall to either side of it.

"Stand at ease."

Cortez brought her knee up to waist height again and brought it down, her feet now shoulder width apart as her hands locked together at the small of her back.

"Take a seat, Sergeant."

Her jaw locked in grim determination in dire opposition to the nervous thumping in her chest, Cortez looked down to her side and saw the chair left for her. She sat down, removing her blue beret, the tans and greens of her combat fatigues seeming almost circus-like in the frivolity of their colors compared to the somber black fatigues of her interview panel. She looked across.

A broad-shouldered man in his forties, with iron-gray temples and the epaulets of a Father-Officer sat directly opposite her. Next to him was a slightly younger, but no less stern looking, Mother-Officer with thick, dark hair. Flanking them were two senior sergeants, both staring at her impassively.

"There are ten applicants out there, Marianna," the Mother-Officer began. "Why you?"

Cortez met her glare evenly and cleared her throat.

"Ma'am. I've served in the fusiliers for over a decade. I've fought on Dawn, in the Third Offensive, on..."

"We've all read your service record," the Mother-Officer interrupted coldly, "we know your service history. We've seen you demonstrate your skills and experiences in three full days of assessments. There's no point in wasting time talking about your military expertise. What I asked you is 'why you?'"

Cortez tried to meet the older woman's stare but broke away. She looked across at the other three members of the panel as if somehow she might find a more sympathetic pair of eyes. There were none. The question was so simple, yet somehow so impossible to answer. She had spent months preparing for every aspect of the assessment; she knew her business as a platoon sergeant inside out. She had learnt every detail of the inner workings of the Order of the Hospital; its tactics, command structure, doctrine, everything. But, having fared mid-pack in every test she had faced in the last three days, she now found herself mute in front of her would-be judges.

"Allow me to assist you, Sergeant," the Father-Officer leaned forward. "Specifically, why are you applying to leave the fusiliers to join the Coadjutor Crosiers?"

Cortez felt the sides of her jaw ache. She leaned backward, immediately felt that her body language was in danger of seeming lackadaisical and unprofessional, and then leant forward again.

"I believe I'll fit in better in the Order, sir," she finally answered.

All four board members momentarily exchanged silent glances.

"Why's that?" asked the younger of the two sergeants on the flanks of the line of interviewers.

"Well... I... I share the values that your Order holds dear."

Cortez bit back on the string of obscenities she immediately felt for such a poor answer. The look on the face of the Mother-Officer only confirmed her suspicions.

"Alright," the older woman said, "then tell me: which passage in the gospels do you think best encapsulates the overall aim of this Order?"

Cortez felt her jaw drop. Fuck! The gospels? She knew that was a part of the Bible but had no idea what. It had been nearly twenty years since she had attended a Christian school - her upper school was not NeoVatican affiliated, and after her grandparents died, there was nobody applying pressure on her and her siblings to go to church. She didn't remember what the gospels were, let alone what they said!

"Ma'am?" she cleared her throat, frantically looking to buy time.

The Mother-Officer visibly rolled her eyes and sighed.

"The gospels, Sergeant. The four books in the New Testament, written by the evangelists. The bit in the Bible that says what Jesus did! For Heaven's sake, Sergeant, you're sat in front of a panel and you're asking to be considered for admission into the NeoVatican's coadjutor Crosiers! You want to be a warrior of God, and you don't know what the gospels are?!"

Cortez sat up straight. For a moment, she was back in upper school, all virtual eyes of her classmates staring at her from the safety of their own homes. Her cheeks felt hot. Then the anger kicked in. She narrowed her eyes, met the Mother-Officer's glare, and leaned further forward.

"I didn't go to a Christian upper school. They taught me about all faiths at my school, but not much. They taught me that being a Christian means believing that Jesus was God's son. Well, I do believe that. I don't claim to be a good Christian, or a knowledgeable one. But I am one, nonetheless. What I do claim to be is a fucking good soldier. So I'm here, as I said earlier, to tell you in all honesty that I have seen enough shit in my time in the fusiliers to begin to question the morality of my orders and the direction of the PMC."

The Mother-Officer recoiled a little, sitting up straight and folding her arms. The other three members of the interview panel watched the exchange in silence.

"But," Cortez continued, "every time I've worked alongside the Military Orders, I've liked what I've seen. I've admired the priority of protecting civilians over all else. I've wished my orders were more... meaningful. I want to be involved in things that I feel matter, instead of pressing home attacks against positions that didn't really need to be attacked, and that we didn't stand a chance against. So no, I can't quote the Bible. I don't know the gospels. And those other soldiers in that room behind me, some of them are faster, stronger, and better at shooting. But as an overall package, I'm the best of the lot. I'm the best soldier you're looking at this week. And I believe in God, and that Jesus was his son. That's why you should select me."

One hour later, the short list of successful applicants was read out to the candidates as they waited awkwardly in the assessment block ante room.

"Novotny. Park. Cortez."

Small patches of mist were already blurring the hills on the horizon as the night continued to cool. The abrupt end of the jungle and beginning of civilization was now more of a green fade, as bulbous plants and thorn-lined vines snaked their way across the cracked, gray concrete of the edge of the suburbs. Even from this distance, Cortez could hear the hissing of lizards and occasional cawing of birds from the dark jungle; across the deserted streets of outer Moravia, the only movement was the occasional marsupial-like rodent, hopping across the silent roads on powerful hind legs before disappearing into the black alleyways between the long abandoned buildings.

Cortez peered around the corner of the public house doorway, tapping her comlog to utilize her lens's zoom function and basic, multi-spectral vision options. Nothing stirred. At the far end of the street she saw a two-story bar; the upper floor was open with only a safety rail and a few circular bar stools surrounding the once thriving social setting. Below was a curious collection of vintage, hands-on arcade machines that had made a huge resurgence in popularity some ten or fifteen years earlier. The neon-strip lights of the bar now remained black and lifeless, as did the rows of cars on both sides of the cracked street, curiously left abandoned in place by ALEPH's traffic control system.

Cortez glanced over her shoulder. At the far end of the corridor, guarding the building's back doors, Lois and May crouched in the shadows with their weapons at the ready. Content they knew their business, Cortez resumed her watch of the front of the building. John Lois, like Cortez, was an ex-fusilier. With six years experience under his belt, he was a good NCO, if perhaps something of a dreamer in Cortez's opinion. His appreciation of the heavily armored knights sometimes bordered on sycophancy. His wife had given birth to their first child six months before, and if Lois was on the promotion signal to sergeant at the end of the year, that would at least allow him to proceed to the Crosiers Training Center on NeoTerra as a drill instructor.

Stephanie May was a bit more of an enigma. A direct entrant into the Crosiers, she had joined at the age of nineteen after spending a year teaching aerobics and spin classes at a gym. This was only her third time in combat, and she kept herself to herself. But, like Lois, she was dependable, and Cortez could ask for no more than that.

Cortez's attention was drawn back inside the building as she heard soft footsteps from the stairs leading down to the basement. The unit's four knights appeared in the corridor behind her, all armed and pulling on their helmets. De Fersen walked quietly over to Cortez.

"I'm taking Surgeon-Sub Officer Stanescu with me to recce the enemy storage complex," he said quietly. "Sub Officers Tocci and Hawkins will be conducting an offensive patrol to try to stir things up a bit to the northwest. You're in command while we're gone."

"Yes, sir," Cortez nodded.

De Fersen tapped his wrist.

"Transponders are on secure channel two, with encryption codes changing every twenty minutes. Both teams will check in with you every twenty minutes, just in case. If either team is overdue by more than sixty seconds, alert the other team. Keep things quiet here. Only power up those dronbots if a firefight is initiated."

"Understood."

De Fersen glanced at both ends of the road before stealthily stepping past Cortez. Stanescu stopped briefly by her, his dark eyes hidden behind his red visor.

"Sergeant Poddar is stable, but Sergeant Nilsson is keeping an eye on him," the surgeon knight said, his higher pitched voice kinder in tone even when distorted by his helmet's faceplate. "Please check in on them. Just in case."

"Got it, sir," Cortez nodded cooly.

Stanescu followed De Fersen silently into the night, quickly fading from view after a few seconds to be visible only as a blue bracket on Cortez's lens and a blip on her tactical map. Tocci and Hawkins followed a moment later, disappearing off to the northwest and melting from view.

***

The inevitable advance of the jungle had punched through the comparatively crude, angular constructs of mankind's engineers and builders, but still something did not quite look right. Closer in toward the city center itself, the lower buildings of the suburbs were now replaced with taller, broader apartment and office blocks. Their regular edges and straight lines - even though softened by curving corners and sweeping bridges over the grid-iron pattern roads - stood out against the relentless tangle of green weeds and bulbous plants forcing their way up through the broken concrete. But, to even the most casual of observers, there was still something wrong that made it patently clear that even without any sign of human life, the city was not deserted. That something was that the city was clean.

The roadways and gutters were swept clear. The off-white walls of the majority of buildings - occasionally punctuated by a somewhat patriotic PanOceanian blue or rogue shade of red - were largely free of grime and dust. Hawkins paused to reflect on that simple observation. Even under new and brutal management, the occupiers still believed that it was a worthwhile endeavor to expend valuable energy and resources on keeping the city's army of cleaning bots at work.

Hawkins's attention was instantly snapped away from his musings on the silent city back to his present surroundings as an update alert flashed across his helmet visor, accompanied by two blips on his tactical map and a pair of red brackets in his field of vision. A line of text scrolled across the corner of his visor;

- *Broadsword Two transmits hostiles, strength two, moving marker Delta.*

From where he crouched in the shadows of the alleyway between an abandoned clinic and a sporting goods warehouse, Hawkins looked ahead at the street corner highlighted to him. He checked his map again; Tocci lurked in the shadows on the far side of the street - the sender of the information that now updated his armor's tactical system. The pair of red brackets moved slowly ahead until, at a small crossroads, two hulking figures appeared in the center of the road.

Both figures stood a little taller than the average human but significantly broader of shoulder. Their light armor was coloured black from the waist down and dark red across the torso, standing out in a slight contrast to their bare, red, heavily muscled arms. Neither figure wore a helmet, displaying shocks of white hair that linked into rough, white beards. Both stocky soldiers carried bulky Combi Rifles. Morat Vanguard infantry - the stuff of nightmares to the general population of the Human Sphere, but nothing more than simple line infantry from the point of view of an elite Knight Hospitaller.

"Let them pass," Tocci's whispered words chimed through Hawkins's earpieces, "I'll take Target Delta One, you take Delta Two."

"Understood," Hawkins replied. "Silent or overt?"

"Silent," Tocci replied, "checking enemy surveillance."

Hawkins did the same, tapping his wrist-mounted comlog to bring up his radial wheel of menus. He cycled through to the N-2 Intelligence menu and quickly brought up the most current tactical map overlay showing patterns of Combined Army drone surveillance.

"We're clear," Tocci said. "Six minutes until we're in the path of the next drone overfly."

"Yes, concur," Hawkins whispered.

The two Vanguard infantry drew closer. Hawkins watched their heads turn slowly from side to side - the shorter of the two occasionally turning to check behind them, walking backward for a few paces. Hawkins narrowed his eyes, patiently waiting for the pair of Morats to approach. He saw his vital signs transmitted onto the lower right corner of his visor and marveled at how calm he was. For the briefest of moments, he recalled walking out to his first ever combat encounter - only a few weeks in the past, but already seemingly so dim and distant - and how his pulse had raced with anxiety. Now, here, in the shadows of the dead, gray city, it was merely a case of parking those emotions and waiting for the optimum time to strike.

The two Morat vanguard soldiers walked past only a few paces away, one of them turning to face Hawkins, and for a snapshot moment, seeming to look directly at him as he crouched in the darkness of the alleyway, hidden behind a grime-covered dumpster. The Morat's eyes scanned past him and the pair continued on with their slow vigil, briefly uttering a few words to each other.

Hawkins slowly, carefully, raised himself to his feet and drew his sword. The joints in his armor silently whirred to allow him to move forward, his feet far apart and his center of mass low as he crept out of the alleyway. He followed the edge of the building for a few paces, seeing his movements replicated by Tocci as she emerged on the far side of the narrow street. Both Hospitallers quickly gained on their prey, darting noiselessly across to move directly behind the Morats and reduce the chance of being seen in the crimson-skinned soldiers' peripheral vision.

One hand tightening around the grip of his sword, the other extended loosely to one side to distribute his balance, ready to strike, Hawkins silently quickened his pace until he was only a handful of meters behind the Morat. That was the moment the alien soldier chose to turn to check behind.

For another split second, time seemingly froze to preserve the memory perfectly as Hawkins stared straight into the eyes of the first alien he had encountered face to face, in broad daylight. The Morat's own eyes immediately narrowed in determination. He shouted out an alert. His Combi Rifle was brought up to aim at the human knight. Hawkins was faster. He propelled himself forward from his rear foot, lashing out with his lethal blade to neatly slice through the Vanguard infantryman's closest arm and sever it between the wrist and the elbow. The bulky rifle swung out to one side and fired a brief, wild burst until Hawkins swept his blade back down to hack through light armor, skin and bone alike. A great wound carved out of the Morat's chest, the muscular soldier was dead even before he hit the cracked road at Hawkins's feet.

Hawkins turned in place, his sword raised and ready to strike at the second Morat. He saw Tocci remove her own blade from her target, the straight, twin-edged sword sliding neatly back out of the exit wound in the chest and then the entry wound in the back. The Morat sank down to his knees and then pitched forward lifelessly. Tocci looked across at the taller knight.

"Could you make any more fucking noise, even if you tried?" she hissed venomously. "Come on! Hide that body before their drones sweep this area again!"

***

The dawn sun peered over the horizon, painting the cloudless sky in hues of warm pink. The horizon to the east showcased the curved and irregular lines of nature's beauty; sweeping hills covered with a rich expanse of green vegetation, accompanied by the faint and distant chirps and squawks of colorful birds as they arose from their slumber. To the north and west, the horizon told a different story. Abandoned skyscrapers reached up to the heavens like white fingers through a sea of smaller buildings, their unnatural intrusion through the jungle planet's dry earth resulting in the eerie, low howls of the wind as it swept through the man-made metropolis.

From his position prone beneath a long-abandoned heavy goods vehicle atop an epic, arching road bridge, De Fersen peered down at the miles of empty streets spanning out below him. The sun crept a little higher in the sky, slowly transforming the pinks and lilacs to pastel shades of blue. Long shadows painted the landscape sprawled out beneath him. The familiar, stifling heat of Paradiso's long days was already in the morning air.

"There," De Fersen muttered, tapping his comlog to highlight his target, "right there."

Lying next to him, Stanescu pressed an armored finger against his own wrist-mounted controls, no doubt to filter and zoom the visual display on his helmet visor in response to the marker De Fersen had sent across to him.

Perhaps half a mile away, on the other side of a narrow river cutting gently through the maze of buildings, a square area of pale blue industrial buildings lay silently within a perimeter of chain link fences topped with crumbling cutting foam. The buildings themselves were long and two or three storys, with roofs made up of black triangular prisms. Motionless, automated cranes painted in grimy black and yellow stripes punctuated the entire site, marking it out as having previously been used as a storage area before the human evacuation of Moravia. The map reference of the site matched perfectly with the numbers provided in De Fersen's intelligence brief.

"If we needed any other confirmation, I guess that's it, sir," Stanescu muttered.

De Fersen pressed a finger against the holographic radial display projected in space above his forearm and refined his visual settings, coupling his own lens to Stanescu's helmet visor. His field of vision flicked across to see exactly what his subordinate could see - a pair of Morat Vanguard infantry walking around the southwest perimeter of the industrial storage area.

"Considering how thinly spread these bastards are, that's certainly of note," De Fersen grunted. "Let's get a closer look."

De Fersen led Stanescu silently across the bridge, threading carefully between the rows of abandoned vehicles to maximize on the shelter they provided from lookouts or airborne surveillance. The two knights moved stealthily down from the bridge to then disappear back into the alleyways snaking in between the tall buildings and main roadways, slowly and silently following their map markers to close on the industrial site.

***

The sun set on the second night of holding sentry duty in Hill 152 forward operating base. The surrounding jungles fell a little quieter; the daytime racket of birds and lizards now gradually replaced with the night time rasp, rattle, and buzz of nocturnal insects. An evening breeze picked up, gently whistling and moaning its way through the abandoned buildings of the suburbs, ever-present but only now audible without the din of everyday life. Nilsson checked her tactical display. Another check-in from Broadsword Two:

- *Ops Normal at my Marker Sierra.*

Tocci and Hawkins were still out, moving erratically across the region, having silently dispatched three patrols of Morats in the last twenty-eight hours. The check in came from Broadsword Zero moments later; De Fersen and Stanescu were nearly back at the FOB.

Nilsson glanced over her shoulder at the far end of the corridor. Sergeant Poddar leant awkwardly by the frame of the main entrance to the building, a pistol in one hand. Despite the instructions left by Surgeon-Sub Officer Stanescu - and the warning message that Nilsson had sent to him to alert him to the fact that his instructions were being ignored - Poddar had insisted on taking his turn standing guard duty. The silent vigil held by the two Order Sergeants did, at least, give the trio of Crosiers a chance for some proper rest.

A lizard the size of a small cat scuttled across the road in front of Nilsson, its squat, emerald-colored body almost comical in its movements as it waddled toward the shadows on the far side of the street. Nilsson rested the barrel of her rifle against the window frame she crouched behind and suppressed a yawn. Even after months to supposedly acclimatize, the relatively higher gravitational pull of Paradiso still occasionally leapt out to increase the weariness she felt in her limbs. She heard footsteps on the stairs behind her, leading up from the basement, and saw Sergeant Cortez's transponder signal moving on her tactical map. Nilsson tapped her comlog to establish a private channel via her geist.

"You should be resting."

"I've had two hours," Cortez replied. "Your injured man needs more rest than I do."

Nilsson risked another look over her shoulder and saw Cortez appear at the top of the stairs. The older woman's jet black hair framed a stern face and intense eyes. Nilsson looked away again, partially to resume her duties properly but also out of just a slight element of intimidation. Cortez was, after all, a real sergeant. A woman who had earned her stripes the conventional way, via a decade of combat and multiple promotions based on merit.

As an Order Sergeant, Nilsson's rank was given immediately upon completion of training. Yes, she was a part of a more prestigious unit with higher entry standards than the Crosiers, but she was not ignorant to the fact that many saw them as 'plastic sergeants.' Not the real deal. An awkward, uncertain limbo that sat in between commissioned officers and knights of the Military Orders, and 'proper' NCOs who earned their rank the hard way rather than jumping straight into it. At least that was how Nilsson saw it; in all likelihood, the overwhelming majority of

Order Sergeants were perfectly comfortable and secure in their role. But that was because the majority had not tried and failed the selection process to become a knight.

Cortez stopped at the top of the stairs.

"C'mon, Anil," she said to Poddar, "I've got it from here. Go get some more rest, like the doctor ordered you to."

"I'm fine here," Poddar replied quietly.

Nilsson turned in place to look across at the two soldiers. She momentarily considered supporting Cortez's challenge but instantly decided against it. A sickening feeling of guilt rose within her gut. She had been perfectly happy to report Poddar behind his back to Stanescu, but now lacked the courage to challenge him to his face, as Cortez just had. A proper sergeant.

Cortez took a step forward and instantly froze in place. Her eyes narrowed. The next second, she snatched her pistol up from her holster and raised it into a two-handed grip, pointing it into an empty space midway down the corridor.

"Lower that weapon," a hissed, unfamiliar voice warned.

Her body tensing in surprise, her eyes frantically scanning around for the source of the voice, Nilsson brought her Combi Rifle up to point along the corridor. At the far end, she saw Poddar bring his pistol up to aim, his face hidden behind his helmet but his stance betraying his confusion and anxiety.

"Lower your weapons and don't power up those dronbots," the hushed, metallic voice warned again. "I'm on your side. You're not even pointing them at me, you're more likely to shoot each other."

Nilsson stared intently along the length of the corridor. Cortez and Poddar remained frozen in place, their pistols ready but aiming at nothing more than emptiness. Nilsson momentarily reached across to tap her comlog but thought better of it. There was no point - somebody was in there with them, using active camouflage. Without a proper multispectral visor, cycling through the normal range of visor filters would give her nothing. The bodiless voice spoke again.

"If I wanted to shoot you, I would have done it by now. I'm a Trinitarian. I'm powering down my camouflage."

The mention of the Trinitarian Tertiaries caused Nilsson to let out a long breath of relief as the puzzle began to make sense. A branch of the Military Orders created in part to deal with stealth, secrecy, and subterfuge. Nonetheless, she kept one finger pressed against the trigger of her rifle as a shape appeared in the corridor. The plaster of the walls and the wooden floorboards seemed to almost shimmer as the shape of a hunched figure appeared, its form made up of exactly the same colors and shades as its surroundings. Nilsson had seen active camouflage at work before, but its power to trick the human eye and the majority of visual spectrums still never ceased to amaze her.

The colors of the figure slowly faded to off-whites and pale blues, solidifying to reveal light armor not dissimilar to that of the Crosiers, covered with a loose fitting coat. The Trinitarian lowered his MULTI Sniper Rifle and reached up to pull a camouflaged hood back from his head, revealing a square-jawed man in his late thirties, with graying temples and cool, gray eyes. Cortez half lowered her pistol, but her posture remained tense and alert. Nilsson followed the more experienced soldier's lead. There were more than enough intelligence reports of unexplained infiltrations and disappearances along the front lines to leave units across the Human Sphere panicked and unsure over the abilities of the alien invaders.

"You're not showing on IFF," Cortez said warily.

"Neither are you."

"Our IFF codes are encrypted. We're on a covert op."

"So is mine and so am I. Are you going to put that pistol away, or do you think I'm Shasvastii?"

"You've shown me nothing to prove that you're not," Cortez growled.

"Other than power down my camouflage? This is Hill 152 forward operating base. It has been assigned for the use of my operation. You're not supposed to be here."

A few seconds of silence followed until the intruder slowly leaned over to lay his sniper rifle to rest on the floor. He held his hands up and walked toward Cortez.

"I'm sending you a link," he said, reaching across to activate his comlog's radial menus. "If you accept it, that'll be all the proof you need. Unless you think I'm now trying to hack you, in which case, we're going to go around in circles all night."

Cortez reached across, her pistol still in hand, and pressed her comlog to accept the file. Her eyes traveled quickly from side to side as she read the lines of text scrolling across her lens. Her shoulders slumped and she holstered her pistol. Nilsson let out another sigh of relief and lowered her own weapon.

"What are you doing here, Sergeant?" the Trinitarian asked.

"We were inserted here two days ago," Cortez replied. "We're here to destroy an enemy supply installation. What about you?"

"Assassination," the Trinitarian replied, "there's three of us in the team. We're here to eliminate an enemy High-Value Unit."

"Where are the other two?" Poddar asked.

The lithe Trinitarian turned to face the other end of the corridor.

"Just out there," he nodded, "waiting on the signal from me. I saw one of you at the window. We were expecting this place to be empty for our operation. I came in here to ascertain exactly who you are. Now I know you're friendlies, I'll call the other two in."

The sniper walked back toward the main entrance, tapping his comlog to open a communication channel before mumbling a few words under his breath. Cortez retreated back toward Nilsson.

"Keep your eyes out," she said curtly, "we're still on sentry, and I don't like this."

Nilsson obliged, turning to resume her vigil by the window. Active camouflage had been demonstrated to her before, but only in training. Her eyes widened as she mentally calculated the only options the Trinitarian could possibly have taken to get inside that corridor. He would have to have physically climbed through the window and right past Nilsson, or crept through the door straight past Poddar. Either way, the operative's skills were mind-blowing. Or, at least, the skills he used to back up the technology he was equipped with. Nilsson turned back to look at Cortez.

"How did you know he was there?" she whispered. "Did you have different settings on your lens? Was there something I missed on the tactical map? Did you..."

"Floorboards. When anybody steps off the top step, the floorboards always creak a little. They didn't, so I figured there was a weight on them stopping the creaking. Eyes out the window, they're coming."

Marveling at the awareness exhibited by her comrade, Nilsson turned to look out across the street again. Two armored figures, hunched low in the shadows, sprinted across the battered road and around the building to enter at the main entrance by Poddar. The first of the two soldiers wore an older, heavier variant of the same issue Order Sergeant armor worn by Nilsson. However, his outline broke up and shifted as he ran, demonstrating a level of camouflage technology not quite as advanced as that of the Trinitarian. The second soldier was more heavily armored - a knight, evident even in the poor levels of light - but in a lighter variant of armor than that worn by the Hospitallers.

The first soldier appeared at the door, stepping lightly inside. Nilsson saw now that his surcoat was colored the dark shade of blue that marked him out as Indigo - Special Operations. The knight stepped in after the Indigo sergeant, his surcoat white and bearing the black cross of the Teutonic Order. A Spitfire grasped in one hand, the knight reached up with his other to remove his helmet. A pale, stern face with cropped short ginger hair was revealed. The knight scowled around at the three sentries.

"What the hell are you idiots doing here?" the Teutonic Knight demanded.

Chapter Seven

Huradak Krakto Zevult returned the salute from the two guards who snapped to attention to either side of the Battalion HQ entrance. The building's interior provided some respite from the mid-morning sun, but the environmental controls had been disabled to save energy. It seemed a logical decision, to prevent the wasteful extravagance of something as pathetic as a human comfort; but given the state of his soldiers, he now wondered if some basics might go some way to providing better rest to keep them in optimal fighting condition. Not a reward, an indulgence, or a sympathy; it was a measure to increase the efficiency with which they fought and killed the enemy.

However, some disgusting non-combatant logistical expert had boldly announced at a meeting that every day a building had its environmental controls disabled roughly equated to the power required to produce three Combi Rifle rounds. And his battalion needed those rounds. Zevult swore under his breath. This was no way to fight a war. The Morats were renowned for their ability in combat, rightly feared for being double-hard bastards when it came to the killing. But war was not about bravery, honor, or any of that outdated shit. It was about logic. Efficiency. Control of every situation at a strategic, operational, and tactical level. And for all of that to occur, logistical support was absolutely essential.

Yet here Zevult was, trying to run a battalion where his ammunition and spare parts were literally being forged in hastily constructed forced labor camps by aliens who would take any opportunity - and quite rightly so - to sabotage their own work. That was the grand plan. Drop off the Morat Aggression Force and leave them to take the planet. Self sufficient force - limited logistical support required. Zevult swore again. What utter, utter shit.

Zevult continued along the corridors of his headquarters building - once a human doctors' surgery before the Third Offensive - following the stripped bare, turquoise walls toward his planning room. He stopped in the broader corridor that ran to the planning room entrance. Two Morat soldiers waited by the doorway, locked in conversation. Both stopped and turned to face him. Zent Guntat and Gehter Ryyak, commanders of his battalion's 2nd and 3rd Companies respectively. The two veteran officers stared across at him silently.

"You didn't call ahead," Zevult stated as he paced toward his two subordinates. "That's... irregular."

"There's been a lot of activity overnight, sir," Guntat said. "We were both in the area and thought it better to tell you directly."

"Ze Hamak!" Zevult snapped. "I'm responsible for a battalion of soldiers maintaining an advance against a determined enemy! I'm not a child, a human, or even worse, some snivelling Shasvastii who needs its fucking feelings managed! If you've got something to report, then fire up your damn golgrapt and send it to me!"

"We're here now, sir," Ryyak grunted, "so here it is. The enemy force - the larger one. It's causing more problems."

Zevult barged his way past his two ze hamaks to open the door to the planning room.

"I know that. I know they took out one of our patrols."

"Three," Ryyak corrected, "three of my patrols, sir. Six soldiers disappeared. We still haven't found any of them."

Zevult spun around, his eyes wide.

"Three! You've lost three patrols! We can't afford to lose soldiers like that!"

The tall officer gritted his teeth for a moment, took in a half breath, and then responded with a controlled, even tone.

"I know that, sir. In fact, that's exactly what I warned you about last time we spoke."

Zevult took two paces across to square up to the taller Morat. Ryyak stared ahead respectfully without flinching.

"We've plotted the locations of the missing patrols, sir," Guntat interjected. "From drone surveillance, we can narrow down the approximate locations of when they disappeared. They're all pretty close to the prison."

Zevult turned to look down at the newly promoted ze hamak. Ryyak was a fearsome bastard indeed and commanded the respect of his soldiers, but Zevult would rather have a company full of Guntats any day. Guntat had spent longer as an NCO, leading in the field. Guntat had a reputation for clarity of mind in planning operations and bloody ferocity when facing the enemy. Guntat was legendary within the brigade for his hand-to-hand fighting prowess. And Guntat also did what he was told without backchat thinly disguised as 'presenting other options.'

"The prison," Zevult mused, "so that's what the bastards are here for."

"Yes, sir," Guntat replied, "and knowing that, we could kill a pair of lizards with a single rock."

"No," Zevult shook his head, "that's not our orders. That would take some justification."

"If we executed the prisoners, we would free up the entire guard force. We would augment our patrols instantly if there were no prisoners to guard. And we would remove the reason for the humans even being here."

"And we would eliminate a significant proportion of our labor force, and thus damage our own already tenuous infrastructure situation. No, we're not killing our own laborers."

"Then what?" Ryyak demanded. "Ask for help from 'A' Battalion? We are here to rest and recuperate as quickly as possible so that we can get back to the front line! Instead we are taking losses that we cannot sustain! Fucking hell! If we don't get this sorted out, we will be asking for soldiers to come back from the front lines to get this shit under control!"

"Shut up, you fucking pain in the arse!" Zevult thundered. "Let me think!"

The battalion commander folded his thick arms across his muscular chest. He took in a breath, pondered his predicament, and then swore again. Ryyak was right. 'B' Battalion was in place to recover and get back to the front line to support 'A' Battalion. Asking for soldiers from 'A' Battalion to actually leave the front line to fall back and support the defense against an enemy covert operation was unthinkable. But there were at least two enemy units in the area. Something bigger was going on. Zevult needed more boots on the ground.

"Twenty," he nodded, "execute twenty prisoners. That'll free up enough to replace the patrols we lost. And get everybody out! Not just the Vanguard, everybody! That means the two of you as well! You're leaders, remember! Get out there and lead your damn soldiers!"

***

Stepping down off the last of the stairs leading to the basement, De Fersen paced across to the armorer's bench and placed his Spitfire down with a metallic clunk. Nilsson looked up at him from where she sat at the far side of the room. Her face was quite the opposite of the eager, optimistic young soldier he had come to know and had last seen before leaving the FOB with Stanescu to recce the enemy storage depot.

"Weekly check on that, Sergeant," De Fersen nodded at the bulky weapon.

It did not need a weekly, but the simple and mundane work would keep the young woman distracted.

"Yes, sir," Nilsson nodded obediently.

Mark Barber

De Fersen looked around the basement. Lois sat up on his bed roll, wiping at red-rimmed eyes groggily as his sleep was disturbed by De Fersen's appearance. May continued to sleep through the entire thing. Upstairs, Cortez stood sentry while Stanescu had stopped to reprimand the still wounded Poddar for doing exactly the same thing. Tocci and Hawkins still had not returned but had checked in on the team's secure frequency on time.

Then there were the new arrivals.

Cortez had already messaged the details to De Fersen. A trio of Military Order operatives from another unit; a parallel covert operation under the operational command of the Teutonic Order. De Fersen grimaced at the thought. There were many amongst the teeming billions of PanOceanian citizens who believed that the Military Orders were nothing more than ill-disciplined, barely controlled, fanatical murderers who reveled in bloodlust and justified their violent actions by spouting out of context Bible quotes they did not even understand. This image, of course, was not helped by that fucking idiot Mendoza and his shitty Maya action movies. But the truth was that if any corner of the NeoVatican was close to that macabre picture, it was the Teutonic Order. At least, that was De Fersen's experience, and his experience was considerable.

De Fersen looked around the dim basement for the knight in question. As he had commanded, the three new arrivals had already jumped onto the same encrypted channel for communications and had aligned their IFF codes to appear on De Fersen's team's tactical maps. With that information, he knew that the other two team members had set up an observation post about two hundred meters away and were watching over the FOB as an extra security measure. That just left their leader, who stood at the far end of the basement with his arms folded. The young knight - a pale-faced man in his mid to late twenties, with red head practically shaved to the scalp, stared across at De Fersen.

The norm in working together would have been to share basic details of team members so that leaders knew the strengths, experiences, and qualifications of their soldiers. The Teutonic Knight staring indignantly at De Fersen had provided no such details.

"You're not supposed to be here!" the red-headed knight pointed a finger in accusation, his Germanic accent marking him out as hailing from the normal recruitment areas of his Order. "This FOB was designated for my..."

"Shut up," De Fersen snapped irritably.

The Teutonic Knight's lip curled into a sneer, and his blue eyes narrowed.

"What did you say?" he seethed.

"Stop!" De Fersen spat impatiently. "Just stop! We can both read each other's rank, and we both know I'm in command here! Now stop your whining, wipe that bloody sneer off your face, and get upstairs, where I promise you that you're about to give me a damn good listening to!"

Nilsson made a stifled, choking noise and failed dramatically to suppress a smirk. The Teutonic Knight stomped past De Fersen and made his way up the stairs. De Fersen followed him and, on reaching the top, gestured for the man to take one of the doors leading into the pub's main bar area. The two knights walked past where Cortez stood guard and Stanescu checked on Poddar's injuries. De Fersen shut the door behind them. The room consisted of a vintage-vibe, wooden semi-circular bar with thick, crude barstools made to caricature a sort of medieval style. The olde world feel was ruined by a series of virtual gaming areas dotted around the surrounding walls.

De Fersen looked down at the shorter man as he turned to face him.

"I've worked with your sort before," he began, "so the whole angry man of war thing does absolutely nothing for me. I promise you that I've seen more war than you ever will, and I'm an angrier bastard than you can ever hope to be. So here's how this will work. This FOB will be shared between us. We both have a job to do, and somebody somewhere has messed up by assigning this base to us both. This is classic left hand not talking to right hand, but now we have to un-fuck this situation and both achieve our aims."

De Fersen paused to allow the Teutonic Knight to speak. The younger man wisely elected not to.

"I'm here to destroy a munitions depot," De Fersen continued. "Now, whatever your objective is, we can box clever and I might be able to time my attack to cause enough of a distraction to take the heat off your team. Now, who are you and what are you doing here?"

Again, the knight paused. De Fersen narrowed his eyes and tilted his head expectantly.

"Brother-Sub Officer Stahl," the man replied. "My team is here to assassinate Colonel Trant Vandakk. He's the highest ranking Morat officer in the region and one of the chief architects of the Third Offensive's push against PanO positions."

De Fersen nodded.

"Alright. We'll support you in any way you can. How do you intend to kill him?"

"We're prepared for any eventuality, but the primary plan is from range. Sniper shot."

De Fersen turned away and tapped his chin idly with one knuckle.

"Keep me informed of your plans. I've lost one soldier already and we've got another wounded. I have two knights still in the field, causing as much of a distraction as possible…"

"That needs to stop!" Stahl snapped. "The last thing I need is defenses bolstered in the area! If they think we're coming for Vandakk…"

"Bit late for that. Now, it appears that both of our chains of command have neglected to inform our sister Orders about our plans which is something of a *faux pas* to put it mildly, but my orders have come from the secretary of defense and are signed by the prime minister and the Pope. So this Morat you need to kill, it's secondary. I suggest you accept that, right now, because there's no way in hell I'm stopping my knights from killing Morats to leave this place nice and quiet for you."

***

"Take a look for yourself," Tocci breathed, nodding to the angular building to the northwest.

From where he lay prone atop the deserted residential building, Hawkins tapped his comlog to cycle through various lens settings and then zoom in to Tocci's marker. It was exactly as she said. A large, cuboid building of reinforced structure surrounded by broken and sagging cutting foam. A handful of smaller structures surrounded the main building at irregular intervals, all sat within the confines of the lines of wire. At each of the perimeters was a guard tower; atop each of them was a lone, rifle-armed Morat stood by a large searchlamp. Hawkins winced. The sentries were all looking inward, toward the enclosed building.

"Well," Hawkins murmured, "they want whatever is inside to stay inside, rather than protect it from the likes of us."

"Yes, I can see that!" Tocci snapped. "Look, there's an entire guard room on the western wall. I can see two of them inside, even from here. This is the largest group of them we've seen since that firefight on the road, on the night we landed."

Hawkins looked to the northwest, past the guarded enclosure and to the heights and spires of the deserted city of Moravia. He vaguely remembered something his grandfather had told him as a child about the cultural significance of the city - something to do with theater, or opera or something.

"Are you paying attention?" Tocci's seemingly relentless disapproval of his every action began again.

"There's a building on the western side. It looks like a vehicle depot."

"I know," Tocci replied, tapping her own comlog, "I've pulled up a map of Moravia before the occupation. This place was a high security prison. It makes sense that the Morats would repurpose this building for exactly what it was designed for. They've just bolstered the security."

"But for who?" Hawkins asked himself quietly.

A low, squat utility vehicle rounded a corner to the west of the main complex before driving up to a security checkpoint. Two Morat Vanguard soldiers walked out to the vehicle. Hawkins scanned his eyes across the complex again, noting with interest that every last security point and guard installation was hidden beneath a dense sheet of white alloy. A simple but effective measure put in place to deny drones or orbital satellites the opportunity of detecting activity at the prison.

"This could be something significant," Tocci nodded, "this could be something bigger than..."

"Just a second." Hawkins exhaled. "Wait... look, down there. My Marker Charlie."

Hawkins ran a finger across his comlog interface plate to align his tactical map with his visor, and then double tapped to mark the latest area of activity. Next to him, Tocci swore.

"Come on," she said, raising herself to her feet, "we need to get a closer look at that."

***

Rubbing his eyes and suppressing a yawn, De Fersen leaned back in his chair. He turned away from the holographic display of the Morat storage depot, his eyes wandering around the bar. Age-old decorations and amenities decorated the vintage-themed bar; a dartboard and a snooker table - both cheaper to replicate with VR - lay dusty and neglected in the far corner. Framed photographs of sports teams adorned one wall, further adding to the relatively successful attempt to replicate the ambiance and vibe of a public house from Earth, prior to the digital revolution.

De Fersen turned his attention back to the holographic map on the table before him. The plan was simple enough. No need to over-think it like an amateur. Tomorrow night, they would go in.

The door behind De Fersen creaked open. He turned and saw one of the three members of the Teutonic team - the sergeant - walk into the room. De Fersen's face cracked into a smile. He recognized the man's specialized armor and his distinctive gait before he had even removed his helmet. The olive-skinned, dark-haired man placed his helmet down on one of the tables and flashed a charismatic, infectious smile.

"I guess they're all small worlds in our little sphere, then!" Konstantinos Karayiannis grinned.

De Fersen leapt to his feet and darted over to tap his comlog against the younger man's in greeting.

"What the hell are you doing here?" He chuckled. "You know you're in a war zone? Proper fighting going on here!"

"Right, right! Good to see you haven't given up on working on that banter! Even at your age."

De Fersen took his seat again and gestured at the chair opposite him.

"You're here with that Teuton, then?"

Karayiannis's genuine smile changed to one carrying an element of wariness.

"Werner's alright, really. Don't let the gung-ho aggression fool you. You know as well as I do what the Teutonic Order expects from its people."

De Fersen nodded in agreement. To the outsider, all of the NeoVatican's orders would likely seem to be mere subtle variations of each other; armored soldiers who wore a different colored surcoat and cross, and perhaps had a slightly differing battlefield role to fulfill. To the men and women living inside those orders, daily existence could not be more different. De Fersen had begun his life within the NeoVatican's hierarchy as a Templar Knight, back when such a thing still existed. The jump to Hospitaller was significant and summed up succinctly by that order's original motto: *Tuitio fidei et obsequium pauperum* - 'Defence of the faith and assistance to the poor.' De Fersen briefly recalled those early days as a Hospitaller, and the change in temperament from a stance of aggression and attack to one of a more humble defender of the helpless.

Then there was the Teutonic Order. Whereas the culture of the Templars could fairly have been described as aggressive, the Teutonic Order was nothing short of fanatical. To the barely restrained killers of the Teutonic Order, the humble and reserved Hospitallers appeared, no doubt, pacifistic - perhaps even weak. De Fersen smiled grimly as he remembered his conversation with Grand Master Gerard. The stories of NeoVatican soldiers hammering crucifixes into the hearts of their enemies. If, God forbid, anybody had ever actually done that, De Fersen would have bet it was a Teutonic Knight.

De Fersen looked back up at his friend.

"What's brought you onto this team, anyway? If Special Operations Command have attached you to this Teutonic endeavor, I'm guessing there's more going on than merely an assassination."

The younger soldier lowered his brow and tilted his head a little to one side. De Fersen grinned.

"I know. You can't say anything. But your silence speaks volumes. Something's going on here, then."

The Indigo Sergeant's familiar smile returned.

"Come on. You didn't think they'd send the great Gabriele De Fersen all the way out here for a simple munitions depot?"

"Nor for a Teutonic mission to simultaneously kill a mid-ranking enemy officer. Tell me this, at least. You and I being here at the same time. How did that happen?"

Karayiannis leaned back.

"That, at least, was a genuine mistake. We knew about your operation in the area but didn't expect you to be using this exact FOB. You know how some Orders don't like to talk to each other."

"I know those Teutonic bastards certainly like to keep things in house!" De Fersen grumbled.

"And your lot, Gabe!" Karayiannis laughed. "And you! Look, all I'll say is that your raid on the depot needs to keep to timings. As you've said, something bigger is going on. You hit the depot, hit it hard, and get out. Then we'll see what happens."

De Fersen cleared his throat and folded his arms.

"And you?"

"Me? I'll be right there with you tomorrow night."

"Oh?" De Fersen raised his brow. "You're helping us out? And what about your target? The Morat colonel?"

The olive-skinned sergeant's infectious smile grew broader.

"Colonel Vandakk is inspecting the munitions depot tomorrow night. We'll take him during your raid. All part of the bigger plan, Gabe, all part of the plan."

***

Skirting the path of the cracked, overgrown road, the two knights followed the ragged precision from the cover of the trees. Some twenty meters ahead, a miserable collection of ten men and women staggered forward in single file, their hands bound and their black overalls torn and covered in grime. All ten were of fighting age - in their late teens to thirties - and all ten limped and stumbled forward, their starved, skeletal frames seemingly barely capable of standing, let alone walking. Flanking the ten wretched specimens were four Morat Vanguard soldiers; huge and muscular in comparison to a human under normal circumstances, but now practically giants of legend compared to the starved, exhausted prisoners before them.

Hawkins glanced back at the prison complex behind them, and then forward again at the sad precession.

"Who are they?" he whispered.

"Zhànshi," Tocci replied without hesitating, "look at their body gloves. Standard StateEmpire issue. They're soldiers. Or at least they were, once."

Hawkins swallowed and shook his head.

"We have to help them."

The anger Tocci felt was clear to Hawkins even from behind her faceplate as she turned to face him.

"What?"

"We can't just leave them like this!" Hawkins gasped. "We're..."

"Two months ago you were killing those bastards yourself!" Tocci snapped. "And now you want to risk our entire operation by helping our enemy?! Hawkins, you need to grow up! Right now!"

"Oh, fuck off!" Hawkins growled, his fists clenched. "They're human beings! People like you and I! When this is all over, we'll be on the same..."

"Don't talk shit!" Tocci shoved a hand against Hawkins's breastplate, failing to move him even an inch. "They're our enemy! Let the damn Morats kill them, it makes the job easier for us!"

Hawkins shook his head in utter disgust.

"And you call yourself a Christian! I'm stopping this! Right now!"

Tocci took a step back, one hand dropping to her holster.

"I'm in command here!" she grunted. "And you'll do what I say!"

"Command?!" Hawkins echoed with disgust. "Because we're the same rank but you've got six months' seniority on me? We're supposed to be a team!"

Tocci's reply was cut off by a shout of alarm from the jungle path ahead. Hawkins span in place and saw one of the disheveled Zhànshi running awkwardly away from the line, dragging one injured leg in a near hop, eyes desperately fixed on the cover of the trees only a few paces ahead. The closest Morat - a giant figure with bare arms of knotted, scarlet muscle - calmly raised his rifle and shot the young prisoner in the back with a single round. The Yujingyu soldier somehow limped on another pace despite the bloody hole in his chest before collapsing down into the long grass. His hands still bound, the dying man desperately attempted to shuffle and kick his way along the ground to reach the cover of the trees. His executor casually walked over from the horrified procession of the Zhànshi's comrades with an expression of almost bored indifference, drew a heavy pistol, and shot the man in the back of the head.

The jungle fell silent for only the briefest of moments as the eyes of the bedraggled line of Yujingyu prisoners stared in disbelief at their fallen comrade. A second Morat - a soldier at the very head of the line, paced purposefully over to the closest prisoner; a short man barely out of his teens. In a horrific display that Hawkins, in a stunned daze, could only assume was some sort of group punishment for the escape attempt, the Morat grabbed the man by his hair, dragged him up off his feet, and slit his throat open with a long, jagged knife. The Morat soldier threw the dying man down into the dust and then planted an armored boot on his head, staring a deadly warning at the remaining eight prisoners as he crushed the Zhànshi's skull underfoot.

Hawkins stood up from cover, smoothly brought his MULTI Rifle to his shoulder, took aim, and fired a burst of three rounds at the closest Morat, blowing the trooper's guts out of his back.

Guttural shouts of alarm echoed from the trio of remaining Morats. The Yujingyu prisoners scattered in panic. Tocci swore viciously and raised her own rifle, firing at one of the Morats. Her first shot missed as the enemy soldier darted for cover, the second caught him in the hip and span him in place, while the third blew off half of the alien's thick neck in a shower of blood.

Bullets whizzed through the foliage to either side of Hawkins. He saw one Morat falling back to cover, firing from the hip as we went. The other had already disappeared. A moment later, a wailing siren sounded from the direction of the prison complex.

"Come on!" Tocci growled, stepping up and forward toward the jungle pathway. "You've started this now! Fucking kill them!"

Hawkins rushed forward through the undergrowth, following Tocci as she advanced on the pair of Morat Vanguard soldiers. The closer of the two appeared bracketed in red on his lens from his firing position on the other side of the path; the final soldier had disappeared entirely. Tocci fired another burst as she advanced, winging the Morat's shoulder armor. Hawkins was close enough to see the alien's expression - one of utter calm and detachment. The close shave did not phase the red-skinned giant, but nonetheless he dropped to a prone position to avoid Tocci's fire. In response, Hawkins slung his rifle onto his back, drew his sword, and sprinted across the thin, dusty path.

Another blast of fire chattered from the prone Morat, yellow muzzle flash blinking in stark contrast to the vivid greens of the jungle. Hawkins felt a thump in his chest, stopping him dead in his tracks and spinning him in place as lines of damage reports scrolled across the upper corner of his lens.

-   *Ballistic impact, torso. Non-penetrating.*

With a roar, the Morat flung himself up from cover and rushed out to engage Hawkins. Tocci dropped to one knee, raised her rifle to her shoulder, and shot the enemy soldier in the head. The impact point of the hit on his chest still smoking, Hawkins rushed off the path and into the undergrowth on the far side, dropping to one knee and grabbing his rifle from his back again.

The jungle fell silent, save for the rattling and warbling of insects and the incessant alarm that still sounded from the prison. Sweat running down his face despite the best efforts of his armor's climate control, Hawkins sheathed his sword and brought his rifle up to his shoulder. His tactical map showed clear of hostiles. A blue blip moved up alongside him as Tocci silently appeared to his right.

"He's gone," she murmured, her helmeted head still slowly turning as her eyes scanned the jungle around them, "that last one has fallen back."

"I thought they never ran?"

"He hasn't. He's fallen back. In an orderly, disciplined manner to regroup with the Morats who are no doubt heading this way right now from the prison. Fucking hell, Hawkins, you've put us in a position now."

Hawkins let out a long breath. The accusation stung, yet he found himself curiously devoid of any feeling of guilt or wrongdoing. As if providence had placed her there to reinforce his thoughts, an emaciated Yujingyu prisoner backed slowly away from the two Hospitallers on her hands and knees, still half hidden in the dense undergrowth. Hawkins stood up and moved quickly over to help her.

A short, equally starved looking man of a similar age to Hawkins shot out from the treeline next to her, standing in between the knight and the female Zhànshi. The shaved headed Yujingyu warrior took up a combat stance, his teeth gritted and his eyes narrowed in determination. He shouted out a challenge and stood his ground defensively. Tocci raised her MULTI rifle.

"Wait!" Hawkins shouted, lowering his own weapon and raising one hand passively. "Stop!"

Insects buzzed and swarmed. Rays of light plunged through the foliage canopy overhead in white pillars. The prison alarm still blared. Hawkins slowly reached up and removed his helmet. The dense, hot and humid air instantly replaced the cool climate of his armor. He fixed his eyes on the fearless, unarmed, and unarmored Zhànshi stood before him. Hawkins slowly brought one hand back to his belt, unclipped his medical pouch and offered it to the Yujingyu soldier.

"Take this," he urged, "quickly. You need to get your people out of here."

The man stayed fixed in place, eyeing the knight with overt suspicion. A third Zhànshi stepped out from behind a tree a few paces away and said something in a language Hawkins did not understand. After another moment's hesitation, the soldier took a pace forward and grabbed the medical pouch. Hawkins waited for the next wave of Tocci's anger and resentment as she stepped forward to join the encounter. Instead, she offered up a pouch of her own.

"Provisions," she said, "they need food as much as medical supplies. Give them everything we've got."

Hawkins obliged. His eyes fell on the two pistol holsters at his waist.

"Our pistols..."

Tocci span around and held up an admonishing finger at her taller comrade.

His eyes still locked on the Zhànshi's, Hawkins took a step back. The would-be enemy soldier's features softened. The young man gave a curt bow of the head and again said something Hawkins did not understand. Hoping one of the Zhànshi watching from the shadows of the forest could understand English, Hawkins offered a smile.

"Good luck. And God bless."

He followed Tocci as she sprang off into a sprint through the jungle.

Chapter Eight

His armored arms folded across his chest, De Fersen stood by the grimy window and looked out across the empty street. The sun was setting and long shadows were cast across the road from dead streetlamps, abandoned cars, and powerless refuge incinerators. He checked his tactical map again. Nilsson and Lois were on sentry duty, while Byrne - the Trinitarian sniper - lurked atop a nearby residential block, providing overwatch. De Fersen glanced up at the eye-tracking controls on his lens to zoom out on his map. A single marker, way off to the north, showed the last time that Tocci and Hawkins had checked in. They were keeping schedule on their Operations Normal checks. Running late, but clearly alive at least.

De Fersen glanced back in at the pub and across the dusty bar. His eyes fell on the long rack of spirits still intact in their bottle rail. He smirked briefly, remembering another life. Almost instantly, the slightest pang of guilt rose up into his throat. He closed his eyes, stood up straight, and bowed his head, his fingers interlocked.

"O, my God, because you are so good, I am very sorry that I have sinned against you. By the help of your grace, I will not sin again."

A thought, a distant memory, forced its way to the fore of the old soldier's mind. He recalled kneeling on cold stone, his head bowed and a mantle of white dangling over his shoulders. A dimly lit, small room. Only one other occupant - the priest sent to accept his final confession before the ceremony. He remembered the weariness, draining even as a youth, from the requirement to remain knelt in prayer for a full twelve hours overnight as a prerequisite to the initiation ceremony.

"Bless me, Father, for I have sinned. It has been one week since my last confession..."

Back in the present, De Fersen's grimace was a lot less fond of this distant memory. For that matter, how long was it now since his last confession?

"What do you wish to confess? I remind you, Novitiate, that this is no ordinary confession. This is your last chance to lay all before God, who sees all. Your last chance to enter that room humbled and absolved. So I ask again, what do you wish to confess?"

Four years. For four years, De Fersen had carried that secret with him, just as he promised he would. For four years he had deftly equivocated, but never outright lied. But there, on his knees in that tiny room, minutes before entering the cathedral to accept his vows as a Brother-Sub Officer of the Knights Templar, there was no escape. There was no hiding. God saw all.

A line of text scrolled across De Fersen's lens, rescuing him from the unwanted memories.

-   *Broadsword One, Operations Normal, inbound to FOB.*

De Fersen opened his holographic radial menu and tapped the keyboard projected above his forearm to send a text reply to Tocci.

-   *Broadsword Zero. Copied. Out.*

Shutting down his menu and content that Tocci and Hawkins were still on track for returning to the FOB in good time, De Fersen turned to address possibly the most difficult individual task of any commander in the field, but also one of the most important. He headed back down toward the basement to attempt to catch some sleep.

***

Nilsson shut the door behind the two knights as they entered the FOB. Tocci immediately pulled off her helmet, revealing eyes darkened with lack of sleep. Her short, black hair was pasted against her pale face with sweat. Hawkins took off his own helmet - as always, his classically handsome features were somewhat ruined by his seemingly permanent expression of vapid bewilderment. The door between the main bar and the entrance corridor opened, and De Fersen and the olive-skinned sergeant from the Teutonic Knight's team stepped in. De Fersen looked across at Tocci.

"You're late."

"Your orders were to kick up hell, sir. So we did."

"So I hear. Couldn't help but notice that you're both missing your medical pouches and provisions."

Tocci exchanged a brief glance with Hawkins before turning back to look up at the team leader. Cortez appeared at the top of the stairway from the basement as De Fersen eyed Tocci wordlessly. Nilsson checked her chrono-watch handover time. At least she could get some sleep. She looked back up as Tocci's stern face broke into the subtlest of uncomfortable winces.

"That'll take some explaining, sir."

De Fersen held open the door and nodded to the bar.

"Explain away, Sister-Sub Officer."

Tocci walked wearily into the bar, followed by De Fersen and the sergeant, who shut the door behind them. Hawkins flashed a brief, friendly smile at both Nilsson and Cortez as he walked past them before heading down to the basement.

"Patrol is back in," Nilsson greeted Cortez as she took position by the door, "they've…"

"If you've got nothing to handover, don't feel you need to," Cortez interjected, "I've got it. You go get some sleep."

Nilsson nodded an acknowledgement to the broad-shouldered woman and headed down to the basement. Poddar and May were asleep. Stanescu stood in the far corner with Hawkins. Just opposite from them, Stahl, the Teutonic Knight, sat on a bench seat, watching the two Hospitallers wordlessly. Nilsson froze at the foot of the stairs. She had seen Teutonic Knights in combat before. And their Order Sergeants, for that matter. She walked over to her armorer's bench, unloaded her Combi Rifle, and laid it down.

"Zhànshi?" Stanescu asked, his brow furrowed in confusion, that solitary word immediately grabbing Nilsson's undivided attention. "Out here?"

"I suppose they move them around?" Hawkins offered, taking a new medical pouch from one of the basement's supply crates. "Maybe they put our prisoners in the territory they've taken from the Yujingyu, and vice versa? It came as something of a surprise to us, too."

"Hopefully they appreciated the intervention," Stanescu smiled.

Hawkins fought back a yawn and fitted the new medical pouch to his belt. His hand moved to the next pouch along, and he took out a set of rosary beads with a fond smile. A small object fell out of the pouch, hit the floor, and rolled across to Stahl's feet. The red-headed man slowly dropped to one knee, picked the object up, and then raised himself back to his feet. He stared across at the two Hospitaller Knights.

"I've been sitting here listening," he began, no attempt to hide the scorn in his tone, "about the exploits of an individual who calls himself a warrior of God. A… *boy* who saw fit to offer assistance to enemies of the Church. The sort of person who carries… *this* around with them in an active area of conflict."

Hawkins took two paces across to stare at the older knight, standing not quite in his personal space but only inches from invading it. His dark eyes narrowed, that earlier vapid look now replaced with one of restrained fury. He held out a hand.

"That's important to me. Give it back."

Nilsson watched in silence, curious as to what the object was but also experienced enough to know that this show of unprofessionalism amidst the higher ranking knights was something she needed to steer well clear of.

"This is important to you? This..."

Stanescu paced over and leaned in with a friendly smile.

"Alright, alright! Let's stop here! Clearly there's some confusion. My friend said that it is important to him. You're still holding onto it, like you're some sort of shitty school bully in an awful Maya teen-drama. So, be a good fellow and give it back. Let's just remember where we are and who we're fighting."

"There a problem here?"

Nilsson looked across at the foot of the stairs. Tocci walked slowly over, eyeing the confrontation.

"No problem," Stahl sneered, "just two of your thugs acting like children and threatening me."

Tocci nodded slowly and walked over to stand next to Stanescu.

"They can't both be wrong, can they?" the young woman said. "So... if you know what's good for you. Off you fuck."

The Teutonic Knight's eyes flitted across all three of his potential adversaries. He smiled and tossed the object over to Hawkins.

"Here's your teddy bear, pretty boy. I suppose the likes of you three wouldn't want to face the worst the Morats have to throw at us without one of those."

Shaking his head in disgust, the red-headed soldier barged through Stanescu and Tocci and walked up out of the basement. Stanescu flashed a broad grin at Hawkins. The younger knight did not reciprocate, his eyes still glaring at the stairs. Nilsson remained motionless in place, wondering if somehow the entire altercation had taken place without any of the four knights realizing she was there; as if somehow staying still had made her invisible. A stuffed bear? That was what this was about? Nilsson exhaled quietly, finding herself mentally siding with the blunt Teutonic Knight. Childish sentimentality had no place in what they were doing.

"Boss wants to see you," Tocci said to Hawkins. "He seems alright with the decision to free those Yujingyu prisoners. Wants to talk to you about it, though."

Hawkins continued to stare at the steps leading up to the surface, his dark eyes narrowed.

"Kyle?" Stanescu ventured.

Hawkins looked across at the other two knights, his brow lifting. "Oh! Right! On my way."

Tocci clamped a hand on his shoulder as he walked past.

"Good job out there," she nodded seriously to him.

Hawkins replied with a grin and made his way up the steps. Stanescu walked across to stand by Nilsson, his smile now seemingly apologetic, even uncomfortable.

"Have... have you worked with the Teutonic Order before?" he began as Tocci walked over to one of the empty bed rolls and began removing her outer armored plates.

"No need to explain, sir," Nilsson replied. "One never wishes to judge an individual based solely on the organization they belong to... but my limited experience of the Teutonic Order is that their culture leads to... fairly standard approaches to most situations. How about yourself, sir? I thought this was your first operation outside of training?"

Stanescu shrugged.

"Yes, well, I had a life before the Order. I was a civilian doctor, briefly. I had a few encounters with the Teutonic Order during my time as a volunteer. But, as you quite rightly said, it is not fair to judge anybody based on the tunic they wear. However, I'm no saint. I'm more than happy to judge a man on his words. Anyhow, I've said too much. I'm going to make some coffee. Would you like any?"

"No. No, thank you, sir."

Nilsson watched Stanescu pace over to the far side of the basement and wondered what would possess a man to leave the safety and high pay of a civilian doctor to take on the mantle of a Hospitaller surgeon-knight. For not the first time in her brief career, it began a chain of thought that ended in her questioning her own decision to turn down a first-rate education to become a soldier of God.

***

The three-dimensional, holographic plan of the industrial site shimmered in place in the center of the bar. De Fersen stood by the plans, one fist placed against his chin, his elbow tucked into the arm held across his chest. His three knights, two Order sergeants, and three Crosiers stood in a loose circle around him in the darkened room. Stahl, Karayiannis, and Byrne studied the plans from the other side of the holographic display. Outside, powered up and ready for action, the Sierra and Clipper dronbots stood guard while their human counterparts briefed the mission.

"The target building is here, designated Objective Alpha," De Fersen began, highlighting the large, rectangular building in the middle of the industrial compound. "The interior plans are taken from before the enemy occupation, so treat them as suspect at best. On our recce, we saw the badge of the Morat Taugak engineering company, so it's almost certain that the interior of the building has been completely re-modelled for its new role. Once we're inside that building, we're unsure what we are facing. However, tactical support from Combined HQ is aware of our operation timings, and the normal network of overhead surveillance will be provided."

De Fersen briefly remembered the pre-assault plan against the terrorist-occupied hotel on the other side of the planet, only a few days before but already feeling like months in the past. What he would have given for that same level of intelligence right now, the real time tracking of targets and numerical superiority that allowed him to assault an enemy held installation and win, without taking a single casualty.

"Sergeant Cortez," De Fersen continued, "you'll set up your team on this rooftop to the east to provide fire support. Three Crosiers, plus the Clipper dronbot. That's our main firing line to support the main push. That push will be a core fireteam - Sub Officers Tocci, Hawkins, and Stanescu. You will gain access to the building and sweep through to the main storage area, where you will lay the micro charges. Silently, as far as possible. The moment the first shot is fired, we're all going in hot."

De Fersen cast his eyes across his team. He was met with a mixture of visible emotions - stoicism from Tocci and Cortez, excitement from Nilsson and Lois, mild confusion from Hawkins, apprehension from Stanescu. The doctor was perhaps his primary worry. He had arrived on front line strength as a 'training risk' - an individual who had fallen short in some areas during various assessments. But the Order always needed doctors. Sometimes at any cost.

The micro demolition charges were a secondary concern. Hospitaller Knights did not routinely lay demolition charges; the equipment was simple enough and was specifically designed to be used by any soldier who was not trained in the utilization of the full-sized charges. The micro charges could blow open a lightly fortified door, or in this case, set off an already volatile item such as munitions or flammable liquids, but they were sometimes unreliable. But, as it was explained to De Fersen in his brief, demolition experts were not available to his team. He would go with what he had.

"The secondary push is here, from the west," De Fersen carried on, "the Sierra dronbot will be in position here, atop this plateau. The Sierra is sacrificial - the moment this all becomes kinetic, the Sierra will enter a Total Reaction program and make as much noise as possible

Mark Barber

Mark Barber

<body>

<p>to keep the defensive force occupied. I will enter the building at Marker

Mark Barber

to keep the defensive force occupied. I will enter the building at Marker Charlie - here - supported by Sergeants Nilsson and Poddar. I will be looking to establish a hacking program to set up an electro-magnetic charge as a secondary means of detonating the stores inside the building, should our primary, physical detonation fail. If the stores stockpiled in this building are detonated, the resulting explosion will destroy the entire logistics depot."

De Fersen paused on that point. He hoped the intelligence analysts had calculated that correctly. This was a long way to come to use micro-detonators designed to blow the locks off doors, in the hands of non-specialists. He turned back to the brief.

"While all of this is going on, Sub Officer Stahl's team have their own objective."

De Fersen looked across at the Teutonic Knight. The younger soldier glanced across at Karayiannis and raised his brow. Karayiannis stepped forward to address the Hospitaller team.

"We'll be on the same IFF channel as you, so you'll see our every movement on your tactical maps. There is an individual at the installation who must be confirmed as eliminated. We cannot rely on chance and the explosion your team will be causing to assume his death. We'll have a sniper positioned at Marker Delta, here to the south, and Sub Officer Stahl and I will enter the building at Marker Echo. That's all you need to know, really."

"Yeah, question there," Tocci snapped immediately. "If our entire operation relies on stealth and our probability of success is drastically reduced the moment the first shot is fired, how does that tie in with you two blundering across our objective area with the express intention of shooting somebody?"

Karayiannis let out a brief, well-natured laugh.

"Erm... I've done a few of these operations before, ma'am. I'm pretty good at it. Don't worry about me blundering anywhere. If anybody sets off alarms, I promise you that it won't be me."

Tocci's brow furrowed. She opened her mouth, but De Fersen cut her off quickly.

"Both teams are here to support each other, Sub Officer. It isn't a case of *if* this operation will descend into a rather loud firefight, but *when*. I haven't told you about the defenders yet."

Tocci took in a long, slow lungful of air and then exhaled.

"Yes, sir. Sorry, sir."

De Fersen glanced across at Karayiannis and issued a brief, apologetic wince before turning back to the holographic display.

"Surveillance has been limited. The defending force has employed the time honored tactic of building extra roofs and horizontal obstructions to hamper the efforts of our air and space surveillance. From what Surgeon-Sub Officer Stanescu and I saw on our own recce, there is a standing force of ten Vanguard soldiers at any one point. This will no doubt be bolstered for the inspection. In addition, our intel suggests that an installation of this value will likely also be covered by covert forces from the Zerat Special Missions Regiment, as well as additional Vanguard assets nearby. Suffice to say, we will be outnumbered and outgunned."

De Fersen tapped the controls on his comlog to trigger the next sequence of holographic animations. A series of blue arrows faded into view leading away from the industrial site.

"Our exit route is here, to the south. A fighting withdrawal, most likely, to Marker Zulu. This plateau is flat, clear of obstructions, and well clear of any fixed defensive weaponry the Morats have. Two Tubarãos will be landing on at zero two hundred for our extraction. If we miss them, it's a long walk. Any questions?"

Hawkins cleared his throat uneasily and pointed to an area of the map within the city suburbs, just to the west of the exfil route.

"This built up area here, sir. It's perfect for losing a pursuing force, if we smoked out the left flank."

De Fersen fought to control his rising temper.

"But we don't have smoke. Do we?"

"That's precisely my point, sir. If we did start bringing smoke…"

"Fucking hell, Kyle!" De Fersen yelled. "You're literally pointing out alternative plans based on equipment we don't have with us! We don't have smoke! You and your little Fusilier buddies used the entire PanO stock of smoke grenades at Alpha Four-Four! There's none left for the rest of us! So how about we go with this plan, *my* plan, which I've put together based on the capabilities and limitations presented by equipment we actually *do* have?! Is that alright with you?"

Hawkins's eyes sank to the floor.

"Sir," he nodded quietly.

"Then if there is nothing else, everybody go pack up all of your shit. We're leaving in ten minutes."

***

Ze Huradak Trant Vandakk did not cut the most imposing of figures by Morat standards. A good head shorter than the average height for a fighting man, a combination of age and previous injuries had also left him with a stoop, further exaggerating the height difference between him and his subordinates. But, Zevult mused as the senior officer returned his salute, the sequence of badges painted onto one arm of his angular, black and red armor was more than enough to demand respect.

There would be many officers - particularly those of the old guard, Vandakk's own generation in fact - who would scoff at what could have been perceived to be a gaudy display of achievement, begging for respect and validation. Zevult did not see it that way. Vandakk's badges merely stated who he was and what he was capable of. Kyosot Killing Platoon, Oznat Hunting Unit, Rindak Emergency Brigade; a wide variety of skills. It was the last badge - Rindak - that was perhaps most pertinent today, for the inspection. Rindak had its origins in the Buklenad Sovereignty, where part of its duties had been to act as a fire department incase of fires in naval shipyards and ammunition depots. In short, Vandakk knew far more about the security of major ammunition and weapon depots than Zevult did, and that placed him on the defensive before he had even exchanged words with the regiment's new ze huradak.

"Let's make this quick, Zevult," the senior officer addressed him in Tykalad, the battle tongue of senior officers. "While the vital importance of secure logistics is no doubt wasted on neither of us, I'm sure we'd both rather be concentrating on the more direct elements of war fighting."

"Yes, sir," Zevult answered.

Zevult briefly recalled hearing Tykalad as a child; the most complex of the four military languages of the Morats. It served as both a way for senior officers to communicate their intentions without junior ranks being privy to the subtleties of command, but also as a trial of sorts, a new and surprisingly difficult skill to learn once reaching the rank of huradak. There was, of course, a third use which came as a second order effect of sorts. The ability to speak in the most senior and prestigious of military tongues after leaving the military, as a show of achievement in civilian life with the trappings that came with it - prestige, networking, elitism... things that Morat society outwardly said were outdated and crass hangovers of the old ways, but secretly had not yet been eradicated. Zevult briefly hung on that thought. He had always considered himself a 'lifer' - a soldier until he died. Now? Older and a little wiser? Perhaps taking his knowledge of Tykalad back home would not be such a bad thing.

The two officers turned to walk from the utility vehicle toward the storage depots. The ex-PanOceanian industrial complex had previously been used for civilian building contractors - after the occupation, the area had been extensively converted to make it suitable for military equipment. The first depot building stored spare parts and perishable items for both Bultrak and Raicho TAGs, while the second and third housed weapons and ammunition respectively.

Ze Huradak Vandakk's two guards walked a few paces behind the aging soldier, while Zevult and Ryyak flanked the shorter Morat on his walk up toward the buildings. Zevult glanced across at Ryyak suspiciously. The ambitious junior officer had been too quick to volunteer to form part of the ze huradak's reception for the inspection. It was decidedly un-Morat.

"It's been rather a long day," Vandakk remarked with something hinting at an almost avuncular smile to Zevult, glancing up at the darkening skies above as the sun dipped beneath the horizon and the first sheets of evening drizzle drifted down from the bulbous, gray clouds. "It's a shame that this is the only time you could fit me into your schedule. But we are here to support the efforts of the front line soldier, first and foremost. So let's proceed."

Zevult's eyes narrowed in confusion. The inspection of the logistical facility had only been rearranged a few days before, and the time and date had been transmitted to him via the Ursphere at the insistence of Vandakk's command team. Zevult had played no part whatsoever in that - why would he want to show his commanding officer around a storage facility at night? He elected - wisely, in his mind - to refrain from challenging the ze huradak's inaccurate statement. This was all logistics - bullshit, really, that should be handled by simpering second-line fools rather than front-line fighting soldiers - and if an administrative mistake had been made, it was an even chance it was from Zevult's HQ rather than Vandakk's.

"Your guard force is relatively light," the senior officer said as the five Morats arrived at the first building. "This storage depot is the main source of ammunition and weapon components for an entire brigade. Do you have the capacity to increase the strength of this facility's security?"

"Every soldier I have is being utilized to their full capacity," Zevult replied, noticing with interest out of the corner of his eye Ryyak's attempt to suppress disgust at the ze huradak's comments. "If I bolster the guard force here, I take soldiers away from patrols when I already have enemy saboteurs in our midst. Or, worse, I take soldiers away from the front lines."

The old soldier looked up at his battalion commander, again with that same pseudo-supportive half-smile.

"They are fighting men and women of the Morat Aggression Force. Warriors. Just give them less sleep, Huradak."

Zevult bit back his initial, insubordinate response. He failed in keeping his mouth shut entirely.

"Sir. My battalion was moved here to regenerate fighting efficiency before returning to the front line. Robbing them of even more rest will reduce that fighting efficiency and *will* have a measurably negative effect when we return to the front line."

"I'm not sure I entirely agree," Vandakk replied evenly. "To put it in simple terms, what would you rather have? Ten soldiers at one hundred percent efficiency, or twenty soldiers at ninety percent? We need to manage this problem together, Zevult. Work the numbers. You've been placed in command to manage your resources in the most optimal way in which they can be utilized to kill the enemy. If that means a few soldiers lose some sleep, even to the point they are perhaps a little sloppy, then so be it. It's more rifles pointed at the enemy. You understand how I see this?"

Zevult looked across at Ryyak. For the first time, he felt the two ex-Rasyat soldiers were bonding over the short-sightedness of their ze huradak. But the debate was over. A military leader could reasonably be expected to challenge a superior's decision - appropriately, of course - only once. If the answer remained the same, then it was clear. Orders were orders. The Morat military excelled due to its resilience and its obedience.

"Understood, sir," Zevult answered crisply.

Vandakk stopped at the entrance to the munitions depot. The two Vanguard soldiers by the door snapped to attention, bringing their rifles up vertically in salute. The senior officer returned the salute irritably. He turned to face Zevult again. Zevult worked to keep his face impassive, sensing another uncomfortable conversation and another delay to getting this damned inspection started, let alone finished.

"You lost two soldiers during a prisoner escape?"

"No, sir, not exactly," Zevult replied. "The prisoners were being marched out for execution. One tried to run and was shot. During group punishment, the guards were attacked by an enemy covert group. Elite soldiers of the PanOceanian Military Orders."

"The prisoners, are they recaptured?"

"No. Sir."

"You have executed more prisoners in their stead?"

"No, sir. I ordered the execution of twenty prisoners to free up more soldiers for patrols. Ten were executed. Ten further prisoners were taken out to be executed. Two were killed, eight escaped. Irrespective, I now have twenty less prisoners to guard and I have freed up more soldiers from guard duty."

Vandakk nodded slowly. The older officer said nothing, but his expression conveyed his disappointment well enough.

" Very well, Huradak. Let's begin the inspection."

Vandakk walked inside the building, closely followed by Ryyak. Whatever momentary bond Zevult had felt moments ago with his company commander had already evaporated into nothingness. Zevult stopped at the door. He half turned and looked up. The horizon was dark, nearly black. The drizzle was turning to rain. He saw two more

Vanguard sentries walking the perimeter of the complex. All was normal.

And yet, something did not feel right.

As a younger soldier, he remembered dismissing such feelings as folly; there was no tangible, scientific evidence that what the humans called a 'sixth sense' could possibly exist in reality. But now that he was older, Zevult accepted that what a lesser soldier might write off as an overactive imagination was actually a warning seeded in years of combat experience. Something was wrong. Zevult unclipped the flap of his pistol holster and headed inside.

Chapter Nine

"So this is really how you're ending this?" Owen threw his arms
out in exasperation to either side.
"No. It's how you're ending this…"

Cortez swore under her breath. She had always prided herself
on her ability to compartmentalize her problems; to pack up and ignore her domestic life the moment she deployed on operations. Yet
now - here, atop a roof in a Moravian industrial estate, miles behind
enemy lines - she found her mind wandering to her ex-fiance and the
relationship breakdown that was confirmed only seconds before meeting up with her team to deploy. One ex-husband, one ex-fiance. Five
years of solitude and mistrust after her divorce, followed by two years
of time wasted by a man she trusted and relied on, who then suddenly
'changed his mind' about the thought of having children…
"Sergeant!"
Cortez looked up as Lois tapped her shoulder. The corporal
gestured down to the narrow roadway below the rooftop, to where a trio
of shadowy figures bracketed in neon blue on her lens rushed westward.
"Bravo Team are moving," Lois muttered.
"Yeah. Got it."
From her prone position between Lois and May, Cortez watched
as the three Hospitaller Knights melted from view in a narrow passageway between a power generator hut and an old administration block.
Behind the three Crosiers, the squat metallic Clipper dronbot swiveled
slowly in place, its targeting protocols deactivated until Cortez gave it
permission to engage. She checked her tactical map.
On the ridgeline to the west, on the far side of the target building
was one of the few areas in the vicinity which had been left by the city's
original inhabitants with some greenery and nature in the sprawling
habitation. There, the Sierra dronbot watched and waited with its heavy
machine gun. Below, De Fersen, Nilsson, and Poddar slowly advanced
on the target building. To the south, Trinitarian Byrne waited atop another three-story building on the periphery of the industrial site, providing

overwatch to his own team with his MULTI Sniper Rifle. Below him, the Teutonic Knight and Sergeant Karayiannis advanced to fulfill their own objective. Only the north side of the building remained uncovered, but the river cutting through the city and the wide, open spaces left that as dead, unuseable ground.

Red dots punctuated the tactical map with some regularity. There were doors at the west, south, and east walls of the target building - the west and south walls were both guarded by pairs of Morat Vanguard infantry. On the one hand, that left Tocci and her fireteam with a clear run to get into the building. On the other, it left Cortez's rooftop team with no clear shot at an enemy. She tapped her comlog and shifted her viewpoint to the field of fire from the Sierra Dronbot on the plateau to the west. She saw De Fersen leading the two Order sergeants slowly from cover to cover. Ahead of them, two Morat soldiers flanked the main western entrance to the depot at Marker Charlie. Three Morat officers with a further two guards had stopped for a brief conversation by the entrance. One of them, no doubt, was the target of the Teutonic team. Cortez glanced up at the eye tracking markers in the corner of her lens to use the Sierra Dronbot's ocular zoom.

The image clarified, giving a clear view of the seven Morats. The Vanguard soldiers stood alert and ready - mountains of red muscle topped by piggish, fanged faces and white hair. The PanOceanian media - and Maya horror movies, for that matter - loved to paint the Morats as merciless monsters of near unstoppable force, countered only by the virtuous forces of the PMC. Cortez had faced them many times in over a decade of combat. They were overrated. They looked terrifying, but when you shot them they dropped, just like anybody else. And since transferring from the Fusiliers to the Crosiers and receiving even the basic Military Orders hand-to-hand combat training package, she had now faced and defeated them up close on more than one occasion. The officers and Senior NCOs, though, that was a different matter. Those bastards had all come through specialist training of some sort. Near untoppable, deadly killers.

"Nordpol Zero from Nordpol Two," Bryne called across the comlog's shared tactical net, "visual feed from Broadsword Sierra confirms target is at Marker Charlie."

"Two, Zero," Stahl replied, "have you got a clear shot?"

"Negative. Visuals relayed from Sierra Dronbot at Marker Golf."

"All units, hold fire!" De Fersen growled. "Wait until my teams are in position!"

The communication channel fell silent. Cortez switched back to her own view. She saw Tocci, Hawkins, and Stanescu arrive at the side door on the depot's eastern wall - the only unguarded door to the building.

"Broadsword Alpha Zero, from Bravo Zero," Tocci called. "In position and ready for entry. Door is locked and alarmed."

"Got it," De Fersen replied, "give me a moment... your door is unlocked, alarm is disabled."

Cortez looked down and saw the three dark figures of Tocci's team fade away into the building.

"Nordpol team from Broadsword Alpha Zero," De Fersen spoke again, "your target has entered the building."

"Scheisse!" Stahl spat. "Nordpol Two, move to Marker Golf!"

"Negative," De Fersen cut in, "you hold your position. Keep the south wall covered. Broadsword Alpha Team is moving to Marker Charlie."

***

The embarrassment of a warning message across his lens was cutting.

- *Warning - heart rate high. Adrenaline level high.*

The self-loathing at that moment was bad enough for Stanescu, but the knowledge that those same warning messages would be relayed to the lens of his team leader was even more galling. This was something he had fought through and, in his own mind, mastered during training at the fortress-monastery. Yet now, moments away from combat, old anxieties were forcing themselves back to the forefront of his mind.

The three knights reached the eastern wall of the main depot building and paused by the door. Tocci glanced across Stanescu.

"You alright?" she whispered.

"Yeah. All good," he breathed.

"Keep it together. Let's go in there and fuck 'em up."

Tocci crept silently up to the door. Hawkins patted a hand on Stanescu's shoulder briefly as he moved past in the darkness. Stanescu knew that it was supposed to be a sign of encouragement, but he immediately felt resentment rising up within him at the younger man's action. A second later, that resentment was gone, replaced with guilt and more self-loathing for inwardly lashing out at his friend, purely for being better at the task they were both charged with.

"Broadsword Alpha Zero from Bravo Zero," Tocci called from a few paces ahead, one hand on the door handle, the other keeping her MULTI Rifle tucked in at the hip and ready to fire, "in position and ready for entry. Door is locked and alarmed."

Stanescu peered across. A rectangular panel next to the door flashed a bewildering array of colored buttons, with a text screen scrolling words in a language Stanescu recognized but could not understand.

"Got it," De Fersen replied to Tocci, "give me a moment."

Two long seconds passed by in an uncomfortable silence. Stanescu glanced up at the vitals read out on his lens. His heart rate was still high. In that moment, he missed the ludicrously high levels of stress and anxiety, but complete and utter physical safety, of medical school. The lights on the lock panel changed again, and a different message in the harsh language of the Morats scrolled across the panel.

"Your door is unlocked," De Fersen said, "alarm is disabled."

Tocci slowly, silently opened the door and then disappeared inside. Hawkins followed her, his sword and bulky pistol drawn and ready. Stanescu took a breath and followed in turn. His helmet's visor filtered the harsh light sources inside the building. A short, wide corridor led to a T-junction ahead where Tocci was already tentatively checking around the corners.

"Nordpol team from Broadsword Alpha Zero," De Fersen's voice chimed in Stanescu's earpiece, "your target has entered the building."

Stanescu's grip tightened around his MULTI Rifle as he anxiously checked his tactical map. Still nothing new or unexpected - all the blue dots of friendly forces were in position as planned. Two Morat guards were represented by red dots, walking slowly along the southern wall. Another two dots guarded Marker Charlie at the west entrance, near where De Fersen was advancing with Nilsson and Poddar. Five red dots had moved inside the building but now flashed on the tactical map to signify that they were last known positions but not up to date intelligence.

"*Scheisse!*" Stahl growled across the comlog channel, "Nordpol Two, move to Marker Golf!"

"Negative," De Fersen grunted, "you hold your position. Keep the south wall covered. Broadsword Alpha Team is moving to Marker Charlie."

Blue arrows appeared on Stanescu's tactical map and on his lens as Tocci plotted a route for the team to advance along. The three knights moved swiftly and silently, following the corridor to the left and toward the center of the ground floor. Up ahead, the corridor met a large, armored double door with another security lock.

"Alpha Zero from Bravo Zero," Tocci transmitted, "we've got another lock. Looks like this could be leading to a main storage area."

There was a moment's silence before De Fersen whispered a hushed response.

"Wait out. We've got a problem."

***

The two broad, powerful Morat guards remained motionless by the western wall door, their eyes fixed in concentration as they scanned the rough ground leading down from the plateau at Marker Golf. From where he crouched with Nilsson and Poddar behind a trio of oil drums, De Fersen checked his tactical map again. Completely against routine and seemingly with no provocation, the perimeter guard team of two further Vanguard Morat soldiers had turned around to reverse their tracks and head back toward his position.

"Merde," De Fersen grumbled.

He risked a quick glance around the side of the oil barrels.

Sure enough, the second pair of enemy soldiers walked slowly toward him, their bulky rifles held across their armored chests. Both guards flashed in red on his tactical map as, on the other side of the continent, a tactical support analyst from a team at Combined HQ utilized the overhead network of surveillance drones to highlight enemy units. De Fersen paused. He tapped his comlog, activating the zoom function on his visor. The Morats both looked from side to side, their scarlet faces holding the same disciplined focus as the first team stood by the western door. De Fersen nodded to himself. If they had been alerted about something, they did not think it was critical. Everything about them yelled 'routine.'

"Broadsword Alpha Zero from Nordpol Zero," Stahl said across the comlog net, "request sitrep."

De Fersen's eyes flickered between the two groups of Morats for a few more seconds. He returned to his comlog and checked his link to one of the handful of tiny surveillance drones secreted in the dark skies above. He flicked through the various lenses on the miniature aircraft but found nothing more of note in their area.

"Nordpol Zero," he whispered, "second enemy guard team is investigating my position. Southern entrance is left unguarded. Recommend you enter the building now to locate your target."

"Broadsword, negative," Stahl replied, "you've got four enemies near your position, and if they're alerted, reinforcements will be arriving directly behind you. I'm moving to my Marker Emil to support you."

De Fersen's eyes opened a little wider in surprise. Perhaps he had been wrong about Stahl.

"All units from Nordpol Two," Byrne called from the rooftop to the south, "I've got eyes on the second Morat team. Content I can take them both if required. I can provide support to Broadsword Alpha team."

That seemed like a logical plan. With sniper support from Byrne, De Fersen could take the two Morat teams with the help of the two Order sergeants, leaving Stahl and Karayiannis to enter the building. He glanced across to Nilsson and Poddar. Before he could speak to them, automatic fire echoed from inside the depot building.

Instinctively, De Fersen leapt to his feet and hugged his Spitfire into his shoulder. He was aware of a casualty notification scrolling across his lens as he wrapped the fingers of his left hand around the grip of his Spitfire, took aim, and squeezed the trigger. The light machine gun thundered into life in his hands, rattling back into his shoulder as bullets spewed out of the weapon. The first Morat by the door was instantly cut down, patches of red blossoming out of impact points across the alien warrior's gut and chest.

The second Morat instantly returned fire, blindly, and only in De Fersen's rough direction. De Fersen corrected his aim and brought the weapon across to bear left, bullets punching into the doorway and wall behind the second Morat before catching him in the hip and half spinning him around. Winged but very much still active, the Morat darted for the door and disappeared into the relative safety of the building. To his right, De Fersen heard the telltale whine-zip of a high velocity sniper round, and he saw one of the second Morat team suddenly brace up, drop down on his knees, and then crumple down into the dust at his feet. Only then did he read the casualty notification message on his lens.

- *Sub Officer Sonia Tocci, dead. Gunshot wound, torso.*

For the briefest of moments, De Fersen felt that familiar and sickening pang of sympathy. There was no time for more. He brought his Spitfire around to face the final Morat from the roaming security patrol as Nilsson opened fire from a prone position at his feet. The Sierra Dronbot from the ridge to the west fired its heavy machine gun with a dull thud, cutting down the last Morat. Then De Fersen heard a second sniper rifle round cut through the rain and the night sky above. He registered the change in pitch and direction of the round even before the second casualty notification scrolled across his lens.

- *Trinitarian Liam Byrne, dead. Gunshot wound, head.*

Shrill alarms cut through the night across the entire industrial site.

***

The familiar sound of gunfire echoed from the far side of the building. Zevult's thoughts immediately jumped from the tedious nature of the site inspection to the focus and determination required to win a firefight. He recognized the weapon's dull thud and rate of fire as, at least, one of his own side's Combi Rifles; but it was immediately answered by the faster, higher pitched banging of two human MULTI Rifles. Alerts began to flash across his golgrapt. Zevult turned to Ryyak and the two Vanguard soldiers.

"Get over there, coordinate the forces in this building, and repel the attacking force. Report in as soon as you have ascertained what we are facing."

"Sir," Ryyak grunted, almost contentedly, before bounding away down the corridor toward the sound of gunfire, closely followed by the two Vanguard troopers. A moment later, the blast of a human Spitfire chattered away from outside, somewhere to the west - very close.

"All units, from C-Two," the voice of one Morat trooper crackled through Zevult's earpiece - calmly, Zevult noticed with satisfaction, "PanO knights in my position. Strength three - one is down. One of my team is dead. Request assistance."

Vandakk turned to face Zevult.

"You and I need to leave. Now."

There was a moment - little more than a flash of a thought - where the primitive, beast-like Morat inside resented the ze huradak for that comment. The Morat existed to fight and to win. Then, the more modern, progressive, and intelligent thoughts swarmed forth to consume the outdated need for mindless violence and tribal validation. Vandakk was entirely correct. If two senior officers were killed in this engagement, the repercussions on the leadership of the regiment would be unacceptable. The simple, efficient solution was to fall back and allow the rank and file soldiers to do their job. Engage and kill the enemy.

He tapped his wrist-mounted golgrapt, confirmed that the general alarm had been raised, and then opened a comm channel to the veteran, dependable Ze Hamak Guntat.

"Guntat, it's Zevult. The industrial complex is under attack from a Military Order force. Activate every unit we have and send a Yaogat platoon to my location."

"Just one platoon, sir?" Guntat asked.

"For now. We don't know what we're facing. This could just be a diversion for something bigger. Get support here and get everything else we have ready to deploy, quickly. And power up every building within a ten block radius. Get the whole area lit up so the bastards can't hide. Wait out for further."

Zevult looked back to his commanding officer.

"There are enemy units to the east and west. They'll have the south entrance and the roof covered, as well. There's no door to the north, but there are windows on the next floor. We'll jump from there."

The aging Morat officer nodded in approval.

"Then let's be quick about it."

***

At the far end of the corridor, one of the two remaining Morat Vanguards leaned around the corner and fired a long blast at the two knights, the high velocity rounds slamming into the walls between them. Hawkins fired a brief burst of ineffectual return fire, but the Morat had already ducked back into cover. The first Morat lay dead at the T-junction at the far end of the corridor, spread eagle where he had fallen to a burst of fire from Tocci's rifle. In turn, Tocci herself lay motionless in a pool of blood halfway along the corridor. Another casualty report scrolled across Hawkins's visor - Byrne, the Trinitarian sniper.

"Give me cover!" Stanescu urged from Hawkins's left. "I'm going to get Sonia!"

"She's dead!" Hawkins yelled. "Darius, she's gone! We need to…"

Stanescu darted forward along the corridor, hunched over low. Hawkins swore and raised his rifle back to his shoulder, firing ahead at where the pair of Morats waited just around the corner. Stanescu reached Tocci and grabbed her by the armpits, dragging her back toward Hawkins in a smear of scarlet across the smooth, white floor. The two Morats leaned around and fired; again, just a little quicker than Hawkins. A round slammed into Stanescu and knocked him down.

The doctor was immediately back on his feet, smoke rising from a hole on one of his pauldrons as he continued to drag the armored figure of his team leader to safety. Hawkins fired again until the ammunition counter on his visor hit zero.

"Loading!" he shouted, dropping to one knee and ejecting the curved magazine from its housing just in front of the pistol grip of his weapon.

Stanescu reached the comparative safety of the corridor's corner and crouched over Tocci's body, pulling a small, mechanical disc-saw from his medical kit.

"She's gone," he said sorrowfully. "I've got to get her Cube out. I've got to…"

Hawkins grabbed Stanescu by the side of his helmet and forced the less experienced knight to look back down the corridor.

"Mate! We are under fire! We need to get rounds down at those fuckers! We haven't got time! We take those two out now, or we're dead!"

Stanescu looked briefly down at Tocci's corpse, then up at Hawkins and nodded. Hawkins looked back down the corridor. He could sit here all night and exchange fire with the two Morats, but it was on their terms. They were defending. Hawkins had a job to do.

"On me!" he growled. "Go!"

Hawkins pelted out of cover and hurtled down the corridor, firing long bursts as he ran and hoping that Stanescu was with him. One of the two Morats again leaned out to adopt a firing position from cover, but the sheer weight of fire blasted the corner of the corridor apart, and through the dust, Hawkins saw the enemy soldier throw himself prone. Nearing the end of the corridor, he flung his MULTI Rifle onto his back and unsheathed his sword. The second Morat leapt out to meet him, bringing his Combi Rifle up to fire from the hip.

This time, Hawkins was faster. With a roar, he shoved the tip of his heavy sword straight through the Morat's gut to emerge in a bloody mess from the soldier's back. Still shouting, both hands wrapped around the sword's handle, he lifted the Morat up off his feet, twisted the sword, and then withdrew it before hacking down through the alien's shoulder. The first blow cut through the middle of the vanguard trooper's torso; the second sliced the soldier in half. Blood sprayed across his visor, his breathing ragged, Hawkins turned to face the final enemy soldier. He saw the Morat pinned on the ground beneath one of Stanescu's armored feet while the doctor fired a full four seconds of ammunition into the alien's body and face.

The corridor fell silent. Hawkins sheathed his sword and recovered his rifle.

"The charges," he breathed, "we need to get to the storage area and lay these charges. Come on."

Sprinting along the corridor, Hawkins and Stanescu proceeded only a few paces until they heard heavy, thudding footsteps ahead and guttural shouts from the coarse, crude language of their enemy.

***

"Target! Five points right of my Marker Tango!" Cortez shouted, pointing the outstretched fingers of her right hand in the direction of the rooftop for emphasis. "Open fire!"

Lois swung the Spitfire around to point to the northwest and crouched low over the weapon, his face screwed up in frustration.

"I can't see him! Mari, I can't see him!"

"Just fire! Hit that marker with everything!"

The Spitfire barked into life, spewing out dozens of rounds across the darkened sky toward the rooftop on the far side of the industrial estate. Acting off its own logic, the Clipper Dronbot behind the trio of Crosiers whirred around on its spider-like legs and tilted its missile launcher upward. With a banshee-like howl, a thin missile shot out of the dronbot's launcher and streaked across the night, slamming into the top of the building and lighting up the sky with a blossoming, orange explosion.

Cortez looked to the south, where Byrne lay dead on a rooftop and the southern wall of the target building was left without cover. Below them, Stahl and Karayiannis darted across open ground toward the depot.

"Johnny!" Cortez slapped a hand against Lois's shoulder. "That sniper is there! He must be there! Keep hitting that rooftop and the upper floor of that building, I'm relocating!"

"Got it!" Lois replied through gritted teeth, firing another long burst through the rain-soaked skies.

May moved across to the lip of the rooftop, raising her own rifle and firing short bursts to support Lois as the Clipper let loose another missile. Confident that she had narrowed down the location of the sniper who had killed Byrne, and content that the base of fire raining down would force him to relocate, Cortez dashed across the top of the roof and swung over to clamber down the slippery ladder leading to the ground.

"Alpha Zero from Charlie Zero," she called as she quickly negotiated the thin, slippery rungs of the ladder, "enemy sniper suspected at Marker Tango, I'm moving to take up a position to cover the south wall."

"Charlie Zero, roger," De Fersen replied calmly. "Do not take up a firing position until the enemy sniper's position is confirmed. Got it?"

Cortez slid down the last few rungs and turned to sprint off across the darkened industrial complex. Of course she was taking a risk in taking up a firing position in the sniper's field of fire. But she trusted in God to protect her. God would be her shield if that was her fate. And if not? Well, fuck it, it had been a reasonable run. Neglecting to answer De Fersen, Cortez ran across to the next building and set about searching for a ladder leading to the rooftop.

Then, without warning, the lighting of every building as far as Cortez could see suddenly illuminated the night. Office interiors within the complex, external security lights, even advertising billboards on the edge of the city to the west all flooded the night with artificial, neon sunshine.

***

Gunfire echoed from inside the building. Another missile streaked across the sky from the rooftop to the east, hurtling through the rain to impact into the same building to the north, blasting the walls with fragmentation. The western suburbs bombarded the night sky with light from abandoned office blocks, residential areas, and the myriad colors of a hundred advertising billboards. From where she crouched in cover behind the barrels, Nilsson risked a glance at the entrance to the depot on the western building. The Morat guard De Fersen had gunned down lay motionless in a pool of blood. The second guard had not dared open the door.

"Listen in," De Fersen grunted to Nilsson and Poddar as he tapped his comlog to update marker positions on the team's tactical map, "they've lit this place up to try to see us. Now the alarm is raised, there will also be reinforcements on their way here. The two of you need to get inside that building and support Hawkins and Stanescu. Stahl and Karayiannis will be moving in from the south to fulfill their own objectives. It'll be chaos in there. Get to Bravo Team and get those charges set. Got it?"

Nilsson looked up at her commander.

"What about you, sir?"

De Fersen nodded to the north.

"I'll sort out that sniper and then double back to you."

"On your own?" Poddar asked.

"The missiles from that dronbot will have forced their sniper to relocate," De Fersen said, quickly checking over both shoulders. "Keep an eye on Marker Uniform for the next twenty seconds. If I make it to cover, get in the building. If I don't, see where the sniper fire is coming from and get both dronbots to hit it. Understood?"

Nilsson nodded. There was a pang of anxiety over the plan, but with a reasonable amount of experience under her belt, she was well aware that snap decisions needed to be made; and more often than not, they involved risk. De Fersen peered around cover again, ducked back in, and quickly made the sign of the cross. That symbol concerned Nilsson more than his brief. Nonetheless, she raised her Combi Rifle and took position at the edge of the barrels.

De Fersen jumped up and sprinted across the open ground toward the cover of the buildings to the north, his armored feet splashing through the puddles in the cracked concrete. Nilsson's eyes scanned the top floor windows of the building at Marker Uniform, her finger held ready against the trigger of her rifle. De Fersen darted low and fast, quickly reaching cover without incident. Nilsson turned and nodded to Poddar. That was as much assurance as they were going to get that the sniper had moved on. She propelled herself up to her feet and ran quickly across to the depot door, slamming her back against the cover of the wall as Poddar caught up with her.

At her feet, the Morat who De Fersen had shot let out a weak wheeze. Nilsson looked down. The alien soldier's eyes were closed, but his chest rose and fell, and a barely audible, guttural grunt escaped his lips. Nilsson unholstered her pistol and shot the Morat twice in the head.

"That other one could be waiting for us," Poddar breathed as Nilsson returned her handgun to her side. "Only thing on the tactical map from Bravo Team is on the east side of the ground floor."

"Yeah, got it," Nilsson exhaled, "I'll take lead. I'm going left. On three... two... one."

Nilsson slammed a foot into the door to fling it open and darted two paces inside, dropping to one knee and raising her rifle as Poddar took position behind her. Nothing. She quickly checked her tactical map as her lens automatically updated her comlog, changing her picture of the inside of the building to reflect the corridor layout she now saw. Long corridor ahead to a ninety degree bend.

A Morat soldier leaned out from behind cover and fired at the two Order sergeants. Fighting to overcome the urge to face the incoming fire head-on with the bravery that had defined her Order for over a thousand years, Nilsson instead applied common sense and dove to the ground. Poddar returned fire, sending a blast of bullets back into the corner of the corridor.

"On him!" the older sergeant growled. "Don't let him get away!"

Nilsson was up again in an instant, rushing headlong down the corridor with her rifle tucked into her hip. She rounded the corner at exactly the same time that the Morat reappeared to resume his firing position. Nilsson pulled the trigger, emptying the remainder of her magazine into the enemy soldier from only three paces away. The white wall behind the Morat was painted in dark red as his guts were blasted out of his back, his muscular arms thrown to either side.

The Morat slumped down against the wall, smoke rising from his bloodied torso. Nilsson dropped to one knee and ejected her empty magazine.

"Loading!" she called as Poddar stepped past her, taking the lead of their duo as they moved slowly toward Bravo Team.

Chapter Ten

The rain intensified. The thumping of synthwave music thudded away from the suburbs, from some automated advert or gaming bar activated by the sudden onset of power. Billboards for everything from taxi services to sporting events to underwear flashed in a myriad of color from projectors along the rooftops of the buildings to the west of the industrial site. The hammering of automatic fire continued from within the main depot building. De Fersen checked his tactical map; Hawkins and Stanescu were making slow progress toward the center of the building. Nilsson and Poddar were moving in from the western depot doors to link up with them.

From his covered position at the corner of one of the smaller storage silos, De Fersen risked a glance to the north. Still no sign of the enemy sniper. Given the ease with which the Morat shooter had taken out Byrne, it was a fair guess that he had some sort of multispectral visor to negate the Trinitarian's camouflage. De Fersen just needed to find the bastard and at best, kill him; at worst, at least use his hacking device to paint the sniper up with a spotlight program. Through the neon glare reflecting off the rows of tall, neat, white buildings, De Fersen made out the beams of vehicle headlamps. He immediately opened a communication channel to all members of his team.

"All units from Zero - enemy reinforcements inbound from the north. Moving to engage."

De Fersen took only three steps out of cover when the howl of a high velocity sniper round cut through the rain only inches above his head. Swearing viciously, De Fersen changed his path and darted to his left to dive for the cover of a row of forklift trucks. His breathing heavy, he quickly tapped at his wrist to bring up his tactical map again, quickly checking rough angles from surrounding buildings to his present location, to at least narrow down the location of the Morat shooter. There - a more squat, rectangular administration building to the east of the sniper's original location. De Fersen dragged his forefinger and thumb across his comlog's touch plate to highlight the area on his team's shared tactical display.

"Charlie Team from Alpha Zero," he transmitted, "Zone Bravo to the north of your location is the most likely location of the enemy sniper."

"Charlie Zero copies," Cortez replied, "I'll get missiles down in that location. I've plotted Route Delta on your map; it's your clearest route away from the sniper to close with the enemy reinforcements."

A series of arrows appeared on De Fersen's lens as he accepted the recommended route from Cortez. Further west, then a sharp turn north through an alleyway between the edge of the complex and a row of empty residential buildings to give a better view of the roads to the north. De Fersen grunted and swore again. He was in command. His place was in the midst of his team to ensure the operation went to plan, not dashing off alone on some glory-hunting mission to kill an enemy sniper and cut off the Morat's entire axis of reinforcement. Well, he was here now. Forcing himself back to his feet, he sprinted along the line of forklift trucks and across a small gap to the alleyway before heading northward.

"I'm eyes on with the reinforcements now," Cortez called. "Two personnel carriers, less than a minute away. Pretty big carriers, we're looking like half a platoon of reinforcements at the least."

"Broadsword from Nordpol," Stahl's voice cut in, "we're moving to assist. I'll set up a base of fire to your west at my Marker Gustav."

It took only the most rudimentary mental mathematics for De Fersen to calculate that, for Cortez to see what she could see, she must have located herself precisely where De Fersen told her to avoid. Fucking idiot. He would deal with that later, if she was still alive. And now Stahl was rushing across to throw himself into the enemy sniper's sights.

"Alright, understood," he replied as a salvo of missiles blasted into the administration building to the northeast, briefly lighting up the sky in a blossoming fireball. "I'm sending the Sierra Dronbot up to support me. We'll keep them busy."

De Fersen plotted a firing position for the dronbot and quickened his pace. Two guns would not hold off half a platoon for long. His team needed to hurry up with setting the charges.

***

The familiar stench of expended ammunition wafted back down the corridor. A Combi Rifle blasted away from just around the corner, answered from a little further away by the boom of human MULTI Rifles. Ryyak rounded the corner to see one of the soldiers of A Company slumped against a wall, half of his head blown off and scattered across the white floor tiles. A Morat Vanguard trooper took cover at the wall of a T-junction, his weapon blasting away at an unseen foe at the end of the corridor. The two soldiers accompanying Ryyak rushed forward to take up firing positions in support of their comrade. Ryyak paced over and clamped a hand on the shoulder of the A Company Vanguard trooper.

"Haza Geruk! Report!"

The young Morat looked over his shoulder and then across at the two new additions to his firing position. He stepped back away from the T-junction and stiffened his posture in reverence to Ryyak, which half impressed the senior soldier and half disappointed him with the futility of the gesture.

"Sir! Two enemy knights are at the end of the corridor. We've slowed their advance, but they've forced us back. They're trying to get to the main munitions storage."

"I can see that," Ryyak growled, "it's a coordinated assault. They've got us surrounded. We need..."

A dull tone sounded in Ryyak's earpiece as his golgrapt was updated with a warning message. He checked his display. Another unit of human soldiers had entered the building from the west. Two Order Sergeants. Ryyak grunted in annoyance. He was already being squeezed between two advances. That would not do. He had a daughter back home - one year old, he had never met her, but she would grow up to be a good soldier and a wise leader. Ryyak was perfectly prepared to die, but there was no way that he would allow that girl to grow into adulthood with the knowledge that her father died in some piss-ant little shoot out to protect a building full of bombs and bullets.

"Sir," the haza geruk said as he loaded a fresh magazine into his rifle, "there's more of these bastards, back the way you came."

Ryyak paused. The knights were the bigger threat. But this situation was almost childlike in its simplicity. Quickly remove the easier threat so avoid being surrounded, and then regroup to face the greater threat.

"Stay here and stop those knights from taking one more step forward!" Ryyak commanded. "Hold them right here! I'll deal with the others."

***

Nilsson reached the corner of the corridor and dropped to one knee, her rifle held up and ready to fire. She glanced at her tactical map as Poddar caught up with her; Hawkins and Stanescu were not far now, but whatever enemy forces lay between them was a complete unknown. At least outside, the constant umbrella of drone-based surveillance managed to detect most enemy forces - all bets were off as soon as the fighting moved inside. She glanced over her shoulder at Poddar. The gaunt man held one hand to his side and let out a long, slow breath.

"Hey!" Nilsson whispered. "You okay?"

He looked down and issued a slow nod.

"God watches over us," he breathed, his smile somehow detectable on the other side of his helmet's faceplate.

Nilsson winced. It had been evident to her even in the brief that he had not yet recovered sufficiently from his wounds on that first night. But he could fire a weapon, and sadly, that was enough right now. She heard De Fersen's voice on the group channel, a hurried message about more enemy reinforcements that was cut off by Hawkins as he spoke on a direct line to her team.

"Bravo Team from Bravo One," she heard Hawkins's voice in her earpiece, "dropped one. Two of them left, but they're retreating toward your location. Set up a firing line, and we'll run them straight into you."

Automatic fire continued to chatter and boom from ahead as Nilsson checked her tactical map. She saw the two blue blips of Hawkins and Stanescu moving slowly forward, while two red dots they had identified retreated toward her and Poddar.

At that moment, a hulking mountain of armor hurtled around the corner of the corridor and smashed into the two Order Sergeants like a hurricane. The towering, red and black figure batted aside a strike from Poddar with a thick, alloy encased fist before slashing open the sergeant's belly with a backhand strike from a squared-off, long blade. Poddar had barely staggered forward a pace before, with lightning fast movements, the Morat warrior stabbed his blade into the mortally wounded man's chest, planted a heavy pistol against the back of the sergeant's neck, and fired a round directly into his Cube.

Throwing aside the feeling of loss and sympathy, Nilsson piled into the huge warrior. She slammed the butt of her Combi Rifle into his gut and then swung the weapon around to connect with the side of his head with a dull clang. The Morat warrior barely moved. He brought the butt of his pistol slamming down into Nilsson's skull with a thud, cracking her head back and leaving her dazed. Desperately fighting through the sea of stars in her vision and sickening nausea in her gut, Nilsson brought a knee up into the Morat's stomach, to no effect. She quickly grabbed for her pistol, but as her hand closed around the weapon's handle, she heard a loud bang, and the space between the two of them lit up briefly with a yellow-hued flash.

Nilsson stopped dead in place, her limbs ceasing to respond. Pain flared up from her body. Warning messages scrolled across her lens.

- *Sergeant Anil Poddar, dead. Gunshot wound, neck.*
- *Ballistic impact, penetrating. Severe wound, abdomen.*

She looked down and saw the Morat's smoking heavy pistol pointed at her lower torso. With a yell of rage and determination, Nilsson brought her own handgun up. The huge Morat batted it aside with ease, kicked her back, and shot her again in the chest. Nilsson collapsed down to her knees and then crumpled to one side, blood flowing up her throat and out of her lips with a bitter, almost rusty taste. The Morat quickly paced over to her. Her eyes fell on Poddar; the man's rear skull decimated by the Morat's cruel, deliberate attack against his Cube. He was gone. Not just dead - but with his Cube destroyed, there was no hope of ever coming back. The same fate that was now mere seconds away from Nilsson.

As the Morat soldier towered over her, Nilsson thought of that moment at her graduation when her mother pretended to be happy with the decision to join the Order. For the first time in over a year of fighting, resolve collapsed entirely. Nilsson found herself crying. She held up one weak, shaking hand.

"...please..."

The Morat recoiled as if struck, insulted. His posture spoke of the instant revulsion in her act of surrender. He slashed down with his long knife, severing Nilsson's shaking hand halfway down the forearm. She let out another cry of agony as blood sprayed from the severed stump.

The armored bulk of a Hospitaller Knight slammed into the Morat like a freight train, tackling him at the waist and sending the two soldiers smashing straight through the thin wall behind them in a cloud of dust.

***

Rounding the corner in a sprint, only a second behind, Stanescu saw Hawkins launch himself forward and slam a shoulder into the waist of a huge Morat warrior in bulky armor. The two soldiers locked in an embrace and smashed through the wall to one side. Stanescu looked down and saw Poddar's corpse sprawled across the floor, a sizeable part of the back of his skull missing entirely. Nilsson lay propped up against the nearest wall, one arm severed just above the wrist and her surroundings awash in dark crimson from multiple wounds.

- *Sergeant Anil Poddar, dead. Gunshot wound, neck.*
- *Sergeant Anja Nilsson, critical wounds, abdomen. Critical trauma, right arm. Death imminent.*

His fingers curling tightly around his MULTI Rifle, Stanescu looked up at the hole in the wall and heard the exchanged growls of rage and thudding of metal as Hawkins and the gargantuan Morat traded blows in the next room. He looked down again at Nilsson. Hawkins stood a chance. Nilsson would die. The only wrong decision was indecision.

"Anja, it's me," Stanescu said calmly, dropping to one knee beside her and grabbing his medical bag. "Look at me. You're going to be alright."

Stanescu tapped on his comlog and opened his primary survey program. A trauma diagnosis visual overlay shimmered into life across his lens, highlighting two high caliber gunshot wounds in blue on a holographic display over the top of Nilsson's torso. Worryingly large exit wounds were highlighted in her back. One through the lung, the other through the intestine. Oxygen level was at seventy-eight percent. The undamaged lung was not coping. Blood pressure eighty-two over thirty-six. Bleeding profuse. Cardiac arrest warnings flashed across his lens. Breathing rate high twenties.

Reaching forward, Stanescu pulled off Nilsson's helmet. As soon as her face was exposed, she spat out a mouthful of dark blood. Her panicked eyes stared up at him as her body shook and blood continued to flow out of both sides of her mouth. Her one remaining hand grabbed hold of his arm weakly, but desperately.

A guttural cry rang out from the adjacent room as a body thudded into the wall. Fighting past the distraction and remaining focused on his primary calling, Stanescu grabbed a sterile tube from his medical bag and fed it into Nilsson's mouth. His diagnosis overlay flashed a sequence of blue arrows to aid him angle the tube down the dying woman's throat. Her grip on his arm loosened. Oxygen level seventy-four percent flashed in warning across Stanescu's lens.

"Don't worry," he said calmly, as his overlay highlighted the tube's end moving down the trachea "nearly got it."

The tube slid into place. Stanescu quickly grabbed his serum gun from his side and checked the load. As standard, the serum load was nanobots optimized to remedy bleeding. He pressed the gun to the side of Nilsson's wounded abdomen and pulled back on the trigger, pushing a vial load of microscopic nanobots into her body that immediately set about repairing severed veins and arteries. Oxygen level seventy-six percent. Stanescu allowed himself a shadow of a smile of satisfaction as he loaded a second vial into the serum gun to attack the exit wounds. Then another casualty report scrolled across his lens.

- *Sub Officer Hawkins, wounded. Severe wound, chest.*

***

Ryyak saw only a blur out of the corner of his eye before the heavily armored human soldier smashed into him. He felt a confusing instant of weightlessness as he was forced off his feet before the two smashed straight through the wall and hit the ground in the adjoining room. Training kicked in. Ryyak instantly fought through the confusion and loss of awareness, and struggled up to his feet, looking around him for his dropped knife. Opposite him, a Hospitaller Knight was already standing and unsheathing his sword.

Ryyak lunged forward and slammed an alloy-covered fist into the knight's face, knocking his head back. He clamped his fingers around the knight's right wrist to hold his sword arm down and then flung his free elbow into the human warrior's face. The Hospitaller nimbly ducked his head beneath the attack and brought it back up to slam into Ryyak's own faceplate, denting the alloy armor with a ringing bang. Ryyak felt a knee slam up beneath his ribs as the knight fought to free his sword arm; the cutting edge technology of the human's heavy armor fought against Morat raw strength as the two fought for control of the lethal blade while trading blows with their spare limbs.

Overcoming his opponent, Ryyak fought back a sneer of victory as he managed to prize the weapon away and fling it to the other side of the room. The Hospitaller responded with a volley of three powerful punches to his face and gut before a sidekick to the chest propelled Ryyak across the room. No time to think - just react. Ryyak pushed himself back up to his feet and darted over to his own blade. He snatched the weapon up off the ground and continued on into a slashing attack against the knight as the human soldier struggled across to retrieve his sword. Ryyak was again faster than his foe, forcing the man to bring up a forearm to block the attack.

The Hospitaller swept Ryyak's hand to one side and then counter attacked with a knifehand blow to his neck, finding a chink between his breastplate and helmet. The strike sent pain flaring across the Morat's throat, choking the air from him. His teeth gritted, Ryyak leapt up to bring a knee into the human's face to throw him back and create an opening. The Hospitaller staggered back a step, and Ryyak lunged forward with his blade again. The human warrior skilfully dodged the first attack, batted the second aside, and then blocked the third. The fourth strike found its mark. Ryyak plunged the knife into the human's chest, driving it through a vent just beneath the rib cage.

The Hospitaller grabbed desperately at Ryyak's wrist. The two combatant's paused for a second, their dented faceplates pressed forehead to forehead. Ryyak looked down into the human's eyes. Through his visor, he saw that the man was young. What surprised him was that he did not see pain or fear. He saw only rage. Fury. Ryyak hauled back on the blade to remove it from the young soldier's body. The Hospitaller held it firmly in place. As Ryyak struggled to overpower his foe for a second time, he felt a thump in his belly as the knight shoved a pistol muzzle into his gut. There was a deafening, staccato bang, and Ryyak's innards were blown out of his back.

Fighting for all he was worth to stop the indignity of crying out in pain, Ryyak fell down to his knees and then pitched over to one side, face down. No time to think. Just act. He urged his limbs back into the fight, willing himself back up to his feet. But it did not work. He found himself writhing in pain, flailing pathetically on the floor in a river of his own blood as his arms and legs refused to respond to the commands his brain sent to them. He saw the knight stagger forward, excess serum leaking from the bloody hole in his surcoat and breastplate as his armored suit's auto-heal functions addressed his injury.

For the first time since his childhood, panic began to set in as Ryyak saw the Hospitaller limp over and recover his sword. All of the training, tradition, Morat evolution, and years of combat experience did not stop Ryyak from yelling out in agony as the human knight plunged the weapon down through the small of his back and twisted it in place.

***

'*Alert! Enemy reinforcements inbound. Broadsword Alpha One - acknowledge.*'

De Fersen growled in frustration. Stahl still was not in position, and now some blithering idiot in their comfortable office building who had been ordered to provide tactical advice to his team had actually activated the direct override function and interrupted him to insist on a response to something so obvious. De Fersen lay prone at the edge of an alleyway, his Spitfire pointing toward the two approaching vehicles. He quickly activated his comlog.

"Combined from Zero! I'm literally pointing a gun at them now! Wait out!"

'*Alert! Enemy reinforcements inbound: Map References Tango Six-Six-Two, Four-Three-Seven. Broadsword Alpha One - acknowledge.*'

De Fersen's eyes widened as he shifted his tactical map to the southwest. Two more enemy personnel carriers were hurtling toward the industrial complex.

"All units from Zero! Enemy reinforcements inbound from the west, moving Sierra to…"

Then casualty reports began scrolling in. Poddar, Nilsson…

De Fersen let out a breath and placed a hand on the cross on his surcoat, looking up into the rain and clouds above.

"Give me strength," he breathed.

Directly ahead, at a third story window in one of the complex's administrative blocks, De Fersen saw a shimmer. A faint sensation of movement. His eyes widened. He quickly zoomed in on the window and made out the hazy outline of a humanoid figure.

"That'll do, thank you, Lord!" he whispered as he brought up his hacking programs on his radial menus.

"All positions from Zero! Enemy sniper is at my Marker Uniform! I'm Spotlighting him... now!"

His fingers dancing across the holographic buttons projected above his forearm, De Fersen quickly finalized the program. With a last click, the outline of the Morat sniper was painted in vivid red, flashing up as an updated alert on the team's shared tactical map. The Spotlight program instantly painted targeting assistance advice on De Fersen's lens, projecting a scarlet line from the muzzle of his Spitfire to the sniper, complete with aiming corrections. A message scrolled across his lens.

- *Clipper Dronbot: priority target assessed. Engaging.*

A missile streaked across the black sky from the right, arcing up and then nosing down to slam into the building ahead of De Fersen. A second missile followed up a second later, smashing through the open window of the third story and exploding with a roar of shrapnel. The red outline extinguished.

Ahead, the two red and black, angular vehicles carrying the Morat reinforcements peeled apart and slowed to a stop in an open line of vehicle loading bays. The familiar hollow thunk of a panzerfaust sounded from De Fersen's right, and a projectile shot across to plough through the driver's cab of the first vehicle. A crumpled explosion sounded from within, and the carrier tipped over to one side, alloy screeching against concrete as it slowed to a stop. The combined fire of a Combi Rifle and a Spitfire blasted across from De Fersen's left, cutting into the skidding vehicle as it halted. De Fersen lined up his own sights on the second personnel carrier, squeezing the trigger to fire a long burst as that vehicle, too, came to a stop. The first Morat to jump out of the back of the vehicle was hit full on by De Fersen's fire, the rounds smashing through the soldier's dappled green and black armor and knocking him back against the carrier in a shower of blood.

Undeterred, Morat soldiers quickly piled out of both vehicles and spread out to take up prone positions to return fire. De Fersen instantly recognized the angular cut of their armor and the extra protection on their lower arms; Yaogat Strike Infantry - more than a cut above the Vanguard infantry in terms of fighting prowess and equipment. De Fersen checked his tactical map; Stahl and Karayiannis continued to pour fire down from a stubby building to the left, while a third blue blip on the map showed where Cortez was rapidly approaching the fight from the south.

His teeth gritted, De Fersen fired another burst from his Spitfire and caught another Yaogat trooper in the head and shoulder, blasting the soldier's helmet apart. His jaw twisting into a rictus grin, De Fersen raised himself up onto one knee to assume a new firing position that gave him better visibility of the six Yaogat soldiers ahead of him, albeit at the cost of the cover he had seconds before.

"Advance!" he growled across the comlog communication channel. "Straight up and into the bastards! Advance on me!"

A thump sounded from the line of enemy soldiers to the side of the stationary personnel carrier, and a projectile slammed into the wall to De Fersen's right. With a deafening bang, a hole opened up in the wall, and a shockwave slammed into De Fersen. A moment later, masonry toppled down to cut off the alleyway behind him. A message scrolled across his lens.

"Gabe, stay in cover!" Karayiannis yelled. "There's a dozen of the bastards with more coming in from the south, and three of us! We need to fall back to the extraction point!"

De Fersen checked the message. Karayiannis had assigned him to Stahl's fireteam on their network's tactical display. De Fersen ducked back into cover and accepted. To the south, he heard the thunder of a heavy machine gun as the Sierra Dronbot engaged the second wave of Morat reinforcements. It was instantly answered by automatic rifle fire.

Chapter Eleven

Her feet slipping and stumbling as the dusty rubble gave way beneath her, Cortez shoved out a hand to one side for balance as she pointed her Combi Rifle upward. The hammering of automatic fire continued ahead of her as De Fersen fired long bursts, answered by the crackles of Morat return fire from the darkness ahead. Hunkering down at the end of the alleyway, Cortez dropped to one knee and raised her rifle to her shoulder. Perhaps a dozen Yaogat troopers lay prone in groups ahead, to either side of two burning Morat vehicles. Cortez checked her tactical map; Stahl and Karayiannis poured down fire from an elevated position to the east, while to the south, the isolated Sierra Dronbot had already engaged the second wave of reinforcements.

"Charlie Team!" Cortez called. "Advance to the depot! Get inside and support Alpha Team in setting those charges!"

"Zero from One, copied," Lois replied.

A thunderous explosion sounded from the south.

- *Sierra Dronbot destroyed.*

Finally reaching her commander, Cortez leaned down and clamped a hand on De Fersen's shoulder as the aging knight loaded a magazine into his Spitfire.

"Sir! We've got to fall back! The Sierra's gone, and there's nothing stopping that enemy push to the south from surrounding us! We've got to pull back to the extraction point!"

"No!" De Fersen growled. "You're a Crosier now, Sergeant! Not a damn fusilier anymore! The job isn't finished! If we're falling back anywhere, it's to the depot to blow it up! Follow me!"

"I've sent my team in there! They can set a simple charge! We *need* to secure our escape route!"

De Fersen fired another long burst at the line of green armored Morat soldiers before raising himself to his feet and backing off out of their line of fire. He quickly tapped at his forearm and then stared down at Cortez.

"We fall back when *I say* we fall back, Sergeant!" he roared. "Our job is not done! Follow me!"

Cortez stared up at the older warrior incredulously, and then at the hopeless situation displayed on the tactical map. So this was it. This was the hill she would die on. For a fucking ammo dump.

"Nordpol from Zero," De Fersen transmitted as he struggled over the debris cluttering the dark alley, "fall back to Marker Charlie! Back to the depot!"

***

Snapping the alloy collar in place over Nilsson's forearm, Stanescu checked the wounded soldier's vitals again. He had stopped the internal bleeding, and one lung was functioning; he had bought time for her, but nothing more. A trio of heavy, unsteady footsteps thumped slowly forward from the adjacent room. Stanescu unholstered his pistol. Hawkins appeared at the hole in the wall and clambered through. The young knight removed his helmet and took in a deep breath. His face was pale and his dark hair dripping with sweat. Stanescu's primary survey program automatically locked in on the knight's wound.

- *Stab wound, left torso. Vital organs functioning. Armor auto-heal successfully initiated. Casualty stable.*

"You alright?" Stanescu asked hurriedly, returning his attention to Nilsson's unconscious form as he fed her severed hand carefully into the open end of the amputation collar. Positioning advice appeared on his lens as he lined up the radius and ulna bones, ready to reattach them.

"I'm fine," Hawkins replied wearily, sheathing his sword and holstering his pistol.

Stanescu nodded to the room behind him.

"Is that bastard definitely down?"

"He's not getting back up again. How bad is Anja?"

Stanescu pressed his thumb against the activation panel on the side of the amputation collar. The tube locked in place, and a jet of serum sprayed into both sides of the horrific wound. The doctor looked up again.

"I've got to get her out of here. I've bought her time, but she needs proper facilities."

"Can you move her?"

"If I have to. I'd rather have another two minutes here."

Hawkins grabbed his MULTI Rifle from the ground and quickly checked it over. The chattering of gunfire outside, to the west, intensified. Stanescu heard shouted exchanges over the comlog channel between De Fersen, Karayiannis, and Cortez.

"I'll be back in two minutes, then," Hawkins said quietly. "I'll go set the charges."

Hawkins turned to leave. Stanescu suddenly felt his calm evaporate, leaving a clawing anxiety at the pit of his gut.

"Kyle!"

Hawkins turned around. Stanescu looked up at him. He remembered their first meeting, when as an Order initiate he was making his way back to his dormitory room. He heard music from another room; strange in that music was normally played through an individual's geist rather than out loud, which was normally just for social occasions. But, also strange in that it was vintage rock music. Not quite as vintage as the expansive collection of music Stanescu enjoyed, and certainly a fair bit harsher in tone, but more than enough to pique his interest. Miserable, tired, and lonely after the first two weeks of intensive training at the Hospitaller's fortress-monastery, Stanescu decided to take the risk and see if the music might lead him to a kindred spirit, somebody to talk to in an attempt to find some escapism from the harsh, new world he had volunteered for. Hawkins became that friend.

"Kyle, I don't know what to do!" Stanescu blurted out rapidly as an explosion sounded from outside. "I need to pick up a weapon and follow you, because I'm a soldier now and I should have your back! But this is my patient, and if I leave her, she'll die! But I don't know if I'm just... just making fucking excuses because I know exactly what I'm doing here, saving her life, and I'm making a mess out of everything else!"

Hawkins offered a small, calm smile.

"Two minutes," he repeated as he pulled his helmet back on over his head, "keep Anja safe. I'll set the charges and be right back. We'll RV with the others and work out where we're going from there. Two minutes."

***

The four soldiers pelted through the industrial site. The sound of gunfire had ceased, now replaced with the distant thudding of music from the bars and leisure facilities forced back into life on the edge of the suburbs to the west. De Fersen checked his tactical map. Hawkins, Stanescu, and Nilsson were still inside the depot. Lois, May, and the Clipper Dronbot were moving toward them from the east. Stahl, Karayiannis, and Cortez were with him, rapidly closing toward the depot from the west. He tapped his forearm to open a channel to the two knights.

"What's going on in there? We're on our way to you."

"Zero from Two," Hawkins replied, "I'm setting the charges now. Where's the RV for falling back?"

De Fersen checked his map.

"Charlie Team, RV with me at Marker X-Ray. We're going to shoot a way through to the extraction point. Alpha Team, catch up as soon as the charges are set."

De Fersen quickly dialed in an order for the Clipper Dronbot, sending it to the western wall. It was just a dronbot. Leaving it behind to make as much noise as possible gave them a better chance of getting out alive. He checked his chrono. The Tubarãos would be in the air now and on the way to pick them up. It was still a long way to the extraction point. This would be close.

***

His eyes flitting between his tactical display and map, Hawkins made his way quickly back from the main munitions storage to the corridor where he had left Stanescu. He reached another corridor junction, checked it was clear, and then silently darted forward again. Pain flared up from his wounded side. Of course he had told Stanescu that he was fine. His suit's diagnostics told him so and that the wound repair was holding. But that did not stop it hurting like hell. But to complain about that would be thoroughly un-English. Far better to keep that upper lip stiff.

Hawkins arrived back with Stanescu. His eyes fell on Poddar's body. He lowered his head and held a hand to the rosary beads in the pouch at his waist, offering the briefest of silent prayers before he looked up again.

"The charges are set," he told Stanescu.

"Yes, I heard you tell De Fersen."

The doctor propped himself up on one knee and carefully hauled Nilsson's body up over one shoulder.

"Do you want me to carry her?" Hawkins offered.

"Probably best that you do the shooting and I look after the casualty."

Hawkins checked his map. Lois and May had already joined up with De Fersen's team. They were all now heading east toward the extraction point.

"Let's go." Hawkins nodded.

He led the way back toward the western wall doorway, where his map told him that the Clipper dronbot stood guard. Still no sound of gunfire. Things were looking up. The two knights and their casualty reached the door; Hawkins checked the route was clear before stepping out into the night and a torrent of rainfall. The Clipper stood a few meters ahead, its logic having selected a pile of upturned barrels to provide some cover as it obediently waited behind to cover the retreat. Hawkins jogged quickly over to it, checking the escape route plotted on his map. He stopped by the dronbot. The automaton remained in place, the long, pod-like body atop its four alloy, crabby legs swiveling in place as its scanners checked its surroundings. All automated, all reactionary, no sentience or feeling - just limited AI. Yet Hawkins felt remorse for the machine.

"Awfully sorry, old chap," he muttered, patting the armored shell before leading the way south to catch up with the rest of the team.

Hawkins and Stanescu had barely managed three paces down the next alleyway before gunfire erupted behind them. The distinctive whine of missiles filled the air as the Clipper exchanged fire with enemy troops that appeared on the tactical map.

"Are we clear yet?" Stanescu yelled.

"Keep going!" Hawkins urged Stanescu as he picked up his pace.

The two Hospitallers reached the end of the alleyway and burst out into the open, where six jungle-green armored Morats appeared at the far side of a vehicle park. Hawkins raised his rifle and fired a long burst toward the nearest enemy soldier as muzzle flashes lit up the night ahead. To his right - eastward, and the path to De Fersen and the extraction point - was a long warehouse blocking his path. Swearing, Hawkins darted westward and toward cover as rifle rounds snapped past his head and kicked into the concrete at his feet. He reached a long row of crates and stopped to check behind him. Stanescu carried on after him, Nilsson draped over one shoulder, a smoking smear on his back where a round had impacted the armor to one side of his spine.

"Are we clear?" Stanescu said again as he carried on past Hawkins, sprinting toward the brightly lit suburbs ahead.

Hawkins followed him, turning to check behind them every few paces for pursuers.

"Clear?! What do you mean? You know that's them shooting at us?"

"I know that, you fucking idiot! Are we clear of the blast zone? Are you going to detonate those damned charges?"

Hawkins's eyes widened in realization. He pressed a finger against his forearm to bring up his radial menu and selected his weapon display. A large, holographic button in red projected above his arm. With a bitter grin, Hawkins pressed a finger against it. A block to the northeast, he heard the explosions. A series of four dull, crumpled bangs in quick succession. Then nothing. Hawkins's eyes opened wide. He checked his map. He checked his weapons display. He pressed the button again.

"Oh bollocks."

The two knights burst out of the industrial site and into a brightly lit, main roadway running along the perimeter of the eastern Moravian suburbs. Billboards advertising clothes, movies, games, and social venues lit up the broad pathway extending north and south.

"Bollocks?" Stanescu repeated as he led the sprint southward. "What does that mean?"

Hawkins checked over his shoulder again.

"It means the charges I set didn't detonate the ammunition! The target is still intact! I've got to go back!"

"Don't be a bloody idiot! We need to..."

Gunfire sounded from behind them as two Yaogat troopers appeared at the edge of the industrial site. Hawkins turned and fired a long burst from his MULTI Rifle in response.

***

The incessant thumping of synthwave faded slowly into the distance as De Fersen led his team through the thickening undergrowth. Karava vine traps flanked the narrow, natural path at the foot of the steep valley. The seemingly ubiquitous bloorbriars that De Fersen had encountered on every corner of every continent of Paradiso weaved seamlessly amongst the palm trees and brightly colored flowers.

Once again, gunfire sounded from the direction of the industrial complex. De Fersen stopped and turned to check behind him. Cortez plowed on tirelessly with her team of Crosiers; Lois and May both showing signs of fatigue as they kept pace with her. Behind them, Stahl and Karayiannis guarded the rear of their small column. The Teutonic Knight had also stopped to survey the edge of the city as flashes of light erupted where fire was exchanged. De Fersen glanced at his map. Three IFF signatures in blue moved slowly westward, directly away from the extraction point as Hawkins, Stanescu, and Nilsson were chased down by the teams of Yaogat troopers. Two lines of text appeared on De Fersen's lens; the first alerting him that the valiant Clipper Dronbot had been destroyed, the second was Hawkins opening a private communication channel to him.

"Kyle!" De Fersen snapped. "You're heading the wrong way! What the hell is going on?"

"The charges!" the young knight gasped as gunfire erupted from close by. "The charges didn't detonate the depot! It's still standing!"

De Fersen closed his eyes and exhaled. He pressed his hand against the cross on his chest and took a moment of silence before replying.

"Nevermind that now. Look, you've got to lose those bastards chasing you down. Those Tubarãos won't wait. You need to evade, cut south, and then directly across to us. I'm plotting you a path now."

"Yeah, well smoke would be bloody good right now to..."

"Not now!" De Fersen growled. "Lose them, head south, pick up the path I've sent to you. Understood?"

"Understood, sir."

De Fersen shook his head as he terminated the communication channel. Stahl had already barged over to him.

"What's happened?"

De Fersen looked down at the younger soldier.

"The charges haven't detonated the depot."

De Fersen could detect the knight's rage even with his pale face hidden behind his helmet.

"*Fick!*" Stahl snapped. "Your man couldn't even set a charge properly? We've sacrificed our entire mission to support you and your team, and you've fucked..."

"Listen up, you insubordinate little shit!" De Fersen jabbed a finger in Stahl's face. "This isn't over yet! So stop panicking like a fucking space cadet and listen! I'm going back, and I'll detonate that building myself. You need to get this team to the extraction point, you understand?"

"You're heading back? Into that? You won't make it a hundred meters!"

"Stealth, not force now," De Fersen hissed, "I only need to get close enough to detonate that place quantronically."

"If you could have blown it up with a hacking program, why didn't you do that earlier?" Stahl demanded.

"Because it takes a bloody age to get through the firewalls, and that place was crawling with guards!" De Fersen snapped. "But now it's our only chance! So I'll say it again - get my people to the extraction point!"

Cortez moved past her Crosiers, her grim face set in determination.

"Sir, look... we can loop around to the south and hit them from the flank. It'll link up with Sub Officer Hawkins's team and provide a distraction for you to..."

De Fersen held up a hand to stop the veteran soldier, his eyes narrowing in frustration.

"Cortez! You've done enough of this shit to know that this far behind enemy lines, pilots don't wait! If you're not there, then none of us are going home! And I don't need a distraction from the south to alert them to us doubling back; I need you to carry on eastward to the extraction point so those bastards don't smell a rat! So all of you, this conversation is over! Follow my orders and piss off to the extraction!"

A flash of seething resentment darkened Cortez's features. Stahl stepped in before she could reply.

"You heard the Father-Officer! Come on! Corporal Lois, on point!"

De Fersen watched as the line of soldiers continued wordlessly ahead, following the narrow ravine as it weaved and meandered uphill toward the dimly lit skyline. He turned and saw one soldier, still, remained by his side.

"Are you fucking kidding me?! Which part of..."

Karayiannis slapped an armored hand against De Fersen's pauldron.

"Yeah, yeah, yeah... you're going it alone. You're a massive hero and you're really grumpy and scary. Heard it all before from you, Gabe. Now, last time I looked, I was the specialist in infiltration and you were the computer nerd. So how's about I lead you through their lines back to the depot, and you make it explode?"

Grunting irritably, De Fersen followed the younger man along the path and back toward the neon lights of Moravia.

***

Marker Zulu showed up on Cortez's lens as she waited in the foliage at the edge of the clearing. She heard the two Tubarãos before she saw them; both tucked down at low level in a snaking valley to the north of the extraction point. An alert scrolled across her lens from the operation's tactical controller.

-   *Encrypted communications establishing... Channel open between Broadsword Team and Hammerhead Flight.*

"Hammerhead One from Broadsword Charlie Zero," Cortez called, "extraction point is cold, you are clear for approach.

"Hammerhead One, copied," the lead aircraft's pilot replied.

Even the gunfire from the south had stopped now. Cortez checked her map and saw that, somehow, Hawkins and Stanescu were still alive and rapidly approaching the extraction point through the dense jungle. De Fersen and Karayiannis were already back at the depot. But, a decade of combat experience told Cortez that this was the worst time for things to go wrong. Proverbial hairs stood up on the back of her neck. She cycled through her lens's various visual filters as the first Tubarão appeared in the night sky and began its approach to the darkened site.

"Keep looking out," she breathed to Lois and May. "I don't like this."

The sleek, sharklike transport aircraft flared to a hover and touched down in the center of the jungle clearing. May raised herself to her feet.

"Wait!" Cortez snapped, slamming a hand on the young Crosier's shoulder.

She looked across at the aircraft.

-    *IFF interrogated - access cleared.*

"Broadsword from Hammerhead, you are cleared to approach."
Stahl nodded to Cortez and May.
"You two first."

Cortez hauled herself up from the lip of ground at the edge of the clearing and rushed across the open ground, hunkered down low in the darkness. Her hands gripping her Combi Rifle tightly, she checked every shadow around the clearing as she approached the aircraft. In the darkness ahead, she made out the rectangular hole in the side of the aircraft where the cargo door was open and an aircrewman waited next to a swivel mounted heavy machine gun. The blast of scorching air from the aircraft's idling jet engines hit her as she approached, the smell of burning replacing the mustiness of the jungle.

Cortez planted a boot onto the fold out footstep beneath the cargo door and hauled herself up. She immediately pushed past the aircrewman and made her way to the cockpit as May clambered up to relative safety behind her. Two pilots sat in the darkened cockpit, only the faint glow of a small number of backup, tertiary instruments breaking up the darkness around the two aviators.

"How long can you wait?" she called to the pilots. "We've had problems."

"How many of you are there?" the pilot to her left replied over his shoulder. "We were told to expect thirteen and two dronbots."

"Nine," Cortez replied, "Four dead, both dronbots gone, and five are still out there. There's only the two of us, and two more at the edge of the clearing. How long can you wait?"

"Shit!" the pilot in the right hand seat snapped.

The first pilot turned to his colleague.

"Calm down. We've got a little time. Patch me through your tactical map so I can see how far away the rest are."

Cortez sent her tactical map contents across to the Tubarão's mission system. Stahl and Lois clambered up into the back of the aircraft. Hawkins, Stanescu, and Nilsson were still some two hundred meters away. Then, up ahead, lines of tracer fire snaked up into the night sky from the jungle to the north.

"Hammerhead One from Two," a new voice cut in across the comlog, "we're taking ground fire from my Marker Golf. Looks like small arms. How long have you got left down there?"

Cortez saw a sparkle in the sky as the HMGs aboard the second Tubarão poured down into the Morat soldiers below.

"How many of them are out there?" the first pilot asked Cortez.

"Couldn't tell you for sure," she replied honestly. "We saw a platoon, but there could be more."

The pilot looked up at his comrades in the second Tubarão and paused for a moment before transmitting again.

"Two from One. There's nine pax in total, so I can take them all. Still waiting on five. If you can keep those bastards busy, then loiter in that area. If their fire starts to become at all effective, then get out of here. I'll stay here for as long as I can."

"Hammerhead Two, copied."

Cortez swallowed and looked out of the cockpit. The engines continued to thrum and roar to either side of her. Gunfire spluttered, chattered, and thudded to the north.

***

The joints in his heavy armor silently whirring, De Fersen sank back down to take cover behind the low wall of a loading bay. Practically right back at the start. De Fersen pushed the weary feeling of disappointment in his subordinates to one side and set about concentrating on the task in hand. Karayiannis leaned past the edge of the wall to glance across at the main depot building.

"Nothing," he breathed, "nobody. Now's your chance, Gabe."

De Fersen brought up the holographic menu wheel of his hacking device and cycled through his software packages. Knowing full well that he faced a lengthy task, he was unwilling to harness the complexities of a full entry into the quantronic realm. As much as he trusted Karayiannis, he needed his wits about him if a Morat patrol appeared. No. This needed to be done old school. A brute force attack straight into their firewalls, while the real payload would be in via the back door. De Fersen selected a pre-prepared line of code, replicated it a thousand times over with an army of bots, and then connected to the depot's mainframe.

Warnings flashed across De Fersen's lens as automated responses from the mainframe firewall kicked in, detecting the hostile connection and eliminating De Fersen's self-replicating army of virtual bots almost as quickly as they were being created. He allowed himself a grim smile. That would keep the system busy. It would also alert the enemy chain of command that intruders had doubled back to create a virtual connection to the target. It would not be long until either an enemy patrol was re-routed to them, or a counter-hacker connected to the system to stop him.

"How long is this going to take?" Karayiannis whispered.

"Patience! I've barely started!"

De Fersen quickly analyzed the capabilities of the Morat firewall and how it was countering his brute force attack. His smile instantly disappeared. The bastards were more hacking-savvy than he gave them credit for. No worry. He would simply have to hit the main firewall a little harder. De Fersen's fingers moved quickly over his holographic keys as he prepared a second wave of virus-ridden bots with a different line of coding, and then threw them into the virtual battle. For good measure, he added a third. Then back to the real task in hand.

The back door - no matter how alien the mind that designed the system, no matter what star system the intelligence evolved from, programmers would always leave a back door. A way straight into the core of a program, sometimes so that the creator or administrator had a quick and easy route to functionality; sometimes as a secret pathway in case of being locked out by a malicious third party. Whatever the reason, it was always there. And now, with the automated defenses struggling to counter De Fersen's somewhat traditional brute force attack, he needed to settle down and find that route.

De Fersen brought across a virtual mesh, instantly translating as much of the Morat code as possible into Latin numbers and letters. He then fired in a passive program, another wave of bots who this time stealthily interacted with the enemy system to rapidly probe the firewall for gaps. De Fersen selected a random sample of the bots, bringing their interactions with the enemy system up on the screen over his comlog to analyze as they searched for the inevitable vulnerability in the defenses.

"I can see why you wanted to use explosives!" Karayiannis muttered. "This is taking an age!"

"And if I hadn't been given a team of buffoons instead of soldiers, we'd be on our way home by now!" De Fersen growled. "Shut up and let me concentrate."

The frustration lay in the fact that the majority of the process was automated. The majority of the hack was attempted via programs concocted before De Fersen had even deployed on the mission. Manually checking over common areas of programs for suspect code was laborious, and ideally not attempted from a crouched position behind a wall, miles behind enemy lines with a raised alarm and enemy troops approaching.

De Fersen's screen flashed another warning.

- *Counter-hacker connected.*

"Alright..."

De Fersen changed focus to connect to his invisible adversary, watching his opponent's opening moves in the virtual game of quantronic chess. The counter-hacker immediately placed another defensive firewall over the network's short-term back up system.

"Ha!" De Fersen beamed. "Thank you, amateur hour!"

"What?"

"Counter-hacker. And he's highlighted exactly where the back door is. Two seconds... I'm in."

De Fersen's screen glowed green as he gained full access rights. Step one - lock out the enemy hacker.

"Gabe!" Karayiannis breathed. "The bad guys are here!"

De Fersen heard footsteps and shouts in that guttural, gruff language from somewhere ahead and to the right, by the depot. He kept his eyes focused on his screen. Step two - disable all building safety programs. Fire protection, surge protection, intruder protection; everything.

Rifle fire chattered from nearby. Karayiannis fired a burst from his own weapon in response. Step three - overload as many main terminals as possible to cause electrical fires. A dull thump sounded from within the building. Then a second, and a third.

"That's it?" Karayiannis growled from behind his rifle. "That's all you've done?"

"I've set the building on fire and there's no fire protection in there! That's all I can do! We need to clear the blast radius! This is why this was not the primary plan, because for all I know, it might take an hour before..."

The entire world turned into vivid yellow as a colossal explosion ripped the storage depot apart. A deafening boom, so loud that even De Fersen's helmet's noise reduction failed to compensate, flooded his senses as the depot's walls were blown outward spectacularly. A moment later, the shockwave of the explosion smashed into the two soldiers, lifting them off their feet and catapulting them up through the air. De Fersen let out a stifled cry as the air was knocked from his lungs, warning messages scrolling across his lens in a blur as he twisted and cartwheeled through mid-air.

De Fersen landed with a thump on his back, staring up through lenses clouded with alert messages at a clear night sky. Karayiannis landed a few feet from him, his surcoat smoking and singed from the impact of the fireball. With a croak of pain, he turned his head slowly to face the older soldier.

"I bet you're glad you were wearing your helmet for once. Otherwise you'd have lost your eyebrows from that one, as well as all of your fucking hair."

"Shut up, you pain in the arse!" De Fersen gasped, struggling back up to his feet. "We need to get to the pick up point."

Chapter Twelve

The thinnest sliver of indigo painted the horizon as dawn approached. Outside the perimeter fence, Hawkins could hear a few vehicles meandering along the all but empty streets as commuters left their homes to set off for early shifts at direct attendance jobs. The town of Hartberg lay nestled on the western shores of the Fairbanks Sea, thousands of kilometers to the west of the bitter and bloody fighting Hawkins took part in only hours before. A small town whose mediocre prosperity was based only on its adjoining military base, the remnants of a once thriving mining industry in the hills to the southwest, and a bizarre, outdated and half forgotten amusement park.

Hawkins let out a breath as he continued along the path from the landing site to the officers' mess. He made his way past an ill-laid out, generic series of storage buildings, a military police building, the region's Underwater Combat Training Unit... all component parts of a sizable base. He still wore his black combat fatigues - the jacket torn and bloodied from where the huge Morat had stabbed him, although the wound was already pretty much healed - with boots and a black beret that had been left for him at the landing site so that he could at least finally discard his ORC heavy armor. He could have waited around for longer at the Landing Site, to speak to the others from his team, perhaps. He did not have to dig particularly deep to work out why he had walked away.

The Officers' Mess reception loomed up ahead; an attractively constructed building with wood paneling covering its curved, slanted walls and sweeping roof. A few military utility vehicles were parked outside as Hawkins approached the main entrance, another twinge of pain flaring up below his ribcage. He entered the brightly lit reception area. He was hit with a cool blast of air, scented with lavender. Smooth steps of black marble flanked with hand rails of highly polished gold led up to an impressive reception area, punctuated with wicker chairs and sofas, and sales display cabinets lined with comlog-linked cuff-links and lapel pins, jewelry, and t-shirts adorned changeable images of all of the regimental crests of units based at Hartberg.

Hawkins removed his beret and stuffed it into one of his trouser pockets. He wearily climbed the stairs and looked for the hall porter's desk to check in for his room. From his limited experience of PMC officers' messes, the junior officer accommodation - the rooms for lieutenants, captains, and when things were getting cramped, majors, too - were of a significantly better standard than the admittedly perfectly pleasant Military Order officers' accommodation. As a Brother-Sub Officer, Hawkins was the direct equivalent of a full lieutenant.

Footsteps echoed from the spiral staircase to the right of the large, open room, and Hawkins saw a young woman in running gear making her way quickly down. His lens immediately auto-populated her details:

- *Amelia Osorio, Captain, 4th Combat Logistics Regiment, Off-Duty*

A reminder to log in to the civilian network scrolled across his lens. Hawkins sighed. He simply did not have the energy to face the hundred invasive adverts, Maya-hints, Sibylla's Advice, or even the missed calls and messages from well-meaning loved ones. He pressed his comlog to accept limited access to the civilian network. The logistics captain's geist immediately painted her digital halo - a square of the information that she wanted strangers to know about her, on Hawkins's lens.

- *Name: Amelia Osorio*
- *Age: 25*
- *Occupation: Government/Defence*
- *Marital Status: Single*
- *Place of Birth: NeoTerra (Canadian Heritage)*
- *Hobbies: Running, horse-riding, painting*

The blonde woman flashed him a friendly smile as she passed. Then her eyes dropped to his torn, bloodied battledress jacket, and she stopped dead in her tracks.

"Are you alright?"

"Yes, ma'am," Hawkins issued a slight smile.

"Are you... Did you arrive on that plane that came in about an hour ago?"

Hawkins paused before answering. That was very much need-to-know. Clearly his silence answered that question, anyway.

"Have you been checked?" the captain asked. "Medically?"

Hawkins nodded.

"Yes, ma'am. I just haven't had a chance to get cleaned up and changed since..."

Osorio smiled sympathetically.

"Well, welcome to Hartberg. Are you here for long?"

Hawkins shrugged.

"I honestly don't know. Could be hours, could be weeks."

The captain nodded to a desk on the other side of the room.

"Isabella will check you in and give you directions to your room. If you're here for a while, please do give me a call if you want showing around, alright?"

"Yes, ma'am. Thank you."

"Amelia," the woman corrected with a smile. "Maybe see you later."

Osorio walked down the steps and outside to meet the first rays of morning sunshine before breaking into a jog and disappearing from view. His spirits lifted a little from the unprovoked show of kindness, Hawkins walked across to the hall porter's desk. He had always found the PMC's regular military personnel to be more friendly than their Military Orders counterparts.

The hall porter's face was punctuated with neat, symmetrical grooves running across matt-white skin. A projection - digitally painted onto Hawkins's lens just as artificially as the arrows that directed him around the establishment. The projected faux-human looked up at Hawkins with a friendly smile from behind the cut out in the wall.

"Sub Officer Hawkins? Welcome to Hartberg Officers' Mess, sir. You're accommodated in SO Suite Twelve."

"SO?"

"Senior Officers, sir. We received communications from Father-Officer De Fersen an hour ago. He insisted that all of his officers were accommodated in higher grade suites, irrespective of rank. The station commander has approved his request."

A series of softly animated blue arrows appeared on Hawkins's lens, guiding him back out of the main building. Upgraded accommodation? Hawkins was not surprised that, given De Fersen's fame and influence since the action at the Horns of Hessen, he could bypass normal entitlements with such ease. The confusing part of it all was that De Fersen was willing to provide such lavish support to Hawkins, particularly given that he had completely ballsed up the micro-detonators and the enemy munitions depot, very nearly writing off the entire operation. That conversation was still to come. De Fersen had, as was now becoming a soul-crushingly demoralizing norm, left him to fester in silence on the entire return journey.

"Thank you," Hawkins nodded to the digital hall porter.

The first yellow line of sun was painting the horizon in pastel shades as Hawkins followed the blue lines some two hundred meters to his accommodation suite. The Senior Officers' suites were independent wooden chalets, only a single story but all backing onto the sandy beach that eased down to touch the nearly still, clear turquoise waters of the Fairbanks Sea. Hawkins walked up the light, pinewood steps of the chalet and opened the front door. The interior - a combined bedroom and living room that would not look out of place in a beach holiday advertisement, shared the same subtle scent as the Officers' Mess main building. Two doors led off into a kitchenette and a shower room.

Hawkins left his beret and boots by the front door and trudged over to the double bed, his eyes falling on the towel folded into the shape of a dolphin left atop the plush duvet. He detached his last pouch from his belt - the only one he had not left in the armory along with his weapons and armor. He carefully removed the contents; his rosary beads and the small, stuffed bear from his fiancee. He placed them on his bedside table and sank to sit down before carefully pulling off his slashed, bloodied battledress jacket.

The stains on the jacket barely showed over the Hospitaller black. Hawkins stared down at them. Deep down, he knew that it was his own blood, yet somehow he found his mind racing and wondering if some of it was somehow from the huge Morat officer he had cut down. He remembered seeing the dead warrior and wondering for a second, just a second, if the deadly alien had a family back home. If that Morat saw Hawkins as the invader, the aggressor. The villain. He shook his head. More likely, that bastard saw him as prey. Undoubtedly, the Morat was content to die fighting. Hawkins remembered seeing Poddar's body, and Tocci's; even burying Kormea right at the start of the operation. He threw the jacket into the waste incinerator in the corner of the room and activated it with his comlog. Instantly, he regretted his actions as he visualized the verbal confrontation with some jobsworth stores clerk who would refuse to issue him a replacement battledress jacket, insisting that exchanges were only permitted on a one-to-one basis and that he needed to see the damaged original.

Hawkins let out a sigh and pulled off his socks, leaving him clad just in his combat trousers and the padded bandages around his torso. He needed sleep. He knew it would evade him. A distraction would have to do. He wished to God that perusing the Bible would provide the positivity he needed, but it did not always work like that. He pressed his comlog and reconnected to the civilian network.

'Sunday... Sunday... SUNDAY!... at the Hartberg Arena! Monster REMs! Mon...'

Hawkins suppressed a curse as he checked his geist's security settings, cutting off the ad with a simple checkbox selection above his wrist.

"Welcome back online, Kyle. You have... 117 messages. Would you like to see your inbox?"

"Yes," Hawkins yawned.

-   *Messages/Personal*
-   *Parents: 15*
-   *Nathaniel Hawkins: 6*
-   *Sarah Hawkins: 3*
-   *Lisette Beckmann: 87*

"Maya - call Lisette."

Hawkins rethought his vocal command a fraction of a second later.

"Maya - cancel call."

That was not fair. With the time difference, she would be asleep. He knew she would insist that it was right to wake her up, but he also knew how hard it was for her to sleep even at the best of times. No, he was only calling her because he wanted to hear her voice, for his own support. It was selfish. It could wait for a few hours. Hauling himself wearily back up to his feet, Hawkins stepped out of the chalet's back door, kicked his bare feet through the soft sand of the suite's adjoining beach, and waded into the warm water of the Fairbanks Sea before sinking to a seated position to watch the sunrise.

***

The normal world swept past the car window. Friends meeting at cafes, joggers weaving their way through the small number of pedestrians on the clean, smooth pavements, pristine ALEPH-controlled vehicles stopping and starting by curbs to pick up and drop off the civilian population of Hartberg. Not a single cloud populated the morning sky above as the sun beat down on the town center and sparkled across the gently rippling waters of the Fairbanks Sea, less than half a mile to the east. The war was far away. The ubiquitous and often deadly jungle of Paradiso, however, surrounded the town on every front, kept at bay only by the automated, near endless sprays of pesticide from the perimeter nozzles and endless procession of small drones.

-   *Would you like conversation?*

"No," De Fersen grunted.

He settled into the back seat of the small, white car as the steering wheel in front of the empty driver's seat gently span in place to navigate the vehicle around a corner. He was paying to be taken to a destination, not to have some soulless AI ask him if he was going anywhere nice that summer.

- *Message received - War Orphans Paradiso wishes to thank you for your continued support…*

"Skip message."

De Fersen was donating ninety percent of his expendable income to charities because it was the right thing to do; not for praise. Nobody needed to know.

The automated car threaded its way along the undulating main road running toward the quaint town center. A soothing hum sounded in De Fersen's ear, alerting him to an incoming call. He glanced up at the accept button in the corner of his field of view, and an image of Isabella, the Officers' Mess hall porter, appeared in a box in the upper left corner of his lens.

"Apologies for bothering you, sir," the synthetic woman began with a smile that combined friendliness with apologies with eerie perfection. "You have a visitor at reception."

"I'm currently outside the wire," De Fersen replied as the hire car took its final turn toward his destination. "Who is it?"

There was a slight pause.

"The gentleman would prefer not to say."

De Fersen rolled his eyes. Some arsehole from HQ, no doubt sent by Eloïse Gerard to take a detailed debrief after the operation. That was scheduled for mid afternoon, and De Fersen saw no reason why he needed to change his plans at zero notice to suit an individual who was six hours ahead of schedule.

"Tell him to make himself comfortable. I'll be back in a few hours."

De Fersen cut off the call as the white car gently slowed down and stopped by a narrow section of pavement. De Fersen winced as his geist alerted him to an inordinate sum of money being transferred from his bank account to 'Gov.Central.Transport.Per.' Shaking his head as he remembered how cheap it was to hire a car twenty years ago, he stepped out of the vehicle and into the blistering sunshine.

The spine tab of De Fersen's red, floral shirt immediately cooled in an attempt to regulate his body's core temperature as he stepped onto the pavement. A progression of blue arrows projected onto his lens to guide him to his rendezvous. He took a breath as for the briefest of moments the arrows triggered a sense of urgency, until he realized that there was no objective marker at the end of the route. Only an old friend.

By Fire and Sword

A long, metallic silver bus crawled past in the light traffic on the broad roadway. De Fersen looked up and saw his own image in the silver alloy, almost comically reflected next to the towering figure of a Hospitaller Knight on an advertisement asking for donations to the Order of St John, projected across the side of the bus. The artificially-generated, idealized knight was a young man in his twenties; tall, broad, handsome, blond hair and blue eyes, a square jaw set in determination, and a look that combined both kindness and strength in his eyes. In that moment of contrast, De Fersen saw himself next to the digital, false knight; a tall, wiry, bald man in his fifties. He unashamedly and unironically wore a red shirt emblazoned with tropical flowers and palm trees that swayed in response to the real world's breeze, detectable only via AR - the style adopted by all of the cool kids in De Fersen's younger days. His lean, hairy legs protruded from beneath beige shorts and ended in broad feet clad within turquoise, thong flip flops. The contrast of the Order's ideal versus the reality elicited a short laugh.

The blue lines guided De Fersen along the pavement to a small, picturesque square dominated by a beautiful fountain of white stone. Surrounding the square was a collection of social venues; cafes, a gymnasium, and a small cinema sat between a hotel and an art gallery. De Fersen trudged wearily up the steps of the closest cafe, wincing irritably as he overheard some turgid conversation between three middle-aged women about their combined disappointment in a local dog grooming parlor.

Konstantinos sat at the far end of a narrow balcony outside the first floor, sunning himself as he lay lazily back across an old-fashioned, white metal chair. He wore trousers of white Solokov linen with a form-fitting t-shirt of sunset peach; a fashion De Fersen remembered from twenty years ago that had now circled back around. The younger man smiled as De Fersen approached.

"You get any sleep?"

"No. You?"

"A couple of hours."

Konstantinos removed his retro-styled, thick rimmed sunglasses and ran a hand through his dark hair as De Fersen sat down opposite him. His geist alerted him to the venue's digital invitation to 'mood music.' He clicked to accept, and a gentle stream of acoustic guitar arpeggios filtered into his ears.

"Nice place you've picked out here," De Fersen remarked, the music briefly attenuating a little with his words. "Very... scenic."

He was immediately aware that, however sincere his words were, his comment sounded bitter and sarcastic. Not the most positive of habits.

"Scenic? You should see this place after sundown."

De Fersen raised an eyebrow.

"What?"

Konstantinos nodded toward the trio of women arguing over dog grooming on the next table.

"As soon as it gets dark, old Ethel, Maud, and Dot over there go crazy. Brawling, knife fights... they're fucking animals. You don't want to be here at night."

De Fersen failed to suppress a gruff chuckle as he connected his geist to the drink menu and ordered a caramel coffee. A carousel in the center of the table gently popped up before sliding forward a cup and nozzle to pour out his drink. Conversation continued gently around them across the sunlit balcony. Cups chinked against saucers. Birds cawed gently overhead. For the first time in days, De Fersen felt tired.

"How are your lot doing?" Konstantinos asked quietly, his face serious again. "Your team seemed... pretty low on experience."

De Fersen made a few brief selections on his comlog to control the privacy settings of their table before replying. He mused briefly on the loss of Tocci, Kormea, and Poddar. If he was honest with himself, they were all people he barely knew; and with decades of fighting behind him, the loss of subordinates was less impactful than it once was. That in itself was perhaps more tragic.

"They're alright. Anja Nilsson is stable. They're hoping to discharge her and send her over here tomorrow. Darius Stanescu is my main concern. Typical freshly-graduated doctor. A fine physician. Not a good soldier."

Konstantinos winced.

"More common than not, though. For an Order doctor, I mean. It takes a certain mindset to drive an individual toward a life of trying to help others in need. And then they come to us, we often end up giving them half the training of other knights because we're so desperate to get doctors out in the field, we put a gun in their hands and then always wonder why it takes them so long to get their shit together."

"He volunteered for this shit!" De Fersen grumbled.

Konstantinos leant forward, meeting De Fersen's stare evenly.

"We all did. And all the training in the world doesn't prepare you for the first time you know deep down that it is for real. That first..."

"Oh, spare me!" De Fersen waved a hand dismissively. "You sound like you're spouting some shit dialogue from one of that prick Mendoza's movies! I didn't come apart in my first firefight. Not one bit."

"That's because you're a complete arsehole."

"That, we can agree on. This coffee is too mild."

Konstantinos exhaled and shook his head slowly.

"And Hawkins? I take it you're going to completely ignore the ninety five percent exceptional performance he gave in driving forward that attack and killing a lot of Morats, and you're just going to shout at him for the mistake he made with the explosive charges?"

"*Putain!*" De Fersen coughed on another mouthful of the sickly sweet coffee. "We've given him ORC armor and a state of the art gun and sword! Killing is the easy bit! We went there to blow up a depot, not swat a few aliens with a sharpened stick!"

Konstantinos slowly folded his arms across his chest and leaned back, his disapproving eyes boring into De Fersen's skull. It should not have had any effect; De Fersen was nearly old enough to be the Indigo soldier's father, and the rank difference was significant. But none of that mattered. Konstantinos had proved himself in combat for over a decade. He commanded respect. De Fersen let out a breath, his shoulders dropping.

"Kyle's a good lad. He's an idiot sometimes, but he's a good lad. They would have kicked him out of training after that ND on the firing range - the second one - if I hadn't stepped in. I'm glad I did. He's... there's something different about him. He's a wildcard. Like you and I."

"I spoke to him on the journey back," Konstantinos said. "Anyhow, we're meeting up tomorrow to go a couple of rounds. From what I hear, I'm in for a kicking. But I reckon I can still teach him a thing or two."

"I don't doubt it," De Fersen agreed, sampling another half mouthful of the disappointing coffee.

He saw Konstantinos's face drop a little as his eyes tracked something down below, on the street behind De Fersen. The old soldier's pulse raised for a second in response to the brief cue. He glanced over his shoulder but saw nothing other than the mundane regularities of daily life for civilians in a quiet, PanOceanian town. Then his eyes came to rest on a young couple, a man and a woman in their early twenties, walking through the square hand-in-hand. He looked back up at Konstantinos. The younger man glanced back up, his smile returning.

De Fersen knew himself well enough to not even attempt to ask how Konstantinos was. How he coped. For years, now. The grim resolve and fearless determination he demonstrated under fire was not about serving God. Yes, it was clear that he believed in God and that Jesus was his son, but that was not what drove him to excel. It was all for her. Niki, the girl who died after a Haqqislamite Hassassin sabotaged a factory, and the Emergency Response Team failed to arrive in time to deliver medical aid to the casualties. An ERT transported in a lunar roverplane that Konstantinos was driving. Anybody could have forgiven him for the error in judgment he made that led to the crash, knowing that he alone was responsible for getting the medical team to the site where his girlfriend lay dying. But Konstantinos certainly never forgave himself. Years later, here he was, still fighting and still risking his life to save up the points for Niki's Resurrection Permit.

A rooftop advertisement on the other side of the square - a tasteful and subtle construct of smooth, white alloy and a lens receptor - changed from announcing the latest series of 'Nubies' on MayaKids to another call to donate to the Order of St John. The image faded from the colorful, animated sort-of-axolotls to Joan of Arc stood victoriously - and perhaps just a touch salaciously - with sword and banner in hand atop a hill littered with the debris of battle.

"Here we go," Konstantinos sighed.

"What?"

"You grunted."

"No, I didn't."

"You saw a picture of Joan, and you grunted. This, again."

De Fersen swore under his breath and rolled his eyes.

"Look. I've known her for years. I've worked with her, been on countless ops, and I've never had a problem with her. I've been pretty open about this. I just query the thought process behind how she was manufactured, that's all."

The younger soldier muttered something in his native tongue and prodded his comlog to order another drink.

"Manufactured?" he repeated. "She's not a bloody REM! ALEPH knew what it was doing when it created her. PanOceania is intertwined with the Church; Joan of Arc is one of history's most inspiring figures. Seems a pretty good idea to me to synthetically recreate a modern version to bring us all together in the common goal of kicking murdering aliens off our land."

"Right, first off... Joan of Arc was French. That's *my* heritage, you Grecian dickhead! Not the Church's! The real Joan was famous for kicking the English out of France, not for fighting aliens! Second, the real Joan was a short, muscular, plain-faced young woman with short, dark hair who never wielded a sword in anger in her life! Not once! Waved a banner bravely at many a battle and risked her life for a noble cause, but never killed anybody.

"So, explain to me the thought process behind why we take historical fact - a plain-faced, non-combative brunette - and thought, 'let's make a slim blonde and make her awesome with guns, and, ooh, how about even just a tiny bit sexy! Because that's apparently what the modern Church wants to associate itself with!' I like Joan, she's a good woman. What I don't like is the marketing bullshit behind her creation. It's not fair on her, and it's twisting *my* history! The Order's marketing... have you *seen* how many different toys and models of her you can buy?"

Konstantinos grabbed a chilled bottle of beer from the table's center carousel and cracked off the lid.

"I know you're always civil to her in person," he said, "and with that in mind, I dread to think about what you say about me behind my back."

"Oh, that's easy. I'll say it to your face. You're an overconfident, glory-seeking twat who cares too much about his hair."

"Yeah. That we can agree on. You want a beer?"

"Yeah, alright."

***

Compartmentalization had not been an issue for years. That vital skill of mentally packing up issues that were not relevant to the moment - issues that were actually distracting - and shove them to one side for later. Cortez remembered Johnny Lois grabbing her by the shoulder on the rooftop overlooking the Morat depot, bringing her back to the task in hand and away from her domestic woes. Only amateurs needed that. It was an embarrassment.

The regular, light tap of her feet atop the concrete path just inside the sandy beach accompanied the hammering of dance music as Cortez entered the third mile of her early morning jog. A few venues were opening up now; surf hire shacks, cafes, and yogurt bars. Another jogger heading in the opposite direction approached Cortez rapidly; a tall man, perhaps a decade older than her. He flashed a comradely smile to the fellow jogger as he passed. Cortez could not find the energy or enthusiasm to return the simple act of civility.

The track in her earpieces changed to 'Last Summer,' a song she remembered from night clubs she used to sneak into with her brothers as an underaged teen. With an irritated exhalation, she tapped her wrist to cancel the audio. Now only the gentle crash of waves to her left and the light buzz of traffic to her right accompanied the rhythmic thumping of her feet on the hot tarmac.

She had lost nobody. The thought came around again as Cortez rounded a corner and picked up the pace in between a sleek, white harbor office complex and a row of jetties with beautiful, expensive looking yachts that sparkled in the low sun. All three Crosiers made it home. Lieutenant Moreno, her platoon commander, had remarked on that in the quick debrief she had as soon as she arrived at Hartberg two days ago. Two dead Order sergeants with a third critically wounded. A dead knight with a second wounded. But the little Crosiers with their entry-level equipment and brief training package, they all came home. When Moreno pointed it out - as a compliment to Cortez's leadership -

he immediately apologized afterward. It was not a contest. They were all one team. Yet the thought had crossed her mind several times already.

A calendar reminder flashed across Cortez's lens as she left the harbor behind and ran uphill toward a sandstone cliff cutting into the clear water. Church service at midday. The Crosiers had taken her under their wing, and she needed to try harder with her faith. Just believing was not enough anymore. She needed to give back to God, to prove that faith was a part of her life instead of just putting a cross on her wall and going to church at Easter and Christmas.

Were all of these things just distractions? The music reminding her of her three brothers, the successes and failures of Operation Aphek, the need to be a better Christian... were these all thoughts she was cramming into her head to avoid facing the fact that her engagement to Owen was over because he did not want children, and she did? They had both been honest and open when things became serious. They both admitted that, looking to the future, they did not really have any strong feelings either way and that was just one more reason they were so compatible. Then he asked the question, she said yes, four months passed, she said she had decided that now she did want children one day, and he was suddenly adamant that he did not.

Another message mercifully scrolled across her lens to rescue her from her thoughts.

- *Marianna?! Marianna Cortez?! From school? You're here in Hartberg? I haven't seen you in years!*

Cortez narrowed her eyes. She checked the recipient and saw that the sender was part of a long, long dormant social group on her geist. San Juan Primary School, Bacala.

- *It's Mia Ruiz. Well, Mia Giordano now. We were at school together. My geist told me that you just jogged right past my office!*

Cortez slowed to a halt on the neat pavement. Her breathing labored, sweat dripping down her face, she leaned over to prop her hands on her hips as she pondered the messages. The waves cascaded across the thin stretch of beach to her right as a middle-aged couple walked their dog across the sand. Gulls continued to caw over her head. The smell of something decidedly unhealthy wafted across from a food vendor to her left as the trader opened her venue's shutters. The war - something she was up to her elbows in only two days ago - seemed so far away.

Cortez remembered Ruiz - now Giordano - well enough. As with the overwhelming majority of Human Sphere citizens, most of Cortez's schooling was carried out online. She remembered her parents both saying that practically their entire education was delivered this way, but changes in education policy over concerns regarding the lack of social development in children now meant that it was mandated for some classes to be conducted face to face.

Giordano had been a relatively loud child - not obnoxious or malicious, just believing herself to be a lot more humorous than she actually was. That, of course, was entirely forgivable in hindsight. Cortez had not seen her since they were eleven years old and moved on to different secondary schools on Neoterra. Now, two decades later and on a different planet, they were somehow within walking distance of each other. Cortez clicked on her geist.

- *Yeah, it's me. Where are you?*

- *Just on my way to you now!*

Her breathing gradually slowing back toward normality, Cortez turned her back on the sun and cycled through her geist menus. Still logged into the old primary school social page. As highly, highly unlikely as it was, that small lapse in personal security could have left her exposed to an encounter far more problematic than this. That was sloppy. Cortez brought up a map of the area and connected it to her conversation with Giordano. Sure enough, a personalized pink mermaid emblem that instantly made Cortez cringe moved steadily across the map, toward her from the north.

Within minutes, a figure that could only be Giordano appeared from an alleyway at the end of the harbor complex and hurried toward Cortez. Giordano was a little shorter than average, a little broader in the hips and the shoulder, and had a wide smile that lit up a face largely hidden behind an eyeshadow that was far too neon, but which matched her ostentatious attire. Giordano squealed in delight on setting eyes on Cortez, and she hurtled over with her arms outstretched. Cortez took a step back instinctively and held up her hands.

"I... I've been running... I'm covered in..."

"Don't care! Don't care!" Giordano yelled before hauling Cortez in for an awkward embrace.

She stepped back and looked her old classmate up and down.

"Mari! Look at you! You haven't changed a bit! You still do your hair the same! My gosh! Look at your arms! You look like you could deck a horse! It's so good to see you!"

Cortez nodded slowly, partially embarrassed by the looks of the few locals passing close by at the noisy reunion, but also appreciative of the effort of her old classmate. Giordano, for her part, had changed. Cortez would not have recognized her if they had passed by. Sure, the face was a logical maturing from what she remembered. But it had been nearly twenty years.

"So... what do you do here?" she ventured.

"I work just up the road! Got married straight out of school. Frank, my husband, he runs three fishing boats out in the bay here. We've got two kids - Ezra and Leeane - they're both old enough for school now so I work just over there for a maritime insurance company."

Cortez accepted the double tap on her geist and was instantly flooded with a barrage of family pictures from Giordano. An older man with a graying beard. A son whose mischievous face - very similar to Giordano's as a child - marked him out as trouble. A daughter with a tragically similar taste in fashion to her mother.

"How about you? What brings you all the way to sleepy old Hartberg? You're not up at the base, are you? I spoke to Dana about ten years ago. She said you'd joined the army or something?!"

"Yeah, I'm at the base. I'm not in the army. Not anymore. I joined up straight out of school, but I left the regular PMC about eighteen months ago."

Giordano's eyes opened wide.

"You were a soldier? That makes so much sense! D'you remember that time you gave Greg Novak a black eye because he was picking on me?"

"No, I don't remember that..." Cortez began truthfully.

"You were always in scraps! I bet you were a good soldier! What did you do? What title did you have?"

"I was a Fusilier. A sergeant."

"What's that?"

"Light infantry."

"Is sergeant high up? Did people have to salute you?"

Cortez took a slow breath. She noticed that her fists were clenched, so she took a moment to uncurl her fingers and calmly compose her thoughts.

"Sergeant is... a rank. It's pretty normal for somebody who had done as many years as I had. Not bad, not great. And no, people didn't salute me."

Giordano nodded, her seemingly permanent grin still tugging at both sides of her happy face.

"So what are you doing now? If you're up at the base, I guess you're a contractor or something?"

"Military Orders. I transferred across from the army to the Neo-Vatican military."

Somehow Giordano managed to open her eyes even wider as her jaw dropped theatrically.

"You're a knight?! Like in the Mendoza movies?! Oh... my... God! Oh! Sorry, I didn't mean to say 'God' like that, I know you lot are..."

"I'm not a knight," Cortez cut in, finding herself working harder still to keep her tone amiable, "I'm in the Coadjutor Crosiers. A sergeant. Direct transfer. I'm doing the same job, just for the Church instead of for the government. Still a soldier."

The shorter woman frantically prodded away at her comlog with the fluency and rapidity of an individual who spent more time connected to Maya than was perhaps healthy.

"There! I've taken the day off work! C'mon, I'll buy you breakfast! I know a great place just down..."

Cortez took another step back and shook her head.

"I... I can't. I've got a debrief in a few hours, I need to have a wash, I can't go to breakfast dressed like this, and..."

Giordano waved her hands frantically.

"No, no, no. I insist. It's been twenty years! C'mon. You said it yourself, you've got a few hours. And nobody will care about how you are dressed. They'll all just be checking out your arms! C'mon, breakfast."

Cortez watched the chirpy woman, the complete stranger that a half-forgotten childhood acquaintance had become, walk quickly away. With a shrug and another long breath, she followed her.

Chapter Thirteen

The children's choir harmoniously built up to the crescendo of the song; not one of the twenty singers even a semitone off key. The two rows of children, resplendent in their dark blue blazers and matching ties, ended on a perfect high 'E,' sustained for a full bar without wavering. The assembled visitors issued a polite round of applause that echoed around the wood-paneled school hall as the thin headteacher strutted proudly out to the front of the stage.

"As you can see, the potential we unlock in each and every one of our students is not constrained merely to sciences. Far from it. Although we are a scientific academy, pursuit of the arts is…"

From where he sat on the back row of the school hall, Darius leaned in close to his father and grasped his hand. The big man looked down and threw him a lopsided smile. The ten-year old looked forward again to the rows of perfectly dressed, seemingly emotionless children who remained seated, as still and fearless as if on parade, on stage in front of a crowd of some two hundred prospective students and their parents.

"Dad," Darius whispered, "I don't think this place is for me."

The burly soldier leaned back over to his son.

"Whad'ya mean?" he whispered.

"I… this place… I… these children all seem so… clever… I'll never pass the entrance exams. I… I don't think this school is for me."

As the headteacher droned on, quoting statistics and policy that Darius did not understand, he saw his father wince uncomfortably. The big man tilted his head closer.

"Never pass? Like, you're not clever enough for this place? Not good enough? Don't think like that. I mean… look at that loser on the front row of the choir. That ugly kid with the stupid face. You think he's better than you?"

Darius stifled a laugh and immediately felt guilt rise up.

"Dad! Don't say things like that! You can't talk about people like that, especially not kids!"

"Bullshit! Look at that girl next to him! The one with the stupid hair! Is that a mullet? You're telling me that you think mullet-girl is cleverer than you?"

Darius laughed again. Another father on the row in front of them turned to admonish the pair over the noise. The look of thunder that Darius's father shot at the man encouraged him to immediately turn and face the front again. The soldier wrapped an arm around his son's shoulders.

"Don't think that you're not good enough. Don't give up. Failure? Yeah, that'll happen sometimes. But never give up. Never think you're not good enough when you haven't even tried. You're good enough for this place. You're good enough to be anything you want to be, if you try hard enough."

That year, the academy was oversubscribed with entrants. Darius never found out if he was good enough. With so many applicants, he was not even given a chance to sit the entrance exams. Instead, he settled for a state school place alongside his primary school friends; a less prestigious school with less impressive exam averages. His father encouraged and supported him every step of the way. Seven years later, he graduated top of his class and secured a place at medical school.

The view out of the narrow corridor's two windows presented the coastline of the Fairbanks Sea in perhaps its best light. A long beach of white sand, with small clusters of tiny islands within swimming distance of the sea's edge, each a unique and scenic piece of paradise covered in bright flowers that seemed as if they had been deliberately draped over the sandstone rocks rather than growing naturally. Stanescu watched as a large yacht he could never even dream of affording came to a gentle halt by one cluster of islands, dropped anchor, and then lowered two jetskis from its quarterdeck.

A door at the far end of the corridor opened. Stanescu looked up from his seat to see Hawkins walk slowly across, the light wooden floorboards beneath his feet creaking. Hawkins was clothed in his working uniform, as was Stanescu; black trousers and hip length battledress jacket of black atop a white shirt and black tie, with rank on the shoulder epaulets and the cross of St John on the upper sleeve. Stanescu tapped his comlog and nodded at one of the other doors along the short corridor.

"You're cutting it a bit fine, aren't you?"

The younger knight sat down on one of the other cheap, uncomfortable chairs that lined one side of the corridor.

"I lost track of time. I was in the chapel."

"Right."

That came as no surprise. Stanescu had exchanged a few brief text messages with Hawkins since they returned. The younger soldier had not said much, but it was clear enough that those who had not survived the op were at the forefront of his mind. The two sat in silence for some moments as colorful birds lining the branches of the bright trees outside the open window sang in the late morning sun.

"Do you ever think about school?" Stanescu asked. "Childhood?"

"Not a great deal," Hawkins replied quietly. "I'm sort of… glad it's in the past, really. Why do you ask?"

Stanescu paused. He had shared a great deal about his upbringing with Hawkins during their basic training, so none of it would come as any great shock.

"Just thinking about my dad. How he got me here. I…"

I let him down.

That part, Stanescu found himself unable to verbalize. His father was a great soldier - that much he knew from what his father's oldest friends told him at the funeral.

"What did you do at school?" Stanescu dragged his mind away from the hurdle he could not mentally jump. "Sport, I mean? I know you were the best at all of that in training. Were you a football guy?"

"No," Hawkins replied, his voice barely more than a whisper, "cricket in summer. Rugby in winter. I was a flanker. Cross country running, kendo, and shotokan karate all year round, too. Never really liked team sports, which probably says a lot about me. It was always martial arts for me."

"Oh! I did cross country, too!" Stanescu smiled, relieved that a sport he actually understood had finally been mentioned. "I was my team captain. I guess you were, too?"

"Oh, no. They never trusted me with leadership or inspiring others or anything like that. I was a pace bowler; I opened for the college. Got the most wickets for two years running. Likewise, I scored the most tries out of any of the forwards. But it was kendo and karate that I competed in at the higher levels. I suppose I was a star player in the team sports. But never a leader."

The despondency in his friend's tone caused Stanescu to turn and face him. When Tocci died, it was Hawkins that pushed them both forward. It was Hawkins that fought the gargantuan Morat to give Stanescu time to tend to Nilsson's wounds. It was Hawkins that carried on alone and planted the bombs when Stanescu wanted to leave with his patient. He opened his mouth to offer something positive, but a door at the other end of the corridor creaked open. He looked up and saw De Fersen, clad in his black working uniform, stood at the entrance to his temporary office.

"Sub Officer Hawkins. Get in here. Don't sit down."

Stanescu tried his best to offer a smile of support and encouragement as his friend stood and walked over to the office. Stanescu knew he was next in line for De Fersen's wrath. As the office door closed, he tried and failed to shift his thoughts back to the picturesque yacht near the horizon.

***

The relentless sunshine poured in through the office window, at odds with the cold air pumped out of the atmospheric control vents. A functional office; desk, chair, large potted plant in the corner, briefing screens, and communication terminal. Somebody had thought to change the default image displayed on the office's sole picture frame to a dramatic painting of the Knight Hospitallers' valiant defense of Malta against the Ottomans in 1565, no doubt in anticipation of De Fersen using the office for the foreseeable future. He paced slowly behind the young knight, his arms folded across his chest and his head bowed in thought.

"Let's sum all of that up," De Fersen said. "You know the pass rate for selection as a Knight Hospitaller is amongst the lowest of any force in the entire Human Sphere. The four years of training that follow see even more people fail. You not only graduated top of your class in all aspects of melee combat, you actually scored the highest grades in over a decade. You were top physically, top quartile in marksmanship, and even came mid-pack in academics. Graduating as a knight gives you a civilian accredited degree in theology. An elite soldier with a commendable intellect."

That was, of course, only half the story. But it was the half that supported De Fersen's current agenda. Hawkins stood to attention, staring ahead at the digitally displayed image of the Siege of Malta behind De Fersen's desk. The aging knight noticed something in his stance; something different. The slumped shoulders of defeat he had seen in him before; the tense posture of fear, too. But not this. There was almost... a slouch.

"So explain to me," he thundered, spinning on the spot, "how an elite soldier of the NeoVatican with a degree-level education fails to blow up a fucking warehouse full of bombs! You were issued with charges! You were trained to use them! What the hell happened?!"

Hawkins's head tilted a little to one side. De Fersen considered screaming at him to stand up straight but was more interested to see how far the attitude would go.

"I planted the charges on an explosive container that was in a non-volatile state, sir," he replied.

Calmly. Quietly.

"You planted them on a container filled with a stable compound... that is only half of a two part explosive material. Inert. Dormant. As was clearly marked in big, fucking red symbols all over the container!"

"Apologies, sir, my Morat storage container label recognition is a little rusty."

De Fersen darted over to stand by Hawkins's side, shoving his face into the younger knight's space.

"Don't get funny with me, you petulant little shit! The Black Friars and the Trinitarians work around the fucking clock to provide us with software updates detailing all of the latest intelligence we need to fight our enemies! Those symbols were one click on a comlog away from being highlighted on your lens! One click! Hell! Even an idiot would have thought to plant their charges on separate containers, just in case one was inert! But no, the same moron who negligently discharged a weapon with live ammunition during training - on *three* occasions! - thought it best to plant his charges on the explosive equivalent of a crate of potatoes!"

Hawkins continued to stare ahead. His eyes narrowed just a little. De Fersen strode around to the front of his desk.

"I'm canceling your post operation leave. Rather than two weeks at home, you'll be staying here for a one week basic explosive awareness course while I think of an appropriate way to waste your second week, the way you nearly wasted the rest of your team with your utter stupidity. I'll probably have you carry a plant around for a week so you can start replacing the oxygen you've been wasting. You're a knight, a commissioned officer of this Order, and you are supposed to be a leader of fighting men and women. You are consistently failing to demonstrate that to me. Your course starts tomorrow. You're dismissed."

Hawkins turned smartly to his right and stamped his foot in place to acknowledge the dismissal before leaving the office without a word. De Fersen considered denying him attendance at the memorial service for the four soldiers killed on their part in Operation Aphek but decided that that was perhaps a step too far. He was actually a good soldier. From the post-op analysis of the lens footage, it was Hawkins who pushed forward after Tocci died, and Stanescu consistently wanted to hold position to deal with casualties. He was good. But if he was pushed hard enough to snap and stop being the 'nice guy,' he could be excellent.

The thought of the memorial service reminded De Fersen of the job he was only halfway through; the next of kin letters for those who had been killed on the op. Tocci was next, and that was proving to be a problem. An orphan with no living relative on file, she had committed herself wholly to the Order. And now? Her Cube would have been vaporized in the explosion at the depot. Now all she was was a name on a memorial in Skovorodino. And a soul in Heaven. De Fersen needed to believe that.

De Fersen was interrupted from his thoughts by a hum in his ear as he received a call from Isabella, the Officers' Mess hall porter.

"Apologies for bothering you, sir. You have a visitor at reception."

"Not now!" De Fersen snapped. "The debrief is already scheduled for this afternoon! Tell them that! I'm not changing the timings now!"

De Fersen terminated the call, immediately hoping that it was not Grand Master Gerard, who he had been warned was traveling to Hartberg to take the debrief in person. Well, if it was her he had just refused to meet, he would be made aware of that soon enough. Back to the matter in hand. De Fersen walked across the office and opened the door. In the corridor outside, Hawkins and Stanescu both turned to face him in silence. De Fersen nodded at the doctor.

"Come on. In here."

Stanescu walked briskly inside the office and stood to attention in front of the desk.

"Never mind that. Sit down," De Fersen said curtly, closing the door and taking a seat behind his desk.

The doctor looked across at him but said nothing.

"How do you think it went?" De Fersen began. "Your performance during the operation?"

"My performance was unacceptable, sir. Terrible."

De Fersen nodded grimly. The falling on the sword technique. A time honored classic tactic to hit yourself hard at the first opportunity so there is nothing left for your commander to reprimand with.

"When we were attacked by the Morat patrol shortly after arriving, I don't recall any problems," De Fersen countered. "For a first time under fire, you remained calm. You dealt with our casualties with efficiency."

"I don't even remember firing my weapon, sir. And it's the second encounter that is the problem. At the depot. I froze, the post-op analysis showed that my firing accuracy was poor, I attempted to prioritize Cube recovery over our objective, I... my performance was even worse than that first firefight! I... I think that it must have been that I had longer to think, longer to mull over it all, whereas that first time it was just on us and it just happened and..."

De Fersen held up a hand to silence the anguished young knight's seemingly ceaseless verbal self-flagellation.

"Let me put it in perspective," he said, at least some effort forced into keeping his tone soft, "because I've been doing this since around about the time you were born. First and foremost, you stood your ground. You never retreated. Second, you killed enemy soldiers. Even with the most extensive training and best equipment in the Sphere, that's difficult. When it's for real for the first time. Especially when you're the sort of person who slogged themselves for years at medical school because your head is wired to want to help people, not shoot them."

De Fersen felt a pang of guilt for his low-level dishonesty; for twisting the same argument regarding the ease of killing with top grade weapons one way for Hawkins, and then the other for the doctor. Stanescu shook his head, his face suddenly contorted aggressively.

"No, no, no! I've got no problem killing these fucking animals! I saw what they did firsthand! I saw it! What I saw when I was a missionary is what drove me to join this Order! I've been waiting a long time to get back at these bastards! First time you put me in combat against other humans? Sure, I can already see how that might be a problem. But these pieces of shit? I have no moral problem with what we're doing here. Doctor or not."

"Then what is it?" De Fersen asked.

He was all but certain he knew the answer. This was a well-trodded path. Stanescu looked to one side, leaning forward to interlink his fingers. He turned to meet De Fersen's gaze again after a few moments.

"It's... unnatural. It doesn't make sense to me. I've spent four years in medical school and a year practicing. Half a decade of prioritizing the patient. The Order gave me two years of combat training where everybody else gets four, yet the same standard is demanded from me on graduation. So now I have two years of training in how to kill. And now I look up to find bullets flying over my head, dying comrades at my feet, enemy soldiers ahead, a gun in one hand, a medikit in the other... If I have to make a choice, I'll go for the medikit. Every time. If there is somebody else there who can keep the enemy busy, then I'll be a doctor. Because we can all shoot, but I'm the only one who can deal with casualties."

De Fersen leaned back in his chair and folded his arms.

"I agree. So, what's the problem?"

"The problem?!" Stanescu jutted out his bearded chin. "The problem is that I ended up running around after Kyle like a clueless idiot! I wasn't a knight out there, I was a bloody space cadet! If it wasn't for the fact I have a return of service to work off, I'd honestly be considering resigning my commission, I'm so poorly suited to this!"

De Fersen narrowed his eyes in concentration.

"And do you think Sergeant Nilsson would agree with that?"

There was no answer. De Fersen continued.

"She's been discharged from hospital and is on a flight across to us as we speak. Perhaps you can ask her yourself. Look, Darius. The fighting arm of this Order is on the bones of its arse for doctors. We don't have the time or resources to train our own from scratch, so we rely on qualified doctors coming to us. Normally from other areas of the Order, but sometimes - like you - from the public healthcare service. Either way, we can't train you and people like you for four years. We need you in the field quicker. That's why we rush you through in two. Practically all of you. And that's why... we turn a blind eye to elements of your final test scores that we deem to be... non-essential."

Stanescu's eyes widened.

"You mean... I failed training? I didn't make the grade?"

"You made the grade for a doctor on a shortened training package. That syllabus was cut in half for emergency purposes. It's now as good as steady state for doctors. So stop putting all of this pressure on yourself and lower your expectations. You're as good as any doctor I've seen straight out of training. It'll just take a bit more time before you have the combat experience to catch up on the shortfalls in your training."

"Which is very easy for you to say, sir," Stanescu snapped. "You're not the idiot who only managed to graduate due to standards being lowered and people looking the other way on exam day!"

De Fersen let out a laugh and then immediately held up a hand to stop Stanescu's angry response.

"Darius - we need doctors. So we get you to a basic standard - basic by the standards of the most elite fighting unit in the Human Sphere. And as an aside... I understand how you feel about this. Perhaps more than you think. I graduated from my training with a combat enhancement implant. And it's not a cheap, entry level model."

Stanescu sat bolt upright in his chair.

"You... you were failing at training?"

De Fersen grinned.

"No. Not at all. The Order didn't pay for my implant. I did. I had it fitted *before* training. So, in that respect, I went into training with a hugely unfair advantage. But the Templars didn't seem to care. Either way, I graduated training with that same feeling of...wondering whether I passed out fairly or because of blind eyes being turned."

"Where did you get the money from? If you have enough money for things like a combat implant, do you even need to be doing this?"

De Fersen smiled.

"You're not the only one who had a life and a skill set before joining the Order. And no, I don't need to be doing this. But... and I am not a man prone to melodrama, so believe me when I say this... I'm here because I believe God called me to be here. This is God's will. You and I are called to this."

The office fell silent. The whine of high-powered engines droned outside the window as a powerboat swept by on the clear, calm waters of the Fairbanks Sea. De Fersen stood and took a step over to the window, watching the vessel dart across the gentle waves. He turned back to Stanescu.

"That's all I wanted to say to you. To let you know that you are meeting the standard. You're doing alright. So stop torturing yourself. Believe me, I don't shy away from telling my soldiers if they're not up to standard. If you weren't, you'd know. I assure you."

Stanescu nodded and stood. He paused for a moment before speaking again.

"So, what now, sir?"

De Fersen sat on the window sill and folded his arms.

"Now? I'll take the debrief with the Grand Master this afternoon. I'll let you know what the fallout is. You? If I were you, I'd compartmentalize all of this. Box it up and put it to one side. Get some of the others together. Go out and have a few drinks. But not too many. I mean that."

Stanescu nodded.

"Yes, sir. And thank you."

De Fersen waved the awkward compliment away and turned to watch the powerboat again as Stanescu left his office.

***

The horizon burned beneath a blood red sky. The crumbled walls of the cathedral still stood in parts, a valiant symbol of defiance against the the cruel, relentless advance of the murderous alien warriors of the Evolved Intelligence's Combined Army. The black clouds in the scarlet sky parted, just enough to allow a shining pillar of heavenly light down across the cathedral tower's cross, through the shattered roof and to the cracked altar.

Father-Inquisitor Mendoza knelt in front of the altar, one hand grasping the handle of his six foot long sword, dug into the stone by his knee, while the other clutched tightly to the lifeless hand of the beautiful, freshly qualified, and now dead knight who lay serenely across the marble. The light plunging through the dark clouds lit up Mendoza's noble face, casting shadows across his strong cheekbones, broad stubbled jaw, and artistically customized heavy armor. The flames outside illuminated the shattered stained glass windows, painting the stone floors and oaken pews inside the cathedral with shimmering shades of reds, blues, and greens. Mendoza looked up at the heavens and cried out in anguish.

"Why, God?! Why did you take her? You should have taken me!"

"Oh, fucking hell," Cortez sniggered.

Giordano shot her a severe look from her seat.

"My brothers!" Mendoza cried out, one shaking fist held up in front of his face. "My sisters! The vile foe bathes in their blood! Yet we will not stop! We will never stop! The glory of God shines down on us! We are chosen! We are righteous!"

Cortez's snigger erupted into a full blown laugh. Giordano scowled at her, tears of raw emotion streaming down her cheeks.

"You're ruining it!"

"I can't ruin it any more than that prick's over-acting! Or the script writer, for that matter!"

Heavy footsteps echoed across the cathedral behind Mendoza. The hulking warrior turned slowly to look over his shoulder. Behind him stood six Morat warriors, their red armor adorned with goats' heads and trident symbols. Mendoza slowly stood. The Morats waited in silence. He turned to face them.

"You dare... you dare defile the house of the Lord with your presence?!"

Mendoza paced slowly down the cathedral's central aisle, his huge sword held in front of him in both hands. The Morats watched him in silence. With a blood-curdling yell, Mendoza sprinted out to face them.

"For PanOceania!"

The first Morat lunged forward, but Mendoza cut the vile alien neatly in half at the waist. A second stepped out, but a hammerfist blow from Mendoza crushed the warrior's skull in a fountain of blood. The third warrior took a pace forward, only to have Mendoza plunge his fist straight through the alien's chestplate to emerge out of his back. Then, with a demonstration of the tactical astuteness the Morats were notorious for, two of the alien warriors rushed him simultaneously. Twirling in place gracefully, Mendoza span around and lashed out his sword to decapitate them both neatly with the same blow. Both Morats remained stood, fountaining blood, before sagging down to their knees and pitching forward at the same time.

The final Morat let out a splutter of panic, crying out in sheer fright and backing away as his terrified eyes searched frantically for an avenue of escape. Mendoza thrust a fist forward to grab him by the neck. With one hand, he effortlessly lifted the armored bulk of the Morat warrior clean off his feet, holding the struggling alien aloft. Mendoza let out a long, deep cry of righteous fury. Flames licked up around his wrist. The Morat screamed in pain as the purging fires melted his insides. Flames shot out of his mouth, nostrils and eyeballs as he died a slow, agonizing, but deserved death...

Cortez pressed a finger against her geist to disconnect from the movie. The gothic cathedral and the burning skies faded away, replaced with the clear, white walls of the small cinema booth. She took a few seconds to stop herself from laughing as her old school-friend followed her lead and disconnected from the movie experience. She looked across sympathetically at Cortez.

"I... I'm so sorry. I didn't think. Did that remind you of the war? Did you have to disconnect because of all of the trauma?"

"No. I had to disconnect because it was so shit!"

Giordano's face dropped. The now elegant, plain white room consisting of nothing more than a door, sofa, and holographic movie projector fell silent. Giordano wiped a tear away.

"You must think I'm so stupid."

Cortez's face dropped.

"What?"

The shorter woman stood up.

"This... a movie like this. This is as close as I'll ever get to a war. We don't all have the courage to stomp off to kill aliens like Mendoza does."

Cortez found herself laughing again.

"No! It's nothing like that! You think those bastards stand at the back of churches, wait for you to run over, then calmly take it in turns to run up one by one and get cut in half? Six of those murdering fuckers would have every entrance of that church locked down in seconds and then execute a perfectly timed, coordinated assault with..."

"That's not the point!"

The room fell silent again. Cortez looked up at Giordano uncomfortably.

"That's not the point," she repeated, more quietly as she wiped her eyes again. "I know there's a war on. We all know. But they're not conscripting or anything, so I guess things are going well enough for us or we'd all be in uniform. But... I don't know what's going on over the horizon. I'm here supporting my husband and raising my children. And I'm proud of that. And movies like this might be stupid to you, but they make me emotional, and I don't think it's fair for you to laugh at me, even if you have got arms like tree-trunks and I'm guessing you've actually killed alien soldiers for real at some point."

Cortez nodded and slowly stood. Her cheeks felt hot. The right words did not suddenly present themselves to her. She tried, nonetheless.

"I'm sorry. I'm not laughing at you. And... none of us out there think we're better or stronger or braver than anybody back home. We all do our thing for different reasons. I didn't choose the army so much as I made a complete mess of my exams at the end of school, and the infantry was the best option for me. I tried to get what you've got. I was married. It didn't work out, because I was away from home so often and he didn't wait for me. I tried again recently, and that didn't work out either because... well, I wanted what you've got and he didn't. So no, I don't think I'm better than you. I'd swap with you in a heartbeat."

Giordano fell silent again, her eyes flitting from side to side as she seemingly processed that information. She looked up again, her expression one of sorrow, and opened her mouth to start that same speech Cortez had heard half a dozen times from her parents and her brothers. She held a hand up.

"Don't... it's okay. I'm okay."

Giordano slumped back down again.

"Would... I'm guessing you don't want to watch the rest of this movie?"

Cortez gritted her teeth, frantically searching for a diplomatic excuse to avoid being faced with any more of Mendoza's acting.

"Or..." Giordano shrugged. "I could tell my husband that he's got the kids tonight, and we could go out and get paralytically drunk instead?"

Cortez grinned broadly.

"Yeah. Let's do that instead."

Chapter Fourteen

A pair of automated fishing boats headed out to sea under the high, midday sun. The beach behind them was a little more crowded now, but certainly not to the extent of some of the actual tourist destinations De Fersen had seen over the years. This was just a few dozen people quickly cramming in an hour's sunbathing or swimming before heading back to work for the afternoon. From his vantage point on the sweeping, elegant balcony of the Officers' Mess, De Fersen found himself momentarily envying that simple lifestyle. Vines and crawlers swept across the outside of the balcony, complete with an array of colorful flowers that matched the coverings of the accompanying chairs.

"Overengineered," a familiar voice said from behind him, "no matter where you go, it's the same problem."

De Fersen turned and saw Gerard walking over with a cup and saucer in each hand. He rushed across and took his coffee from her.

"Thank you, ma'am."

The building inside was busy enough now with officers from a dozen regiments heading downstairs for lunch. Gerard, to her credit and in stark contrast to her predecessor, had arrived with no pomp or ceremony. De Fersen could see the Hospitaller Standard flying from the base's flagstaff, to warn all personnel that a high-ranking visitor was present somewhere on the base. These visits would normally involve parades, inspections, tours of the base; Gerard had insisted on none of this. She was purely passing through to speak to one of her subordinates face-to-face. And now, dressed in the same black uniform as De Fersen - lacking any of the braiding or other appendages she was entitled to wear - she carried over his coffee for him.

"Haven't you brought an aide with you to do that sort of thing?" De Fersen asked.

"He's already on a job. I've sent him off to the Underwater Combat Training Unit to make some inquiries. Just an idea I'm toying with. Anyway, overengineering. Did you know that this base has recently had a major catering overhaul that cost enough to keep a Seraph in the field for a month? And now the drinks dispensers have broken down and the contract says they have a full two weeks to get them fixed."

"Military suffers at the hands of poorly written contract shocker," De Fersen chuckled, sipping his coffee.

She was entirely correct, of course. The thought of the Grand Master of one of the most powerful fighting organizations in humanity, spending her valuable time pouring out coffee and hand delivering a cup to a Father-Officer was ludicrous. The double doors to the sunlit balcony opened as two junior officers in combat fatigues walked out. The taller of the two stopped dead in his tracks, eyes open wide as he recognized the rank symbol on Gerard's epaulets.

"Sorry, ma'am! So sorry!" he spluttered, dragging his colleague back into the main building.

Gerard exhaled. De Fersen grinned.

"This is what happens when you turn up somewhere without a visit program. Your humility is causing anarchy."

Gerard pressed her comlog.

"They'll get over it, I'm sure. Anyhow, I don't have long so I'll cut to the chase. You're going to be here for a few days. Not long. You're going back out soon."

An alert scrolled across De Fersen's lens to warn him that Gerard had now isolated the balcony, allowing conversation to continue up to Secret level. De Fersen checked his own security settings before continuing.

"Your part in Op Aphek was a success," Gerard continued. "As you were briefed, it was part of a larger, coordinated series of attacks. Eight out of ten were successful. Not only will the success of Aphek cause significant logistical complications to the EI, it has also shown them that we can and will hit them right in their own back garden. Int reports are already indicating that some enemy units who were rotating through a period of rest are now being used to bolster the defenses on the EI interior on Paradiso."

De Fersen briefly thought on Karayiannis's comments on the Op. That it was part of something bigger. But De Fersen was not supposed to know that.

"Alright. So what's next?"

Gerard cleared her throat and looked down into her cup.

"Next? I'm moving you and your team to Firebase India Two-Five. It's about ten miles north of Damberg. It's not much more than a couple of fields with a TAG hangar and a grass strip runway."

De Fersen took another mouthful of his cheap, instant coffee.

"We're going back in to Moravia, then?"

"That's right. You're going in to blow a hole in that prison your team found, free everybody, and get them home."

De Fersen fought to keep his expression nonchalant. Prisoner of war breaks were the stuff of history books and war movies, not reality. Not when it came to fighting against the EI.

"You don't need me to tell you what we'll need in terms of resources," De Fersen said. "Demolitions, TAGs, combat drops... It'll be worse now that we've alerted them into bolstering their defenses. And, also, how do we even know they haven't moved the prisoners? That's SOP for these bastards. They don't keep their POWs in the same place for long. That's assuming they haven't all been worked to death or executed by now."

Gerard nodded and leaned back against the balcony railing.

"I know, I know. But... we had a rather interesting correspondence from the StateEmpire. You see, one of the Yujingyu soldiers that was freed by your team was a junior officer whose uncle is a prominent politician. This act of... hospitality by your team has gone down rather well. The StateEmpire has provided us with all of the details given by their escaped POWs. So, we know a little bit more about that prison that we otherwise would have."

De Fersen grunted and shook his head.

"No, no. This stinks to high heaven of a set up. The enemy of my enemy is not my friend when we were already enemies. This is just the Yujingyu setting us up for a massacre."

"The same thought crossed my mind. And the collective minds of the PMC general staff, it would appear. The matter has already been investigated by Strategic Security. They've confirmed that the source of the intelligence is legitimate."

"So we're trusting Hexas now?" De Fersen grumbled. "I... this doesn't sound right. Intelligence from the enemy, confirmed by the shadiest of all PMC sources, for us to move against a heavily defended target behind enemy lines, and then face the logistical challenge of somehow getting one or two hundred casualties home?"

Gerard finished her tea and placed her cup down.

"They're mostly our people in there, Gabriele. We owe it to them to bring them home if we can. I've approved Operation Paran, and you'll be leading it."

De Fersen placed his cup down and folded his arms. A small bird chirped away on the rail of the balcony, only a few feet away. The idealistic life of the citizens of Hartberg continued serenely below.

"I'll need more people," De Fersen said, "and more firepower."

"I know. You'll have it. Leave that with me. I know we're taking a big risk with this. We lost eight knights on the various elements of Aphek."

"And several sergeants," De Fersen reminded the Grand Master about the lower ranks.

Gerard raised a disapproving eyebrow.

"I'm well aware of that, Gabe. But knights take four years to train. They are extremely difficult to replace. Crosiers and Sergeants are not. I'm not talking about human beings and lives here; once they're dead and gone, there is nothing I can do about that. That's in God's hands, and I trust in God for their souls. But I need to deliver effect against the enemy with what I have, and there is no room for sentimentality there. So, a knight's life is worth more than a Crosier's or a sergeant's life."

De Fersen exhaled slowly.

"When are we going in?"

Gerard tapped a finger against her comlog, her eyes flitting from side to side as a message came through.

"You won't have anything for a couple of days, at least. Give your people a proper break while you can. I'll be in touch when we have a more detailed plan to discuss. Right. Problems down at the Underwater Combat Training Unit, and my flight leaves in less than two hours. I have to go. Good job with Aphek, Gabe. Make sure your people know that their efforts are appreciated."

A chime in De Fersen's ear announced an incoming voice message.

"Apologies for bothering you, sir. You have a visitor at reception."

De Fersen suppressed a curse. He looked across at the Grand Master.

"How many people did you bring here with you?"

"Three others. I've got one at the UCTU and two on a job outside the wire. Why?"

De Fersen shrugged.

"Just... somebody trying to track me down for a couple of days. I thought it was one of your team. Nevermind. Thanks for the update, ma'am, it's much appreciated. I'll wait out on the order to relocate."

"Speak soon."

De Fersen watched the Grand Master head back inside, a small group of engineering officers on their lunch break instantly parting like the waves of the Red Sea to allow her through.

"On my way," he replied to the hall porter.

De Fersen walked back into the main building, where an open area for social events was lit up by sunshine pouring through skylights above. The large area was surrounded with groups of sofas and tables where officers chatted over post-lunch coffees before returning to work, a few of them watching him and his black uniform with interest as he passed. Down the broad staircase ahead, he saw a handful of figures waiting by the hall porter's desk. Four of them were officers pulling on their blue berets to go back outside and walk to their places of work for the afternoon. One figure was dressed in plain clothes.

An old man in a shabby suit that looked as though it was cut for a larger frame. The man was tall but stooped, with a thick, white mustache that contrasted his thinning hair. He would almost have been a sympathetic looking figure, old and in need, if not for the dark look in his eyes as he watched De Fersen approach. The old man's halo gave away very little. No name, no background, merely a line on De Fersen's lens to confirm that the man held military veteran status.

"Are you the man who has been trying to get hold of me?" De Fersen asked warily as he approached, an uneasy feeling driving him almost to be ready for physical confrontation.

The old man looked up, folded his arms, and smiled. It was not a pleasant smile. That was the point that recognition dawned on De Fersen. The broad face and nose, the thin lips and pale eyes. It had been over thirty years.

"Hello, Gabby."

De Fersen looked across at Trevithick but said nothing. He worked to keep his face expressionless, refusing to give his former colleague and friend the satisfaction of appearing surprised.

"If you had anything friendly to say, I rather imagine that you would have found me sooner." De Fersen sniffed as another couple of officers passed them by to head out of the main entrance, oblivious to the severity of the meeting they blundered past in the foyer. "So what do you want?"

Trevithick took a step forward, clamping his hands at the small of his back.

"Rob's dead. He killed himself last month."

De Fersen let out a breath. Now the surprise was impossible to hide. He swallowed, remembering his first meeting with Gillan, and those last exchanged words in the hospital room in Mauritius, when he was barely out of his teens.

"I'm sorry," De Fersen said quietly, but genuinely.

"Sorry? You did it. You might as well have put a sword through his gut. At least that would have been more honest."

De Fersen rolled his eyes and swore.

"Oh, here we fucking go! *I* did it! *I* was the one who forced him to con millions out of thousands of honest people! To become the king of white-collar crime and dismiss it all out of hand because there was no direct violence involved! Rob made all of those choices! And you knew! You knew all along!"

Trevithick locked his cold eyes on De Fersen. He remained silent for a moment before answering.

"I know, do I? Let me tell you what I know. Rob Gillan plucked you out of failure and obscurity, and gave you friendship and value. He - no, shut your mouth, you ungrateful little shit, I'm still talking. He gave you a job, a home, he paid you for your skills. You took his money and turned your back on him. That night you apparently found God, that night *I* rescued you from drowning. You blew all that money on a combat implant that has gotten you where you are today. You stand here as some sort of heroic soldier-of-God, whose success is based solely, *solely* on the money you took from Rob Gillan."

De Fersen coughed out a laugh of sheer derision.

"So that's you," Trevithick continued, "but let's talk about Rob. A self-made man who ended up with a ten year prison sentence based on evidence given from a source who was not named at court. A source I am entirely sure was you. Rob was released after seven years on good behavior - because he was a good man. With his connections burned, his name in tatters, and his fortune gone, he spent the next two decades trying and failing to drag himself up out of the gutter. I stood by him. I helped him. I offered to find you for him. But Rob would have none of it. 'Gabby did what he thought was best. Leave Gabby alone.' That's what Rob insisted."

De Fersen clenched his fists, his jaw clamped shut and his eyes narrowed as he glared at the old man.

"What do you want from me?" he spat. "You want me to say I'm sorry for what I did? I'm not. The pair of you dragged me into something I didn't understand. And when I realized what we were, I told you both face to face. I told you both, and I walked away. And when I had my back against a wall, years later, and I *had* to tell the truth…"

Trevithick held up a hand.

"Save it. I don't care. Rob made you all that you are, and now you're a war hero and he's dead after you destroyed his life. It's that simple. He told me to leave you alone. But he's gone now. So here I am. To tell you face to face - to have the spine to look you in the eye while I do it, the spine you never had - that I don't forgive you. That this isn't over. And that now Rob is gone, I don't see the need to leave you alone."

De Fersen took another step forward, folding his arms across his chest, his eyes still locked on the former soldier stood before him.

"You've come here to threaten me? Like some cheap gangster in a shitty movie? Grow up, you idiot. You can't touch me. You think that after three decades of fighting, that I can't protect myself? That with my connections, I can't make one call to find out everything about you?"

Trevithick shook his head as he took a step back.

"And you think I didn't anticipate all of that? I'll be seeing you around, Gabby."

De Fersen watched in silence as the old man turned and walked out of the Officers' Mess main doors, a slight limp slowing his pace as he made his way toward the base's main gates.

***

The All Ranks Bar was situated toward the middle of the base, not far from the sports center and the parade square. It consisted of a central bar with a handful of tall, circular tables and bar stools decorated with regimental crests, and more secluded booth seating along two of its walls. The dim lights partially hid a number of old war trophies suspended from the crimson walls - a machine gun from the NeoColonial Wars, a

Helot ceremonial banner, and a blackened armored plate from a Squalo TAG. Only a few other patrons were present in the bar, the low hum of conversation partially suppressed beneath the soft tones of jazz which wafted through Stanescu's earpiece as he sat in the booth opposite from Hawkins.

"What's that you're drinking?" he remarked as he sat down his cold beer.

"Tea."

"You not playing on sleeping?"

"It's decaf."

"Oh. Better than those energy drinks you were hooked on in training, I suppose."

The younger man did not answer. Stanescu found himself frantically searching for a neutral topic of conversation. He found none, so went in blunt.

"What's wrong?"

Hawkins looked up. He scratched his neck beneath the soft collar of his black fiberweave shirt.

"Same as always," he replied quietly. "I... struggle to switch off from... all of this. I know that nobody forced us into this vocation, but... the loss of life we're surrounded with causes me to think over things a great deal more than I ever thought I would."

Stanescu nodded, searching again for the right tone to address the issue.

"Oh man... look... I... I'm in no place to lecture anybody on war and soldiering. I've got two years of training and theory, and a handful of days of firsthand experience. But... there's some crossover with my previous existence. I mean, I was only a doctor for just over a year, but I saw a lot of upsetting things in that time. And I had some good advice from people far more experienced than me. That advice generally centers around accepting that you can't do everything for everybody. You can just do your best. Sure, if something goes disastrously wrong that you're accountable for, then you have to take a pretty serious look in the mirror. But, day to day... you've got to accept that doing your best is good enough."

Hawkins looked down into his cup of tea and nodded in agreement, but still said nothing. Stanescu returned to his frantic search for a distracting subject of conversation.

"I saw that since you've logged back into the civilian net, that your halo shows you're engaged. When did that happen? You never said anything."

Hawkins looked up, his face lighting a little with a smile.

"Yeah! I popped the big question a couple of weeks ago, so it's all very new. I didn't mention anything because, well, you remember at school when some chap landed a girlfriend and then went on and on and on about it? I just didn't want to be that guy. So I've sort of kept it to myself."

"Oh, don't think like that. If I wasn't interested, I wouldn't ask. What does she do?"

"She's... err... a session musician," Hawkins said, breaking eye contact for a moment, "guitarist. And a fantastic singer, too. I'm actually waiting for a call from her any minute now. She's a bit... down. You remember that altercation we had with that Teutonic Knight about that little bear I dropped? That was from her. I told her and she's, well, a little bit angry with Stahl. Probably best I talk her down a bit. She's quite... complex. She gets emotional about some things."

Stanescu found himself more interested in the musical aspect than the brief psychological overview - as a piano virtuoso himself, music had always been a huge part of his life.

"I'm sure it'll blow over. Do you have a picture of her?"

"Yes, sure!" Hawkins said, his entire demeanor now animated and radiating positivity as he brought up the radial menus above his comlog. "This is from a few weeks ago. We climbed the western face of Scar Peak and then took a couple of kayaks down the rapids to the base. It was fantastic!"

Whatever Stanescu was expecting on the picture holographically projected over Hawkins's forearm, this was not it. He had known Hawkins for two years, and it did not come as any huge surprise that the young knight had found himself in a committed relationship almost immediately after leaving the fortress-monastery. But Stanescu would have predicted Hawkins to settle down with a quiet, modest sort of woman of a similar temperament to his own.

The picture atop the orange rocks of Scar Peak showed the two in climbing gear, arm in arm with a low sun behind them. Hawkins's dark-haired, blue-eyed fiancee was staggeringly beautiful, but her pout and pose emanated a real arrogance that threw Stanescu off his guard. He found himself surprised and perhaps even a little disappointed that his friend was more shallow than he thought.

"I'm... really happy for you both," he managed.

"Thanks. But enough about me. How's your grandmother doing?"

Stanescu appreciated the question; after all, with his father being deployed for months on end and his mother having left them when he was only two, it was largely down to his grandmother to raise him. That was something he would never forget.

The conversation was interrupted as a newcomer approached the table.

Stanescu looked up in surprise.

"Hello, sirs," Nilsson smiled politely.

"Anja!" Stanescu shot to his feet. "Hello!"

The young woman wore a simple dress of woven, rustic brown, with an eye-catching cross pendant around her neck decorated with nordic swirls. A smooth, but sturdy alloy medical collar extended from the knuckles of her hand up to her elbow, covering the still healing wound of where her hand had been severed.

Hawkins flashed a friendly smile and issued a slight wave.

"I didn't want to interrupt," Nilsson said, "I just saw you both on the map and thought I would say hello."

"Grab a seat," Stanescu offered.

"I'll get you a drink," Hawkins added, "what are you having?"

"Just a… gin and tonic?"

"Right."

Hawkins headed over to the bar while Nilsson sat down in the booth. Stanescu shuffled along the booth away from Nilsson to leave her a respectable amount of distance.

"It's good to see you looking so much better," he began. "How are you feeling?"

Nilsson looked over her shoulder as Hawkins reached the bar. A young woman in a short dress whose halo revealed to be a Fusilier second lieutenant immediately walked over to engage him in conversation. Nilsson winced and smiled awkwardly.

"Yeah, I'm fine. Sir."

"You don't have to call me 'sir,' not here in plain clothes," Stanescu offered. "Just call me… doctor."

"Alright," Nilsson replied hesitantly.

"It's a joke," Stanescu swallowed. "Sorry. Not funny. Darius. My name is Darius."

"Oh! N…no, sorry, I should have picked up on the humor! Erm… Sub Officer Hawkins is taking a while with that drink. Do you need to go rescue him?"

Stanescu looked over to the bar and saw Hawkins smiling uncomfortably as he edged away with Nilsson's drink, the Fusilier officer in the red dress practically barring his path.

"Oh, he gets this all the time," Stanescu laughed, "I think he plays a good part with the stunningly handsome, but humble and unaware thing. But I think deep down he knows. We went through training, and there were a fair few women pursuing him. Whenever we had a live fire exercise, he always found some excuse to remove his helmet and stand heroically, sword held high and pistol brandished, with one foot planted up on a conveniently placed, tactical rock. I'm sure he does all of this deliberately."

Nilsson laughed.

"Well. Looks aren't everything. Far from it. And… while he's out of earshot… I wanted to say thank you for what you did. Back at that depot. I really don't want to dwell on this at all. I just wanted to thank you."

Stanescu leaned back and smiled, nodding in acknowledgement.

"It's in the oath. It's a cliche, but it's just doing the job. I mean, it's the best part of the job! Not many people outside the medical profession get to have a conversation with another person, knowing that person is alive and well and with their family because..."

He tailed off as he searched for a humble way of describing his skillset and failed to find the words.

"I know what you mean, I think," Nilsson interjected to save him.

Hawkins reappeared, placing a tall glass in front of Nilsson.

"Awfully sorry about that," he grimaced, "there was a terribly friendly lady at the bar. She bought me a drink and everything. I feel really quite rude, leaving her there now."

Stanescu flashed a quick conspiratory smirk to Nilsson before looking up at his friend.

"Terribly friendly?"

"Oh, don't be like that!" Hawkins frowned. "You need to try to see the best in people. My halo clearly states that I'm engaged."

Nilsson sampled her drink and looked up.

"Some women see that sort of thing as a challenge, sir."

Hawkins shook his head adamantly.

"Nope. People are fundamentally good."

"Only one way to be sure," Nilsson offered. "If you go back there and spend a full minute talking about your fiancee and how wonderful she is, see if your new friend sticks around. Sixty seconds. If she's still here, then she's... fundamentally good. Sir."

Stanescu suppressed a laugh as Hawkins indignantly strode back to the bar. He looked across at Nilsson.

"So, you think I'm right about this?"

"Oh, I know you're right. You don't go to a bar dressed like that and buy a guy a drink if you've got noble intentions. She's here for a warm up drink before going into town."

Stanescu watched as Hawkins engaged in animated, one-way conversation, his face lit up with enthusiasm as he talked. After some twenty seconds, the young Fusilier held up a hand and pressed a finger to her ear before apologizing and quickly walking away. Hawkins walked back over.

"I suppose we'll never know. She received a call from work. Had to dash off."

Nilsson looked up at Hawkins incredulously. Stanescu joined her in her silence. Hawkins's face dropped.

"There... there was no call, was there? Bloody hell! Am I that naive?"

"Wisdom comes with age, don't worry," Stanescu offered.

Hawkins looked down at his comlog.

"Oh! I've got a call now. I've been waiting for this call for a while, really sorry I've got to go. Nice to see you both!"

Stanescu watched as Hawkins quickly departed the bar. He looked across at Nilsson.

"He... he's a nice guy. I think that's why we got on so well in training. There were some real egos. Most, in fact."

"I can imagine," Nilsson said, swilling her drink in its tall glass. "I found my training pipeline difficult enough. I'd have loved to be a knight, though, at one point."

"You still could," Stanescu said.

He considered making a joke about how he was the living proof that anybody could be a knight, but bit back. That was disingenuous. Selection as a knight required the absolute highest standards of intelligence, physicality, and faith. As a graduate of a prestigious medical school, the academia never challenged him. His grandmother raised him with a strong faith and knowledge of scripture. By the time he applied to become a doctor in the Order, he had already achieved decent results in twelve iron man competitions, so strength and endurance were likewise not an issue. Stanescu's face fell as he recalled that earlier conversation with De Fersen. It was only his complete inability to shoot and wield a sword that resulted in the invaluable piece of technology that was uploaded into his brain.

"Stanescu," Nilsson asked, "is your family name Eastern European?"

He looked up again, appreciating the distraction.

"Romanian. My father was of Romanian heritage. My mother's side of the family are descended from Bulgarian stock, but neither really had much interest in those historical links. My dad always just said we were PanOceanian. Perhaps NeoTerran, at most, given that I was born and grew up in San Pietro."

"Oh, my family love all of the history!" Nilsson said wistfully. "My father's side of the family traces its ancestry back to Sweden. My mother's is also Nordic, but a combination of Swedish and Norwegian. You should see my father's study back home - literally has replica Viking swords and shields on the wall! I'm kind of interested in it too, just not as much as he is. Do you speak to your parents very often?"

Stanescu felt his smile fade. He looked down at his drink and tapped the tips of his fingers against the top of the table for a few moments as he gathered his thoughts.

"My dad passed away not so long ago. My mum... she left us when I was about eighteen months old. My dad was a soldier, so he was away a lot. My grandma raised me."

Nilsson's face fell.

"I'm so sorry for bringing that up."

"Ah, don't be! You weren't to know! And I don't ever want to stop talking about my dad. A finer man I'll never meet. My grandma always told me that, growing up."

"She must have been proud of him." Nilsson nodded.

Stanescu looked up again.

"Proud of him? Oh, no. My maternal grandma. My grandma was my mum's mum. She sided with my dad after my mum left us. She said that my mum could only ever come home when she faced up to her responsibilities as a parent. Well... she never came back. I've never heard from her."

Nilsson looked down into her drink.

"I'm sorry. I don't know what to say."

Stanescu forced a smile.

"Don't be," he said, crossing over two of his fingers. "Me, my dad, my grandma, we were all this close. I still talk to my grandma all the time."

"Is that why you left the medical service to join the Order?" Nilsson asked. "Because of your father?"

Stanescu leaned back in his chair and looked up.

"No, it wasn't that. He tried to talk me out of it, actually, but when he saw that I'd made up my mind, he helped me prepare for selection as best he could."

"What do we do now?"

Stanescu paused as a memory forced itself to the front of his mind; the very moment that started him down the path to a vocation in the Military Orders. He remembered that feeling of helplessness that he never wanted to feel again. But that was a story that he was not even remotely willing to share. When he thought on it, he realized that he had already said far too much. He barely knew Nilsson. She seemed like a lovely person, but he found a hollowness inside suddenly when he realized that he had spoken about his past far more than he wanted to. Even worse, she could be forgiven for thinking that he was concocting some sort of bleeding heart sob-story to gain sympathy from her, with ungallant intentions in mind. No. Best thing to do - the most gentlemanly thing to do now - was politely extricate himself from the situation.

"Well," Stanescu smiled broadly, finishing his drink and then standing, "that does remind me, I do need to call my grandma. Then head to the chapel for evening prayers. Thanks for swinging by, it was nice to talk."

Nilsson watched him turn to leave, a look of mild confusion across her pale face. She stood up.

"Darius?"

Stanescu turned back.

"I don't want to dwell on this, but... thanks again. For getting me out of that depot and back home. I watched the Op debrief, so I know what happened. You didn't need to stop and stabilize me. You didn't need to get me out of there."

Stanescu grinned, broadly and genuinely.

"Yes, I did," he said, before leaving the bar.

***

Shutting the door to the communications booth behind him, Hawkins sat down on the white, faux-leather armchair and pressed a finger to his comlog to accept the call. Immediately, a voice-only communications box appeared in the upper right corner of his lens with a brief animation of the company logo of the chat service provider. Hawkins suppressed an exhalation for fear that his frustration and disappointment would be audible at the other end of the chat channel. Voice only. Again. He knew what that meant.

"Hey!" Beckmann's voice came through into his earpiece. "I got you! I tried earlier but couldn't get through."

"I'm so sorry," Hawkins replied, "there was a... memorial service."

The line fell silent. Hawkins leaned forward, one fist in the other hand, his chin rested on his knuckles.

"I read the post action report," Beckmann finally said, "you lot were in it pretty thick."

"Yes. We were."

Silence again. Hawkins swallowed and looked around the small, empty room and its plain white walls.

"I'm here, though," he added, well aware of what was causing the uncomfortable silence. "I made it back."

"Looked pretty close at times."

"But I *am* here."

Hawkins knew where this was going. He had enough self-awareness, he hoped, to know that he was no veteran of combat. But he had survived a couple of very, very kinetic encounters now which, coupled with the best training and equipment available in the Sphere, gave him a good chance of coming back each time he went out. Just as he had assured his doubting fiancee before he left.

"Kyle. I need to talk to you about something. I need you to stay calm. I *really* need that right now. I'm going to turn the video feed on, okay?"

Hawkins knew his long, drawn out breath must have been audible. More fighting, more injuries to show from her explosive temperament and the lack of legal consequences that came with her position. He tapped to accept the visual feed. His lens faded briefly to white, and then he saw her stood before him in a cramped communications booth. Her face was perfect, unmarked, completely healed from the previous injuries he had seen before deploying on the Aphek raid. For less than a second, he felt relief. Then he saw her clothing.

Beckmann wore combat fatigues of desert sand, ruddy brown and olive green, their cut just slightly different from the standard issue worn by Fusiliers. She wore a pack and full webbing. A holster on one thigh held a pistol. A MULTI Sniper Rifle hung on a sling over one shoulder.

"What the hell is going on?!" Hawkins bellowed, jumping to his feet.

"Just, give me a second..."

"Where are you? Where the fuck have they put you? You're ill! You're not fit for this!"

"Kyle, just take a moment to calm..."

"They can't do this to you! You need help, you're supposed to be..."

"Sub Officer!" the Hexa Major thundered, the force of her command making Hawkins instinctively stand to attention.

Beckmann's blue eyes bored into his. Her face was twisted in anger, her brow low. It took a few moments before her features softened again, and she closed her eyes, her head sagging.

"Kyle, I've got to do this. I owe this to somebody. I was asked to come out here on a job. I signed the waiver to say that I'm fit for duty."

"But you're not!" Hawkins exclaimed desperately. "If you'd broken your leg, they wouldn't deploy you! How is being medically downgraded as mentally unfit for duties any different? You need serious help! Not this!"

Beckmann looked up again, met his accusatory gaze for a moment, and then looked away.

"You know that things have happened in my past. People helped me out of some things I couldn't escape, and I owe them. And... I believe in what I'm doing here. There's some people who, well, if this team confirms what they suspect and they utilize me... some people don't deserve to live."

Hawkins sank back down to the chair and ran the fingers of both hands through his hair. He tasted bile lodged in his throat and felt his hands shaking. This was not the way it was supposed to be.

"This isn't right," he whispered, "this isn't fair."

"Fair?" Beckmann sighed. "Fair isn't reality. Nothing is fair. Come on, we both knew what we were committing to. We both knew that the path we've chosen together is... complicated. This is... this is us. This is the way it is. You're right, it isn't fair, but it's what we've got."

Hawkins looked up again.

"That's not what I meant. I wasn't complaining about it not being fair on us. On me. I meant that this isn't fair on you. You were supposed to be getting help. Not this."

Beckmann bit her bottom lip and looked up for a second.

"Look, Kyle. I'm an old hand at this. I've survived God knows how many ops, a lot of them when I didn't even want to. But now I actually want to survive? Now I've deleted that DNRR from my records because I've got a reason to come home? I'll be fine. I'm always fine. It's you who needs to take care, just like I've been saying for weeks."

The tall woman suddenly looked over one shoulder.

"I've got to go," she said, "I'm so sorry. About all of this. I didn't want to put pressure on you, but I promised you that I'd always tell you the truth, so that's why I had to call you. Just... you look out for yourself and don't try to be a hero. Fucking amateurs try to be heroes. Just keep your head down, look after the people around you and get the job done. Nothing more. Got it?"

Hawkins closed his eyes and nodded.

"Got it."

"And... I sent you a parcel. Don't look into the tone of the wording in the letter, okay? I was in a dark place. If you pick up any anger, it's not aimed at you. It never is. Shit, I've got to go."

Hawkins opened his eyes and stood. He looked across at the digital image of his fiancee, somewhere thousands of miles away near God only knew what danger. She smiled softly at him.

"*Ich liebe dich*."

"*Ich liebe dich, auch*," he whispered the simple and sincere reply.

Her face hardened again, and she nodded curtly.

"Give them hell."

The transmission ended and the image faded. Hawkins gritted his teeth and just about succeeded in holding back a cry of frustration, then slammed the heel of a clenched fist into the wall next to him.

Chapter Fifteen

The sleek Tubarão pitched slightly nose down and transitioned from the hover to forward flight, the blast from its engines kicking up the dust of the short landing strip cut into the jungle. In its wake, two mulebots scuttled through the dust cloud on their crab-like legs to the pile of resupply crates the crew of the aircraft had dropped off. From the entrance of the TAG hangar of Firebase India Two-Five, De Fersen watched the two automatons quickly and efficiently set about opening the crates, scanning the items within, and sorting them out into piles for onward distribution.

Day two at Firebase India Two-Five; a grandiose, punchy name for a hole cut in the aggressive Paradiso jungle, partially filled with some permanent buildings that were designed to be temporary. A TAG hangar, a secure communications building, a power generator, and a smattering of accommodation habs converted out of old storage containers. Two days of waiting and still nothing through on the communication terminal other than a warning order that stores and personnel were arriving that afternoon. So far, as far as De Fersen could tell, the stores were parts and tooling for arms and armor, and more field rations. He would need a lot more than that to crack open a Morat POW facility converted out of a purpose built prison building.

De Fersen's only companion at the entrance to the hangar brought her arm up and activated a radial menu on her comlog.

"Maintenance parts, ammunition, and domestic stores, sir," Cortez confirmed.

"Thought as much," De Fersen grunted.

Cortez, like De Fersen, wore the black combat fatigues of the Hospitaller Order, left looser and in their more natural state rather than shrunk to fit beneath armor. Both also wore the black berets of the Order, stifling under the fierce Paradiso sun despite the breathable material.

While De Fersen had not spoken much to Cortez in their last couple of days at the firebase, he had at least found her to be an agreeable colleague. He knew literally nothing about her personal life, domestic situation, goals, ambitions... because she never talked about any of them. Not like some of the whining, bleeding hearts he had to put up with elsewhere in his team. Cortez did her job efficiently, to a high standard, and without feeling the need to prattle on about her personal life. De Fersen respected that.

"Hang on," Cortez nodded toward the clear, blue sky to the west, "there's another one coming in. No, two."

De Fersen strained his eyes but saw nothing. He changed the zoom of his lens and scoured the western horizon a second time until he saw the familiar, almost shark-like profiles of a pair of black Tubarãos. The aircraft hurtled toward the firebase before flaring to decelerate, then descending over the landing strip and turning into wind together to make a final approach to land. The whine of the powerful engines dominated the humid air. As the noisy aircraft descended to a low hover, De Fersen suddenly found himself lowering one hand to his pistol holster and turning in place to scan his eyes across the surrounding treelines. He muttered an expletive under his breath almost instantly. Yes, Trevethick had been a dangerous man in his day. But his military service was left behind decades ago.

Keeping well clear of the two mulebots and their stores, the Tubarãos landed at the upwind end of the strip. Their cargo doors opened, and De Fersen saw personnel in the black uniforms of the Order begin to file out of the aircraft. Even behind passenger helmets and visors, De Fersen recognized Britt Heijboer, Luca Romano, and Francois Aubert. They walked out toward the edge of the landing strip at the head of a column of eight soldiers. There was another young Hospitaller Knight whom De Fersen did not recognize, along with five sergeants. An even longer line filed out of the second aircraft; seven Crosiers followed by Stahl, another Teutonic Knight, and Konstantinos Karayiannis.

Cortez strode out to meet the unit of Crosiers. De Fersen cut across to intercept the soldiers walking away from the first aircraft as the recently delivered passengers removed their safety helmets for collection by one of the aircrewmen. Heijboer walked out to meet him.

"I got a message that you needed help from somebody who knows what they're doing!" she shouted above the din of the engines with a grin.

"Funny!" De Fersen growled. "Come on, let's go for a walk!"

The two Tubarãos lifted to the hover in a cloud of dust and leaned forward to power away, taking their infernal noise with them as the remainder of the soldiers filed into the hangar with their heavy packs. Heijboer thrust her hands into her pockets as she followed De Fersen across to the narrow, dusty path running around the firebase perimeter.

"You've got Luca," he began, "whose the other one?"

"Abdi Tibar. I've never worked with him. I've sent you his record. Two years experience, solid soldier. What about your two? How are they doing?"

De Fersen snorted out a laugh.

"What, you mean the idiot who can't set off an explosive charge and the conscientious objector who is spending more time with his medkit than his weapon?"

Heijboer's face dropped as she planted her clenched fists on her hips and looked up at the older knight.

"No. I mean the two knights who stood by you and got the job done. Show them some respect, you cantankerous old bastard. We all had to start somewhere. Even you."

De Fersen swore in French and shook his head. He had forgotten how much of a pain it could be sharing a detachment with an officer of equal rank. Before he could reply, one of the team's engineers appeared at the tall doors of the hangar and looked across at De Fersen.

"Package is imminent, sir," he called across.

As the two Tubarãos turned downwind to depart the area, De Fersen saw a third coming in low across the trees from the west. He saw a large, streamlined package suspended a few feet beneath the aircraft's belly. As the aircraft decelerated on the final approach to the landing strip, De Fersen made out the familiar lines of the comparatively tiny body and the long, sleek limbs. The shape lurched forward from beneath the Tubarão as it slowed to a high hover. Then the huge load dropped. Instantly, metallic arms and legs spread out as the load unfolded into the form of a towering Seraph TAG, the Armored Cavalry of the Military Orders.

The gargantuan, slender fighting machine, over twice the height of an armored knight, thudded into the earth and immediately stood tall. Even without its weapons or the banners of the Order, the bipedal fighting machine was an awesome sight to behold. The small team of engineers at the hangar entrance observed closely as the Seraph paced down the shallow embankment from the landing strip and into the hangar. At the control terminal inside the building, Sergeant Patricio, the diminutive TAG pilot, guided the fighting machine down toward the doors.

De Fersen allowed himself a slight grin. With the support offered by the Seraph - and the small team of parachutists that were being forward positioned on an orbital launch platform - they at least stood a decent chance of success.

"You should go unpack your kit," De Fersen offered, "we've got a lot of planning to work through."

"I'll sort my kit out later." Heijboer shrugged. "Let's get to work."

***

Sat with his back to the hangar wall, Stanescu stared with grim curiosity at the root of the same karava vine trap he had been assessing - through sheer boredom - for three days now. To begin with, he merely thought he had seen a small advance - perhaps only a couple of centimeters - as the edge of the living jungle jealousy advanced to reclaim its territory from the human invasion that had set up the firebase. Then, the next day, he had marked the edges of the roots with small divots kicked into the ground and returned that evening to see the results. Now, on day three, not only were the roots well past the divots - even the earth had recovered from the damage he had inflicted, and only a faint line remained.

Outside the hangar, work continued on preparing the towering Seraph TAG. The monstrous machine's arms had been fitted with a close combat weapon resembling a twin-edged, longsword of old, and a long-barrelled heavy machine gun. From their mission briefing an hour before, Stanescu had learned that the Seraph's ECM kit was failing to initialize properly, which was causing all manner of problems for a war machine that was holding an alert state and was ready to deploy on combat operations within sixty minutes. However, the team had been poised and ready to go at sixty minute's notice for two whole days now, and Stanescu was left wondering if the operation would ever be green-lit at all. The brief had been simple enough - four teams and the TAG would air deploy at low level to the prison, with the Hospitallers assaulting overtly while the Teutonic team infiltrated the walls to attack from within. Kill the defenders, free the opposition, airlift home again.

He returned his attention to the letter to his grandmother that he was crafting on the holographic keyboard projected above his comlog. On the far side of the hangar, Lieutenant Morenoand Sergeant Cortez valiantly attempted to keep their team of Crosiers keen and engaged with some impromptu training session on E/M mines. Close to the edge of the firebase's clearing, Stanescu saw Hawkins walking aimlessly along the perimeter, his eyes narrowed and his face twisted in concentration. He had been the same ever since they arrived; lost in thought, quiet, and uncharacteristically easy to anger. Stanescu had tried twice to ask him what was bothering him, but had been forcefully pushed away on both occasions.

"You up to much?"

Stanescu looked up and saw De Fersen stood at the edge of the hangar, wiry arms folded across his chest. Stanescu shot to his feet. De Fersen held out a hand to stop him from talking.

"Just checking in. Just seeing what you're up to."

"I... was just writing a letter to my grandmother. Sir."

The older man's eyes narrowed - not unkindly, but more as if he found himself defused by a statement pertaining to family rather than war-fighting or faith.

"It's... good that you are close to your family."

Stanescu issued a slight shrug.

"Yes, sir."

Stanescu watched De Fersen for a few awkward moments. It seemed as though he was pondering over whether to open up on something, but before he could decide, he was saved by the timely arrival of Heijboer. The Mother-Officer flashed a sly grin.

"Just had an Int update. I reckon we'll be job-on in the next few hours. Things have escalated."

"Oh?" De Fersen remarked. "How so?"

"There's been a coordinated series of attacks by the EI across several civilian targets." Heijboer's smile faded as she reported that part of the update. "Us, the StateEmpire, Haqqislam... the EI hit cities across the planet. All came in this morning."

Stanescu's eyes widened.

"What do we do now?"

He quickly surpassed the agonizing memory and looked across at his two commanders. Hawkins walked over and stood by the three other knights.

"Sounds like a response to our raids on them," Heijboer continued. "Twenty coordinated attacks on civilian targets. Every single strike on PanO territory met a prepared defense. Civilian casualties have been light, thank God, but the firefights in our cities... jeez. It's been a massacre. Hexa and Indigo hit teams lying in wait. We hit them *hard.*"

Hawkins stepped forward, his eyes wide.

"W... wait... what do you mean? EI attacking our cities? Our civilians? And there were Hexa teams there waiting for them?"

"Yes, there were..."

"What do you mean, 'massacre'?" Hawkins insisted. "Who was massacred? The enemy or our Hexa teams?"

Stanescu turned to face his friend, bewildered by the line of questioning and the panic in his tone.

"Bit of both, by the sound of it," Heijboer replied casually, "but I wouldn't worry about it. The main thing is that civilian casualties were really light, so it's a job well done. A lot of dead Morats. As for Hexas... well, if you'd worked with them before, you'd know that they're... they barely qualify as human. I wouldn't lose any sleep over a load of Hexas going to meet their makers."

De Fersen flung himself forward to block Hawkins and push him back just as the young knight exploded into a rage-filled onslaught.

"Leave it!" De Fersen yelled. "Drop it, Hawkins!"

"What the fuck did she mean by that?!" Hawkins roared, shoving the senior knight to one side and clenching his fists as Heijboer stared at the two in surprise.

"Drop it!" De Fersen jumped back to push him away. "Now!"

Stanescu stood frozen to the spot, shocked into inactivity. The group of Crosiers stared across at the altercation from the far side of the hangar. Heijboer took a step closer, her eyes wide.

"I… I'm sorry. I don't know what I said to upset you. I'm sorry."

"Sorry?!" Hawkins yelled.

De Fersen grabbed the young knight by the scruff of his black t-shirt.

"I told you to drop it! I…"

Hawkins grabbed De Fersen's wrist and twisted it to force the Father-Officer into a half-turn before shoving him down to the ground. He towered over De Fersen's prone form and pointed a finger down at him.

"You touch me again, and I'll drop you like a sack of shit! Now one of you tell me what the hell happened to those Hexa strike teams, or as God is my witness, you will see me lose my fucking temper!"

De Fersen slowly stood and straightened his uniform jacket. He took a breath, then nodded slowly before turning to Stanescu and Heijboer.

"Give us a few minutes," De Fersen said calmly.

Heijboer's face still displayed her utter confusion over the situation that had developed seemingly from nowhere; a sentiment that Stanescu shared entirely.

"Gabe, I…"

"A few minutes," De Fersen repeated, his tone still serene and composed, "please."

Heijboer nodded silently.

"I'm sorry," she said again and turned to walk away.

Stanescu followed her.

***

In the four years that they had been acquainted, De Fersen had dragged Hawkins to one side countless times during training. Always with the younger man hanging his head despondently for a failing on his part. As the two walked away from the hangar toward the tree line, De Fersen felt Hawkins's eyes boring into the back of his head, as if the rage-filled soldier was only one comment away from lashing out and striking his commander.

De Fersen stopped near the edge of the humid, dense jungle. For not the first time that day, he found himself quickly scanning the trees for an imaginary assassin sent after him by Trevithick. He growled under his breath and shook his head. The old bastard was winning just with a handful of threatening words. De Fersen was experienced enough to know better. He turned to face Hawkins. The muscular soldier stood only a few paces away, broad arms folded across his barrel-chest, and dark eyes boring into De Fersen's. The older warrior shook his head and then pointed a finger in accusation.

"You listen here, you stupid bastard!" De Fersen began. "You need to sort out..."

"Fuck off!" Hawkins snarled, stepping in closer as if he was about to strike. "Just fuck right off! I've put up with your shit for years now! I've done everything you've asked, I've taken your shitty insults and patronizing comments, I've bit my lip when you've hid behind your rank to talk to me like I'm a damned space cadet... and for what? Hmm? So you can feel like the big man. As I recall, I took you down on the mats twice before in sparring. When I was playing nice. Right now? In the mood I'm in? You're about two seconds away from spending the next month eating through a fucking straw, so whatever you've got to say had better be good!"

De Fersen paused, his eyes narrowed. Exhaling slowly through his nose, he mulled over every word the younger knight had said. Yes, Hawkins had the edge in a fist fight and would probably win. That did not intimidate De Fersen even a little, not with the injuries he had bounced back from over the previous decades of combat. It was Hawkins's other accusations that were of more interest. De Fersen nodded and opened his mouth to reply.

"Alright."

Hawkins's angry face contorted further into a confused scowl.

"Alright, what?"

"Alright. I've been a dick. You've called me out on it. So... alright. I'm not apologizing to you. But I'll reign it in. So now what?"

Hawkins's brow unfurrowed a little. He took a slow breath.

"Well...now I get in the shit for insubordination, and then we carry on."

"Don't be such a fucking drama queen," De Fersen grunted. "Like I said, you called me out on being a dick. Look, I'll give you a free pass on this one on one condition. If you want to rant and rave at me again, you take me to one side and do it. Never again in front of subordinates, are we clear? It's not how a fighting force runs."

Hawkins nodded, his shoulders slumping a little.

"Yes. Clear."

"Alright."

De Fersen brought up his comlog and opened his command menu. He whirled across to his folder of Op Orders and brought up everything he had on Operation Aphek. Initiating a program to quickly list every hidden user who had opened the file within the last month, it did not take him long to find a small number of accounts with highly classified personal data. Opening another hacking program, it took a good pair of minutes to identify three of those users as high ranking officers within Strategic Security. Another few minutes of awkward silence later, and he had hacked one of their data protection firewalls to access all linked operations up to Top Secret classification.

"Your fiancee is part of a Strategic Security plan codenamed Operation Cian Thunder," De Fersen told Hawkins. "Typically cringe-worthy Hexa codename, but it appears that Op Aphek was always a precursor to it. Everything we've done, we were used to provoke a response from the El. ALEPH predicted that a series of strikes behind El lines would result in attacks on civilian targets. Op Cian Thunder pre-positioned Hexa and Indigo strike teams to inflict maximum damage on the El attackers."

"What about casualties?" Hawkins insisted. "Is she listed?"

De Fersen shook his head.

"First off, this isn't easy to access. Second, if I'm caught, then I'll go to prison. I'm finding out all I can. Wait."

De Fersen scrolled through another sub menu to access the casualty records but immediately hit another firewall. A second later, his hacking program squawked at him to alert him to a defensive program booting up to combat the intrusion into the secret files. De Fersen immediately severed his connection and ran through a number of stages to cover his tracks.

"Sorry, Kyle. I don't know. I couldn't access the casualty records. Look... I've never met your fiancee but I know her unit by reputation. She's a survivor. Stay focused, save that anger for the enemy, and as soon as we're done, I'll get you home so you can find out. That's all I can do."

Hawkins swallowed and nodded slowly. He turned away and shut his eyes, his lips moving in silent prayer for a few moments before he looked up at De Fersen again. An onslaught of conflicting emotions seemed to wash over the younger knight's face for a few moments of silence as anger wrestled with guilt.

"Thank you for trying, sir."

De Fersen grunted uncomfortably.

"Gabe. Save 'sir' for when we're in front of subordinates. My name is Gabe. Best we get ready; I think Britt is right. We'll get the green light to move soon."

De Fersen whacked what he hoped was a comradely slap on the younger soldier's shoulder, and walked back toward the hangar.

'Glory be to the Father, and to the Son, and to the Holy Spirit, as it was in the beginning, is now, and ever shall be a world without end. Amen.'

Hawkins looked up and opened his eyes. He knelt on one knee near the edge of the firebase, long grass of yellow-green reaching up to knee height around him, wafting and rustling gently in the hot afternoon breeze beneath the blazing sun. On the far side of the hangar, Mother-Officer Heijboer led the other Hospitallers in prayer; the team of Teutonic soldiers had somewhat typically boycotted the gathering to pray independently, while Hawkins had abandoned both groups entirely to be alone.

What kind of bastards judged a person based on the reputation of the organization they were forced into? Who gave any of them the right? They had never even met her. They did not know who she really was behind the game face. The irony was not lost on him; surrounded by self-appointed men and women of God who felt that their rank and status within the Holy Orders gave them the right to judge any and all around them. Hawkins swore under his breath and shook his head. He raised his rosary beads to his lips and muttered one final request.

"Lord, please protect her."

He stood and walked back to the hangar and its surrounding collections of improvised accommodation blocks and storage containers. The two separate gatherings were dispersing now as the mid-afternoon sun began its slow dip toward the horizon. Insects buzzed and rattled, birds sang and warbled from the surrounding trees; something much larger from within the depths of the jungle let out a cry somewhere between a rasp and a roar, but would no doubt keep its distance from the perimeter. The creatures of the jungle knew better than to enter the clearings made by the human occupiers.

Hawkins reached the hangar and was immediately intercepted by one of the TAG technicians. A young man of a similar age to Hawkins, thin and wiry with a mop of dirty blond hair. He carried over a long box awkwardly.

"Sub Officer Hawkins?" he asked. "I'm sorry this is late, sir. This came in with our own stores. We weren't expecting any personal deliveries, so I'm afraid this has sat at the back of the hangar for the last couple of days. I'm so sorry, sir, it was..."

Hawkins took the crate and walked past the technician, leaving him behind in silence. He paced back out into the shade of the hangar doors and put the long, gray box down before sitting next to it. A rifle container; the type used by PanO army units but not the Military Orders. He scanned his comlog across it - yes, addressed to him. The action unlocked the container.

Hawkins opened the long box and looked down to see a Cinet-icS Tunod MULTI Marksman Rifle snuggly fitted into the packing foam, complete with a separate scope and collection of empty ammunition magazines. He removed the weapon and looked it over from barrel to butt. A message scrolled across his lens.

- *Two documents for download: confirm?*

Hawkins accepted the documents with a tap of his comlog. The first was the maintenance and user setup guide for the MULTI Marksman Rifle. The second was a letter.

Kyle,

I'm sorry that I'm back into the job. I honestly thought I'd be taking a long break, but something came up and I had to help. I feel terrible, as this must look so dishonest of me. Honestly, when you left, I did not know this was coming. But it is something I have to do. I know that with our security clearances it is not fair that I know everything you are doing and you know nothing about what I'm doing, but it won't be for long. We'll both be back and together soon.

In perhaps the least romantic gesture ever carried out between two people engaged to be married, please find attached a CineticS Tunod MULTI Marksman Rifle. Yes, I am trying to get you to back off the enemy a bit with something with a bit more range, because I know that statistically most of your unit's casualties occur in close assault actions. So yes, this is purely selfish on my part. Please use it, I'll leave it to you to explain it to your chain of command.

Finally - how do I write this - I'm still fucking angry about that little shit of a Teutonic Knight you mentioned who had ridiculed you for the cuddly toy I sent your way. Please do tell him that I've now sent you a gun as well, and then use it to cave in his fucking skull. If you don't feel like doing that, then just mention Rava Valley, two years ago. Yes, I've had a friend look up who he is and what dirt we have on him. If he pisses you off again, the whole world will know what happened at Rava Valley, starting with his mother.

Take care, stay safe, don't do anything stupid, and know that I love you with all my heart.
Lisette

His hands working almost mechanically with well-drilled preci-sion, Hawkins fitted the telescopic sight into place, uploaded his bio-metric data and individual targeting settings, slotted two empty magazines into place, and then rose to his feet. The rifle held to one side, his eyes set on his target, he strode through the hangar and over to where the soldiers of the Teutonic Order congregated. Stahl stood with another knight, a sergeant, and Konstantinos Karayiannis. A short woman with a shaved head - the Seraph TAG pilot - stood at the periphery of the gathering.

The red-headed Teutonic Knight looked over at him as he approached with a faint smile. Karayiannis, perhaps seeing the look on Hawkins's face, rushed out in an attempt to bar his progress.

"Sir, I don't think..."

Hawkins barged past the older soldier and stood at the edge of the ring of Teutonic warriors.

"You're actually going to *marry* a Hexa?" Stahl spat. "By..."

"Rava Valley," Hawkins interrupted. "Who my fiancee is is none of your fucking business - all of you - but Rava Valley, two years ago, that's of interest. Isn't it?"

Stahl's smirk disappeared in an instant. His eyes opened wide and his chest heaved as his breathing quickened. Still completely unaware as to the story behind the threat, Hawkins took another step closer.

"A soldier with as many years served as you should know all of the golden rules of fighting for the PMC," he continued. "And one of the most important of all - don't fuck with Strategic Security. I don't need my fiancee to fight my battles for me - just say the word, and I'll be happy to kick the fuck out of you right here and now - but you're in their crosshairs now. They know about Rava Valley. You talk shit about my fiancee, my family? Alright. Let's bring family in. Let's see what your mother thinks about what you did."

Stahl's face dropped. His hands visibly shook.

"Don't... don't do that. Don't do that to my mother. It would finish her off."

Hawkins leaned in with a vicious grin and pinched Stahl's cheek like an elderly relative greeting a child.

"Best you stop acting like a twat then, hey?"

Hawkins barged his way past and stomped off angrily toward the firebase perimeter again. In only a few paces, an immense weight of guilt descended on his shoulders as soon as he realized what he had done. Yes, Stahl was insulting his fiancee. Yes, he did the right thing to stand up for her. But involving the man's mother? With a bluff he knew nothing about? And an insinuation that the woman was already ill? Hawkins swore and ran one hand through his dark hair. Resting his new rifle across one broad shoulder, he paced along the perimeter restlessly, replaying the last hour of conversations and confrontations over and over in his mind.

"Kyle?"

Hawkins span around. Stanescu stood a few paces away, a path cut through the high grass behind him where he had paced out to meet Hawkins.

"Kyle?" he repeated. "What's going on? You've been miles away for days, and now... now you're picking fights with other members of our team, and... *De Fersen?!* You're challenging *him?*"

Hawkins opened his mouth to speak. No words came. He shrugged and turned his back on his friend.

"They're saying your fiancee is a Hexa," Stanescu continued, "an assassin. A Black Ops killer. Now, I know that's not true because you told me that she's a session musician, and we've been close friends for two years now, and we've never lied to each other."no

Hawkins hung his head for a moment. His temples pounded. His throat was dry. He looked up again.

"It's true. I didn't lie to you. But it's true. Lisette is a Strategic Security operative. Her cover, the life she lives between operations, is as a session musician. They all need cover lives and occupations, and that's hers."

Stanescu exhaled, then shook his head slowly.

"Why didn't you tell me?" he urged quietly.

"Why the hell are you making this all about you?!" Hawkins snarled, throwing his arms to either side and staring in accusation at his friend. "Why the hell should I tell *you*? That's her secret to tell, not mine!"

Stanescu paused. There was not even a rudimentary effort to conceal the hurt he was clearly feeling.

"I wasn't making it about me. I wish you'd told me so that I could have listened. I could have been a friend when you needed it. I could have stood next to you, to have your back when you were facing down these arseholes who are giving you a hard time. I could have been there for you."

Hawkins took in a lungful of humid air. His head sagged forward. Sweat ran down his neck. Again, he swore under his breath. He felt utterly, utterly exhausted. Not physically: he had graduated top of his intake in training in all things physical, both speed and strength, and was in peak physical shape. In terms of strength and endurance, he felt ready for anything.

But mentally, emotionally, he was spent. He had nothing left. Four long, relentless, unforgiving years of possibly the toughest training regime in the Human Sphere, four years of endless discipline, put downs, reprimands, belittling debriefs, being told the best was never good enough... four years of misery followed by two high intensity combat operations with death at every turn. He had hit his limit. Hawkins swallowed. He searched frantically for a way to apologize to his friend. A message scrolled across Hawkins's lens.

- *Operation Paran initiated. Air transport activated, ETA 45 min-utes. All units form at assembly areas.*

Wordlessly, Hawkins and Stanescu headed back toward the hangar for their weapons and armor.

***

The first of the four sleek Tubarãos flared to the hover over the landing strip before touching down and taxiing over toward the assembly area outside the hangar. The second aircraft was already on final approach as the lead Tubarão came to a halt, the starboard side cargo door on the fuselage slid open.

- *Stick One, embark aircraft callsign Cheetah One.*

The instructions scrolling across De Fersen's lens were accom-panied by animated blue arrows leading across the ground toward the lead aircraft, where they hit a red 'x' at the edge of the Tubarão's safety zone. After a few internal checks were completed by the Tubarão's air-crew, the red stop sign was replaced by more blue arrows leading to the open cargo door.

More comfortable now within the cool, environmentally con-trolled interior of his ORC heavy armor, De Fersen stood and walked out from the assembly area to the aircraft. Behind him, five knights and six sergeants followed him to embark the lead aircraft.

Something bluesy - or at least what De Fersen assumed was 'the blues' - played across the bar's main music channel. It was not his sort of thing, but with little more than total ambivalence to music in gen-eral, De Fersen did not feel the need to change the channel. Perched awkwardly atop a tall barstool, leaning over the polished, marble effect bar and his gin and tonic, De Fersen gazed into the mirrored panels behind the rows of bottles.

His hairline had now receded to the crown of his head. He winced at the thought. On the one hand, it was affordable enough to fix, and he did not want to be the guy who had lost all of his hair be-fore he was twenty years old. On the other hand, a primeval, macho instinct urged him to leave things alone and steer well clear of cosmetic procedures. But, he mused as he took a sip from his glass, perhaps that was why he was sat alone in an empty bar, early on a Saturday evening, with his first date with the latest girl he had connected with on Maya-Meet suspiciously absent nearly half an hour after their planned rendezvous time.

The doors to the bar opened. De Fersen turned on his stool and saw two men walk into the bar - one wearing what De Fersen assumed was an expensive suit, based solely on the dapper waistcoat and accompanying silk tie - the other wearing a heavy, dark coat that matched his thick mustache but seemed at odds with the heat of the summer evening. The man in the suit - of medium build and perhaps only half a dozen years older than De Fersen - smiled at him as if they were old acquaintances and walked briskly across to the bar.

"Gabrielle? Gabrielle De Fersen?"

De Fersen narrowed his eyes.

"If you're Linda, you really need to update your profile picture."

The man chuckled and sat on the stool next to De Fersen.

"No! Afraid not. My name is Robin. Robin Gillan. I'm the CEO of INCRA-Systems. The company you hacked last week."

De Fersen leaned back instinctively, sitting straighter on his stool. He immediately cursed himself for such an obviously guilty reaction. He stammered some sort of pathetic denial, but the young CEO held up a hand.

"No, no. Honestly, stop. I owe you the apology. You see, the whole thing was a set up. I set a challenge - a quantronic trap, in a way - within our accounts. Something subtle. I set it up nearly a year ago, hoping somebody would come poking around. It's a dummy account, the one you found."

"I know," De Fersen admitted warily, knowing full well that if he had been found in the first place, Gillan must have evidence of his illegal tampering, "but you copied the quantronic hierarchy from your real account, and that's how I got in."

"I know that, too," Gillan said, "but I certainly wasn't expecting it. That's why I'm here. It's taken my man over there by the door a week to track you down, but I'm here now."

De Fersen glanced over at the broad, dark figure by the door. The man folded his arms, tilted his head a little, and stared back with none of the gregarious nature of his employer.

"This, right now," Gillan continued, "our little chat here. This is your job interview. Answer my questions well enough, and you can drop out of college tomorrow morning. This is your chance."

'Your chance.' Where would life have taken him if he had rejected that chance. De Fersen strode out toward the open cargo door, Spitfire attached to the back of his heavy armor.

The second Tubarão landed on and taxied across toward the hardstanding as the first stick of troops walked out to the lead aircraft. De Fersen led, followed by Heijboer and Romano. Stanescu was next, his eyes fixed on the aircraft ahead that would ferry him to his next firefight. An aircrewman at the cargo door issued a thumbs up to De Fersen, and the veteran soldier walked past the idle starboard engine nacelle to enter the aircraft.

Stanescu felt the warm blast of the jet engine as he passed, fed back to him from the sensors of his armor. Again, seemingly from nowhere, an isolated phrase from his past forced its way to the front of his mind.

"What do we do now?"

Stanescu paused by the open cargo door.

Screams echoed through the jungle, wafting across the hot night air from the direction of the bright lights of the fires. Tongues of yellow flickered across the eastern horizon, silhouetting running figures and hulking, monstrous aliens with guns and blades. His legs wading slowly through the thick, swamp-like water, his heart hammering with fear in his chest, Stanescu crept slowly away from the sight of the massacre.

A tiny hand clutched desperately to his shaking fingers. Stanescu looked down at the small girl, no more than six or seven years old. Behind her, her mother carried the sobbing younger brother, tears streaming down both of their faces. Another blast of gunfire ripped through the night followed by screams from the refugee column some two hundred yards to the east.

"Darius?"

Stanescu stopped and span in place. He looked up out of the water-filled ditch at the lip of earth above. A solitary figure was stood above him, clad in a similar long, white coat to his own. He recognized her even in the darkness - Marryat, the senior consultant of the medical expedition. The middle-aged woman flashed a relieved smile. Darius beckoned frantically for her to join them in the relative cover of the ditch.

Marryat's smile faded. Darius stared up at her questioningly. Then he heard the noise behind her. A grunt, an alien snarl, and exclamation in the darkness. Marryat's eyes filled, for only the briefest of moments, with terror and despair. Then the veteran doctor slowly smiled, and flashed a grin and a wink down at the young child holding

Stanescu's hand. The wiry woman turned to face the unseen monster in the darkness.

"Do it," she challenged fearlessly, stepping away from the ditch. "Do it, you coward."

A shot rang out, and Marryat crumpled to the ground. Stanescu let out a stifled cry. His shoulders shook and his breath froze in his bile-filled throat. His limbs remained immobile, refusing to respond to the frantic orders from his brain to turn and flee. The little hand clutched desperately to his.

"What do we do now?"

Stanescu only managed to let out a terrified whimper.

"Doctor Darius? What do we do now? Please!"

Up on the rim of the ditch above, an enormous, bulky shape of a monstrously proportioned humanoid appeared. A muscular body encased in angular armor of red and black, with a red-skinned face barely visible in the darkness, crowned in a mane of white hair. The alien warrior stared down at Stanescu, and the small family he had failed to save. Stanescu remained frozen in place. It was no longer fear. He simply gave up. They were dead. There was nothing that could be done.

The blast of gunfire made him jump and cry out. The alien soldier's arms were flung to either side, and he span around in place before falling to the ground. A figure emerged from the trees to the left, wearing slim fitting armor of black and wearing a beret of purple-blue. The soldier raised a finger to his lips, and then beckoned for Stanescu and his three companions to follow.

That was the moment Stanescu resolved to never again, for as long as he lived, fail to have the courage or the skills to help those who needed him.

Grabbing the fuselage handrail and planting one foot on the flip-out step below the cargo door, Stanescu dragged his armored frame up into the Tubarão. He quickly moved across to one of the passenger seats and strapped himself in as the third aircraft came to a hover and moved to position above the Seraph TAG. Stanescu narrowed his eyes. His first performance in combat had been a failure. He had not lived up to that promise he made to himself to never again fail those around him.

But that was out of his system now. The shock of the first fight was gone. This one would be different. Up to two hundred prisoners of war now had the chance to go home to their loved ones if Stanescu did his job properly. This time it would be different. Even if it killed him, Stanescu resolved to not let a single soul down in the upcoming fight.

***

Strops lowered from the belly of the hovering Tubarão to line up with the attachment points on the Seraph TAG stood beneath it as the aircraft responded to the verbal con of the aircrewman leaning out of the open cargo door. The line of Hospitaller Knights and sergeants filed toward the lead aircraft, its engines growling at idle setting. De Fersen, Heijboer, Romano, and Stanescu had already clambered onboard the drab-colored aircraft.

Hawkins reached the edge of the Tubarão's safety ring, co-loured red on his lens. A green halo around the aircraft itself gave him clearance to approach and embark. He reached the cargo door and planted one armored foot onto the retractable footstep folded out from the fuselage. His eyes fell on the holstered handgun on his leg.

Hawkins was not sure how long he had dazed in that transition-ary, half-awake state that lay somewhere between proper sleep and beginning the day. Tinny, melodic notes chimed away quietly from the far side of the room. The bed next to him was still warm, but notable in its emptiness. Hawkins yawned quietly and sat up, wiping at the sleep in his eyes and then reaching across to the bedside table next to him to find his lens.

The doors leading to the grand bedroom's balcony were open, but the normal morning greeting of blazing sunshine in a clear, blue sky had been replaced by an overcast, homogenous mess of gray clouds and driving rain pattering down over the lush trees and flowerbeds of the exclusive coastal housing estate. Hawkins stood and wandered wearily toward the balcony. The hot, natural air of the outside world won the fight with the house's environmental controls, wafting against him as he reached the open balcony doors. Below him, rain pelted down into the back garden's swimming pool and the ornamental flower gardens that reached down to the house's private stretch of beach.

Beckmann sat on a chair on the covered balcony, the source of chiming emanating from an unplugged vintage electric guitar sat across her lap. Her fingers danced across the maple fretboard of the 2096, olympic white Fender Stratocaster, the most valuable guitar in her ex-tensive collection. The notes of the minor pentatonic scale matched the dreariness of the weather. Hawkins looked down at his fiancee. Her eyes stared off out to sea, unfocused and unfeeling.

Hawkins quietly dropped to one knee by her side. A few mo-ments passed. She finally looked across at him and smiled broadly, a completely unconvincing gesture that failed to marry up with the tears that ran down her cheeks. It was perhaps half of their mornings togeth-er. A little time to deal with the nightmares of past events. Hawkins re-turned the smile and rested a reassuring hand gently on her shoulder.

Beckmann stopped playing and gently placed the guitar down on the stand next to her. She leaned across to rest her head on his shoulder and then burst into tears.

"Kyle?"

Hawkins looked up to see Stanescu stood by the aircraft's cargo door, staring down at him where he had stopped by the footstep folded out from the lower fuselage.

"You okay?"

Hawkins jumped up into the Tubarão, barging his way past his friend. A short, portly aircrewman directed him assertively toward one of the aircraft's seats. Hawkins pushed the guiding hand away.

"I know how to use a chair, dickhead!" he scowled before taking his place and attaching his safety harness.

His thoughts wandered instantly off, away from the task in hand. He was numbly aware of a message scrolling across his lens, warning him of his own elevated heart rate. Although that warning would have been automatically transmitted to his field commander, De Fersen still said nothing as the aircraft taxied back to the runway to line up for take off.

Chapter Sixteen

The flight of Tubarãos swept across the undulating terrain at treetop height, fanned out in a loose tactical formation as their pilots followed the contours of the ground toward their target. The late afternoon sun shone down through an orange, cloudless sky as the aircraft and their passengers crossed the front line of the conflict - merely another clump of miles of jungle, indistinguishable from those all around it - to advance on the prison.

Minute after minute dragged on as the aircraft hurtled through enemy skies. In the cabin of the lead aircraft, De Fersen checked his tactical map. He scrolled out a larger range setting, noting the waypoints for each of his teams to drop, advance, and then extricate. A message scrolled across his lens.

- *Halo Team, ready to drop.*

De Fersen smiled grimly. The trio of airborne soldiers - Crusader Brethren - who stood in wait miles above on their orbital platform, ready to jump down through the upper atmosphere to their objective marker. That objective was to ensure that the central guidance system to the prison's anti-aircraft guns was disabled. De Fersen checked his watch. All was on schedule.

- *Halo Team from Broadsword Zero: jump, jump.*

- *Halo Team, jumping.*

Four minutes. At some one hundred and fifty miles per hour in their descent, it would be four minutes until the airborne crusaders were in combat at the small command center two miles from the prison. De Fersen checked his timer again and opened a channel to his teams.

- *Broadsword Zero to all - five minutes to target.*

The aircraft pitched nose over to dive down into a valley, banking sharply to the right as it did so. De Fersen was flung up against his harness, hovering a few millimeters above his seat for a second before thumping back down again. Swearing under his breath, he remembered when such minor white-knuckle thrills actually used to be fun, back in his youth.

The Tubarãos continued on, a panoramic view of lush, sparkling green beneath the orange skies visible out of the cabin's few armored windows. Three minutes to go. De Fersen tapped his comlog to briefly check on the status of his soldiers - a handful of elevated heart rates marginally beyond what we would expect from combat veterans, but nothing to concern him. He glanced forward, past the two pilots and through the cockpit. The city of Moravia was now a gray smear across the horizon; an enigma of abandoned skyscrapers and suburbs, a quarter reclaimed by the aggressive advance of Paradiso's jungle, possibly still housing the sparse remnants of human society that did not flee the initial EI occupation, and were not killed in the fighting or taken elsewhere.

Two minutes. The parachutists would be eyes on their target by now, lining up to hit their drop zone and move straight in to sever the Morat command and control of automated weapons covering the prison. As if in response to the thought, a blue diamond appeared on De Fersen's lens, ahead of the aircraft and much higher up, descending rapidly toward the ground.

A second later, a green marker appeared on the lens, in the aircraft's twelve o'clock position. Marker Alpha - their drop point. Get in, secure the prison walls, and get the TAG in the courtyard. Secure the courtyard as an LZ for extraction. Get the prisoners to the LZ and hold the facility until extraction complete. Four aircraft would wait to the south to be called in to extricate the first half of the prisoners. Another flight of four Tubarãos would be launching soon to come in for the second half and De Fersen's team.

De Fersen took the opportunity to briefly bow his head and recite the Hail Mary silently, taking the extra effort to concentrate on the meaning behind the words rather than simply reciting them mechanically.

One minute.

***

The thumping of gunfire could be heard even above the whining of the Tubarão's twin engines as the aircraft came to a hover. Return fire chattered away from the HMG mounted at the open cargo door, firing long bursts down into the prison courtyard. Even the most fleeting of glances down into the courtyard showed the old exercise areas overgrown with foliage; evidence of the mistreatment of the POWs held within the walls. The Tubarão hovered over the lip of one of the western prison wall; a tall, thick barrier of concrete connecting two guard towers and extending up some fifty feet from the dusty ground. Heijboer was the first out of the cargo door, jumping down the two or three feet to the walkway running along the length of the prison wall before sprinting forward a few paces and then dropping to one knee, her Boarding Shotgun raised to one shoulder.

Romano and Tibar followed. Stanescu was next to egress. He hopped down the short gap to land on the prison wall before rushing forward to follow the green marker on his lens, directing him toward the nearer of the two guard towers. Above him, three more Tubarãos arced around to approach their own objectives; one with a Seraph TAG secured on strops beneath its belly. A pair of multi-barrel autocannons blazed away from their mounts on a battered industrial estate further up the hill toward the city center, lazily following the paths of the circling aircraft but failing to find their mark - they were now manually aimed, showcasing the success of the trio of Crusader Brethren in the opening stage of the assault.

A pair of hulking figures appeared atop the tall, northwest guard tower ahead of Stanescu. The chattering of rifles drifted across the hot, early evening air from the Morat guards at the top of the tower, before a third and then a fourth figure appeared. A moment later, the rapid thumping of a machine gun sounded, and the first casualty message scrolled across Stanescu's lens.

- *Sub Officer Luca Romano, wounded: critical. Multiple gunshot wounds, torso.*

"Darius!" Stanescu heard De Fersen's voice in his helmet ear pieces. "Double back to us! Kyle, Abdi - covering fire!"

Stanescu turned to look back and saw the Tubarão transitioning into forward flight away from the top of the prison wall, its shark-like frame silhouetted by the setting sun as machine guns chattered from both of its open cargo doors. Tibar crouched over the prone form of Romano, pouring fire up into the top of the guard tower. De Fersen dragged Romano toward the relative cover of the wall buttress, leaving a trail of blood on the cracked, dusty concrete behind him while the six sergeants dashed across for cover by the edge of the wall.

His shoulders raised instinctively as if hunkering down would somehow ward off bullets, Stanescu dashed back toward the other Hospitaller Knights. He clipped his MULTI Rifle to his back, removed his medkit, and pressed his comlog to bring up an injury analysis program to send to his lens as he ran. It was with no small amount of surprise that he saw Hawkins, clearly operating under his own initiative and completely without orders or a waypoint, charge headlong the other way past Stanescu, toward the guard tower and the team of Morat shooters.

"Fucking hell!" De Fersen growled. "Britt! Stay with him!"

Heijboer leapt to her feet and ran after Hawkins, her long shot-gun held across her stomach. Only a few paces away from his casu-alty, Stanescu felt a tap - no, more like an aggressive thump - on his shoulder. He span in place to see who was trying to grab his attention but saw nobody. Then his eyes focused on the smoking hole in his pauldron.

- *Ballistic impact, right shoulder. Non-penetrating.*

"Doc," De Fersen yelled, "down! Get in cover!"

Stanescu flung himself to the ground, beneath the level of the wall buttress, and rapidly crawled over to De Fersen, Romano, and Tibar. The air stank of burnt propellant, and the combined banging and whining of rifles and De Fersen's Spitfire echoed across the wall top. Stanescu reached Romano and knelt over him, quickly checking the holographic wound diagnosis that projected onto his lens. Three hits - two penetrating. One straight through the stomach, with a large exit wound. Airway clear, casualty in shock and bleeding out.

"Doc!" De Fersen yelled. "We can't stall here! We need to keep moving! Can you save him?"

Stanescu held up two fingers.

"Two minutes! Gimme two minutes! I'll have him on his feet and firing again!"

***

His eyes fixed on the doorway at the base of the guard tower, Hawkins ran headlong across the top of the prison's western wall. Gun-fire blasted away from behind him, above, and ahead of him as knights and Order sergeants exchanged fire with the growing number of Morats atop the tower. The gunfire seemed dim and distant; secondary to the sound of his rapid breathing and his armored feet slamming into the dusty concrete beneath him. His eyes narrowed, his fists clenched, he closed the gap to his target.

- *Mother-Officer Heijboer has formed Duo Team with you and is in command.*

Hawkins ignored the message on his lens. He did not need a team, or a leader. He just needed to close with his enemies and kill them. He reached the door at the base of the tower, just as one of the Tubarãos was descending into the prison courtyard, lowering the

Seraph TAG toward the ground. He pressed his back to the wall to one side of the door and quickly leaned across to try the handle. Locked. No time for subtlety. Hawkins turned to face the door and pivoted in place to lash out with one foot, propelling an armor-augmented side kick into the door. The first kick buckled the door, the second knocked it off its hinges. Teeth gritted, his pistol and sword drawn, Hawkins darted inside.

Empty weapons racks lined the far wall; armor lockers were crammed beneath a set of stairs leading up to the corner of the tower, where they turned at right angles to follow the wall to ascend toward the roof. Hawkins pelted up the steps just as Heijboer appeared at the door.

"Wait!" she ordered curtly.

Hawkins continued onward, up toward the hammering of gunfire from the roof. He had taken only a few steps when rapid, heavy footsteps slammed down against the metal staircase from above. Hawkins quickened his pace to meet them. At a corner in the stairs, a towering Morat Vanguard turned to rush down toward him, another two of his comrades close behind. Hawkins let out a yell and surged up into them, raising his MULTI Pistol to shoot the first adversary twice in the chest.

The felled alien soldier crumpled forward to fall down past Hawkins. Without pausing for breath, the Hospitaller continued his reckless charge up the stairwell, beating the second Vanguard trooper to the draw and hacking his heavy sword into the soldier's gut. He sliced the blade across to sever halfway through his opponent's torso, splashing a wave of scarlet up across both of them. Still shouting in rage, Hawkins barged his way past the mortally wounded Morat and brought his blade hacking down on the back of the huge warrior's neck to behead him.

Fearlessly, the third vanguard soldier dove into Hawkins, knocking him off his feet. Locked in a deadly embrace, the two armored warriors tumbled down a few steps as they both attempted to overpower each other, Hawkins regaining control over his words as he shouted at the alien.

"Die!... Die... you fucking..."

Heijboer's shotgun pressed against the Morat's gut, and a loud blast reverberated throughout the confines of the tower as the alien soldier's entrails were blown out of his back. The senior Hospitaller grabbed Hawkins by his upper arm and dragged him to his feet.

"If you won't listen to me, then *you* take the lead!" she snarled, her eyes visibly blazing from the other side of the lens in her helmet faceplate. "Get up there and kill them! Kill them all!"

Spitting out a string of obscenities, Hawkins loaded two fresh rounds into the rotary magazine of his pistol and then resumed his charge up toward the roof.

***

From her vantage point on the eastern wall, Cortez could see the exchange of fire developing along the western palisade. Red triangles instantly appeared on her lens from the top of the northwest tower as soldiers from De Fersen's team highlighted Morat soldiers firing down on them - a casualty alert scrolled across her lens before their Tubarão had even departed. Seconds later, red triangles appeared at the top of the southwest tower to box the knights and sergeants in along the wall.

"Come on!" Lieutenant Moreno shouted to his team of Crosiers as they disembarked from their own Tubarão along the opposite prison wall. "Keep going! Advance to my Marker Echo!"

The green triangle of an objective marker appeared on Cortez's screen, at the northern edge of the eastern wall, just at the foot of the northeast tower and the top of a set of concrete stairs leading down to the prison courtyard. Their first objective from the brief - clear the tower, get to the courtyard to link up with the TAG and the Teutonic Knights.

"Broadsword Delta team!" Cortez shouted from her position crouched at the edge of the prison wall. "Advance on me!"

Cortez sprang up to her feet and dashed along the wall, followed by four of the other Crosiers. She risked a glance to her left, down into the prison courtyard. Below her, the third of the Tubarãos lowered the Seraph TAG into position, the sleek fighting machine extending its limbs out below the aircraft like a horrific alien warrior awakening from its slumber. The strops holding it to the belly of the aircraft were released, and the TAG dropped to the ground with a thud, its knees buckling beneath it with an almost human poise as it landed.

"All teams, Mace One on scene and operational," Sergeant Patricio transmitted from the safety of her hangar command terminal back at the firebase.

A door at the foot of the southeast tower opened, and a team of Morat Vanguard soldiers sprinted out into the courtyard. The TAG swung around at the hip and raised its heavy machine gun.

"Mace One, engaging."

The courtyard lit up with the flickering yellow muzzle blasts of the monstrous fighting machine's huge machine gun, an almost solid line of bullets tearing into the Vanguard soldiers. The first two were cut down in showers of blood; the second pair of Vanguard troopers peeled apart with well-drilled precision, diving for the cover of cracked barricades and leaning around to return fire with their Combi Rifles. Its deadly sword raised high, the Seraph propelled itself forward off of one sleek limb and sprinted out toward its foes as a second team of enemy soldiers began firing at the TAG from the cover of the doorway.

Cortez was the first to reach the top of the staircase leading down the inside of the eastern wall toward the cracked, vine-infested courtyard. The rest of her team - Lois, May, Sharma, and Thatch - were only seconds behind. She tapped her comlog to set up another way-point in the courtyard itself to direct her team to a covered firing position in support of the TAG. Behind her, its cargo of Crosiers and two dron-bots now safely deposited on top of the prison wall, the Tubarão transi-tioned away to position downthreat to await orders to return. Both dron-bots commenced firing down from the wall into the courtyard, sending streams of bullets and missiles into the Morat defenders as Moreno's team of Crosiers rushed across the wall to join Cortez at Marker Echo.

***

With a roar, Hawkins barged open the door with his shoulder and charged onto the tower roof, his sword held high in both hands. A firing line of four Vanguard troopers leaned over the tower wall, firing down into De Fersen's team on the main palisade below. One Morat waited behind the quartet of shooters, facing the doorway. The soldier raised his Combi Rifle to a firing position and shot Hawkins square in the chest.

- *Impact: chest, non-penetrating... Impact: chest, non-penetrat-ing... Gunshot wound, shoulder...*

Pain flaring up from the injury below his collarbone, Hawkins continued his charge as his armor fired off its one shot of serum into the bleeding wound. The Vanguard trooper lunged forward to meet Haw-kins's charge. The Hospitaller swung his sword down to cleave straight through his adversary's rifle, the tip of the blade tearing through the alien warrior's gut. Seemingly impervious to fear and injury, the Morat lashed out with half of the Combi Rifle, swinging the impromptu club at Hawkins's head. Hawkins brought his blade up to block, pushed the Morat's arm to one side, and then stepped in to plant his armored fore-head into the warrior's face with a snapping of bone.

The attack forced the Morat warrior back, and Hawkins rushed in to bring a knee up into his wounded gut, tearing open the lacera-tion. Face to face, eye to eye, Hawkins finally saw pain in the soldier's eyes. He spat out a breath of uncontrolled obscenities as he drove his sword through the Morat's chest, twisted the blade, and withdrew it in a stream of blood and tissue.

Hawkins saw the first attack coming in from his right-hand side as another Vanguard trooper lunged in with a long, curved knife. The

Hospitaller deftly dropped his wounded shoulder to avoid the blow and pivoted on his hip to swing his sword around and sever his opponent's arm just above the elbow. A blow from another unseen opponent came from somewhere to his left, and Hawkins found himself on his back with blurred damage and injury texts scrolling across his lens. Unsure of where his enemies were and what he was facing in his dazed state, he rolled rapidly to one side and up onto one knee, grabbing his MULTI Pistol from its holster.

Heijboer advanced on a Vanguard soldier with a sniper rifle, firing her Boarding Shotgun from the hip with each step and blowing the alien warrior back, and then over the edge of the roof. Another soldier dove into her to tackle her to the ground. The two final Morats lunged toward Hawkins, one of them bleeding profusely from the severed stump of his amputated arm. Hawkins brought his pistol around to bear on the uninjured soldier and squeezed the trigger.

The high-powered pistol barked out a blast, the weapon's immense recoil soaked up by the power and stability of the knight's heavy armor. The Morat took the round square in the chest, stopping him dead in his charge, his eyes wide with shock from the force of the blow. Hawkins quickly fired a second shot, blowing the top half of the soldier's head apart.

With courage bordering on insane, the one-armed Morat flung himself in to attack Hawkins with one fist. The blow connected with Hawkins's jaw, a deafening clang reverberating around his helmet as he was knocked off his feet, his pistol flying across the rooftop. The screaming, salivating warrior lunged down on top of Hawkins, one huge fist clenching around his throat. But there was no contest in skill - not even before the fearless Morat had lost an arm. Hawkins thudded a palm strike into the warrior's elbow to break the bone and then rolled on top. Holding the blood-soaked alien soldier down with one hand, Hawkins raised his free fist to bring it crashing down into the soldier's face again and again. All technique thrown to the wind and replaced with blind, animalistic rage, Hawkins brought his clenched fist down repetitively, each blow rewarded with more damage, blood, and the crunching of bone, until finally he realized that his adversary was long dead.

Sweat pouring down his face, his breathing uneven, Hawkins staggered up to his feet to limp across the rooftop to recover his pistol and sword. Heijboer struggled over to him from the carnage of dead enemy soldiers, pulling a Morat knife out of her side as serum flowed down out of her rapidly repairing wound. Hawkins holstered his pistol and rushed over to her.

"Ma'am, you're..."

The older knight pushed him away forcefully.

"You listen here, boy, and you listen fucking well!" she snarled, her Dutch accent thick with rage. "There was a plan! There were orders! You don't just run off to do your own thing! We're a team! Gabriele is in command, not you! You got that?"

Gunfire continued to chatter away from the palisades and the courtyard as Hawkins turned away, his breathing gradually slowing again. The plan... Orders? He remembered landing on the western wall. He... there was a plan... He... had no recollection of what happened between landing and charging into the base of the tower.

"Ma'am, I..."

Heijboer held up a hand to silence him.

"Broadsword Alpha Zero, from One," she called. "Northwest tower secure."

"Roger," De Fersen's voice echoed through Hawkins's helmet, "engage enemy units at my Marker Hotel."

A marker appeared atop the southwest tower. Heijboer pointed at the MULTI Marksmen rifle on Hawkins's back.

"I don't know where you got that weapon," she breathed, "but put it to good use. Stay here and provide covering fire to Alpha Team. Stay here. Covering fire. Await further orders."

Hawkins nodded.

"Yes, ma'am."

The wounded Mother-Officer limped back toward the stairwell leading back down to the prison wall as Hawkins hurried over to the edge of the tower roof, bringing his rifle up to his shoulder and focusing the scope to pick out a target from amidst the squad of Morats firing down from the tower to the south.

***

The incessant dripping of water from a broken pipe on the other side of the dim, gray room prevented any chance of sleep. Sleep - Zevult scoffed at the thought from where he lay in the corner on a torn rollmat, damaged to the point that all functionality was lost and merely a simple, primitive long cushion remained. What a notion sleep was, he mused as he cast his eyes across the small chamber, converted from a storage room for cleaning drones at a fast food outlet. Sleep was something necessary, but overindulgence became a luxury. An admission of weakness. At least, he once thought that.

As a freshly qualified soldier, Zevult was just as guilty as his peers in taking great lengths to avoid sleep. Of course, societally it would be abhorrent to then point that out to other soldiers - a crass, vulgar display of strength that was reduced to nothingness if it was pointed out as a boast. But... if sleep could be ignored, shrugged off, and the ability to silently shoulder all hardships and still have the ability to kill the enemy... well, if that could be achieved and subtly pointed out in other ways to peers, *that* was the way of the young, hot-headed Morat warrior.

But, as the older blades of the soldiering fraternity were quick to point out, that was evidence of the old ways. Even if done silently and subtly, it was still a boast. Still a need for validation as an individual. Still... pathetic. The modern fighting Morat knew that sleep was necessary. If a lack of sleep increased bragging rights at the cost of a mere one percent of fighting efficiency in that individual, then the soldier became a selfish fool and not part of the team. The Morat soldier's job was to retain peak fighting efficiency - not bragging rights - and being rested enabled that soldier to do a better job of killing his opponents. But now? The wrong side of middle age, with decades of experience replacing the vigors of youth, a simple cracked water pipe prevented Zevult from even a moment's slumber. The days of being able to sleep anywhere and through anything were long gone.

A buzz on his golgrapt roused Zevult from his mental turmoil. He struggled up to a seated position on the near functionless rollmat, pain shooting up his ribs from the half-recovered gunshot wound that had prematurely ended his part in leading the attack on the PanOceanian city two days' ago. The bastards were waiting for them. A trap - a dishonest way of waging war, but a pragmatic and efficient one - had seen most of his force cut down from the shadows as soon as they had dispersed from their landing site. The same occurred across all of the sites - well done, PanO. Or, more specifically, ALEPH. You know how your enemy thinks. Strike them in their own back garden, and they shall do the same to you to prove they have the same capability and, in the case of the EI, a lack of outdated scruples regarding civilian losses.

But they were waiting. Zevult, his team, all of the forces involved, they walked straight into the trap.

The golgrapt buzz sounded again. Zevult struggled wearily up to his feet, feeling the advance of years more in that moment than ever before. He checked the unit on his wrist and saw that he was being hailed from the other side of his door.

"Yes?"

Ze Hamak Guntat opened the door, snapped to attention briefly as a mark of respect, and then eased into a more natural position in acknowledgment to Zevult's nod.

"Sir. I thought you would want to be informed eye to eye. A PanO force has just committed to an assault on one of our positions. Prisoner Detention Facility Two-Six. Military Orders, supported by armor. Airlifted, low level transit to remain beneath our sensors on the way in. Orbital deployment of a small team to disable our automated defenses."

Zevult nodded, wearily for a moment, before he remembered who he was and what was expected of him. He stood up straighter.

"Casualties?"

"Heavy."

"Reinforcements?"

"I've ordered everything in the area to move in immediately to support. Kyosot, Suryat, and both of our Bultraks. There is another platoon of Vanguard soldiers moving in from Firebase Three-Two, but that will take some time."

Zevult nodded again. They were bled almost dry. It was well beyond the point of considering keeping forces in reserve. He looked across at his subordinate. Good that it was Guntat. Ryyak had been a good soldier and a good leader, but he was substandard as a subordinate. The older, more experienced Guntat was his better in every way. A good Morat to face the best of the Human Sphere alongside.

"Eighteen soldiers, including the two of us. And two armored units. If it were light infantry we were facing, I would not flinch. But for the enemy to attempt to break out prisoners? It will be their best. Their knights."

Guntat's face twisted and contorted for a second, before quickly returning to a neutral expression.

"You wish for us to await the arrival of more reinforcements?"

Zevult span around to face his subordinate, his teeth bared.

"I did not say that. But a fool underestimates his foe. Enough. Let's go."

Chapter Seventeen

Edging around the corner of the bleak, gray corridor, Nilsson brought her rifle up to her shoulder from her prone position on the cracked-tile floor. A red diamond was painted on her lens to signify an enemy soldier waiting around the next corner at the far end of the corridor, but from the sheer volume of fire they had already received, she reckoned on it being at least three Morat troopers. Knelt just above her, Brother-Sub Officer Tibar leaned around the corridor corner with his own weapon raised at the ready.

"Nearly there," De Fersen's voice grunted through the earpieces of her helmet, "another few seconds."

The hammering and thumping of gunfire sounded from outside where, in the courtyard, the Seraph TAG reigned supreme against small teams of Vanguard troopers who valiantly attempted to combat the towering fighting machine. But as for the core of the Hospitaller team - save for a few soldiers left behind to keep key positions on their egress route secure - they were now in the bowels of the prison, fighting to keep the Morat guards at bay while negotiating a succession of locked security doors. The crackle of rifle fire sounded from somewhere close behind as another group of Morats attempted to find another way around to attack the surrounded Hospitallers.

A darkened silhouette quickly leaned around the far corner of the corridor, briefly illuminated in a series of staccato flashes from the damaged lighting above it. The angular-armored Morat fired a burst down the corridor, chewing into the plaster-covered walls by Nilsson and Tibar. Both Hospitallers returned fire, sending rounds back at the Morat aggressor and forcing him to duck back into cover. Her pulse racing, Nilsson briefly wondered who was keeping who pinned in place - the Hospitallers fighting for time to open the doors to the main cells, or the Morats who undoubtedly had reinforcements on the way at that very moment.

"Alright," De Fersen called, "we've…"

Tibar was the first to shoot as three Morat soldiers sprinted around the corner up ahead, firing their weapons from the hip as they ran. Nilsson picked the closest target and fired a burst of four rounds, her accuracy rewarded with sprays of blood erupting from wounds on the soldier's chest that flicked across the wall to his side as he turned and fell down. The second Morat was gunned down by Tibar as the knight sent a trio of rounds tearing through his gut. A fraction of a moment later, Tibar fell as enemy fire cut across his own chest and knocked him back away from the wall.

Nilsson jumped up to one knee, her rifle still thumping in her hands as she fired another burst at the final enemy soldier. A shot winged off the alien warrior's shoulder, but he did not slow for even a single pace.

Nilsson froze in place.

She remembered the Morat who she had failed to defeat, who had lopped off her hand and left her for dead.

Her moment of fear lasted for less than a second. With a shout, she flung herself up into a sprint to meet the enemy soldier head on. The Morat's roar echoed down the thin corridor as he barged into her. Nilsson pivoted on the spot to deflect the charge, whipping the butt of her rifle up into the Vanguard trooper's face. The blow connected with a sickening crack but again failed to stop the inhuman mass of muscle. His eyes wide and ablaze with fury, his sharp teeth clenched in a sali-va-dripping snarl of rage, the Morat brought a massive, clenched fist up toward Nilsson's stomach.

The Hospitaller Sergeant took the blow against her rifle, dropped one hand to her holster, and rapidly raised her pistol to the Morat's chin. She fired a round up through his head, blowing a spatter of blackened blood up against the ceiling before then pressing the muzzle against his forehead and shooting him a second time for good measure. The Morat slumped down to his knees, eyes drawn almost comically up toward the mass of bloodied flesh atop his head, and then pitched forward onto his face.

Nilsson holstered her pistol and looked around to see Tibar clambering back to his feet, blood and medical serum streaked over the white cross of his red surcoat. The wounded soldier nodded to Nilsson as rifle fire continued to chatter from behind them.

"Alpha Team!" De Fersen's voice growled. "Advance to my Marker Juliet! Go!"

***

With the final security door hacked and open, De Fersen looked up and saw the lights flickering into life along the ceiling of the narrow corridor up ahead. To either side, lines of cell doors punctuated the cracked, off-white walls at regular intervals up to the corridor corner some fifty meters ahead. Each cell was designed for a single occupant - two at a push. From the information De Fersen had just gleaned from the prison's database, the Morats had elected to cram ten prisoners into each cell - irrespective of faction and gender. One thing they had maintained in working order was the soundproofing around each cell. The poor bastards inside no doubt had no idea that the rescue was underway.

De Fersen looked back at his team; two other knights and three sergeants still accompanied him. The other had been left scattered along the route back to the courtyard to secure key junctions. He briefly checked his comlog map for an update on the progress of the Teutonic team; the four soldiers had progressed around to the far side of the cells to secure the area from a counter attack from the north.

"I'm opening the cells," De Fersen announced to his team, "be ready for confusion from our people, and hostility from the Yujingyu and Haqqislamite prisoners."

"What do we do if any of the enemy prisoners attack us?" Romano asked. "Are we…"

"No."

De Fersen shook his head. Decades of fighting against the other factions of the Human Sphere had, he knew, instilled a deep and lasting hatred within his heart. He had enough self awareness to recognize that, at least. But then the EI came. The great leveler. The outside threat, more deadly than any internal, that should have united the forces of humanity together as brothers and sisters against a common foe, celebrating their shared values instead of killing each other over their few differences. But the human condition was always victorious. Even over morality, integrity and common sense.

"No," De Fersen continued, "they have no arms and armor. They're starving. Hell, they're disconnected from Maya, like neanderthals. They're not a viable threat. No, don't hurt them. If any enemy prisoners are stupid enough to attack us, just knock them down."

With a final press on the green 'unlock' symbol displayed above his wrist, De Fersen unlocked the doors. Twenty cell entrances slid open along the corridor in front of him, and around the corners of the T-junction ahead. Confused voices mumbled from within the two nearest cells. De Fersen paced over to the closest entrance.

"Come on!" he growled. "Time is not on our side! Out, against the walls!"

He looked in and saw ten prisoners, clothed in dirty and torn bodysuits and combat fatigues. The ten men and women were bruised, bloodied, and exhausted looking. Hope flickered across their eyes as they looked up at the armored knight in the doorway.

"Out!" De Fersen repeated. "Come on!"

Romano rushed along the corridor, shouting at the prisoners within. Slowly - too slowly - the dazed and starved soldiers limped and staggered out into the corridor. Dozens of bedraggled soldiers from

PanO regiments, and Yujingyu and Haqqislamite units, filed out, staring along the passageway with mixtures of hope, confusion, and suspicion. De Fersen watched warily as four Yujingyu prisoners immediately formed a small group and muttered quietly to each other as they eyed their Hospitaller rescuers. De Fersen paced over to them.

"You even *think* of causing problems for me, I'll gun you down myself if it means saving everybody else."

Any reply from any of the soldiers who might understand him without a comlog to translate was cut off as a tall, thin man with graying temples and green combat fatigues limped over to De Fersen.

"You're in command here?" the soldier inquired. "I'm Lieutenant Colonel Claver of the 6th Light Infantry. I'm the ranking prisoner here."

De Fersen unholstered his pistol and switched off the IFF safety before offering it to the comlog-deprived battalion commander as rifle fire snapped and echoed from the corridors behind them.

"Understood, sir. We've secured a route back to the courtyard for your extraction. We'll be shuttling you all out via air, taking the courtyard as our LZ."

Claver accepted the handgun.

"And the courtyard is secure?"

De Fersen shook his head.

"Not yet, but it soon will be. We've taken the walls and we have a TAG in the courtyard, against only sporadic resistance. A handful of survivors from the guard detail."

The middle-aged colonel's eyes narrowed.

"But they'll have reinforcements on the way here already. Armor of their own."

De Fersen nodded.

"That's why we have to move quickly."

Aware of the prisoners' lack of Maya connectivity, he leaned in close to the colonel.

"Sir," he muttered, "I need to prioritize evacuating all PanO prisoners. The rest... we'll do what we can. Can you arrange these people into sticks for airlifting out? PanO front and center?"

The lieutenant colonel nodded.

"There's nearly two hundred of us here. This will take time."

"We'll hold the site for as long as we can, but we need to move."

Claver turned to the lines of prisoners.

"Captain Lewis! Lieutenant Viana! On me!"

***

"How many of them are there, Basek?" Zevult asked as he stared down through the armored window at the prison below, long shadows cast against its dusty walls.

The two bulky Ostarak utility aircraft shot over the abandoned suburbs of City-B-Six, their cargo compartments packed with as many troopers as Zevult could muster in such a short space of time.

"Couldn't confirm for sure, sir," replied Hewza, the freshly promoted basek reporting to him from the firefight at the prison, his voice calm and assured in Zevult's earpiece, "but there are three groups. One on the eastern prison wall, another has taken the courtyard, and the main force has pushed into the facility to free prisoners."

The lead Ostarak banked sharply over an overgrown residential area, its powerful engines whining in the turn. The prison was just ahead now, not far from the river bank and in the low ground at the city's edge. The grim, angular industrial site that had been utilized by the Morats since immediately after their successful invasion snaked out eastward along the river bank; the very reason that prisoner labor was required. The second aircraft was visible off the left wing of the first, carrying Guntat and his Kyosots. The two red and black Bultraks of the 33rd Armored Regiment sprinted along the main road below them, visible only to Zevult on his tactical map. Zevult returned his attention to the prison.

"How many troopers do you have left?" he spoke into his golgrapt.

He knew the answer would be sub-optimal based solely on the fact that a freshly promoted junior NCO had taken command of the prison defenses.

"Eleven of us left, sir. I have command of five attempting to cut off the route from the cells to the courtyard. The others are in the courtyard engaging their TAG and light infantry on the east wall."

Zevult raised one thick hand to his chin. He could hear the crackle of small arms fire from his position looking down across the industrial site and the prison.

"Alright, Basek," he replied in Nylad, the basic military dialect of the common soldier, "consolidate your position at my Marker Two-Four. Get both groups together and retake the eastern wall."

"Sir."

Zevult opened a channel to Guntat.

"You heard all of that?"

"Yes, sir."

"We'll land on and proceed on foot from here. I'm not losing half of our forces to a missile taking out an Ostarak. I'll lead the Suryat and take one Bultrak to assault the north gates. You lead the Kyosot and the second Bultrak to take the south gate. Keep an eye out for their secondary force moving in from the gun battery."

"Yes, sir. And above. They'll be attempting to evacuate by air."

Zevult nodded.

"Undoubtedly."

Zevult heard Guntat shouting at the soldiers in the back of his own aircraft, muffled shouts preparing them to disembark. There was almost a joyful tone to his commands - something more than merely the anticipation of battle. Zevult smirked. Of course. Commanding Kyosot in battle. Guntat's family history was deeply connected to the Kyosot Movement from a time before the Axe Expansion when their ways were considered... unacceptable.

Zevult raised his golgrapt again, zoomed in on his map, and quickly plotted waypoints to coordinate the attack on the two prison entrances. A data transmission came through the Ursphere to his device. A file showing the briefest footage of the TAG in the courtyard - Seraph class, armed with a heavy machine gun. Zevult grunted. Military Orders. The fanatic zealots of a backward race who still clung to archaic beliefs about gods and religion. It was their greatest weakness. And their most dangerous strength as a foe.

***

Stood boldly in the center of the cracked, vine-covered prison courtyard, the Seraph TAG pumped another burst of high-caliber machine gun rounds into the Morat position in the northwest corner. Fist-sized holes punched into the walls to leave a spider web of cracks across the concrete as the fighting machine laid down a deafening hail of fire, the flickering yellow muzzle flash of the huge weapon lighting up the machine's cold, impassive head module. From her vantage point on the eastern wall, Cortez peered over the sights of her rifle and down into the courtyard. There was no return fire.

The line of ten Crosiers lay prone along the top of the wall, eight weapons pointing down into the courtyard while two soldiers kept a lookout for enemy reinforcements to the north and east, from the city itself. The two dronbots had repositioned onto the northern wall, their weapons likewise pointing out toward the city in anticipation of the Morat reinforcements which were sure to arrive. If the courtyard was secure, they could finally move down to their objective.

A snicker of laughter was issued from a soldier two places down the wall to Cortez's left, in the firing line.

"They've run!" Crosier Arias exclaimed, a grin lighting up her face. "They've given up!"

Cortez whipped her head around to stare across at the rookie trooper.

"Morats don't run, you fucking idiot! They're regrouping to hit us somewhere else! Keep that weapon up and ready!"

A silence descended across the prison. The late afternoon winds, light though they were, whistled through the tall, derelict buildings of the city center to the north. Birds sang and chirped away from the immense jungle to the south and east, a carpet of vivid green sprawling out to envelop every contour to the hazy, orange horizon. The faint hum of aero engines sounded from the south, where the Tubarãos waited patiently to be called back in to land on and embark the prisoners.

- *Clipper to all units. Enemy forces inbound from the north, strength two, heavy armor. Uploading marker to map.*

"Shit," Lois grumbled from the end of the firing line.

Moreno looked across at Cortez.

"Sergeant, take Sharma and Dieguez with you. Get up on the north wall and get eyes on that enemy armor."

"Sir," Cortez responded, jumping up to a crouched position and dashing low across the prison wall toward the northeast tower.

The three Crosiers rushed up to the corner tower, Cortez glancing across at where the weapons systems of the two dronbots slowly tracked the still unseen enemy advancing through the industrial complex to the north. Dieguez was the first to reach the tower. He raised his rifle in one hand and placed his other on the door's entry pad.

"Wait!" Cortez hissed.

Her eyes narrowed, hairs on the back of her neck raised, she stared around in the eerie silence to either side, unsure exactly where the feeling of unease had suddenly leapt up from, but knowing from years of experience that it was not to be ignored.

The door burst open, and two hulking Morat troopers rushed out, guns blazing. Dieguez was thrown back in a hail of fire, spinning around and crumpling down in a spray of blood. Cortez brought her own rifle around to fire a burst from the hip, but the rushing Vanguard trooper hit her like a meteor, slamming a rifle butt into her head and knocking her down to the ground as the world around her exploded back into its regular cacophony of gunfire.

***

- *Zero, from Overwatch. Enemy reinforcements inbound from the north; two TAGs, two medium transport aircraft.*

The message scrolled across the top of De Fersen's lens from one of the surveillance operatives overseeing the operation from that safe, cozy ops room thousands of miles away. A few moments later, another message scrolled across.

- *Clipper to all units. Enemy forces inbound from the north, strength two, heavy armor. Uploading marker to map.*

"*Merde,*" De Fersen spat.

The awkward, unwieldy procession of nearly two hundred men and women staggered and stumbled through the corridors leading from the cells back up to the courtyard above. Alpha Team had largely re-formed now, with five knights and six sergeants escorting the prisoners toward the LZ. Up top, the Crosiers held the firing line along the eastern wall, with one knight up on the northwest tower and Patricio's TAG in the courtyard. That left the two dronbots on the north wall, and the Teutonic team moving back through the cells to join them. An effective defensive set up that could fold in on itself quickly to evacuate with the second flight of Tubarãos when the time came.

Still, De Fersen sighed, what he would not have given for some drone surveillance from above - even old school satellite coverage, anything - to give him more situational awareness of his battlespace. But if there was one, single thing that Morats knew how to do well, it was wage war. As brutal - even primitive - as they may have looked up close, they knew well the importance of the cyber battlespace, and the area around Moravia was locked up tight, with counter measures to the PMC's eyes and ears posted everywhere.

The ambling line of injured and emaciated prisoners continued to progress forward with painfully slow progress, past the dead bodies of Morat guards and bullet hole strewn walls of previous firefights. Then the casualty messages began scrolling across De Fersen's lens.

- *Crosier Andres Dieguez, dead. Gunshot wound, chest.*
- *Sergeant Marianna Cortez, unconscious. Head wound, blunt trauma. Critical.*
- *Crosier Fanish Sharma, dead. Gunshot wound, head.*

Swearing again, De Fersen brought up his tactical map and saw a flood of red dots surging out of the northeast tower and onto the eastern prison wall.

"Shit!" Heijboer snapped. "We need to get up on that wall now and..."

"Wait! Wait!" De Fersen held up a hand. "This is damn Morats we're talking about! They don't just blunder into an attack, this is coordinated! No, they're bringing those TAGs around to try to get into the courtyards."

De Fersen's second-in-command looked across at him.

"Through the gates?" Heijboer asked.

De Fersen narrowed his eyes.

"If it's Bultraks, they might be going over them."

Raising his comlog again, De Fersen selected a communication channel to all of his forces, save the Crosiers in the fight atop the eastern wall. They would have enough to worry about without having to deal with him screaming out commands over a tactical net.

"Alpha One, Two, Three - get to the courtyard and assist Mace One with securing the south gate! Four, hold position and provide covering fire. Five, get up on the eastern wall and provide medical assistance to the Crosiers. Sergeants - get the prisoners to Marker Kilo and await further orders. Caesar Team - reinforce the east wall."

"Caesar Team, copied," Stahl replied.

Heijboer laid a hand on De Fersen's shoulder as Romano and Tibar rushed past to sprint toward their objective.

"Gabe," she urged, "this is your show and I'm not trying to take over here, but… the north gate. Reinforcements are coming in from the north. These bastards would be insane not to try to push a Bultrak right through the north gate and into the courtyard."

De Fersen flashed a smile that he wished was visible outside his helmet's faceplate, and tapped a finger against his hacking device.

"I'm absolutely counting on it."

***

Stanescu paused in place as the orders came through his earpiece, his ears picking out the one line that was aimed directly at him.

"…Five, get up on the eastern wall and provide medical assistance to the Crosiers…"

He had already seen the casualty reports lining up on his lens - two dead and one critically wounded. He swallowed, fighting to keep his breathing even as he visualized the carnage of the fighting in the courtyard and up on the walls. The fighting he needed to face to bring his skills to his comrades' assistance.

If you falter in times of trouble, how small is your strength…
Proverbs 24:10.

Propelled back to the here and now, Stanescu looked up and along the line of sickly, wounded, and starving prisoners. The worst of all of them - a young soldier who had only managed to croak out his nickname to Stanescu, clung weakly to one of his armored shoulders. Stanescu turned to find another of the rescue team.

"Sergeant?"

Anya Nilsson rushed over to him.

"Sir?"

The doctor looked across at the critically injured prisoner.

"Patch, this is Anya. She'll take care of you now. I'm sorry, I've got to go."

The young soldier wheezed, his eyes struggling to remain open as Stanescu carefully eased him onto Nilsson's shoulder. Patch slipped an arm around the Order Sergeant and looked up weakly at the doctor.

"Th...thank... you..."

Nilsson checked along both ends of the line of prisoners and then looked up again at Stanescu.

"Kilpatrick can take care of him, sir. I can come with you. You'll need another gun to get to that wall."

Stanescu shook his head.

"Father-Officer De Fersen's orders are clear. We can't mess around with the plan. Take care of this one, please, Anja. I'll see you up top."

Grabbing his MULTI Rifle from his back, Stanescu turned to sprint past the line of bedraggled prisoners and toward the stairs leading up to the courtyard.

Chapter Eighteen

"Two One, Two Two - picking up the pace. In position in ten."

"Two One, visual with you. Suryats in position. Ready to raze and crush. Hoo-ha."

"Hoo-ha."

From where he waited behind the wall of an old generator building, Zevult glanced across at Iriakk, the senior NCO commanding the troop of heavily armored, veteran Suryats. The old warrior, his features hidden behind his black and red helmet, grunted and shook his head in disapproval, his long, plaited white beard swinging across his barrel-chest. Zervult swore. Fucking Bultrak pilots. Fucking youths. Hoo-ha...

Zevult looked at his map again as gunfire echoed down from the firefight on the eastern wall, as the Vanguard counter attack pushed back the line of Military Order light infantry. A few more seconds to get the second Bultrak caught up with Guntat and his Kyosots in position to the south. He felt excitement coursing through his veins at the thought of leading eight Suryat warriors - veterans, the old guard of the Blink Wars and the Flash Wars - into battle against the most dangerous of all human foes. He quickly suppressed that feeling; that outdated exuberance that tragically seemed alive and well in the Bultruk pilot world. He raised his rifle.

"Bultrak Two One takes lead, suppress AI defense on the north wall. Then straight through that gate."

"Aye, sir," Iriakk grunted.

The square representing Bultrak Two Two moved rapidly through the undergrowth flanking the outside of the western wall to catch up with the Kyosots. All forces in position. Zevult opened a channel to all teams.

"All units from command, execute the assault."

"Two One copied," the closer Bultrak pilot replied, "watch this."

The towering war machine paced out of cover from behind the generator building, raising itself to its full height and bringing its carapace mounted magnetic cannon around to line up with the two squat, robotic defenders on the north wall. The familiar but always anti-climactic series of rapid clicks sounded from the internal mechanism of the long-barreled weapon as it spat out a hail of high caliber projectiles.

Rounds smashed against the top of the north wall, blowing chunks out of the primitive human-engineered construct, and sending clouds of dust and debris flying up into the hot air.

A barely visible muzzle flash lit up from amidst the dust clouds as return fire swept down from one of the enemy REMs, followed by white streaks of smoke as missiles whooshed from the second unit. The ground thudded with the impact, and the tinny ring of alloy on alloy sounded as rounds pelted against the thick armor of the Bultrak.

"Suryats," Zevult grimaced, "on me."

***

The crackling of rifle fire battled against the deeper booming of Morat weapons, the combined din echoing down across the courtyard. Below, the Seraph TAG stepped backward toward the western wall. Its heavy machine gun tilted upward as the fighting machine desperately attempted to gain a clear line of fire to the enemy infantry that were just too high to jump up to engage. From the north, a salvo of projectiles slammed into the prison outer wall, blasting concrete apart and covering the two dronbots in dust and clumps of masonry as they desperately attempted to return fire against the Morat reinforcements.

From his position isolated on the northwest tower, Hawkins stared down the sights of his marksman rifle at the eastern wall. Sweat rolled down both sides of his face, despite the constant relief of the cool air blasting through the inside of his armor. His suit diagnostics warned him that his blood pressure and pulse rate were reading amber, although the rigidity provided by his armor negated any real effect on the accuracy of his fire as a result of his labored breathing.

"Come on, you fuckers... come on, you fuckers..."

His rifle raised to his shoulder, leaning against the edge of the buttress, Hawkins ignored the increased din of fire from his left as the enemy reinforcements closed.

- *Crosier Joseph Thatch, dead. Gunshot wound, torso.*

Fire kicked up against both ends of the wall as the Crosiers fought against the advancing Vanguard troopers, the latter keeping to the outer segment of wall to avoid the withering fire of the TAG below. There - one of the bastards was up and running. A red diamond painted over a broad, dark figure surging forward into a charge, covered by his comrades behind. The sensors of Hawkins's scope projected a red crosshair just a fraction ahead of the target to allow for a little lead. Track the target, just for a moment. Take the shot, don't waste the chance.

Hawkins fired. A burst of red mist flew up from the top of the Morat's head, and the enemy soldier fell down. The briefest feeling of relief for doing his job properly and assisting the battered Crosiers was almost instantly replaced with a bewildering sensation of guilt for taking another life. The Morat was just another soldier following orders. Then Hawkins remembered the attacks on civilian populations. He quickly buried any other intrusive feelings about specific individuals that would further distract him from his task. No. No guilt.

In the courtyard below, blue diamonds highlighted the arrival of De Fersen and a handful of knights charging up the steps from the corridors to rejoin the fight.

-    *Clipper dronbot destroyed.*

Hawkins looked to his left and saw the tattered remnants of the top of the north wall. Amidst the smoke, all that remained of the Clipper was a scattering of spider-like, mechanical legs and a torn armored carapace, ripped apart by enemy gunfire. The Sierra dronbot valiantly fought on, despite having one of its own legs blown off. Below, a line of red diamonds advanced rapidly across the opening leading to the north gate.

-    *Enemy reinforcements inbound from the north at Marker Mike. Heavy Infantry.*

Hawkins opened a communication channel.
"Alpha Zero from Four, request..."
"Stay where you are!" De Fersen yelled.
Hawkins swore again and brought his rifle back up to track across the eastern wall.

***

An explosion sounded at the left side of the towering, corrugated alloy gate. It quickly motored itself back into its recess at the side of the guard tower. Before it was even halfway open, Morat heavy infantry poured through the gap and into the courtyard. Taller, broader, more powerful looking than even the Vanguard troopers, their black armor was trimmed with blood red. Their plaited, long beards and the horn-design on their helmets marked them out as Suryat - veterans of years of combat, drawn from the ranks of less prestigious regiments; specialists in assaulting fortified positions.

De Fersen swore. That screwed his plan. Somehow the scenario became even worse when a Bultrak TAG leaned down to squeeze beneath the north gate's archway and follow the seven assault troopers into the courtyard. The lumbering armored fighting machine raised itself back up, both arms carrying long, green-edged close combat weapons. A long-barrelled cannon swiveled over the top of its curved, red cara-pace.

"Knights, targets front!" De Fersen yelled as he reached the top of the stairs leading up to the courtyard. "Advance!"

An explosion sounded behind De Fersen. He stopped, dead in his tracks, and turned to see Heijboer, Tibar, and Romano hurtle past him as behind them the south gate swung open. A second Bultrak TAG appeared in the entrance, a section of ten green armored Kyosot troop-ers advancing through the gap with their rifles and submachine guns already blazing.

"Mace One, targets south! Engaging!" Patricio called.

In a show of spectacular initiative - no doubt influenced by see-ing the knights charging across the open ground toward the enemy force at the north gate with unchecked enemy soldiers firing into their backs from the south - the Seraph responded. The sleek, deadly war machine pivoted in place from its position near the north gate and fired a long, continuous burst from its machine gun into the green-armored Kyosots. The Morat soldiers scattered, two of their number gunned down where they stood in showers of blood.

The Seraph's intervention was cut off seconds later when the Bultrak with the northern force charged into it, slamming an armored shoulder into the PanOceanian TAG and knocking it back a pace. The Bultrak hacked down with an angular, heavy close combat weapon to slice against the Seraph's arm control-cables, sending severed pipe-lines snaking out in a spray of hydraulic fluid.

De Fersen looked south, then north, then keyed in an objective marker on his comlog.

"Knights! Take enemy unit Alpha!"

The trio of Hospitallers resumed their rapid advance toward the Suryats, weapons blazing as they advanced. De Fersen sprinted out to their left, vaulting over a waist-length partition wall and firing a burst from his Spitfire as he closed. Romano was the first to fall, gunned down by the Bultrak at the south gate with a long burst of fire from its magnetic cannon. A casualty notification message on De Fersen's lens confirmed the worst.

Heijboer flung herself screaming into the closest Suryat, duck-ing beneath a sword strike and then digging her own weapon into the Morat's belly before withdrawing it in an arc of crimson. Tibar rushed across to her side, deflecting an attack from a second Suryat and then bringing his own sword around into a high strike to the neck.

The thunder of gunfire blazed away from the northern gates ahead, the southern entrance behind, and the continuing firefight between the Crosiers and the Vanguard troopers up on the wall to the right. His teeth gritted, De Fersen fixed his stare on one of the black-armored enemy soldiers ahead. A round impacted his armor over the left hip, half spinning him in place and knocking him down to one knee. Ignoring the damage notification message from his armor's sensors, De Fersen jumped straight back on his feet.

Ahead of him, four figures in whites and blues shot out of the northern gatehouse, hurling themselves into the bloody melee with the Suryats. Stahl's Teutonic Knights - enough to even the balance. Above them, the thick, angular figure of the Bultrak TAG remained locked in close combat with the tall, lithe Seraph. The Morat TAG pilot, suspended from the front of his machine's torso like some morbidly humorous baby carrier, pushed his control sticks to command his fighting machine's arms into life, swinging two heavy blades down toward the Seraph. The PanOceanian TAG, controlled remotely from the hangar hundreds of miles away at Firebase India Two-Five, deftly avoided the first strike and then blocked the second before thrusting its own glowing sword out at the Bultrak, lancing through its upper torso in a shower of sparks.

His eyes narrowed, his thin lips twisted in a determined smirk, De Fersen raced toward the fighting TAGs and activated his hacking device.

***

A mere trio of knights charged out to meet Zevult and his Suryat veterans at the prison gate, their archaically-styled swords held aloft. The combined fire from Iriakk and one of his troopers cut down the first knight, stitching a line of fire across the human's body and sending him sprawling down in the dust. The second knight, a woman judging by her thinner frame and slightly different pattern of armor, rushed in to face Iriakk and, after a mere few moments of exchanged blows, cut the fifteen-year veteran down with a slice across the belly.

Zevult took two paces toward the woman - not for vengeance; emotion had no place in such decisions - but with the intent of killing her quickly, now that she had identified herself as a significant threat. Then he detected movement in his peripheral vision - a flash of white out of the corner of his eye - and span to the left. Three more human soldiers, clad in white surcoats with black crosses over their chests, hurtled out of the northern gatehouse building to engage his Suryats. A fourth soldier, dressed in lighter armor of blues and whites that faded and pulsed as evidence of his reactive camouflage, hung back by the doorway and took aim with a Combi Rifle. The soldier fired two rapid shots into a Suryat's chest in quick succession, followed by a third shot to the face to fell the elite warrior.

Raising his own heavy sword, Zevult charged out to meet the Teutonic Knights head on. The first warrior sprinted across to meet his challenge, swinging down with his straight, twin-edged blade. Zevult took the attack onto his own sword and pivoted in an attempt to fling his attacker off balance, but the expert warrior had already withdrawn his blade and ducked beneath Zevult's own counter attack. Eyes narrowed, teeth gritted, Zevult barged forward into his attacker to slam a shoulder into him and knock him down. Again, the heavily armored soldier moved with surprising agility for his size, and Zevult felt pain tear across his back as the human soldier's sword cut down through his armor.

Undeterred, never phased, the Morat commander turned into the attack and swung out again. And again, the Teutonic Knight was faster. Zevult let out a yell that he hoped would sound like unbridled frustration before swinging out with a wild, uncontrolled overhead strike. His adversary easily stepped aside, and Zevult followed through to dig his own blade into the ground. The Teutonic Knight stepped across to take advantage of the Morat's seemingly ill-executed attack.

Zevult brought his free hand up and slammed a clenched fist into the knight's face with a clang of dented alloy, taking advantage of the knight's eagerness to capitalize on a faked error. The Teutonic Knight's head was flung back by the sheer force of the blow, and both arms flew to either side. Zevult quickly hefted his sword up and cut a great wound across the knight's torso, cleaving through from his hip to his opposite shoulder.

The human soldier's armor immediately sprayed its automated healing serum across the wound, but Zevult had his opening now. With a genuine roar of determination, he sprung forward into another attack, plunging his sword through his adversary's gut. The knight fell forward limply, his sword falling from his hands. Zevult stepped back and withdrew his blade. The Teutonic Knight sagged down to both knees. Zevult smirked and nodded. Good man. Good fighter. Deserving of a quick and proper death. Rather than going for his Cube, Zevult showed his respect by standing over the felled human and slicing open his throat, nodding again in admiration as he saw the dying man's hand grab at his pistol, even in defeat.

Zevult stepped away from his fallen prey, turning quickly in place to search the bloody melee around him for his next target. He saw four of the human knights - two Hospitallers and two Teutonic Knights - formed back to back, holding their ground as the five remaining Suryats rained attacks down on them. Again, Zevult saw the female Hospitaller exploit the tiniest of mistakes in one of the Suryats and punish an opening by beheading one of the Morats. Enough. She needed to die. Zevult charged across to fill the gap left by the fallen Morat warrior.

He had closed only half the gap when he picked out a handful of words, a single uttered sentence across the tactical communications network that stood out from all of the other commands and alerts given in Nylad.

"Two Two, from Two One, got a problem... controls are locking up... I... wait..."

Zevult froze. He turned to face Two One - the Bultrak pilot who had accompanied him and the Suryats in assaulting the northern gate - and saw the tall, powerful machine stop in place in front of the enemy TAG. The Hospitaller Seraph, in turn, had ceased fighting against the shorter war machine. Stood a few paces from them both, Zevult saw another Hopitaller knight stood alone and detached from the main fight.

"It's locked up!" the Bultrak pilot called, a decidedly un-Morat-like tone of alarm in his communication. "Nothing's responding! Wait... I..."

The Bultrak stepped across with its left leg to assume a stable stance and swung its magnetic cannon around to aim at Guntat and his Kyosot team at the south gate.

"I've been hacked! Two Two, I've been hacked! Get everybody clear of my arcs of fire, I can't control it!"

"Get out, Askar! Eject!"

"I can't eject! I can't stop the weapons systems! Kill me! Quickly!"

The tall, thin Hospitaller crouched down by the Bultrak pressed a holographic symbol projected above his comlog. The Bultrak's hyper-rapid magnetic cannon clicked into life. A stream of projectiles blasted across the prison courtyard, sweeping through the Kyosots by the southern gate. The first caught a burst of fire through the chest, lancing a hole straight through his armor; a second Kyosot was decapitated by a round straight to the face. The others scattered.

***

Gunfire snapped and thundered across the prison courtyard, dominated by the deep boom of the Seraph's machine gun as it fired long bursts at the Bultrak to the south. Knights and Suryats were locked in a swirling melee by the north gate as behind them, the hacked second Bultrak fired its carapace mounted magnetic cannon at the Kyosot troopers advancing across the courtyard. To the right, rifle fire exchanges continued up on the east prison wall as the battered Crosiers continued to battle against the Vanguard troopers dug in at the northeast tower.

At the stairs leading up from the cells, Stanescu stared wide-eyed across the carnage of the courtyard. He could charge the Suryats down. Drive into them from behind and hack them to pieces with his sword; the weapon he only knew how to use proficiently from the artificial programming shoved into his head. But proficient he was.

No. His orders were to provide medical assistance to the casualties on the east wall. But was he following his orders obediently, or looking for an excuse to avoid the dangers of direct combat? Shit, not now. Not the time to overthink. Time to just get stuck straight into it all.

"Sir!"

Stanescu turned and saw three sergeants pelting up the steps behind him. He let out a gasp of frustration.

"Sergeant! Your orders were to stay with the prisoners!"

"It doesn't need all six of us," Nilsson replied. "We need more guns up here. We need to get you to the east wall, now."

Stanescu looked at the bloody fighting by the north gate, up to the east wall, then back at Nilsson. He nodded. The young sergeant turned to face her two squadmates, tapping her comlog as she did so.

"Francois, Rory, take targets at my Marker Sierra. Sir, let's go."

Sergeant Kilpatrick took position by the top of the stairs and fired his Combi Rifle into the Kyosots advancing across the courtyard. A second later, a rocket from Aubert's launcher whooshed out of the tube and across the open space between the Military Order soldiers and their enemies. The projectile slammed into the back of one of the Kyosots, who was swallowed from view in a brief blossom of yellow and black which spat out body parts in a macabre spectacle of crimson.

His MULTI Rifle held across his chest, Stanescu hurled himself over the last step and sprinted toward the southeast tower. He had taken barely four steps when red flashes appeared along the left edge of his lens, alerting him to incoming enemy fire. Bullets snapped and cracked over his head while puffs of dust kicked up by his feet. Stanescu pivoted in place, bringing his rifle around to face the line of green armored Kyosots taking cover by one of the courtyard partition walls. He fired a long burst of return fire, his rounds punching holes in the wall and blasting up slivers of masonry.

"Keep going!" Nilsson shouted as she sprinted past him. "Don't stop!"

Stanescu turned again and ran after the more experienced soldier. Somehow, from somewhere, an invisible hand grabbed at his right calf, but he wrenched his foot clear of the assailant.

- *Projectile impact, lower right leg. Non-penetrating.*

Shit. He had been shot. No time to think about it now... no. Fuck 'em. The bastards.

Stanescu turned again and brought his rifle up to his shoulder, picking out one of the Morat troopers crouched over his submachine gun by the wall. He centered his sights and fired, swearing in his father's native tongue as he did so. The target jumped in his sights as the Morat's camouflage warped and twisted the outlines of his image.

"Sir!" Nilsson urged again. "Keep moving! Don't stop!"

Projectile impact - abdomen. Non-penetrating. Projectile impact...

Stanescu's third shot caught the Morat soldier right in the center of his face, blowing a fistful of flesh and bone out of the back of his head. Rounds kicked up around the next Kyosot as fire poured down from the northwest tower.

"Darius!" Hawkins shouted over the com channel. "Keep moving! Don't stay in the open!"

Two of the remaining Kyosots turned to fire up at Hawkins. Stanescu took his cue and pelted across the last few yards of open ground until he reached the base of the tower. Nilsson crouched by the tower entrance, hurriedly loading a fresh magazine into her Combi Rifle. She looked up at Stanescu and shot him an encouraging smile, which also revealed her labored breathing. Then Stanescu saw the alert message on his lens from ten seconds before.

- *Sergeant Anja Nilsson, wounded. Gunshot wound, torso.*

"It went straight through," Nilsson gasped as she tucked her rifle back into her shoulder. "Don't stop! Get up there and help them! Don't stop..."

Stanescu pressed his comlog to bring up a diagnostics overlay. She was right - pistol caliber bullet, straight in and out above the hip bone. Bleeding, but not on death's door. Personal favoritism had nothing to do with triaging a casualty. She was right. He needed to move on. Stanescu pressed a syringe into her side and pushed a vial of serum into the wound.

"I'll be back as soon as I can," he breathed before rushing up the steps toward the east wall.

***

"Two Two from Command!" Zevult growled. "Do *not* target our own damn units!"

The Suryats moved forward like a wall of steel against the human knights, the melee having almost formed two distinct lines like the battles of ages past. That at least gave Zevult a few seconds, the breathing space he needed to swing the fight back in his favor.

He brought up his golgrapt and quickly activated his mission command sub-routine, selecting the menu for his armored units. Two Bultraks; good. No callsigns assigned, just chassis numbers. Zevult swore. No... there. There were callsigns. He needed to keep pace with technology. Just an incredible ability to gun down and club to death his adversaries was not good enough these days.

Zevult selected Bultrak Two One, keyed the command override menu, and shut the machine down. To his right, where it stood treacherously alongside the Seraph, the Bultrak's limbs locked in place. Zevult rebooted its control and mission systems. Motors whirred as the fighting machine powered back up into life.

"Two One!" the pilot excitedly transmitted. "I'm back in the fight! I..."

The Seraph turned in place and fired its heavy machine gun directly into the Bultrak, blowing off one of its arms and puncturing the torso with high velocity rounds. The tall, graceful human fighting machine then stepped in and swung its heavy blade down, hacking the pilot's position in two. The Bultrak leaned over and crashed to the ground, sending up a cloud of dust around its fallen body. Its symbol faded from Zevult's tactical map display.

Almost immediately, a rapid volley of fire from the remaining Bultrak traced across the dusty courtyard, firing over the heads of battling soldiers and smacking into the flank of the already damaged Pan-Oceanian TAG. Holes punctured through its thick armor as sparks flew up from the impact, tearing into the machine's torso. A leg buckled and it dropped down to one knee, its sword digging into the dry earth at its feet for support. The war machine attempted to struggle back to its feet, bringing its own heavy weapon around to line up with its attacker. The Bultrak fired a second volley, blasting through the Seraph's head and shoulder, destroying both the central sensors and the Crabbot link to its pilot. Zevult allowed himself a grunt of satisfaction as the towering fighting machine toppled over and fell forward, clattering into the ground not far from the wreckage of the Bultrak it had destroyed only moments before.

Zevult narrowly avoided the full force of the blow that came hurtling out to strike at him from his left. He brought his own blade up to deflect the attack and looked up to see the female Hospitaller Knight who had already felled two of his veteran Suryat warriors. For a brief moment, their swords locked together, he saw her dark eyes through the tinted visor of her helmet, wide open and filled with rage. He rapidly planted a fist into her stomach and brought his sword down onto the back of her neck.

The Hospitaller deftly stepped aside, slashing her sword toward Zevult's ribs. Zevult reacted with equal speed, batting the attack aside with his blade and again connecting his free fist into his adversary, slamming his knuckles into the side of her helmet. Relentlessly the woman bounced back onto the offensive with an overhead attack toward Zevult's skull. He darted to one side, but just not quick enough, feeling the blade bite through his shoulder armor and carve off a sliver of his flesh. The veteran Hospitaller, clearly an old hand, did not rest on her laurels for a moment and followed up on the wound with a lancing strike of the tip of her sword toward Zevult's chest.

Again, he turned to avoid the thrust but succeeded only in escaping the worst of it, feeling the blade puncture the armor over the same shoulder and bite in, just below his last wound. The woman withdrew her blade and tirelessly continued with a series of expertly timed attacks, forcing Zevult back pace after pace.

Until he saw his opening. Zevult brought his blade up horizontally over his head to block another high attack, then surged forward to barge his shoulder into his assailant. Her guard was opened, just enough for Zevult to grab his sword by the blade and club the woman heavily across the face with the crossguard of his weapon. Her head flung to one side, her helmet was dented and torn open by the blow. For the first time in their fight, she did not leap straight into a response. Taking advantage of the stunning blow, Zevult grabbed the woman by the throat and drove his sword toward her gut.

A hammer blow like nothing he had felt in years smashed against the side of his skull, knocking him flying back and sending him rolling through the dusty earth. His vision blurred and his ears ringing, Zevult forced himself back up to his feet. He spat out a mouthful of blood and looked up. The wounded Hospitaller lay breathlessly on one knee, clutching at a wound by her side where Zevult had nearly succeeded in finishing her off. Stood by one side was her savior; a tall knight wearing the same red surcoat and white cross of the Order of the Hospital.

The tall warrior took off his helmet, threw it to one side, and raised his sword. He fixed his cold eyes on Zevult. His face was wrinkled, his head bald, and his gray eyes narrowed with a burning hatred that Zevult had seen on a hundred human warriors before. The two force commanders rushed into each other with their weapons held high.

Chapter Nineteen

Of the ten Crosiers in Delta Team, four were already dead, three injured, and only three left firing. Two dead bodies lay sprawled across the midpoint of the eastern prison wall, evidence of a failed and bloody attempt to charge the Morat position at the northeast tower. A third Crosier lay with them, on her back and screaming in pain. Two more corpses lay by the tower, along with one critically injured NCO.

Ignoring the chattering of rifle fire as he dashed across to where the surviving Crosiers crouched by the door to the southeast tower, Stanescu applied a diagnosis overlay to each of the surviving casualties as part of his triage process. Blue holographic filters shimmered instantly into life on his lens, detailing the extent of the injuries to each casualty.

- *Lieutenant Hector Moreno, critical. Gunshot wound, neck. Airway compromised. Death imminent.*
- *Sergeant Marianna Cortez, critical. Blunt trauma impact, head. Brain hemorrhage. Death imminent.*
- *Crosier Joao Arias, critical. Gunshot wound, lower torso. Kidney ruptured. Gunshot wound, thigh. Death highly likely.*

Stanescu dashed over to where Moreno had been dragged into the tower, a pool of blood around his head as his eyes stared unfocused at the ceiling. Stanescu knelt down by the mortally wounded officer, grabbed an airway hose from his medical bag and tore off the sterile covering. Behind him, Corporal Lois yelled out a warning as the rifle fire continued. Stanescu filtered the words out. Whatever it was, it had to wait. For Moreno's sake.

"Alright, pal," Stanescu said, well aware that the unfocused eyes were no reliable indication that Moreno was not at least partially conscious and terrified of his predicament, "let's get you all sorted."

Slowly, carefully, ignoring the sudden increase in the flow of blood from the neck wound, Stanescu fed the flexible tube into Moreno's mouth and down his esophagus. He checked the oxygen level. Sixty-six percent. Not rising. Stanescu quickly returned to his medical bag and took a miniature pump, clipping it onto the end of the pipe. The pump whirred quietly into life, connecting to Stanescu's medical diagnostic overlay, calculating the optimal rate of air insertion for recovery and then sucking in air from outside to pump into the casualty's lungs. Oxygen level sixty-eight percent. Some progress; moving in the right direction.

Next, the bleeding. Stanescu fired a vial of serum near the wound. The smart solution would be straight to work, but the rate of bleeding was unacceptable. Time to go old school. Stanescu took a pad from his medical bag, applied it over the wound, and then fixed it to either side; careful not to compromise the airway in any way. Oxygen level seventy-one percent. Rate of blood loss reducing.

- *Death probable.*

Alright, an improvement in the outlook. Getting somewhere...

Stanescu had no idea what prompted his next reaction. He did not see or hear the Morat counter attack, but from nowhere, a pair of the red-skinned warriors hurtled into view, sprinting up the stairs from the tower's next floor down. From his kneeling position, almost bewildered by the rapidity of his own automatic reaction, Stanescu whipped his pistol up from his hip and into a two-handed grip before shooting the first enemy combatant six times in the chest and gut.

The knight was on his feet before the first Morat trooper had even hit the floor, running toward the second enemy soldier. The Morat fired his Combi Rifle from the hip, catching Stanescu but failing to punch through his armor. Stanescu smashed into the Morat, screaming aloud as he locked the alien in a deadly embrace. The two soldiers tumbled back down the stairwell to the floor below.

Stanescu was the first to react when they stopped. He rolled on top of his enemy, wrapping both armored hands around the warrior's thick neck. The Vanguard trooper looked up with anger and determination, smashing his huge fists into Stanescu's elbows in an attempt to break the lock. In the contest of technology versus raw strength, the augmentation provided by the knight's ORC armor won. Stanescu squeezed harder, his teeth gritted as sweat rolled into his eyes, his pulse hammering in his temples. The Morat smashed a fist into Stanescu's face. The knight held firm, choking the life out of his foe.

"...I will use my power to help the sick to the best of my ability and judgment; I will abstain from harming or wronging anyone by it..."

For the briefest of moments, Stanescu almost eased the pressure as the words of the oath he once swore forced themselves to the forefront of his mind. Then another memory took their place.

"What do we do now? Please..."

Stanescu released one hand, raised it above his head and then brought his clenched fist down into the Morat's face. Bone broke. Blood splattered up over the cross on the knight's chest. He punched him again, and then a third time. Dazed by the force of the armor-augmented strikes, the Morat offered little resistance as Stanescu strangled the life out of him. The alien warrior fell limp. Stanescu pressed his pistol against the Morat's forehead and shot him, just to be sure.

No time to think. People depended on him. Stanescu shot back to his feet and ran back up the stairs.

- *Lieutenant Hector Moreno, oxygen level eighty-eight percent. Bleeding stemmed. Casualty stable.*

Stanescu looked along the top of the wall to where the next casualty lay screaming, holding onto her bleeding gut. The third - Sergeant Cortez - was unconscious at the base of the next tower. Corporal Lois lay over his Spitfire, firing from a prone position by the doorway as two other Crosiers fired bursts into the top of the northeast tower. The cacophony of gunfire continued from the courtyard as the Seraph TAG was gunned down, falling to the earth next to a felled Bultrak.

"Mace One, damage terminal! Connection severed, I..."

Patricio's final transmission was cut off as the Seraph lay still in the dust.

"Corporal!" Stanescu shouted. "I need covering fire! I need to get to that casualty on the wall!"

"No, sir!" Lois shook his head. "There's five of the bastards still up there, I think! You'll get gunned down before you're even halfway! We need to secure the wall first!"

"Corporal!" Stanescu growled. "It's not a request! I'm moving to that casualty! Covering fire!"

"I'm with you."

Stanescu span around to see Nilsson limping up from the stairwell below.

"I'm with you, sir. You need another gun. Covering fire from here, you get serum into that Crosier to stabilize the bleeding, then we move forward to recover Sergeant Cortez. Sir?"

Stanescu looked across the wall at the weight of fire still spewing out of the opposite tower. He briefly remembered panicking over exams in his final year of medical school and suppressed a short laugh. He nodded.

"Covering fire in five, Corporal."

***

The two heavy blades bit into each other with a dull, almost anti-climactic clang. De Fersen was quicker to bring his sword around into a second attack, forcing the huge Morat back a step. The veteran Hospitaller saw in an instant that the Morat commander had moved back just a fraction too far, trying to dupe De Fersen into over-extending or losing his balance. De Fersen responded by sweeping his sword around in a wide arc toward the towering Morat's belly. With a surprising agility for a warrior of his size, the Morat darted away and narrowly avoided the strike.

Quick to follow up, De Fersen lunged in but saw the counter strike a moment too late. A red, clenched fist slammed into his face and knocked him back a full pace, a crack sounding from the left side of his jaw as pain flared up across his face. De Fersen turned the momentum of the attack into a counter of his own, spinning around in place to bring his armored foot up into the Morat's face. His heel connected with the alien commander's mouth, eliciting a stream of blood and broken teeth as his adversary was flung back.

De Fersen advanced again, raising his sword in both hands above his head and then swinging down in an attempt to cut the Morat's head open and into two. The crudely angular, heavy alien blade came up and met the full force of the blow to stop De Fersen dead in his tracks. The Hospitaller Knight linked a series of blows to keep the enemy commander on the defensive, forcing him back step after step until a counter came from below, the square-tipped Morat blade lashing out to hack across De Fersen's breastplate.

Just as quickly as he had seized the initiative from his towering opponent, De Fersen found himself forced back across the dusty courtyard, twisting his blade in both hands as he struggled to defend himself against the flurry of blows from his tireless attacker. For the first time in years, De Fersen found a seed of doubt plant itself in his mind as he realized the full extent of the skill, experience, and raw aggression present in the hulking Morat he faced.

***

Five Kyosots remained, hunkered down by the cover of the partition wall that lay about halfway between the southern gatehouse and the center of the courtyard. The Seraph lay in a smoking ruin next to the Bultrak it had destroyed moments before its own demise. Stahl and Karayiannis had dragged Heijboer to the relative safety of the northern gatehouse; Romano and two of the Teutonic warriors were dead. Tibar lay unconscious in a pool of blood. Around them lay the bodies of all eight Suryats. Only De Fersen and the towering Morat commander remained in the open, trading blow for blow in an even and relentless display of skill and aggression.

At the eastern wall, gunfire was continuously exchanged between the handful of remaining Crosiers and a team of Vanguard troopers dug in atop the northeast tower.

Hawkins returned his attention to the south gatehouse. Five Kyosots, an officer or senior NCO of some description, and the second Bultrak. Sporadic fire snapped away from the steps leading down to the cells, where Sergeants Aubert and Kilpatrick continued to target them, but their fire seemed all but ineffectual. Hawkins checked the ammunition counter of his MULTI Marksman Rifle on his visor. His eyes widened. How he had managed to expend so many rounds was beyond him. He took in a breath and crouched over his sights from his position atop the northeast tower, centering his crosshairs over the enemy officer with the green-armored Kyosots.

The officer ducked back into cover, as if somehow sensing his own peril. Hawkins gritted his teeth, and then quickly checked over both shoulders in case he, too, was under threat. Just as his veteran sniper tutor had instructed him to do. Not that he could ever even hope to emulate her marksmanship.

He narrowed his eyes. All of the technology in the world, all of the drone and satellite surveillance, the out of theater assistance and third-party targeting, all of it became moot when a tactical level leader made himself a target by pointing and shouting a lot. And wearing a different color and type of armor from the soldiers he was commanding. Hawkins concentrated on slowing his breathing and watched the wall where the enemy officer lay. He swore. There was no time for this. Yes, his orders were to provide covering fire from the tower and yes, he had largely remained undetected and untargeted by the enemy, but he was wasting time. Nearly two hundred prisoners needed to go home, and a flight of aircraft were marking time to the south, wasting fuel and waiting for clearance to close with their Landing Zone. An LZ that remained unsecured.

A Kyosot dashed quickly across the gap between two lengths of wall - a green blur whose reactive camouflage armor threw off Hawkins's targeting assistance and appeared on his lens as two identical figures, phasing in and out of solidity. Hawkins took his opportunity and fired. His first round flew high; his second punched into the wall mere inches from the Kyosot before he reached the safety of cover.

Immediately, the remainder of the Morat shock team's soldiers took up firing positions by the cover of the low wall and shot back up into the tower. Rounds from marksman rifles and submachine guns tore into the masonry around Hawkins, spitting clumps of dust across his helmet's lenses. But it was another opportunity, and one not to miss. He quickly centered his sights over the closest of the enemy soldiers, steadied his weapon, and squeezed the trigger.

What looked like dust sprouted out from high on the Morat soldier's chest, not far below the throat. The Morat staggered to one side, a geyser of blood spraying out of the wound before he collapsed lifeless into the dust. Then the Bultrak opened fire.

A withering stream of projectiles swept up like the rains of a hurricane, smashing across the dusty tower and plowing into the wall below Hawkins. The floor trembled from the impact, and his left arm was thrown back as a projectile nicked his pauldron, tearing a chunk off the armored alloy. Hawkins, fighting to overcome his anger with his enemy and his paralyzing sense of duty, dug deep within to find that lost kernel of common sense and flung himself down beneath the lip of the tower wall. Chunks of rock and concrete fell down onto his back as the rapid fire of the mobile, armored gun continued to target him.

His breathing fast and ragged, rage clawing at his mind, Hawkins fought to see through the anger and formulate a plan. A mobile gun. Of course. A Bultrak was a mobile gun, designed for speed but ultimately to move into a position to support infantry from behind. It was not designed primarily for close assault. It was no Gūijiă. And, albeit with help, Hawkins had fought one of those bastards to a standstill when he managed to get up close, back at Alpha Four-Four.

Hawkins shouldered his rifle and unsheathed his sword.

"You equipped me with strength for the battle; you made those who rise against me sink under me."

Crouched low to avoid the hail of enemy fire, Hawkins dashed across for the stairs leading down to the courtyard.

***

Muzzle flashes twinkled along the top of the northeast tower, flickering sporadically to momentarily hide the dark shadows of the firers against the backdrop of the setting sun. Her feet pounding against the cracked concrete of the eastern wall, Nilsson fought to ignore the pain flaring up from the injury above her hip. She thumbed the switch on her Combi Rifle's sight, rapidly cycling through the visual settings until it appeared as a red pencil-beam on her lens.

Bringing the red beam up to align with the enemy soldiers on top of the tower, Nilsson pulled back on the trigger of the rifle tucked into her hip and fired a long burst, walking it onto her target despite the years of training and experience which urged her not to do so. Her rounds, coupled with the covering fire provided by the Crosiers behind her, blasted across the top of the tower. A pace or two behind her, Stanescu followed her example and fired a succession of bursts from his own weapon as they reached the halfway point of the connecting wall.

- *Surgeon-Sub Officer Darius Stanescu, wounded. Gunshot wound, upper arm.*

"Keep going!" Stanescu yelled from behind her. "Don't stop!"

The pair ran past the bodies of the fallen Crosiers from the previous attempt to cross the wall, and the corpses of the Morat Vanguard soldiers only a few paces from them. Up ahead, Nilsson saw where Cortez had fallen. Another salvo of enemy fire kicked up the wall-top walkway around the Military Orders soldiers, and Nilsson felt a thump against her armored kneepad, knocking her off her pace.

Stanescu raced past her, loading a fresh magazine into his MULTI Rifle as he ran. Not far now, only a few paces. Her throat dry, her heart racing with fear, Nilsson raised her rifle again and fired another long, barely controlled burst of fire across the top of the enemy-held tower. She thought she saw an impact against one of the Morat soldiers but could not be sure.

Stanescu reached Cortez and crouched low, dragging her away from the enemy arcs of fire atop the tower. Nilsson was only seconds behind him, slamming her back into the wall of the tower and reloading her rifle, her breathing ragged from pain, fear, and exhaustion.

"Do all you can for her, sir," Nilsson gasped, "I'm going up there."

Stanescu's helmeted head shot up to stare at her from where he knelt over Cortez's prone form.

"Don't go up there! They'll cut you to ribbons! You need support!"

Nilsson shook her head.

"Need to... keep the attack going. Keep pressure on the bastards. I'll..."

"I need covering fire, not another casualty to deal with!" Stanescu snapped. "Stay here and stop those bastards from shooting me! I need to drill a hole in her head!"

The wounded doctor pressed a syringe into the Crosier NCO's temple, and then pulled a tiny drill from his pack which whirred into life on the pull of a trigger.

***

Another right hook smashed into Zevult's cheek, cracking the bone of his eye socket and tearing the skin. A follow up strike came in the form of a knee to the gut, denting his armor and digging the bent alloy into his belly. Returning the gesture, Zevult slammed an elbow around into his attacker's jaw, flinging his head to one side and sending a stream of blood from his torn lip.

Separated from his dropped sword, Zevult grabbed his fighting knife from the sheath at the small of his back and darted in for the human knight's throat. The bald human warrior punched the Morat in the wrist, flinging his hand to one side, then whipped a kick around into the side of Zevult's head to knock him down into the dust.

Mark Barber

With a snarl of rage, the Morat was straight back up onto his feet. He flung himself forward into the human commander, tackling him around the waist and knocking him down. Both soldiers grabbed at the vicious, serrated kyosot knife as they rolled over each other in the dust.

"...One Zero... command... reinforcements inbound... fall back... staging post to north of prison..."

Zevult wrapped one hand around the knight's throat and brought his blade down with the other. The Hospitaller slammed a palm into Zevult's elbow, breaking the bone and freeing the hand from around his throat, but not quickly enough to prevent the Morat driving his blade down into the gap between the knight's breastplate and shoulder pauldron. The blade dug in, all the way to the hilt, forcing a snarl of pain from the veteran knight.

Both adversaries rolled away from each other and struggled up to their feet in the prison courtyard; Zevult glancing down at one of his thick arms made useless now by the broken elbow joint, while the human pulled the knife out of his shoulder and threw it to one side. Both warriors looked around them, searching for their dropped swords.

Zevult saw his blade, only feet away. Only then did he register the last communication in his earpiece; orders from Ze Huradak Vandakk to retreat back out of the prison to await reinforcements. It was the damn Bultrak. Vandakk thought that Zevult's force was defeated, and he did not want to lose the second Bultrak. Zevult spat out a mouthful of blood, eyed his fanatical adversary, and then lunged forward for his sword.

***

Cortez sat bolt upright, grabbing for the pistol in her leg holster.

"Stay down! Stay still!"

Her vision swam in and out of focus, a dull pounding on the side of her head and an intensifying feeling of nausea in her gut. It was sunset, the sky above was orange, and gunfire crackled away from above her and off to her left. Yet, she had no idea where she was. She turned and looked up at the helmeted face of a knight, blood splattered across his own cheek from a wound on his upper arm. A bloody medical drill was in his hand. Stanescu? Was that the name?

"Stay down, Sergeant!" the doctor repeated.

"She's stable, right?" another familiar voice called from her right. "Sir! We can take that tower!"

Cortez looked across. Nilsson, one of the Order Sergeants, her back to a tower wall as she looked across at the doorway leading in, a bloody bandage around her waist. Stanescu looked back to the far end of the wall, up above, then at Nilsson.

"Alright. Let's go."

Cortez staggered to her feet, her vision swimming and her head pounding. She looked around, saw her Combi Rifle, retrieved it, and then recollected that they were fighting Morats. That was it.

"Sergeant!" Stanescu yelled. "Stay down! You're concussed and full to the brim with medication! *Stay! Down!*"

Cortez looked up at the knight and threw him a sloppy grin.

"Not a fucking chance, sir. I may not be able to shoot straight, but I'll at least be something else for them to shoot at. Gives you two a better chance to drop the bastards."

Stanescu returned his drill to his bag and pulled out a syringe. The bastard. He was going to put her back to sleep...

Stanescu jabbed the syringe into her neck. Cortez's vision swam sharply into focus. The doppler-effect of her hearing snapped back to normality. The pain in her head intensified to the point that she screamed out loud.

"Aaargh! What the fuck was that?!"

"You want to shoot? You can do it without anesthetic in your system! You want to come with us, you'll do it without painkillers making you sloppy!"

"What happened to my head?"

"I drilled a hole in it!"

"Why the fuck did you do that?"

"You're going to tell me how to be a combat physician, now? Shut the hell up and follow me!"

Hisses of pain escaping through gritted teeth, Cortez followed her comrades as Nilsson led the charge inside the enemy held prison tower.

***

"Fall back?"

"Two Zero, Command, affirm. Fall back."

The tone in Vandakk's response to Guntat invited nothing but total obedience. His breathing ragged, pain wracking his body from half a dozen bleeding wounds, Zevult looked over both shoulders as he took another step back. Behind him, the Bultrak fired another long burst into the north gatehouse, forcing the handful of surviving human knights to take cover. The few remaining Kyosots fell back to the southern gatehouse, firing bursts as they covered each other's orderly retreat toward a path outside of the prison and then up to meet the reinforcements.

It pained Zevult to admit - much more than the pains inflicted from the wounded, ragged knight stood in front of him - that retreating felt... wrong. That was the old ways, a primitive and faintly ridiculous urge to be seen to be a fearless warrior. A professional soldier obeyed orders. Vandakk had ordered a retreat to regroup, and that was what Zevult would do, no matter how it 'felt.'

Ahead of him, the bald, aging knight raised his sword again, blood dripping from one side of his mouth, his broken nose, and two deep cuts to his torso. Zevult almost smiled. Whoever the bastard was, he was good. Possibly the most capable warrior Zevult had ever faced. Enough for him to even briefly contemplate the thought of defeat. He took another wary step toward the southern gatehouse, careful to keep the bald knight between himself and the enemy guns to the north.

Out of the corner of his eye, Zevult saw one of his soldiers stand up, slowly, and step out from the cover of the southern gatehouse. Zevult turned to glance over his shoulder. Guntat looked across at the two opposing force commanders. The veteran trooper threw his rifle down and drew his sword, his face twisted into a scowl and his eyes wide open. He paced forward purposefully.

Zevult finally allowed himself that smile. Guntat was of the old school of soldiering, a time when the old ways were entertained, if not truly permitted. The old ways of blind aggression, never falling back. And loyalty to one's commander in the field. And if Zevult wanted any soldier to fight by his side against the deadly human knight, it was Guntat. A true master of hand-to-hand fighting.

Guntat's determined walk broke into a sprint. With a baleful, rage-filled roar, the towering Morat raised his squared-off sword and sprinted headlong at the aging human knight. The bald man turned in place, a weariness showing on his wrinkled, bloodied face, and raised his own weapon.

Seemingly from nowhere, a second human knight clad in a red surcoat with a white cross appeared from the western wall. The knight hurtled toward Guntat, pelting directly for Zevult's deputy with purpose and drive.

"Guntat!"

Guntat responded to his commander's warning and looked over to see the new challenger. The veteran of a dozen campaigns fixed his angry stare on his new adversary and peeled off to his left, his roar now louder. With a speed and agility that Zevult thought impossible from a soldier clad in PanOceanian heavy armor, the knight planted a foot on the courtyard partition wall and propelled himself into a jumping kick.

The knight's foot rapidly passed Guntat's guard and slammed into his face, snapping his jaw clean off one side of his skull. The knight then span in mid-air to bring his other leg around into a more powerful kick. Zevult heard Guntat's skull break even from that distance. His eyes rolled back in his deformed head, his jaw hanging off one side of his face, Guntat fell down to his knees and then pitched forward into the dust.

The human knight thrust his sword into the small of Guntat's back, twisted the blade, and then withdrew it. Still, Guntat trembled in place on the ground. The knight drew a heavy looking pistol and shot the Morat officer twice in the back of the head. He then looked up, his visor fixed firmly on Zevult. And with one attack of a ferocity Zevult had never seen from a human, one of his most experienced and capable officers was dead and gone.

A hail of fire swept across the courtyard, forcing the second human knight to dive back to the cover of the partition wall. Zevult looked up at the older knight. If the second human warrior joined the fight, Zevult was dead. He needed to dispatch the enemy force commander. Once and for all. And quickly.

***

The moment of doubt that forced itself into De Fersen's head as the second Morat officer charged toward him evaporated as Hawkins hurtled out to cut off his advance. In seconds, the young knight had reached his target and dispatched him with two quick strikes, a sword blow, and two bullets to the back of the head. Then the Bultrak's hyper-rapid magnetic cannon chattered into life again, its buzz of bullets forcing Hawkins to dive and roll back into cover.

"Alpha Zero! Sir! Fall back to cover! I can take the shot!"

De Fersen's hands curled tight around the handle of his sword.

"Gabe!" Karayiannis' voice shouted into De Fersen's earpiece. "Clear the line of fire! Get out of the way!"

Aching from his bleeding wounds, perhaps even feeling his age, De Fersen stepped in to face his gargantuan foe once again.

The Morat commander was quicker this time, sweeping his sword around for a feign which forced De Fersen's blade up to block; a fraction of a moment later, the Morat's fist smashed into De Fersen's face, cracking his broken nose for a second time in their face off. De Fersen staggered back, his eyes watering from the pain and his guard faltering. The Morat was straight in, slashing across De Fersen's chest and then battering him in the side of the head with the pommel of his sword, again tearing open the skin and drawing a stream of blood.

"Gabe! Get down!"

With a determined roar, the red-skinned alien soldier slammed a knee up into De Fersen's stomach, bending him over double with the force of the blow. The knight saw the Morat's sword raised high for the killing blow out of the corner of his eye. With a bitter growl, De Fersen launched himself forward to barge his shoulder into the Morat and knock him down into the dirt.

The two commanders fell down, their swords flying from their grasps, locked in an embrace as both attempted to pummel each other with their armored hands. De Fersen slammed a fist into the Morat's face again and again, breaking his cheek bone as he struggled to free his other hand. The Morat let out a guttural yell and sank a thick, sharp tooth into De Fersen's neck. The knight responded by forcing his thumb into one eye socket and crushing his opponent's eyeball. The hulking Morat threw his head back instinctively, tearing himself away from the Hospitaller for a precious moment.

De Fersen reached out into the twilight dust of the prison courtyard, wrapping his armored fingers around the handle of a sword. He raised the blade, instantly recognizing its unfamiliar weight and balance as not his own. Holding the Morat's own, square tipped sword aloft for a moment, he then brought it slicing down to impale his enemy through the chest. The Morat let out a great cry, both hands scrabbling frantically at the heavy blade emerging from his bleeding ribcage.

De Fersen crawled away, broken and bloodied, to quickly recover his own slim, deadly blade. Rolling back up to his knees, he raised his sword to the darkening heavens above, and he drove it down with all of his remaining might to pierce the great Morat warrior's chest for a second time. Staggering back up to his feet, unsteady from pain and loss of blood, De Fersen looked down at the silent, still Morat who lay sprawled on his back, two opposing blades emerging from bloody wounds in his chest.

Looking around in a weakened daze, De Fersen saw the southern gatehouse now lay unoccupied; devoid of enemy soldiers. Atop the northeast tower, he saw three blue diamonds on his lens that signified a trio of his soldiers had successfully routed the final Vanguard troopers. He fell to one knee, raising his comlog to open a channel to the Tubarão flight circling to the south.

"Cheetah One from Broadsword... Alpha Zero... LZ secure... commence run in from the west. Keep a lookout for... enemy forces to the east... one TAG plus infantry support... prisoners on their way to the LZ..."

His breath coming out in wheezes, pain racing through his chest, De Fersen collapsed down toward the ground. An arm wrapped around his shoulders and pulled him back up to one knee. He looked across wearily and saw Hawkins, helmet removed and looking down on him.

"I had them... I had them both... you bastard..." De Fersen gasped.

"Yeah, yeah," Hawkins nodded wearily, "great banter. Like a buddy cop movie. Come on, get up. Let's get these soldiers home to their families before the Morats send another wave in."

Chapter Twenty

Another of the ceaseless procession of Tubarãos nosed over gently to transition from the hover into forward flight, accelerating across the top of the dusty runway and then pitching up to climb away and head westward. The growl of the engines receded into the distance as the aircraft became nothing more than a speck on the horizon, and the shrill calls of jungle birds was once again heard from the surrounding mass of trees. The mid-morning sun blazed down on Firebase India Two-Five and its new, hastily constructed accommodation and medical blocks.

De Fersen paced slowly along the encampment perimeter, wincing a little with each alternate step from the wounds he sustained at the prison break two days before. Heijboer, Tibar, and Moreno had already been evacuated with the first wave of freed prisoners, and now a steady stream of airlifts slowly whittled down the population at the firebase. The sick and wounded were the first to go, then the Yujingyu and Haqqislamite prisoners, off for processing and then exchanging with their own chains of command for something beneficial to the PMC. De Fersen would never find out what.

Sixteen soldiers from De Fersen's team were still at the Firebase, alongside fifty or so prisoners who were still waiting for their chance to return home. Seven dead. De Fersen had exchanged the lives of seven soldiers to free nearly two hundred. Of course he was sorry for the seven. Of course, once he returned to the firebase and the adrenaline seeped away, he prayed for their souls and quietly, in private, lamented their loss. But if he knew that he would have ordered seven men and women to their deaths so that two hundred would live; he would have changed nothing.

De Fersen made his way back from the side of the runway and down to the hangar, where the control suite for the team's Seraph TAG was now packed away and ready for transit home. He saw Nilsson and Cortez by the hangar entrance and walked across to them, wincing for a moment before his lens compensated as the change of direction placed the sun directly into his field of view.

Both soldiers stood straighter as he approached.
"Sir."

"Sir."

De Fersen offered a half smile.

"Sergeant Cortez. You're still here. With a hole in your head. Despite my orders for you to go home."

The dark-haired woman's eyes narrowed a little.

"Surgeon-Sub Officer Stanescu has fixed up the injury, sir. I'm all but fully fit. And I'll be damned if I delay one of these poor bastards from going home to their family because I've got a bit of a headache. Sir."

De Fersen nodded.

"Yes. Fair enough. Sergeant Nilsson, a few minutes, please."

The blonde woman followed De Fersen back away from the hangar, out of earshot of the others. De Fersen looked down at the nordic soldier, her bright eyes wide and keen, enthusiastic to hang on his words.

"Sir?"

De Fersen smiled again, a little more genuinely this time.

"You did well out there, Anja."

"Well... we all did. We got these people home."

"But you led an assault on an enemy position when you were already wounded."

Nilsson's smile faded.

"Twenty-six of us went in there, sir. Twenty-nine if you include the air drop on the guns. Seven dead. Eleven wounded. All the wounded carried on fighting." She shrugged.

"But most of us were encased in top of the line armor with auto-serum systems. You weren't. Your role is light infantry, and you led a charge like an assault trooper."

Nilsson looked up uncomfortably. She remained silent.

"I know you went through selection to become a knight," De Fersen continued, "and I'm sorry it didn't work out. I can't reverse that, and maybe one day you'll go for selection again. But until then, the least I could do was recognize your potential, and acknowledge all you've done. I'm sending you on two weeks leave. Then you're starting your training with the Crusader Brethren."

Nilsson's eyes widened.

"Airborne? You're sending me Airborne?"

"That's right."

Nilsson looked down at the dusty ground by her feet, then up again with a broad smile.

"Thank you," she said quietly, "thank you so much."

"Alright. Enough. Fucking hell, you'll make me start crying. Good job, Sergeant. Off you go."

Nilsson took a step back, her smile somehow growing.

"Sir."

She turned on her heel and dashed off to where she had left Cortez. De Fersen continued on past the hangar, enjoying the warmth of the morning sun as he made his way past the accommodation area and onto the temporary medical facilities. The medical bay was little more than half a dozen generic containers - now largely empty, thankfully - with some rudimentary beds, monitoring equipment, bots, and stores. De Fersen saw Stanescu stood outside the first container, a cup of coffee in one hand.

"Just the man."

Stanescu turned to face De Fersen as he quickened his pace across. The doctor's eyes were red-rimmed and glazed, but a stoic confidence was painted firmly across his face. The confidence of a man in his element. Behind the doctor, a trio of medical orderlies and their accompanying palbots tended to the handful of lightly injured former prisoners who were still under Stanescu's care.

"All alright here?" De Fersen asked.

Stanescu nodded.

"All fine. Those I was worried about were packed off on the first flights. These here are perfectly stable. Nothing to worry about."

"And your arm?"

"Right as rain."

De Fersen exhaled and glanced briefly across at the half dozen patients in the closest medical bay. He then returned his stare to Stanescu.

"I heard from the Grand Master a few minutes ago. She's delighted with the outcome of the operation. She's a tough woman to please."

Stanescu nodded.

"We achieved the objectives."

De Fersen's eyes narrowed a little. He took a moment to formulate his response.

"We don't do praise very well, not in the Order. I don't do praise very well. I just wanted to say that your performance was good. Nobody ever doubted you as a physician. But you're also a good soldier. That's my opinion, at least."

"Alright. Thank you."

De Fersen glanced down at his comlog. Another message from command. A request for clarity in one of his post-operation reports. It could wait. He looked up again.

"Where's Hawkins?"

"Over on the other side of the runway, last I saw."

"Oh. Doing topless katas to impress the ladies, no doubt?"

Stanescu's face hardened.

"Building a memorial to our fallen. Sir."

"Right. I... sorry."

De Fersen trudged up the embankment to the firebase runway and then across to the other side of the dusty strip. After only a few moments he found Hawkins in a small clearing at the edge of the jungle. A stream trickled down over a series of smooth, light gray rocks to briefly parallel the runway before disappearing off into the mass of vegetation. A cube plinth, waist high, with a cross fixed atop it had been built, no doubt cobbled together out of packing crates and spare parts. A plaque was fixed to the front with the simple wording recessed into it: Operation Paran. Hawkins sat in the shade by the memorial, a knife in one hand as he scratched away at an alloy strip in his other hand. He looked up and offered a half-hearted smile.

De Fersen looked down at the small plaques on the grass by Hawkins. Some had names already carved in.

Brother-Sub Officer Luca Romano
Brother-Sub Officer Hans Weber

"You could get the machine bay in there to print those into your plaques," De Fersen suggested.

Hawkins shook his head.

"It would be too quick. Each one of these plaques is taking me about half an hour to carve. Half an hour to think on their name and pray for them isn't much to offer."

"You want some help?"

"No. At Alpha Four-Four, I spent so long worrying about the lives I'd taken that I never stopped to think about the friends who died around me. I need to think about them this time, and from now on. And... I need the distraction."

"Distraction? From what? We're done here."

"From not knowing whether my fiancee is dead or not."

De Fersen turned away and looked up at the sun. Of course he knew he was a complete bastard to so many people, but for some reason, it was so difficult to apologize for it. He looked down at the younger soldier.

"You mind if I stay here for a while?"

"No, not at all."

De Fersen sat down in the shade beneath the trees at the edge of the clearing. He momentarily contemplated replying to that recent request for clarity on his post-action report. He could not be bothered. He looked over.

"You ever play computer games as a kid? On Maya?"

"Still do sometimes."

"RPGs? Those party-based adventure games?"

"More into beat 'em ups."

"Ah, well. I used to play those fantasy adventure games," De Fersen smiled, "when you made an elf or a dwarf or some shit like that. I loved them when I was in my early teens. There was a formula to those games. Go do heroic shit, fight waves of bad guys, beat the end of level boss... but the bits I really loved were the bits in between. Those 'rest at the campfire' scenes where you could interact with your party. The game designers would always find some beautiful, picturesque setting for you to rest on your laurels from having completed the last level, learn more about the lore. The companions were always so real. I really just beat the fight scenes so I could get back to those peaceful, picturesque bits in between the levels and enjoy those victories with virtual friends."

Hawkins glanced across from his carvings.

"They make games just about that stuff, you know."

"Yeah, I know," De Fersen drawled, "but it's not the same. Not without risk. Not without a sense of achievement. And here in the real world, well, I guess this is the equivalent. The bit where you should get to know your party of adventurers a bit better. So... I'm sorry, Kyle. I'm sorry for being such a dickhead to you sometimes."

Hawkins stopped carving and looked across.

"I'm sorry I didn't become everything you hoped I would," he replied, his tone sincere. "I know you put a lot of faith in me."

De Fersen shook his head.

"No. Don't think that. Don't become like me. Don't become just another angry soldier of God who has forgotten God's message. God's way. God's peace. Be the guardian that you were at Alpha Four-Four, not the killer you were at the prison. Don't ever change."

Hawkins paused, perhaps to contemplate the words, then returned silently to his carving. De Fersen chuckled briefly at a memory.

"Do you remember when we first met?"

"First year of training," Hawkins replied, "unarmed combat. On the mats."

"No," De Fersen replied, "it was a couple of days before that."

The classroom consisted of rows of separate desks, each finished in a dark wood to give some sort of old worldly vibe that De Fersen neither cared for nor understood the need for. The twenty knight-aspirants shot to their feet and stood to attention, their black uniforms devoid of any rank or qualification badges save the cross of the Order on their shoulders. Twenty men and women, the majority of them being eighteen years of age and straight out of school, who had passed the cripplingly high standards required for knight selection and were now two weeks into a grueling four year training syllabus.

"Sit down," De Fersen ordered.

The trainee soldiers returned to their seats silently.

"Father-Officer Valconi has been called away on other business," De Fersen began, "I'll be filling in for him. My name is Father-Officer De Fersen."

De Fersen would have been lying to himself if he denied the smug feeling of satisfaction that was drawn from the excited smiles from the rows of knight-aspirants at the mention of his famous name. He continued regardless.

"The subject of this lesson is 'Ethics and Morals.' You are here to be more than soldiers. You are here to be knights of the Order. Soldiers of God. Upholders of morality. Enforcers of God's will. To do so, that morality must be beyond reproach."

De Fersen paced down from the lectern and holographic screen at the front of the classroom, his lesson notes and syllabus key points scrolling along his lens as he did so. All eyes followed him as he continued.

"Our morality is drawn from God's word. The Bible. Beneath this, we draw our rules from the Catechism. But you need to progress onto both of those, despite what you all may think you already know. So let's begin with a ridiculous and unrealistic hypothetical.

"A time machine is invented. You are selected to go back to a set point in time. The birth of a dictator. Pick one, if it helps you visualize the question. Hitler, Stalin, some piece of shit like that. You can go back in time to their birth, rip them from their mother's arms as a baby, and then execute them to prevent their future atrocities. Would you do it?"

Silence ensued. Then a few chuckles from the braver trainees at the ludicrous nature of the question. A hand shot up.

"Sir!" *Knight-Aspirant Santis, already established as the academic leader of the class, boldly began.* "I would do it. I would make the tough call. Knowing what we know."

De Fersen looked down at the confident young woman.

"The ends justify the means?" *he offered with a grim smile.* "Machievelli."

"You'd kill a newborn?" *Knight-Aspirant Forczyk spoke up.* "No. Just… no. Not under any circumstances. It's wrong."

"What, to save billions of lives?" *Santis snapped.* "Perhaps you ought to question whether you're in the right place if you can't make a call like…"

"Like what?" *Knight-Aspirant Maze butted in.* "You don't know it'll make things better!"

"Err… yeah! We do! Listen to the question, pal! We're traveling back in time so we know the outcome if we don't act!"

"No," Forczyk retorted, "haven't you ever seen a single time travel movie? We know one possible timeline! For all we know, somebody has already gone back and killed an even worse dictator, because this one is somehow the lesser of two evils!"

"It's not a time travel question, dickhead, it's a question of ethics! You've completely missed the point!"

Suppressing a chuckle, De Fersen paced around the classroom for some minutes and watched a room largely filled with young men and women used to being the top of their peer group, now forced together in fierce competition. As tempers flared up, he stepped in.

"Hands up. Who would make the kill? Alright. Who wouldn't?"

De Fersen nodded slowly at the split opinion. One knight-aspirant sat on the back row in silence. De Fersen paced over to him and looked down at the seated youth.

"And what about you?" he sneered. "Everybody else here is actively taking part. You've just sat here for the whole debate, umming and arring, doing a great job of facial acting to pretend you're on the precipice of some great philosophical contribution. Well? Are you even listening to this?"

"Yes, sir."

"You didn't put your hand up. For either answer. Why?"

The trainee, a muscular, good-looking young man with dark hair and eyes, looked up at De Fersen.

"I'd go back, sir. But I wouldn't kill anybody. I'd take with me what I knew, and I'd spend my life supporting the baby and their parents so that the outcome changed. I'd try love and compassion rather than killing, just as Jesus taught us. Because I honestly believe that one act of love and compassion can change an entire world."

De Fersen stared down at the trainee in silence. A contemptuous laugh was issued from the front of the class. De Fersen looked up.

"Knight-Aspirant Santis, we're a team, not individuals looking to mock our brothers and sisters. Report to the gymnasium, get a thirty kilo pack on your back, and then straight into twenty laps of the parade square at best pace. Off you fuck."

De Fersen returned his glare to the quiet boy on the back row. He checked the trainee's name on his lens.

"There is no correct, 'staff' answer to this hypothetical question. But if there was one, I believe you, Knight-Aspirant Hawkins, may have found it."

De Fersen smirked at the memory. It should not have surprised him when, at the very end of the prisoner of war rescue, with the very last Tubarão leaving the prison courtyard just as the second wave of Morats was arriving, Hawkins risked his life and jumped back out of the aircraft. To rescue a dronbot. A Sierra dronbot that, missing two legs, limped pathetically toward the last Tubarão. Not out of desperation to be saved - it felt nothing, after all - but simply because it was programmed to do so. But Hawkins... De Fersen sighed as he recalled the incident - he went back under fire to help retrieve the dronbot. Almost certainly because he felt sorry for it. Soppy, sentimental bastard.

Hawkins placed his third carved name plaque down and picked up a fourth to commence work. De Fersen looked across at him and then brought up his comlog. A few taps later, and he was navigating his way through a series of sub-menus, delving into programs that he rarely used and was perhaps even a little rusty with. But, as they said, like riding a bicycle, committing stealth-based hacking always seemed to come back quite quickly. Defenses changed, but programs updated to keep pace with them. The technique remained largely the same.

Minutes drifted by in silence. On the battlefield, hacking was an active, dynamic endeavor. The enemy knew who you were, and counter-hackers were often in place to keep things in check. Even if not, battlefield hacking was an overt and obvious art, and commanders could - as the Morat had at the prison - shut entire programs down to restart them to defeat a hacker with high level auth codes rather than actual quantronic skill. And if all else failed, there were always bullets.

But hacking a department's entire database? Particularly a government department that was created specifically for dealing with secrets? That was anything but dynamic. It required a trait that came with age: patience. That was De Fersen's mistake when he had tried to help Hawkins before the assault on the prison. He had rushed things. This time, he moved with caution. It was perhaps half an hour before De Fersen spoke.

"Kyle? You know that I'd be in a world of shit if I hacked the mainframe of the Strategic Security Division to access Top Secret records?"

Hawkins looked up.

De Fersen held up the holographic display above his comlog.

"Operation Cyan Thunder... Casualties... von Beckmann, Lisette, Major... Wounded in Action, minor injuries... estimated time for full recovery, one week."

De Fersen severed the connection. Hawkins leaned forward and planted his face in his hands. He took in a few deep breaths and then looked up again, his eyes glazed. He exhaled and stared across at De Fersen.

"Thank you, Gabe. Thank you."

***

The line of soldiers stood patiently in the sun by the edge of the dust-strip runway, the few who had personal possessions with camouflage bags by their feet. It was getting late, with an orange sky above that was almost identical to the heavens that spread over the top of the prison complex in the firefight only days before. A low hum issued from the western horizon as another aircraft swam into view, ready to run in on final approach to pick up the waiting soldiers.

Stanescu looked across to Hawkins. The younger soldier issued a smile.

"I'm sorry," he said quietly, "again. Sorry for... the way I've been in the last few days. For not telling you what was going on."

The doctor flashed a broad, friendly grin.

"It's alright. Honestly. It's alright."

"When are you getting away from here?" Hawkins asked as the aircraft drew closer.

"Tomorrow, hopefully. Then some leave. Off to see my grandmother."

Hawkins offered his hand as the shape above the horizon swam into view and grew into the familiar silhouette of a Tubarão. Stanescu accepted his friend's hand and shook it firmly.

"Pass all my kindest regards onto your grandmother, please," Hawkins said, lifting his pack up over one shoulder, "and I'll see you soon."

"Take care," Stanescu smiled.

He turned and began to walk away from the airstrip as the howl of engines grew louder. He looked down the embankment, toward the accommodation area, and saw Nilsson dashing up the incline toward the airstrip, a pack over one shoulder. She stopped a few paces away from Stanescu.

"That's my flight!" She smiled. "So... I'm off. Take care, Darius."

Stanescu swallowed and nodded. He had heard that Nilsson had been selected for Airborne. A dangerous task, fit only for the most fearless in the Order.

"Take care, Anja. With everything."

Nilsson nodded but remained stationary a few paces from him for a moment more. Then she smiled again and took a step back.

"Well... see ya."

Stanescu returned the smile and pivoted on the spot to walk away. Before he had really formulated a plan, he found himself spinning back around and blurting out an ill-thought out request.

"Anja... I... would it be awfully forward of me, or inappropriate, if I wrote to you? From time to time?"

The young woman's near perpetual smile broadened further.

"No, no it wouldn't be forward. It would be really welcome."

Nilsson turned and dashed off to catch up with the line of passengers as the howling Tubarão flared to hover over the landing strip. His own spirits lifted, a sudden optimism and happiness back in his core, Stanescu watched the aircraft depart and then returned to the temporary field hospital to continue supervising its dismantling.

***

A cool breeze blew across the tarmac of the dispersal area at the civilian aerospace port at Valkenswijk. A band of sky blue ran across the horizon, darkening as it eased up toward a starlit panorama above in a cloudless, evening sky. The aerospace port was lit up with a plethora of twinkling lights, running along the edge of the active runway and highlighting the various taxiways linking it to the dispersal areas. Scanner dishes rotated in their emplacements just outside the port's perimeter fence, and behind them were the peaceful skyscrapers of the city, reaching gently up to the stars above. Hundreds of passengers moved through terminal buildings as another huge airliner took to the skies, packed with holiday makers as, somehow, with the threat of open war against aliens being waged on that very planet, normal life still went on - albeit with highly sanitized and specially selected airways.

Self-conscious in his uniform of black battledress, Hawkins walked briskly toward the dark painted Rhincodon transport aircraft at the far end of the restricted area. His beret was tucked into one epaulet of his battledress jacket - having been shouted at several times on several airfields for FOD awareness, whatever that was - and he carried a single red rose in one hand. Which, he mused, made him feel perhaps ten times more uncomfortable as he continued on through the restricted area hired out by the military, a succession of cameras and drones watching his every step.

Three figures in a mismatched concoction of combat fatigues and civilian clothing busied themselves outside the huge transport aircraft, carrying crates down the aircraft's ramp to the tarmac below, and then sorting through different dumps of equipment. All three figures turned to regard the new arrival in the pristine Military Orders uniform, awkwardly carrying a flower.

- *Security Clearance Interrogated - Access Cleared.*
- *Security Clearance Interrogated - Access Cleared.*
- *Security Clearance…*

The closest of the three operatives, a tall man with the logo of the Akalis Commandos on his t-shirt, nodded to Hawkins and then up the ramp and into the aircraft.

"Thank you," Hawkins replied, looking around at the three Strategic Security Operatives - Hexas - and wondering how little they must be thinking of him at that moment.

Then, recalling his experiences only a few days before, Hawkins came to the sudden realization that he could very probably kick the shit out of them all if he had to, and so found himself standing that little bit taller. His booted feet clumping on the walkway up the ramp, Hawkins found himself smiling as he heard a familiar voice.

He saw his fiancee standing inside the aircraft, clad in jungle-green combat trousers and an olive green armor undershirt, pointing in accusation at a shorter, blonde-haired woman as she spat out a string of obscenities. Both operatives turned to face Hawkins, and Beckmann's face lit up in a smile. Hawkins knew the requirements of professionalism well enough - it did not matter that they were engaged to be married, what mattered is that they were both in uniform, and she held a significantly higher rank.

"Ma'am," he nodded respectfully,

Beckmann rushed over to him, wrapped her arms around his neck, and kissed him. She broke away after a while, still smiling, her eyes glazed with tears.

"I am so happy to see you," she whispered.

Hawkins offered her the rose.

"You're going to make me cry in front of this bunch of fucking arseholes," she laughed quietly, accepting the rose and looking down at it with an ever-growing smile, "but thank you!"

Hawkins nodded to her bandaged forearm.

"You got hurt..."

She looked up at him.

"I've already seen your post-op lens footage, Sub Officer. Don't you dare try to lecture me on risk taking."

"Yes, well... fair enough."

The tall woman took a step back.

"Let me get my bag, okay? I'll be right back. I've already got us tickets out of here. How long have you got off?"

"Not as long as last time, but long enough."

Beckmann dashed off toward the front of the aircraft, leaving the cavernous cargo compartment. Hawkins looked across at the cargo bay's other occupant. A slim woman of medium height, mid to late twenties, with vivid blonde hair that clashed with a delicate face that looked to be possibly of Filipino heritage. The woman paced over slowly, her dark eyes regarding Hawkins cooly, with curiosity.

Hawkins knew exactly what Beckmann was. What she was capable of. What she had done in her past. But he also knew that it was not really who she was, and it was something she was desperate to break free from. But the woman stood in front of him now? She, he figured, was the real deal. A real, cold, remorseless, state-sponsored murderer.

"So, you're the one," she said quietly.

Hawkins remained silent.

"Let's get things out in the open, shall we?" the woman continued. "I've known Razor for a long time. We've been through a lot. More than your little cult will ever expose you to. So, if you ever hurt her…"

"Let me stop you right there," Hawkins seethed, stepping forward. "I've seen you in a photo in her living room. Your graduation. I know exactly who you are. I also know that she was medically downgraded and non-deployable because of her mental health. But that was overridden. Because she thought she 'owed' somebody."

The assassin's lips twisted into a barely detectable smile.

"So," Hawkins continued, "don't you even dare give me the romcom 'don't hurt my best friend' bullshit. There's only one fucking villain here. And it's you. If you ever force her into danger like that again, and Heaven forbid something happens to her, as God above is my witness, there is not a power in existence that will stop me finding you. Is that out in the open enough for you?"

Hawkins kept his stare locked on the older woman's eyes. She did not flinch for even a moment. He jumped as a hand fell on his shoulder gently. He looked over. Beckmann shot a venomous stare at the blonde Hexa, then turned to smile at him, her blue eyes narrowed in concern.

"Come on," she said softly to him, "let's get you home."

Hawkins turned to follow Beckmann toward the ramp leading back out of the aircraft.

***

The Tubarão taxied across the dirt landing strip of Firebase India Two-Five, backtracking down the runway to position for launch. One of the very last stick of passengers, De Fersen leaned across in his seat in the back of the aircraft and looked out of the cargo door at the base that had been his home for nearly a week. The medical facilities were gone, the accommodation blocks removed; all that remained was a battered, empty TAG hangar with a crane arm suspended from the center of its holed roof.

De Fersen looked around the cabin at the other occupants. Stanescu was already asleep. He did not blame him one bit. The doctor had worked tirelessly in leading the small team who took care of the precession of freed prisoners, triaging their conditions and then working around the clock to tend to them as they were slowly processed and repatriated.

The only other passenger was Cortez. The veteran sergeant stared silently out of the window as the aircraft wheeled around to line up for take off. The cargo door was shut, and the environmental controls immediately pushed out a refreshing stream of cool air into the cabin. The engines powered up to either side of the long, slim fuselage, and the Tubarão accelerated down the runway. The engines tilted and the aircraft lifted, suddenly feeling smooth in transit as the rumbling wheels broke free of the uneven runway. The Tubarão banked around to the left, and De Fersen mentally bid farewell to yet another temporary home in a far flung corner of Paradiso. The last thing he saw as the base disappeared past the cargo door window was the memorial cross by the stream in the clearing. He closed his eyes and silently uttered an Eternal Rest.

The aircraft climbed and accelerated, punching up through a thin wisp of cloud in the early morning sun. De Fersen looked across at Cortez.

"You taking leave?"

"No, sir."

"So, what now?"

"B Company of my battalion are heading out. I volunteered to go with them."

De Fersen frowned.

"You don't want to go home? After all this?"

Cortez looked out of the window again. It was a good few minutes before De Fersen realized that she was not formulating an answer in her mind. She was just ignoring the question.

***

Birds sang outside. A gentle wash of air drifted down from the old-fashioned fan rotating up on the slanted, white ceiling above. Sunlight poured in through the open balcony. Waves crashed gently on the beach outside. The air smelt of vanilla, reminding Hawkins of hotel lobbies from those family holidays as a child. He opened his eyes wearily and rolled over on the huge bed, sleep retreating slowly as he took in and recognized his surroundings as the main bedroom in his fiancee's house.

Beckmann lay next to him, her head propped up on one hand as she watched him.

"Hey."

"Morning." Hawkins smiled groggily, sitting up. "How long have you been up?"

"Oh, all night." Beckmann's eyes narrowed coldly. "I've been watching you sleep for hours."

Hawkins opened his mouth to reply, searching for the best words in his limited arsenal for the scenario.

"Joke," Beckmann winced, "it was a joke. I've been up for about an hour."

"Oh! Well… that's a lot easier to… process."

His fiancee smiled.

"You sleep okay?"

Hawkins exhaled and shrugged.

"Okay, I suppose. Still a few things whirling around my mind from the last few weeks."

Beckmann nodded and sat up, taking one of his hands in both of hers.

"It's bound to take some time. Just… make sure you talk to somebody if it's not getting any better. Don't leave it late like I did. I'm always here to talk, if you feel you can."

"Thank you. Honestly. I'm alright, though."

The birds chirped from the branches of the palm trees surrounding the swimming pool below the bedroom balcony. The waves lapped across the hot sand not far from them. Chloe, Beckmann's black kitten, purred from her position on the end of the bed. Hawkins stood up and walked over to the space between the end of the bed and the open balcony before dropping down to the floor to assume the position for his morning press-ups.

"Instead of doing that," Beckmann offered, "how about we take the kayaks out across the bay? It's flat calm, not a cloud in the sky, and there's a beach cafe a couple of miles up the coast that I haven't taken you to."

Hawkins jumped up again.

"Sounds great! When did you want to go?"

"Whenever you want. I've already packed a couple of bags and dragged the kayaks down to the waterfront."

Hawkins sat down next to her again and wrapped an arm around her shoulders. The images of the past weeks were still there, lurking, not far away from the front of his mind. As was the sense of loss. The memorial had done something to deal with that, and he felt no small sense of guilt when he wondered whether building the memorial and carving the name plaques was out of respect for the dead, or a coping mechanism for himself.

Either way, life needed to go on. He needed to grab every opportunity for happiness with both hands, no matter how brief. They both did. One day, the fighting would stop for them both. But that day was not even beginning to peer over the far horizon yet. And rather than wishing away his life, wasting his chances for happiness in the brief interludes between the danger, fear, and misery of loss, Hawkins would make sure that he would take every chance for the happiness of a normal life that God gave him.

"Moving a couple of kayaks is no big deal," Beckmann said quietly. "I mean... this one time, I took down a fucking Yujingyu TAG to impress you. And you weren't even watching."

Hawkins instantly pushed the pain of that memory away so that he could laugh at her joke.

"I was watching! I was cheering you on, on the sidelines! I was all, like, *'Yay! You go, Hot Girl! You go blow shit up!'*"

She smiled in response. A few moments of silence passed before she spoke again.

"I said from the start that this would be complicated. But we've got each other's backs."

"We always will," Hawkins replied.

***

The simple, wooden door swung open with a creak. It was not much of a home. But it was home. De Fersen walked into his quarters at the PMC Barracks, Vedi, and lowered his heavy bag to the floor by the door, beneath the trio of coat hooks on the wall. The lights blossomed into life, automatically brightening to a pre-programmed, evening dim setting. De Fersen looked across at the living room-office, adjoining his bedroom. A simple armchair, sofa, a light, bookshelf, drinks cabinet, rug... not much to show for after over three decades of service.

The aging knight walked over to his drinks cabinet, pausing to fondly cast his eyes over the framed paintings on his walls. *The Battle of Montgisard in 1177*, a graduation present from an old friend when he was knighted into the Templars. *The Battle of Austerlitz, 1805*, a nod to his family's French heritage.

De Fersen paused by his bookshelf. Two old-fashioned, paper books held pride of place on the top shelf, above a series of memories and mementoes from the past thirty years. The Bible and the Catechism. There was just something different, something special about owning paper copies of books with such importance. Abandoning the idea of pouring himself a small cognac, De Fersen picked up the Bible and sat down on his ancient armchair.

He smiled as he recalled a method of Bible study that he used to partake in with his coursemates during training in the Templars. Open the sacred book on a random page, read the text, interpret the meaning and the lesson. De Fersen carefully opened the book.

"...For the Lord will execute judgment by fire, And by His sword on all mankind, And those slain by The Lord will be many..."

Isaiah 66:16

De Fersen let out a long, slow breath through his thin nostrils. By fire and sword, those slain will be many. A prophetic declaration, a promise to God's people that judgment would be swift on all enemies of the Church. De Fersen exhaled and nodded. Not a random page at all. It was a well-read page, hence it falling open, as the paragraph was hammered home again and again to Knight-Aspirant Hospitallers in training, just as it had been to him as a Templar. The Military Orders were the tool of God's will, used to execute judgment by fire and by sword.

But, exactly as Gerard had said, they had lost their way. Their role in a modern Human Sphere should be one of guardianship, compassion, bravery, and sacrifice. Not of unbridled aggression and violence, at least, not in the first instant. There was a time for fire and sword, and tragically likely there always would be, but with restraint. Control. Proportionality. And if the Hospitallers had truly lost their way, De Fersen knew deep down that he was one of the primary reasons why. He was a legend within the Military Orders, an inspiration, a role model. And for that reason, he needed to change. To turn away from the mindless violence and to act as Christ had shown - with humility, compassion, sacrifice, and love. And those values were needed across humanity - now more than ever - irrespective of whether people had faith and religious beliefs, or none at all.

De Fersen carefully closed the book and returned it to its shelf. It was late and it had been a long day of travel. A long week. He stood and poured himself that cognac. Just one. Always, after the exuberance of his youth, always just one.

"Maya, play 'Carmen,' by Georges Bizet."

The haunting, familiar soprano melody began in De Fersen's earpiece as he took a sip of his cognac from the squat, crystal glass.

"Gabriele," his geist said, "it's your father's birthday in one week. Do you want to send him a greeting?"

De Fersen glanced across to the doorway to his bedroom. Eight years. He had not spoken to his father for eight years. And if De Fersen was not getting any younger, his father certainly was not. Time would inevitably take what it always took. And he would be left with nothing but regret. No, a simple greeting was not enough. He would call him, first thing in the morning.

The doleful melodies of Bizet's 'Carmen' accompanied De Fersen as he walked wearily through to his bedroom. He flicked an eye over the scant few messages scrolling across his lens. Mainly adverts that had somehow survived his filters. But one message, one was from the War Orphans charity he supported. That would be well worth reading. The lights in his bedroom slowly illuminated to evening dim. He stopped in the doorway, dead in his tracks.

A bullet lay on his bedside table. Propped up, on its square base of propellant. Wide awake, his senses now heightened with alarm and adrenaline, De Fersen checked to either side.

"Maya, lights on full."

The lights of all three rooms of his quarters brightened. There was nobody there. No sinister package, no evidence of disturbance. Just a single bullet. He walked over and picked up the projectile. A single word was scratched into the round.

Gabby.

"...this isn't over. And that now Rob is gone, I don't see the need to leave you alone. ... I'll be seeing you around, Gabby..."

De Fersen put the bullet back down and swallowed. He took a few moments to collect his thoughts, process the situation, and think of a way ahead.

"Maya, call Konstantinos Karayiannis."

"Are you sure you wish to call Konstantinos Karayiannis? His time zone location indicates that he is most likely asleep."

"Yes. Call Konstantinos Karayiannis."

It was a few seconds until a familiar but groggy voice came through.

"Gabe... it's... it's pretty late. And you're calling me on a civilian channel. What's up?"

De Fersen looked down at the bullet.

"Something's cropped up. And I'm going to need your help."

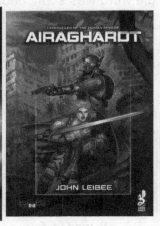